CHARTING A MARRIAGE

Charting a Marriage

A novel

by

JOANNA KADISH

Adelaide Books
New York / Lisbon
2021

CHARTING A MARRIAGE
A novel
By Joanna Kadish

Copyright © by Joanna Kadish
Cover design © 2021 Adelaide Books

Published by Adelaide Books, New York / Lisbon
adelaidebooks.org

Editor-in-Chief
Stevan V. Nikolic

For any information, please address Adelaide Books
at info@adelaidebooks.org
or write to:
Adelaide Books
244 Fifth Ave. Suite D27
New York, NY, 10001

ISBN: 978-1-956635-31-7

Printed in the United States of America

One

Shelli Matson drove up the long windy drive to the family home and turned off the ignition. She found herself trapped in the driver's seat of her black Mercedes SUV, three precocious youngsters jumping on her lap, feeling like she was fighting for her life, or at least for a good lungful of air. A tornado of arms and hands flew, a handful of bagels spilling. Right at the moment, she was rethinking what it means to be a parent, trying to maintain her good humor.

"Look you've ripped the bag," Shelli said. "Can't you wait until we get into the house?"

"Hey, Mom," Seth said, the morning sun streaming behind him, "Stop accusing me. I didn't do the ripping. You did."

"I'll rip you a good one," Nate said, giggling, followed by Seth, and then Micah. They kept the laughter going by tickling each other and falling into Shelli's lap.

"You grabbed the bag out of my hand," Shelli said. "That's how it ripped."

"It was like total Battles Kingdom," Micah said.

The twins were identical to the exact location of the moles on their backs, but all the boys, including Nate, had similar features and blond hair cut long. They looked so much alike that people often asked if they were brothers. But no, Nate was the son of Stefan's younger brother, David.

"Can I have some of your energy?" Shelli said.

"Sure," Seth said, slapping her hand. "That'll cost you. Five bucks."

The boys bounced off each other like ping pong balls. The differences between the twins were stark, a matter of Seth being more outgoing, and always first to comment. Micah came off more thoughtful, the peacemaker. Micah generally looked to his brother for leadership, and agreed with most everything his brother said, which Seth both resented and craved, thus creating friction between the two, adding to the usual jostling that occurs between brothers. Nate was careful to pay attention to both twins and willingly seceded control to Seth.

They went up the stone walkway, trees all around, plenty of lush grass. Through the line of trees with its cutouts, the iridescent purple-gray ocean shimmered. Shelli took in the air dense with the smells of brine, kelp, and decaying seaweed, the cawing of seagulls sounding a symphony. The place was buried in a heavily forested area marked by Victorian and contemporary houses nestled into steep hillsides where everyone knew each other and socialized, block parties and so on. Shelli considered her neighborhood to be paradise. She loved interaction with the neighbors, many of them having become her friends.

The Matsons moved from the concrete heart of Manhattan to the garden state of New Jersey eleven years ago when Shelli was six months pregnant with the twins. Living in the Highlands they were close enough to walk, jog, pedal, paddle or take a water taxi to Sandy Hook Bay, which looked so much like Big Sur in California near where Shelli grew up that sometimes she got confused, knowing that she was in her psychic happy place. One thoroughfare provided access to Sandy Hook's three beaches where tourists mix with locals to sunbathe along the six miles of barrier spit on vast swaths of sand, wetlands, and grasses linked by trails, part of the Gateway National Recreation Area. Past Rumson, casting a long shadow stood Mount Mitchell, the crowning jewel of the Highlands said to be the highest natural point on the Eastern Seaboard south of Maine at 266 feet. The towns and villages of the New Jersey Shore were ancient, dating from pre-revolutionary times, and charming, an antidote to the noise and the claustrophobic feel of the city.

New Jersey, the most densely populated of all states, has 130 miles of ocean front, stretching from Sandy Hook to Cape May. Some of the historic buildings predating the Revolutionary War have been preserved and protected by law and still remain. At one time, Redcoats stormed through narrow cobbled streets of these villages, and later on, those same Colonial-era houses sheltering at one time bootleggers and pirates became the home to the clamming industry. The rickety fishermen's shacks and boxy bungalows with stubby porches and narrow chimneys mixed uneasily next to ornate Federalist cubes replete with widow's walks, many restored and upgraded by generations that value these manmade indictors of time's passing. In the towns where building codes were more relaxed, marble-clad palaces sprang up on gigantic lawns where Victorians once stood. All this history on East Coast lies open begging for attention from the peripatetic who come to gawk. And they do come in droves from all over the world. Movies and books chronicling life on the Jersey Shore only add fuel to the fire.

Many of the Shore's communities were built as resorts in the late 1800s, and still have plenty of the frilly, peaked Victorian architecture that Shelli found so charming. Part of the Highlands near where the Mattson lived lies along a bluff topped by the castle-like 150-year-old Twin Lights Lighthouse, surrounded by a picturesque village with a colorful past of explorers, pirates and, most recently, clammers. Downtown has become a tourist destination about three-quarters of a mile long with some twenty restaurants and an equal number of gift shops, housed in quaint old-world style buildings built from brick and wood. The marinas and bar-restaurants with live entertainment line Shrewsbury Avenue, cutting off Bay Avenue and following the shore. To the north, along Sandy Hook Bay, lies another old clamming village, with Bay Avenue as its thoroughfare, and lined with restaurants, as many of these towns do, with old standbys like a hardware store and municipal building, Rumson, purchased by early settlers from the Native Americans who lived there in exchange for a few barrels of rum back in 1665. So much of the history that happened along this stretch of coast had been preserved, not fossilized. Most of the old hotels along this part of the shore found new life as B&Bs; and pre-revolutionary war boardwalks maintained, playgrounds restored.

On a summer day, the sun-washed beaches along the Jersey Shore remind Shelli of the coasts of California and Florida, having much the same views: ditch-traversed marshes and the brambled islands of palm trees and oaks; seagrass growing in profusion in the same lovely chaotic way backed by dunes white as salt and above it all the horned edge of ocean. And the breeze is just as sublime; the powerful waves as evanescent, and the salt spray just as strong. Except for the southeast winds that develop mid-day, which can, for the uninitiated, generate a cruel deception, in minutes, the change in wind direction often sends temperatures plummeting to as low as the upper 50s, often under clear skies, creating a great disparity between the chilly surf temperatures and adjacent off-shore air temperatures. What is too cold in May becomes in a late summer, a refreshing sea breeze, with temperatures dropping, perhaps, from the 90s into the upper 70s.

Seth placed the bagels on the grayish-white stone countertop under three-story high ceilings, the ripped bag having somehow held up. Shelli brought out the cream cheese and lox, white fish, and cut-up scallion to be assembled on bagel halves and eaten like open-faced sandwiches. She handed bagel halves with cream cheese smeared on, her head swimming from images from the night before, this vision of Stefan talking about having two women wouldn't leave her, the relish in his voice, the way he said it, throwing out words like 'threesomes' as if he was filling in for the likes of Jeffrey Epstein, and tried to put these images aside like one would dock a boat on dry land, but couldn't. The boys started running around, screaming, and soon the room felt as they infused the air with their endorphins, making Shelli lose all concentration. In the center of this maelstrom, Stefan came into the room, changing the dynamics. Shelli was stuck by his sense of calm; features brushed by a humorous something, a wordless desire to be liked that was evident in his ready smile, drawing her to him like a hummingbird to nectar. He liked to laugh, and he laughed often. He had an almost feminine way of moving, as if reluctant to use his strength. She went to give him a hug, and ended up dispensing hugs like a gumball machine, hugging David, Stefan's brother, reaching his arms out and flicking his fingers, before going on to the rest of the room. Her hug to Carmen, David's wife, a dark beauty with a face like Penélope Cruz, with the dark eyes and full lips, and long brown hair pressed to look stick straight, lingered, their arms locked around each other. Carmen was the same size as Shelli. Carmen smiled when Shelli said they were sisters. They sat at the kitchen table facing the wall-to-wall windows looking over the bay. Steve passed around the French roast and everyone filled their cups. The coffee smelled earthy and vibrantly chocolatey.

"The DOW's heading in the stratosphere," Stefan said in his deep bass, unperturbed by the noise the children were making, he would be easily heard over their cries. "And tech stocks are the strongest they've ever been. Every time I think they can't go any higher, they do."

His face was inscrutable, his demeanor as calm as a summer day. He had a way of vibrating his body, as if he was a puppy looking to be petted, and flashing the warmth of his eyes to whomever he was speaking and batting his eyelashes like a girl, and when Shelli was the lucky recipient, she felt she would melt into a puddle on the floor. Right then he seemed the most caring, sweetest guy in the world. What goes on in the bedroom stays in the bedroom, Shelli thought, isn't that what they say?

"A few of the companies I'm hot on right now: Yahoo, Microsoft, and Apple," Stefan said. "Not all of them have come into their own, but I'm betting on the leaders like Jerry Yang, Bill Gates, and Steve Jobs as long term plays. Sometimes I'm wrong, but most often I'm right."

Stefan worked near the World Trade Center as a broker, a position he derided as analogous to a used car salesman. ("I never let my customers look under the hood," he said often by way of explaining his extraordinary success, "It doesn't matter about the engine when I have them drive a forested mountain road overlooking over a gorgeous valley. That usually does it.")

"Things are pretty good for you right now, eh," David said, "your lucky dog."

David was a little less than six feet and broad shouldered; shorter than Stefan but not by much, and with a delicate face, his hair blond and his visage fair like his Polish grandmother on his father's side. Both men looked like they worked out incessantly.

Carmen quietly nursed her coffee, and hardly ever spoke, which puzzled Shelli, since Carmen knew enough English to get by, obvious she learned it as a child. She thought perhaps Carmen felt she had no words to describe her life in Brazil, raised by a German mother and father who was, like many Brazilians, a hodgepodge of races. Whenever Shelli asked, Carmen said life was slower, with little to do other than lie on the beach and soak up the sun, but for the few years she worked in a factory sewing clothes. That period she wouldn't talk about.

David said he had read a troubling story in the *Financial Times* that said that globalization was working against the interests of the poorest nations.

"When did you start reading the financial papers?" Stefan said.

"I've become a reader of *Financial Times* and *Wall Street Journal* to get a different perspective," David said. David was a psychiatrist who worked with troubled teenagers and exuded a caring demeanor. "Weren't you the one who told me to read Helene Cooper, the reporter with the WSJ?'"

"She's a fresh voice."

"I don't know if you read the item in the other day's paper— might have been Monday's—that where she said there's a massive mobilization against globalization being planned for the end of year Seattle WTO conference. And then I read an item in the London *Independent* newspaper that savaged the WTO and seemed to side with the organizers of protest. I thought you might find that interesting."

"I didn't see that."

"You used to work in Africa. What do you think?"

Stefan used to teach modern farming methods to villagers in Africa for the UN back in college.

"I'd love to take Shelli and the boys, but the travel can be exhausting…not to mention mosquitos, and tigers that will eat you without a thought, and while there's medication to prevent malaria, typhoid and rabies, getting sick over there is another matter. Very few doctors and hospitals there."

"Dad," Micah said. "Where we going?"

"Nowhere."

"I want to see the tigers," Micah said.

"I was saying I'd like to take you two to a faraway country where I worked once upon a time, long before you were born."

"But you promised," Micah said.

"I didn't," Stefan said.

"Really?" Seth jumped in. "Before I was born?"

"How do you think you got here?" Stefan said. "You were the twinkle in my eye."

"Dad," Seth said. "I want to do a magic show for you." He rocked his dad's knee.

"Sure, I'd love to see."

"Okay. Look at these cards," Seth's hazel eyes glowed with slivers of copper and green, looking like stars from the sky had taken residence there. "Take the bottom card, memorize it and then put it anywhere in the stack of cards. I'll bet I can find it."

Stefan took the bottom card, looked at it, and winked at Seth.

"Put it anywhere," Seth said with a flourish. "Anywhere at all."

Stefan selected a spot for his card. Micah and Nate gathered around. Seth went through the deck and quickly selected one card.

"Is this it?"

"Wow! You're good."

Shelli knew where her son had learned his magic tricks, she had purchased the magic set after their 18-year-old babysitter had performed magic tricks for them, and they begged her to get it. Then after some playtime outside, they said goodbye to David, Carmen and Nate. Seth and Micah stayed outside. Stefan came into the kitchen where Shelli was cleaning up.

"I'm looking forward to spicing our lives up a bit," Stefan said

"What did you say?" Shelli lifted her head from the expresso machine.

Turning around, holding the half and half in one hand, and closing the refrigerator with the other, Stefan spoke in a loud whisper. "We should receive a couple of CDs I overnighted that came highly recommended. Can't wait for the boys go to sleep tonight. I have a quite the surprise for you."

"I'm supposed to know what you're talking about?"

"Sweetheart, I'm just an erotic guy who wants to live out his wildest fantasies."

The Matsons stood in their yard watching the bright lights of the cars move down the hill absorbed in their private thoughts. A typical summer evening on the Jersey Shore and the ocean breeze sweeps the humidity away like cotton fluff that the sugary air spins out of seeming nothingness. Shelli looked up at the trees swaying in the cool breeze and felt comforted by their presence. The darkening sky was clear; only few stars visible. Moving her eyes down the sloping hillside Shelli imagined they were the only ones at the top of the hill. It was easy to imagine this. The neighbors' houses were hard to spot under the large-limbed trees. Her eyes flitted down to their garden that she had planted in front of the house, a potpourri of tulips of every hue, and the occasional candy colored daylilies popping around the lady's mantle, crowding out the delicate whimsy of baby's breath, her favorite. The wind picked up making her shiver. She smelled the sweetness in the air caressing her skin like a baby's kiss and moved closer to Stefan's tall athlete's body, looking up at his broad face with the creased laugh lines, pausing at the magnificent chin to brush the roughness of it with her lips. They were the same age, 40, and looked like they were in their twenties; that's what everyone said anyway. Her head just reached his shoulders; she felt like a twig next to the big oak of his frame.

When she asked him if he had enjoyed the evening, he said, "I always have to watch what I say around you, so you won't take it the wrong way."

"Why do you say that?" Shelli said. "I didn't say anything."

"The look on your face said it all. I couldn't help but be affected."

"That's what happens when people are in a relationship."

"Well, okay, why the sad face?"

"You were getting very cozy with Mattie, and you neglected to see how I was doing with that."

"We've been friends for years. She's like a sister to me."

They were speaking of their friend, Mattie, married to Stefan's best friend, Rick. Stefan and Rick met in college and had been tight ever since. They both worked near Battery Park in the financial district. Mattie was a psychologist and Rick worked at a bank with global interests in their investor relations department. And now they lived four blocks away, so virtually neighbors.

Usually Stefan was lightning-quick with jokes and humorous asides, but when he lost his cool, like now, the bushy eyebrows grew into a hedgerow that looked to have turned prickly, and his big chin jutted out.

"I love her, too. But could you acknowledge me once in a while? I feel like you ignore me when we're with these friends."

"I wish you weren't so clingy."

She didn't know what to say to that, just looked at him, brows furrowed. All he had to do was look at her and give her a smile or some indication that she mattered to him, and all would be right in her world. Then she wouldn't care so much about what he said to Mattie or how he looked at her.

"What would you say if a couple of cheerleaders for the New York Mets showed up and said they wanted to join us?" he said, his voice teasing.

Wrapping her arms around him, inhaling his musky smell, she pressed the fullness of her breasts into his chest, feeling her sadness at his intransigence filling her eyes. They headed into the house. He opened the door for her, which he didn't do very often, and she felt somewhat vindicated.

"Ha. That's a big fantasy for guys."

"You don't have fantasies like that? I thought women were all bisexual."

Her mind froze at his blithe statement. Was that another one of his jokes? She wished she had a witty comeback but couldn't come up with anything. They stepped inside. The darkness pressed in through the wall-to-wall windows.

"Come with me to the kitchen, I need to gather the wine-glasses."

"Don't tell me you're going to wash dishes."

"No, no, I'll wash them tomorrow, I'm just gathering them in from the patio. It'll take a just a minute. I don't like leaving them outside."

Stefan helped carry the glasses in. The plates had been rinsed off earlier that evening and deposited in the sink. Shelli rinsed the glasses and left them on the counter to be washed in the morning. He poured them both a shot glass of vodka with a twist of lime. They went back outside and sat on the patio at the table illuminated by the flickering light of the candles. Around them the heavy musk from their night garden on the hillside below the house filled the air.

Opening on average an hour before sunset, there was a rush of these beauties lifting their faces to the sky: evening primrose, night-blooming water lilies, and jasmine, transforming their garden with strangely intense colors that appeared to glow as the darkness deepened, staying open through the night, spraying their scents like bitches in heat. Shelli surrendered to the evening primrose taking center stage, their pale greenish-yellow goblet flowers dancing the mambo on red and pink stems, crowding out the starry blossomed jasmine shrubs with their strong, sweet fragrance attracting moths and butterflies by the dozens. It was their feasting time.

Shelli's favorite was the night blooming tropical water lily, its maroon flowers a deep psychedelic sheen floating on the dark still waters in the pond, looking like incandescent stars reminding her of Georgia O'Keeffe's vulvalistic paintings. Also calling to mind the sensual, Imogen Cunningham's images of roses and lilies with their thrusting stigmas and fainting petals might appear suggestive to the casual eye, but neither painter concerned themselves with social mores, or political correctness, they just painted what they saw, without patina of morality, flowers exposed in all their naked glory. This was way before the #metoo movement sought to give women freedom from sexual harassment and ended up instead stratifying sexual expression, making men afraid to show their appreciation of good-looking women.

Looking at Stefan, she thought she detected a hint of the impatience that seemed to plague him lately when they were alone.

With a big showy wave of his arm, he placed the bottle of Gray Goose between them, his movement disturbing the stillness of the night.

Earlier in the evening, Mattie Sherman held the guests in thrall with her story about a couple she met at a psychotherapy conference, minor celebrities who had gone public with their open marriage: "He's got several lovers and tells her that he doesn't care for any of them, yet he likes having someone new to sleep with, so they made a deal that he can see these other lovers two nights a week, provided he's home by 2 a.m." Mattie's green eyes glittered. "Other nights, he's with her."

A former model and now a psychotherapist, Mattie was of a class of women who exude good health and femininity, tall and slender, long limbed, with this innate gift inherited from her father, the gift of passing on good cheer, if she had been an intellectual, she would have hosted salons, but she was quite content to throw lavish dinner parties where people didn't have to put on airs or dress up, where they could look as slovenly as they liked, and just be themselves provided they had a few jokes to share. Mattie started the practice, and now they took turns, every month one of them played host. This particular night, the party was being held at the Matsons' house.

A dozen eyebrows shot up at Mattie's comment. The very idea of that veiled suggestion made Shelli's heart do a backflip. The peace she felt whenever she viewed the steepness of Mount Mitchell rising some distance away was shaken for a moment. What was Mattie thinking? She of all people should know that this sort of talk was asking for trouble. Although the next minute, looking up at that huge unshakeable mountain, she thought she could take on anything as long as she remembered to breathe. The mountain was located unusually close to the shore, created from erosion-resistant volcanic rock mixed with sand and clay by the folding of the earth during the collusion of continents, 65 to 490 million years ago.

"That's quite the arrangement," Stefan said, looking around a table made out of reclaimed oak that looked like a big boat set with fancy crystal and resplendent china, his voice adopting a caressing quality as if he was touching all the women at the party and possibly all the women in the world. They were passing around the makings of a feast: rib roast with mustard horseradish sauce, root vegetable mash with garlic, and creamed peas with mushrooms and onions.

"When it comes to sex, males and females rarely see eye to eye," Mattie said, her eyes sweeping the room. "Males are programmed to spread their seed, females to build a nest. For two nights he gets to spread his seed. The question is: can he stop at two nights?"

"What guy wouldn't go for that," Stefan said, his voice vibrating with good cheer.

Shelli didn't often resent Stefan's high-spirited ways, most of the time she liked it and wished she could join in the fun, but she had too much fear in her heart, principally that he would leave her for anyone who looked twice at him. He routinely ignored her bids for attention, but she tasted the bitter and remembered only the sweet. She had hoped he would teach her the finer points of socializing, as he had been raised in a house where socializing was valued, and hoped he would teach her, but he didn't seem to want that role. Maybe the task was too big for him.

A silence fell as people took that moment to eat. Shelli looked at Rick, Mattie's husband, sitting at the other end of the table to see if she could guess his thoughts on the matter. Rick and Stefan were best friends from college and spent a lot of time together getting high and listening to music. He was slimmer than Stefan, but otherwise they looked much alike, even to having the same height, although one was dark and the other fair. They wore the same uniform: battered jeans and shirts emblazoned with images of rock and roll—Stefan with the image of Ian Anderson in his one-legged pose and Rick in a Mick Jagger's open mouth tee shirt.

"I won't touch that with a ten-foot pole," Rick said to Shelli. "I have enough on my hands with one woman."

Rick's sandy hair was slicked back as usual, and his trademark smile, that effusive mouth that said, 'I'm on your side, whatever it is, I mean no harm,' was very much in evidence. Some might call his smile ingratiating, and maybe it was, but Shelli thought he was genuinely seeking the goodwill of others, and meant that smile in the sincerest way, though it made him appear soft, less of a decision maker, more conciliatory.

Rick's remark and the smile that accompanied it warmed her and allayed some of her fear. She gazed out at the extensive plantings in the backyard around them, and heard what sounded like laughter from the flowers, a heady sound barely above a whisper over the sashaying heavy-limbed trees and knew instinctively that when they're happy they sing. This was one of those times. She loved entertaining their friends.

"I wouldn't mind checking that out," Stefan said, putting the fear back into Shelli's gut once again.

"She doesn't like most of the men she had been with and wants to end the experiment, but he's talked her into staying the course at least for the time being," Mattie said with a wicked gleam in her eyes. "It's complicated by the fact that she loves him and doesn't want him to leave her."

"Why be married then?" Shelli asked. "What's the point?" Thinking that if this idea was promoted, most of the marriages around this table would likely be shattered, she turned to look at the other women, Julia Klein and Leah Green, the ones not saying anything.

Shelli felt secure in challenging Mattie, although she would not do so without thinking though her response. The last thing she wanted to do was alienate someone she loved and whom Stefan cared for as well. Early mornings before their children were up they often jogged together.

Out of the clear blue a voice intruded into her thoughts, and could only be compared to caramel, sweet and sticky: "They have children?" Leah said. She had a voice like a bubblegum pop princess.

"Three," Mattie said.

"What guy wouldn't go for that, kids or no kids?" Stefan said, crossing his arms over his chest and leaning back in his chair, his smile expansive. "No big deal. You'd leave your kids with the babysitter and go on a date. Back home with the wife later that night. The kids wouldn't the wiser."

"That's exactly what he says," Mattie said. "He likes having sex with other women but doesn't want them for keeps." A few blonde tendrils popped out of Mattie's chignon and floated around her delicate features.

"I can't believe they're misbehaving with children in the house," Julia's high voice piped up, looking as moist and soft as a cupcake, and striking with her flaming red hair and alabaster skin, green eyes and full rosy cheeks.

Like Julie, Shelli's mom had been a registered nurse, and talked longingly about that time, saying that they were the best days of her life. Shelli wanted to be a nurse at one time, but she couldn't bring herself to volunteer at the local hospital which might have led to nursing school, other interests took priority. Through the years, a kind of simpatico took hold between the two women, and Shelli often called to ask about the minutia of her days, and to sympathize.

"He can't have it both ways," Shelli said, feeling the fear crawl up her spine and lodge in her shoulders making her torso rigid with the rightness of her belief. Her hands tensed around her wine glass as she spoke. "What is it about guys? Is sex with strange women really what you want, to the exclusion of a real relationship?"

"I'd be lost without Mattie," Rick said, cocking his head toward Shelli.

Who says it has to be either or," Stefan said, his fingers doing a jittery dance on the table, "It's the woman who insists on monogamy." He suppressed a grin and winked at Mattie, "If it was up to me, things would be more fluid."

"Let's be real, she bears the children," Mattie said; her voice strong and clear as the trilling of a bird. "The whole of civilization hangs on her loyalty to her children. And her man needs to a good father and provider for them."

"Just for the record, I wouldn't throw you out of bed." Stefan pursed his snail's foot of a mouth the way he did when amused. "In case you're thinking of misbehaving."

Stefan was rugged looking and had a great sense of humor. People were drawn to him, most of the time he seemed to be laughing over a private joke, something benign to bring joy to the world. Normally Shelli loved his outrageous comments and realized that Stefan flirts with all the pretty women, some more than most. That thought was quickly replaced by the certainty that she wouldn't care so much if she sensed from him that he really loved her even as his sexual interest in her had waned.

She didn't think there's anything wrong with flirting, though the implications scared her with its suggestion of betrayal, but on the other hand, what would be the harm of releasing pent-up feelings that otherwise would fester, and maybe not harm the marriage at all, perhaps even strengthen it? When did flirting turn malignant?

"I read a study that found women tire of monogamy more quickly than men do," Shelli said, "and when their libido fails them, instead of having affairs they just avoid sex altogether."

"Yea, right," Stefan said. "Where did you read that? Don't tell me, you don't remember."

"I can look it up on my phone," Shelli said, putting down her fork. "Just give me a minute."

"So basically, you're saying there's no hope," Stefan said, setting down his wine glass and grimacing.

"Daniel Bergner in his article for *The New York Times* cites several studies," Shelli said. "And says it's societal not biological. Women like novelty, too, it turns out. But it's up to both parties to make the effort to keep it going."

"Hah, that just supports my theory," Stefan said.

"What?"

"Shouldn't have to be so much work," Stefan said.

Shelli didn't know what to say to that; the way he spit those words out, they sounded like turds. She thought it odd that her innocent remark said in the hopes of launching a discussion abruptly caused the conversation to end. In any case, she knew he certainly won't appreciate her carrying on about it. It made her think that she had to stop thinking the thorns were removed from her life; they could easily reappear again, in more virulent guises. Looking over the dark Atlantic Ocean in an immense diaphanous sky, she watched the gulls soaring high, swooping and cawing. Crickets chirped into the deepening of the evening. An ocean breeze flooded the patio lifting her spirits, dispelling her negative thoughts.

"There's this restaurant with the best ribs," Mattie said to Stefan. "I get right to the bone."

"I'll bet you do," Stefan said, his body vibrating the way it did when he was tickled and wanting to make people laugh.

There he goes again, Shelli thought, pushing the boundaries of what a woman can tolerate. Her fingers itched to slap him. Why did it bother her so? Everyone would think he was joking, and she knew he liked to toss off-color remarks into the stratosphere. And while it turned Shelli on to watch him, she felt he said those things to Mattie often enough that she wondered if he dreamt of doing something about it. And it wasn't just that one comment; it was the accumulation of comments, and the way he looked at Mattie. Of the ladies, Mattie was clearly the most striking, and she had a way of entering a room—her movements light and quick like a crane ready to take flight at the slightest sound, adding to the sense that she never stayed rooted in one place for long. And she had a buoyant personality, the kind that Stefan found attractive. Listening to her, Shelli all at once felt dull and witless, all her good sense having failed her. Shelli thought if Rick hadn't gotten to Mattie first, it was likely Stefan would have gone for her.

He used to direct those jokes at her, but that ended years ago—she couldn't pinpoint exactly when that happened, or how, but one day she realized that things between them had changed. Now, the sexual vibes had to be orchestrated. Still she marveled at his audacity and the fact that he could get away with it, and that everyone, including herself, found his wisecracks amusing. When he said crazy things it didn't sound awkward, the way it would have if she had said it. He understood the power of persuasion and knew how to engage its tenets to maximum effect. He wasn't using his powers to flirt simply as an end in itself, at least that's what Shelli used to think—until now.

It seemed the more she accommodated his behavior, the worse it got. One time he told a cute teenaged girl behind the Starbucks counter that in a few years he'd be dating her.

Shelli glanced over at Rick, Mattie's husband, who was sitting on her other side, to see how he was taking this. Would he say she should lighten up already? Rick rarely liked to see conflict he was all about kumbaya. The only criticism of him that floated around, he was so plaint that Daniel called Rick a water boy behind his back. Rick was probably the last person she should ask.

Daniel right then was talking to Julia. Shelli would have liked to hear what they were talking about, but with the noise level this high she couldn't pick out individual voices. People made allowances for Daniel, saying he thought too much of himself, regularly dissing the waitresses and porters, forcing them to deal with his obvious irritation, the withering looks and barking commands conveying the sense he thought they were lower than scum. He said he was the only one in his family to achieve anything; his dad spent his entire life working behind a deli counter in Michigan and the rest of the family didn't do much better. After starting a career in advertising, his brother became a heroin addict, and his nephew, too. Daniel ran a clinic at a hospital in New Brunswick that specialized in congenital heart disease and taught at the medical school a couple nights a week. And while his medical license was in good standing, at the same time he was a bit of a charlatan, mostly worked as an administrator in a supervisory role, and yet liked to heap shame on everyone else, like he was some sort of god.

"What do you think would happen if all the computers in the world shut down?" Stefan said, effortlessly controlling the conversation and everyone not only let him, they applauded it. "Imagine just one day, for whatever reason, all digital transmission ceased."

Stefan was speculating about the Y2K bug. The crux of the problem: in the past programmers had represented the four-digit year with only the final two digits, which made the year 2000 indistinguishable from 1900. Then someone had the bright idea of recalculating 2000 as a leap year. There was a mad scramble. Years divisible by 100 are not technically leap years, except for years that are divisible by 400. Thus, the year 2000 was a leap year.

There was silence around the table as the enormity of what this meant sunk in.

"A friend in IT says it's a simple adjustment," Joe, a pharmacist, said, waving one hand in dismissal, "one of those things that get blown up to epic proportions. People in the media are forever escalating things."

"Everyone's an expert," Daniel said in his disparaging way.

Julia mentioned that she was on maternity leave and planned to go back to work part time in a year.

"It makes me *meshuggah* to leave my sons in the care of someone else," Shelli said in an aside to Mattie.

The Swedish-born Julia converted to Judaism when she married Joe and become more Jewish than anyone else at the table, including Shelli, having mastered the perfect blini.

Shelli felt compelled to break in with a comment. "Stefan might take maturity leave."

"Hey, I'm the most mature one in the bunch," Stefan countered.

"That's a scary thought," Shelli said after a pause, trying to keep her tone light and airy like Stefan.

"Best to stop while you're ahead," Stefan said. "I can see the smoke coming out of your ears."

Shelli looked over the table at Julia, who was sitting across from her, to ask if she wanted wine, thinking she'd fill both their glasses, partially to give her time to come up with a good comeback. Feeling as left out as when her brothers told her she couldn't play football, not unless she could catch a football thrown like a bullet, which she claimed she could do but couldn't. One of her brothers threw a ball really hard and fast and it popped out of her hands despite her best efforts. A friend of her brothers, bigger and older than her, said she wasn't good enough and ran her off the field. The devastation she felt so long ago came back to her and a sob escaped. She wiped the lone tear, returned to the table with a couple of bottles, and manufacturing a smile poured more wine for the people who asked, all the while thinking: Why was she never good enough?

Often when she felt pressure to come up with something clever, her brain froze into a block of ice. At that moment, she felt helpless in the grip of the adrenaline that flooded her veins. But Julia said no, she wasn't drinking; her baby didn't like the taste of alcohol in her breastmilk.

"I remember those days," Shelli said. "My boys were always hungry. Having two at once drove me *meshuggah*."

"Everything these days makes me *meshuggah*," Julia said, lifting her hands as if supremely exasperated, having so many children at once can do that to a person. "Triplets are impossible, but somehow I manage with only two breasts. I could use a couple more."

"What's this with the Yiddish?" Leah, who had been silent until now, her broad eyebrows lifted in mock disdain, her wide mouth puckered, sitting so far away Shelli could hardly hear her soft voice. "You know what they say about converts. They become more Jewish than the Jews who're born to it."

Shelli had a problem pronouncing the language, and memorizing the prayers, but the myriad rules and regulations around the cooking of food and various mitzvahs didn't faze her, she simply ignored them. Of the group, Leah and Daniel were the most religious and observed the dietary laws but there was minimal discussion, too many ways to get around the problem of mixing dairy and meat, which led to Shelli developing a taste for non-dairy creamers. Even to giving up pork, which only applied to food cooked in one's kitchen, didn't bother her, easy to give up bacon, too fatty anyway. When they went out to restaurants, if the dish had pork, they shrugged it off, saying what you gonna do? The rabbi said it was fine when you're eating out, impossible to track what's in the food. And she was happy to see that Stefan's mother ate lobster whenever she could, but always out at restaurants, never in the home.

"It's hard to keep up with Shelli," Mattie said. "She knows more Yiddish than I do."

"Stefan makes fun of me when I try to speak it," Shelli said. "My mouth can't do it right. I keep working it, hoping it'll kick in."

"Speak from deep in your throat, and bring up phlegm to do it right," Stefan said helpfully.

"Easy for you to say," Shelli said.

"You don't have to speak Yiddish," Leah said. "It's not a requirement."

"Yeah, but it helps me feel more Jewish," Shelli said.

"If you're not born to it," Stefan said, "you might get confused and do the sign of the cross instead."

"When have you seen me do the sign of the cross?" Shelli said pointedly, stopping herself from expressing the pain and hurt she felt and bottling its rise in her throat. Why did she always have to prove herself worthy? "You know I believe like you that Jesus was a prophet for the ages, like Moses, but not a god born of a virgin birth."

"See, I'm right, you don't have a sense of humor," Stefan said.

"Isn't it interesting that so many of us have multiples?" Mattie said with a worried glance at Shelli.

"It's the water," Julia said.

"Mine were naturally conceived," Shelli managed to squeak out, "And by the time-honored methods, born premature, but luckily they had fully developed lungs. All they lacked was their sucking reflex, but they were skin and bones, and hungry all the time. I pumped my milk and used preemie nipples, it wasn't easy, but I managed." Shelli went on to point out that naturally conceived twins occurs once in one hundred births, and the incidence of identical twins, one in every 285 births.

"That's because they were metabolizing your milk so quickly," Julia said.

"Oy vey, I had to feed them nonstop."

"Infants are incredibly fragile, and delicate and beautiful, every single one of them—did I mention that I worked with preemies less than 28 weeks gestation right out of nursing school? I had to give them injections. It was scary; their skin is extremely delicate. They can develop debilitating scar tissue later if the injection isn't done right."

"The shock of having to do those injections," Shelli said.

"It's sobering," Julia shivered.

Stefan was drawn into a conversation with Rick and Joe reminiscing about the time they drove down to Fort Lauderdale on Spring Break and drove around endlessly trying to find a grocery store at midnight. Stefan said several times, "you had to be there," and laughing so hard he had to wipe away the tears.

The sun set behind a hill and cast a long shadow over the patio. Shelli lit candles.

"She doesn't need *me* anymore," Joe, Julia's bear-like husband, said, his moist eyes behind thick lens reflecting the tremulous candlelight.

"It's true," Julia said. "This baby has everything I need. Feeding her is more pleasurable than sex."

"I wish they could have taken the breast," Shelli said. "I kept trying but they wouldn't suck—the doc said babies generally develop the sucking reflex in the last month of gestation."

"Breastfeeding was so good I could just *plotz*," Mattie said with a wink at Shelli.

"But they could breathe on their own?" Julia said.

"They were in my tummy for eight months. Apparently, that's long enough to develop fully functioning lungs, thank god," Shelli said.

Joe's throaty response sounded loud next to Shelli's ear. "Well that's certainly true of Julia," he said. "With the triplets, it was physically impossible for her to rely solely on breastfeeding."

A frown crossed Stefan's face. "Shelli, is that a new dress?"

"It's an old shmatte I've had forever," Shelli said, not happy that he would question her like this in front of their friends.

She chafed at the memory of the last time she told him about a purchase. It was not on sale, and he said she wasn't a "good mother." He wanted her to buy only sales, and sometimes she did comply, but sometimes she saw something she didn't want to wait for, knowing it wouldn't go on sale for months. He didn't say "wife," he said "mother" when she was the most adoring, loving person around her boys, never laying a hand on them, hating to reprimand them for anything. To insist that she was a good mother would fall on deaf ears, but she did it anyway and it led to a big fight; Stefan was never moved by what he considered selfish behavior, and thought all material acquisitions—with the exception of computers, phones, and cars—to be mostly unnecessary. Over to Shelli's right, the deep emerald of a carefully tended expanse of lawn ringed by the prickly brown-gray brambles of unshorn greenbelt sprang into view. The idea of the softness of colonial bentgrass ringed by thorns struck her as a metaphor for life. These days, she didn't feel threatened as much by the encircling thorns; the proximity of Stefan made her feel protected from whatever life threw at her. The dotcom boom was at its peak and nearly every man and woman at this table waxed giddy from the precipitous highs of their holdings, and yet Stefan was tight about expenses. The couples in their group, all in their 30s, were celebrating a unicorn IPO offering—having reached a billion-dollar market value—that everyone had their eye on. Most of them stood to make big gains. Yet in buying that dress, she did the forbidden. His mother never bought new, only shopped thrift stores. Even her wedding ring was gold-plated, and she didn't have an engagement ring. And the curious thing was, Shelli's mother was much the same way, after the first three kids were born, she stopped caring about clothes or anything else except she clung to religion. And back when they were poor, Shelli had no jewelry other her engagement ring, a half carat with flaws sold at a discount and a narrow 14k gold wedding ring. Back then she wore jeans and a tee shirt virtually everywhere, except work where she rotated three or four outfits purchased on sale. When her closet was frugal, that's when he loved her best.

"That's women for you," Joe said with a shrug at Stefan's kvetching.

"I know it's shameful," Shelli said, with a sigh. "I'm trying to cut down."

But why was he needling her in front of their friends? And why, when she did comply, did his attitude turn contemptuous? It was a low tactic.

"Shelli loves to buy expensive things," Stefan said. "Half of the dresses she buys she wears once and then it gets tossed when there's no room for the new stuff. So goyishe."

Right then, the fist curled in Shelli's lap trembled as if she suffered from a neurologic disorder. She wanted to scream. Instead, she smiled as if he were joking.

"Shelli has great taste in clothes," Julia said. "If I could fit a size 2 I'd be begging for handouts from her closet."

"I don't shop designer labels," Mattie said. "Not unless there's a 70 percent off sale."

"I do that too," Shelli said. "But it's hard to find extra-small on sale." Her voice sounded tinny to her ears, like a whipped dog. Pointedly disregarding Stefan's frown, she tried to control her trembling limbs, realizing that he knew the conversation unsettled her, and thought she saw him gloat, mouth curling.

She fled to happier thoughts: early that day, she ran across an amusing story. After the sale of his first short story, "The Debutante," Fitzgerald purchased white flannel presumably to have it made into a white three-piece suit, according to his granddaughter Eleanor Lanahan. Perhaps he bought it as a nod to Mark Twain, who immortalized the three-piece white suit, but Fitzgerald was never photographed in it, so no visible proof. Tom Wolfe adopted the three-piece white suit in homage to both authors, and added a distinctive twist of his own, wearing a white or lavender button-down with an impossibly high collar, sometimes adding a black-and-white checkered or completely white silk tie and/or black kerchief or some variation thereof in his breast pocket, always with an eye for pattern and design. And Mary McCarthy shopped Balenciaga and Lanvin in Paris for little black dresses and silk tops, silk scarves and buttery leather gloves from Hermès. But in those days, designers were more reasonably priced. Shelli had a piece or two from these designers, and would have liked more, but she couldn't afford it, not at retail, maybe when it had been marked down by eighty percent, and even that was a stretch. She also loved the minimalistic knits that the younger Joan Didion favored, and that's the direction she tended to go. The aesthetic of Phoebe Philo's designs for Céline fit her sense of personal style to a T. But it wasn't just the women with a literary bent who dressed well; Samuel Beckett had a Gucci bag, and F. Scott Fitzgerald dressed in three-piece Brooks Brothers' suits, as did many other men in the literary world of yesteryear. The fascination with white suits was interesting though. Fitzgerald believed the color signified not only purity, but wealth and breeding; after all, it takes money and a pristine lifestyle to keep white clean. His characters Daisy and Jordan are described as wearing white silk or cream chiffon, Gatsby in a white flannel suit, silver shirt and gold-colored tie.

Thinking like this made Shelli happy. Whatever slings and arrows Stefan might hurl would not pierce her soul.

And then he went for the kill. "Remember that resort in Cabo?" Stefan said. "That cost me thousands of dollars. What was it called?"

"You had a good time when you got your mind off how much it cost," Shelli said, feeling it was useless; she could never convince him that going to an expensive resort was a good idea.

"How could I forget?" Stefan said. "It was 500 a night."

"The resort was on the nicest beach in all of Cabo."

"And that's not saying much," Stefan said. "Cabo has the worst beaches."

"You were the one who wanted to go to Cabo," Shelli said. "We learned after we got there that people don't go for the beaches. We could have taken a boat to see a coral reef, but we went the wrong time of year."

"Only evidence of your poor planning," Stefan said.

"You were the one who said to go in April," Shelli said. "Remember? To take advantage of Spring Break."

"So?" Stefan said.

"Instead we went on a boat ride to see dolphins. That was fun wasn't it?"

"It was okay."

"Well, you said it was okay before we left, but when we got there and you heard how much it was going to cost with all resort fees, the taxes and everything, you wanted to leave." A note of desperation sounded in Shelli's voice. She didn't like that she was put on trial in front of his good friends and of course they would automatically defend him.

"Too rich for my taste," Stefan said. He took a bite of the rib and sipped his cabernet. Shelli refrained from telling him how much the wine cost. "We could have found a cheaper hotel," he added.

"Since then, he refuses to go on vacation with me or the kids," Shelli said as if Stefan hadn't spoken, her voice cracking," unless it's to visit his parents. And we stay at a Motel 6."

"Nothing wrong with Motel 6," Stefan said. "We're just there to sleep; we're hanging with the folks during the day."

She suspected this was payback. Every time she brought the subject of vacations just the two of them or with the children, he said he was too busy, unless it was to visit his parents. The reason was plain: Stefan didn't care for the trappings of luxury. When he talked about money, his expression reminded her of Stefan's father, Henrik, who refused to replace his black and white television set even when the image on the screen was grainy and hard to see. And even though Stefan kvetched about his father, but there was a note of pride in his voice.

The public shaming worked. A few days later in a discussion about this very thing, Shelli agreed no more luxury hotels, and further agreed that they would only buy used cars and although she decried the idea of buying laptops that were on sale with the minimum gigabytes of hard drive, pointing out that he would have to replace computers more often, he said he didn't care, he would rather spend less money up front. His tone derisive, Stefan said that only goyim shop retail, and it dawned on her that he didn't enjoy spending money, period, there was no rationality in the decision to buy as cheaply as possible, no consideration to ascertain whether the product was defective or inferior, but she swallowed the bile that had lodged in her throat, and said she could see it in hotels and cars, but not computers.

She had been unable to convince Stefan to get a computer for each of their sons. He said it was too expensive, nothing she said convinced him that this was a justifiable expense, although he could afford it, but no, he told them they would have to share. She hated having to referee, telling them they had to switch every half hour, and then hearing their screams when one wanted a couple more minutes, which they always did, and then having to find something else for the other kid to do while waiting his turn, all of this had become a big headache for her, but what was particularly galling, having to stop everything she was doing to tend their squabbling, which often ended with tears and heartache. The whole thing was avoidable, but Stefan wasn't moved by the idea that computers are relatively cheap and easily affordable by someone with his salary.

This went on for several months. Then Shelli heard him say he thought his own computer was too slow, the one he had bought six months previously already outdated.

"So this time make sure your new laptop is loaded with at least four GB of RAM, that's what the *PC Magazine* says," she said. "And has processing power, and plenty of storage."

"I don't care what the magazine says, I'm looking for the best deals," he said. "This is for home use, I don't need much storage."

But by that time the relationship between the brothers was forever stained by long-harbored resentments. Shelli blamed Stefan for the nasty fist fights that occurred periodically between them. She couldn't understand why Stefan kept buying computers with the lowest possible of everything; she didn't buy the argument about spending less money upfront. She pointed out that getting the latest technology would pay for itself; he wouldn't have to replace laptops every six months. But she was glad for once that he wanted a new computer and suggested he give his old one to one of the boys, so both would have their own. He agreed to her proposal, and suddenly there was peace between the boys.

They were barely done with that crisis when a new one surfaced. Later that evening he said he wasn't going to put more than $30k into their college fund. He wouldn't budge when she pointed out that a couple of financial gurus he respected said that a minimum of $100K was standard, even after she showed him articles that argued this point. Stefan wasn't swayed. Shelli decided that this man was irrational when it came to money. He gave generously to his favorite charity, otherwise he was determined they would live frugally, even to the types of schools her sons might aspire to. Even though he could afford it, Harvard was out. Surely, he had to be kidding. Shelli had a problem believing that when it came down to it, he wouldn't fold up his Scrooge-like mentality like an old tent and do was right for his children. He would only give generously to charity cases from far off lands, people he didn't know, but not to his children, why was that?

Shelli thought his interest in saving was maniacal; yet his fear of not being perceived as generous in a public way to people in need overrode his fear of being poor and came at the expense of his children's future. They would get nothing, because at the rate he was giving to charities the accountants said there wouldn't be enough for the children's education if he didn't put a cap on his charitable giving. But it was obvious he liked being feted at the charity balls, and having his name etched on buildings, the way he preened at these events, and glowed when people gathered around to compliment him, but forget when it came to his own kids. Stefan's generosity ended at his front door. He was the type who preferred to give cards at birthdays, never presents, saying why spend the money for something the person getting the gift would be repurposing. Their furniture came from Goodwill and Craig's List. Not that there was anything wrong with that, she wouldn't have cared about the rest of it if he had supplied both boys with computers powerful enough to run their games and put enough money into their education funds so they could go wherever they wanted, and encouraged them to do so. She might not have cared to buy expensive dresses. She picked up her wine and took a mouthful of the cloying liquid, tasting the interplay of elements, the tingling on the tip of her tongue, and the slightly oily sensation that lingered, allowing the wine to continue roiling her taste buds a bit longer, delighting in the forbidden. All matter of unpleasant thoughts fled, and she started thinking about the things that made her happy. She recalled stopping by one of her favorite stores and buying a dress that wasn't on sale, something incredibly beautiful, one of a kind. Everything he would object to. The memory of that purchase buoyed her spirits. Whenever she felt neglected, or hemmed in by his insistence that they live as frugally as possible, she felt the urge to buy herself another dress, since she couldn't look forward to a vacation, and he forbid her from buying anything more for the house. But what drove this impulse? Just that morning she learned that Stefan had placed their money on a handful of choice properties, investing in the IPOs on opening day—all of them, pre-IPO, doubling and tripling. It seemed their money flowed like water out of a tap. A pity they couldn't spend it.

Rick turned to Julia, who spoke up just then, asking Rick about his new car, another Jaguar.

"All I can say," Rick said, "you want to own something that's a treat to drive and has plenty of horsepower, this would be my recommendation. It gets slightly better mileage on the highway then a Porsche, or a BMW 550. But in the city, it burns gas, lights your dollar bills on fire."

"We could use a good car," Julia said, "driving down to Florida."

She was planning the usual visit to the grandparents, looking forward to lazy days filled with mahjong and lemon tea, and evenings playing miniature golf, meanwhile showing off the youngest who would be three months by then. Having the entire family there would mean plenty of help on hand, nothing like what she faced at home. That night was a good example of what she had to deal with when she went out with hubby. They left the infant and triplets with her two aunts that night, who were wonderful, she said, but she felt guilty about it. "I worry the kids are too much for them."

Mattie started picking up the dishes, and then all the women were grabbing plates as if they were in a contest to see who could pick up the biggest load, and going into the kitchen honking like a gaggle of geese as they rinsed and stacked. Rick pulled Stefan away from his circle of admirers to reminisce about their latest achievement, a weekend to complete two hundred miles over hilly terrain.

"You were riding a Serotta, weren't you?" Rick said.

"And not just because it's made in America," Stefan said, his eyes twinkling, the corners of his mouth twitching. "It's unbelievably smooth, and fast, the metal contoured to increase the wind's velocity." He rocked back on his heels as he was wont to do when kibitzing with friends.

"I'm looking to buy," Rick said. "What did you pay for yours?"

"Five thousand for the frame, hand painted. The racing wheels were separate. A thousand each." As Stefan spoke, he rolled forward on his heels, inclining his head toward Rick, and crossed his arms, moving into his figurative rocking chair, his go-to position when launching into a favorite topic.

"I've been riding a Trek, but I'm ready to test ride other brands. I also have a Pogliaghi from the seventies. But it stays on the wall."

The other men spoke admiringly of Rick and Stefan's prowess in sports, even as that designation didn't include them. Joe was round and soft; Daniel had some muscle, occasionally he went to the gym, but nothing strenuous. Matsons and Shermans were fit and looked it. They spent their free time after work and weekends on their bicycles training, and when they could fit it in, they lifted weights.

Stefan poured more wine for Mattie, apparently having had couple of glasses already and now mushing her words together, her movements loose. Stefan followed her and she did a little dance, swirling her hips in a sexy way in the far corner of the kitchen. Her bra strap was partially visible; her dress didn't completely cover it, making his blood jump. He pulled the back of the bra strap as a tease, letting it snap lightly.

"Ohh." Mattie twirled around, her hair streaming strands of white gold, and her green eyes widened, her smile morphing into an exaggerated look of surprise. "Bad boy," she said playfully. She looked as sweet as spun sugar, but she kept her luminous gaze on Rick. "You'll protect me, won't you, honey?"

Shelli's shocked expression turned onto one of amused tolerance, at least that's what Stefan thought he saw. It was the response that he favored the one that said, "My man is a cut-up and I'm thrilled to be with him." That look said all things are forgiven and gave Stefan a warm feeling; sometimes Shelli proved a good audience, but very rarely these days did she let loose, she was proving to be prudish through and through. She had turned sourpuss, no sense of humor. Not like when they were dating, she used to laugh at everything.

"The winner gets to see Mattie naked," Stefan said, pulled her strap again, letting go with a guffaw. What is it about pulling a bra strap that had him in hysterics? He had devolved into a child. Looking around him, he thought he saw people laughing with him, hugely entertained by his antics. He glowed inside, his body quivering.

"You should charge admission." Stefan stepped back, his grin lighting up his face. "Your turn," he said to Rick, massaging his fingers.

Mattie's hips swiveled in a tight rotation, moving like one born to perform, her silk dress floating around her body lighter than air. "I used to model," she said, wearing a lovely, wide, mischievous smile.

"Yea, well, I spent a summer in Milan dating lingerie models," Rick said. "Come to think of it, isn't that how I met you?"

"Ah, so you do have a few skeletons in your closet," Stefan said with a wink.

"Honey, I've already seen you," Rick said. "Is there something else you can do for me?" What he saw must have been encouraging, because his own smile burst open like a flower in warm air.

"Hah," Stefan said, placing his hand on Mattie's ass, and squeezing. "Joe, you might be right about Big Pharma. But it's not worth anything, not unless you got a piece like this one." He squeezed again, making his nerve endings roil. "Know what I'm saying?" With his other hand, he reached down to squeeze Shelli's ass, being careful to steer clear of Julia—he didn't know how she'd take it—but his fingers on Mattie's rear understood this was one that he hadn't yet explored but dreamt about endlessly, creating a buzz in his groin that had him feeling dizzy like he had been deprived of oxygen.

"My turn," Daniel said to Mattie, and he snapped her bra, causing her head to spin. The men fell into hysterics.

"That's wicked," Rick cried, his face reddening.

"Know what?" Stefan said. "I'm starting to like this game."

"Enough of that," Mattie said, slapping Stefan's hand playfully. "Didn't your mama teach you any manners?"

"When it comes to you, nearly everything goes out the window," Stefan said, thinking he was one of those guys who needs a haram, one woman not enough. But how to make that work? Pleasing even one woman a minefield.

Mattie beamed at him as if he had paid her the highest compliment.

But then the whole group gathered around him, even Shelli seemed to be looking at him with complete adoration, and he felt an incredible joy suffuse his entire insides, his spirits lifting. But there was this tiny, secret fear that he couldn't squash. Can anyone tell what really is in someone's heart? She was always rushing to do things for him, but she did that with everyone. When someone tells him they love him, what does that mean in raw, unabridged no-holds terms? And she was perpetually assessing everything he said with an eye for inconsistencies, he hated being judged like that, by an unsparing mind, it stressed him out. Why couldn't she enjoy life without putting a name to it? She had turned out to be more of an intellect than he had realized; he liked to dabble in the comfort of generalities, often he resented her tendency to drill down. Why does everything have to be so serious, he said more than once, and rarely got an answer. What exactly held them together, did she really share his love of cycling, or was she just doing it to please him? Did she really enjoy his jokes? He watched her pick up some dishes, her movements tentative, like she was afraid of disturbing the air. He wished she could laugh more. Her temerity made him fear for the future.

Two

"What were we talking about?" Shelli said, breathing in floral essence. "Oh yes…your fantasies." She sipped from her glass. The susurration of leaves made a sound like murmuring voices over her sandaled feet sliding against the hard rock of the patio.

"Honestly, I'm starved for some fun." Stefan flashed one of his smiles for which he was known; its ghost seeming to linger at the corners never completely vanishing from his broad mouth.

"What are you saying?"

'To put it bluntly, I want to live a little, do something wild. And I'd like to do it with you." That smile again.

"We have children now. We're alter-cockers." She felt herself melting under his sunny gaze, what he was driving at exactly?

"You call 40 an alter cocker?"

"What is it you want to do?"

"Have a threesome."

"Really?" She had to pause for a minute. The idea of a threesome shocked her. She had to put his words on pause for a moment longer. It wasn't about the morality of it; it was more about what that might do to their relationship. Why did he suggest that? Would having another woman change his feelings for her? If he wanted another woman, why not have an affair and leave her out of it? She sipped her drink thinking what in the world could she say that he would understand, other than something as roundabout as he had been. Finally: "Didn't you get that out of your system in college?" her throat constricted, and she could barely get the words out.

The first night they slept in the Highlands house, they waited until the boys were fast asleep to go outside and sit on a bench overlooking the water lilies in the pond, and kiss nonstop, galvanized by the beauty around them, before being driven indoors by the midnight chill to make love in their warm bed. He hadn't been bored then. Back then the whole family had been so totally in love with each other in the days the boys looked to their parents as gods. She had given in to their desire to push their twin beds together in their shared room and told them how lucky they were to have each other.

Gazing at the garden's magnificence, in her heart she cried bitter tears. What is it about flowers? In the words of John Lennon: "Love is a flower." Juliet says to Romeo that "A rose by any other name would smell as sweet," which begs the question: Is it true that "a rose is just a rose," as Gertrude Stein famously said? Or was Wittgenstein correct in theorizing that it's how we use the word that gives it its meaning and context changes the meaning (depending on how the word is used), and the manner in which it's said, something that Leo Strauss also believed. These kinds of thoughts she couldn't share with Stefan, he was more of a pragmatist, and took things way too literally, and didn't trust nuances.

She channeled Sappho, remembering his analogy that a woman was like a "hyacinth in the mountains that the shepherds trample with their feet." Why was it that these shepherds didn't value the woman once they had her? And more to the point, why are men's relationships with women problematic? Seeing his father's ghost makes Hamlet reevaluate his relationship with women, and not just his mother, to whom Hamlet said, "Frailty thy name is woman." In the same vein, he tries to shame Ophelia for wearing makeup, and urges her to join a nunnery. Her response is to throw flowers all over Elsinore (the port city in eastern Denmark that serves as the setting for this play), and twine flowers around her hair and body, giving out armfuls of flowers to everyone she comes across. Then she jumps in the river to her death.

Stefan shattered the quiet: "As a teenager I didn't do anything fun, you know my friends, they're the most conservative people."

His friends were the children of his parents' friends, having grown up in the flatlands area of Brooklyn within blocks of each other, attending the same high school and college, and providing him with a sense of community that made her feel secure, something she had longed all her life for herself. In her heart she thanked Stefan who had made this possible with a wave of his magic wand. Marrying him led to so many good things, including being introduced to this amazing group. Making friends didn't come to her as easily as for Stefan; it wasn't a matter of intelligence, but more of a personality thing, the ability to attract people like bees to honey. Oftentimes she felt tongue-tied next to Stefan.

The group's friendship was anchored by tribal connection, a cultural affinity, a nebulous state of mind based on Torah. The Christianity that she remembered from her youth sought to incorporate the values of peace and brotherhood of Torah superposed on the Greek ideals as articulated by Aristotle and Plato, chiefly the striving for courage and effectiveness. Maybe the Jews and Greeks might have joined together on that, but they couldn't agree on the god thing. Even before she met Stefan she was attracted to Judaism and took Hebrew language classes, and classes on Jewish history and culture, but had trouble pronouncing Hebrew and the occasional Yiddish.

She practiced, but there were mishaps. And while most people applauded her attempts, Stefan told her she should give up already. Shelli pointed out in vain that she was dyslexic and had trouble pronouncing words in general. He just laughed.

Shelli sipped the colorless liquid. It went down smooth, but it had a kick, making her head feel like it was filled with helium and about to float away. The idea that Stefan wanted another woman to join them in bed filled her with the kind of dread she reserved for spiders and scorpions. Did that mean he didn't find her body exciting anymore? Personally she liked her lean runner's body, but had to concede that perhaps he was tired of having sex with the same type of body day after day, a woman with her singular personality and doing the same things, something he kvetched about from time to time. He wasn't shy about neglecting to spare her feelings.

"I read in some British tabloid that a sexologist," Stefan said, "god, I forgot her name, and I never forget names…."

"A what?"

"A sexologist, they're a thing, I can't remember her name, but I do remember that she was a woman. Anyhow she said that threesomes are basically the male version of walking in a new pair of Jimmy Choos while eating cake."

"You flirt with everyone but me."

"And you act as if having sex is a chore."

In the space of a gasp for breath, Shelli turned her head looking for the red shimmer of water lilies to gaze at them full on, her mind on hold long enough to uncover the gross exaggeration of his accusation. "That's not what you said to me one of those nights we stayed up all night fucking."

"What night was that?"

She felt her head spin. With a strange pervasive sadness in her heart she listened to his accusation and felt her response well up in her throat: "The night you said that it's not true that the way to a man's heart is through his stomach. We were living in the apartment in Metuchen, remember those days? Screwing every day and I don't remember you complaining." As she said this, she felt her heart lurch.

"That was before we married. You've changed. Now you make sex as romantic as doing laundry."

She thought back to the previous day when they were walking down the street together and she stopped to tie her shoe. She stood up and saw him look at a woman's legs. The woman's face broke out in smiles; obviously flattered by the attention. Shelli tried to take it in stride and told Stefan he had good taste. He responded, "Well, I married you, didn't I?" She found his response gratifying, and her heart swelled to hear that sort of backhand compliment, making her feel that he still thought her sexy. But there were other times when he slighted her in a manner that she thought showed indifference to her feelings.

Now, she thought, is the time to bring it up: "Let me tell what's not romantic, seeing you misbehave around that super cute 20 year old ballroom dance teacher…stopping the dance lesson to ask her to spank you."

"She said I was being a bad boy, so I told her to spank me. You wouldn't have minded if she had been a dog."

Relieved that they were finally talking about their problems, she decided to hear him out. It was difficult not to interrupt and insist he was wrong.

"You shook your butt in her face. We can't take lessons together if you act like that, it's too embarrassing."

"What are you, my mother?"

"Oy, somebody has to teach you manners, apparently she didn't." Shelli didn't hide her outrage. "Your mother, indeed."

She felt an overwhelming urge to try and out-shout him, but his voice was louder and drowned her out, she found her throat getting raw and her voice cracking, so she shut up and let him talk until he finished.

"Remember when we first met," Shelli said, "you talked to me about empathy, and you had me thinking you were the kindest, sweetest man in the world with your precious moral maxims—oh, you fooled me the way you fool everyone. Now we both know it's' bullshit."

"You know the problem with you? You've no sense of humor. I have to walk on eggshells around you."

With prodding, she accepted that she was emotionally challenged, and needed help to undo the legacy of the Religious of the Sacred Heart of Jesus, an order of cloistered nuns, with whom she lived as a student for a couple of years. She had to admit she had no idea what that did to her sensibility. In her attempt to be open-minded about his proposal, she hoped her remarks would suggest a plan of action to him and pave the way to a change of attitude, and perhaps to a more inclusive spirit. But a persistent little voice inside suggested that maybe he was right, she usually hated ideas that came from him, and while she thought she was showing love, to others she may have appeared cold and distant.

Stefan slugged back a shot glass and filled both their glasses to the brim. Shelli promptly downed her drink.

"I know I need help," she said. "I'm so uptight."

As she spoke, he refilled their glasses with a flourish.

A good deal of his uneasiness had to do with self-image. He had a lot of questions about his own performance before he married Shelli (she wasn't as bad in bed as he said, but he liked how his assertion appeared to shake her complacency), now those questions rose up to haunt him again like feverish ghosts. He knew that Shelli liked the things they did together—her passionate embrace did a lot to boost his morale—but he also suspected that most of the women he had dated hadn't considered him much of a stud. No one raved about his sexual prowess, yet no one had ever kvetched much, either. They simply didn't talk about it. He didn't know what any of them thought: to hear nothing, no feedback, made him wonder. He worked feverishly on his cycling. His ass and legs had gained lasting power (at the end of each summer he clocked at least three hundred miles with over ten thousand feet of climbing.) Now after years of practice, he could last forever, and mastered the art of cunnilingus. Shelli had assured him that he was fine in all regards, yet a sliver of doubt remained.

"We do it a few times a week," Shelli said slowly. "That's more than most people, you've said that yourself." His flippant remarks had her thinking that she had to pay attention to the subtext, what was he saying below the surface? Was she too passive? She didn't know what else she could do, he kept telling her to mix it up ("don't spend too long on any one thing"), and that made her feel less sure of herself.

"You don't have any fantasies then?"

"I fantasize about having sex with two men. How comfortable are you with that?" As she said this, she thought, "Good, now he'll see what it's like."

"That you would want that never occurred to me." He said this slowly.

His response surprised her. Oh, so it's all about *him*.

Shelli flung her hands up knocking over her glass, spilling the contents, the glass shattering. "I didn't mean to do that. I'm so tired." Shelli bent down to pick up the broken glass. "I don't want anyone to step on this in bare feet. Can you help me please?"

"Sure." He brought out the broom.

Overcome by a sense of nausea, fighting a deep unease in her gut, knowing that the old inert fragility of the glass eluded her, slipped through her fingers, and broke into pieces, thinking her malaise suspiciously like the transparency of glass, but wasn't, she moved as if she was about to drop another glass. Stefan came behind her and gripped her wrist. He unwound her fingers from the glass and placed it gently down. During that time, the sounds, the smells, and the tastes that her senses picked up were suspiciously not there, especially when they ran quickly through her like startled hares, but the minute she experienced them they were gone, vanished as if they had never been. Were they never real, never themselves, nothing but themselves? In her mind, always that sense of ambiguity and confusion.

It started with name calling and then the fight went out of control. Their limbs shook with conviction and their faces twisted into the sharp lines of hatred, their eyes squinting arrows while they ransacked their memories for weapons to rip the scabs from old wounds. Then they ran out of gas. They stopped talking and listened to the whispering leaves.

He took her into his arms, and she pressed her face against his chest and allowed herself a couple of sobs.

"I'm sorry to burst your fantasy, but I couldn't watch you put your hands on another woman." She looked up at his face and stroked his back with the arms she wrapped round him, breathing in the smell of him that melted into his thin gray tee shirt, a moody cloudbank covering the comforting presence of his shoulder. They headed upstairs to their bedroom. He went to the bathroom to pee and she plopped on the bed, inside a swirl of conflicting emotions. Who cares if they watch porn together as long it satisfies his itch? She could get used to porn. She liked it when it was done well.

There were no clear guidelines to what's right, or best, or even if there was a best. The whole thing had her feeling apprehensive.

In questioning what her mother taught her, everything was up for grabs. Bubbles, her gray Persian cat, a nurtured male, began kneading her leg, raising his squashed-in snub nose, his teary eyes running, demanding to be petted. He was bred to be a lap cat, and looked like a doll that children might want to dress up, but he didn't like the boys, not unless they acted the part of sedated puppies. Shelli petted his gray body blurring into the semidarkness and realized that she really didn't give a shit what the world might say about their sex life. It's a private matter between her and Stefan. Her decision to fashion a response to the question and throw away the anti-sex message mother used to preach gave her a lot of pleasure. After all, how did it work out for her mother? Not so well. At that moment she felt some of her tension slip away. She thought that she must go out and find a cute puppy for them, one that Stefan could tolerate, he was more of a cat person, but she had to run the idea past him first. At first he had qualms about getting a puppy, thinking it would be a lot of work, the house training and so on. She was certain she could talk him into it, but it'd take some work.

It started to rain. Not just a light rain, but a major soaking, a drumbeat on the windows that sounded a fusillade of bullets. It got too loud to hear their voices. Neither boy paid the rain much mind, they just talked louder. With the twins, food often took a backseat to discourse. A question about the Power Rangers came up. Seth was so outraged when Shelli said fights were staged, he stopped eating his bagel, and peppered Shelli with questions. Micah did the same.

"Didn't you notice the enormous physical space between them," Shelli said, "they couldn't hit each other. They're playacting?"

"They are hitting each other," Seth said, mouth held open in an exaggerated and extended pout.

Micah looked equally aghast. "You're wrong," he said empathetically.

Witnessing their outrage, Shelli changed the subject. She wouldn't have traded places with anyone, but their energy was so massive that when it came time to pack off them off on the bus, she was happy to let the teachers deal. She helped them get their rain jackets on, pointing out the rains were in full force, as if they needed reminding. But the minute they climbed on the bus, her old worries returned like the fevered whispers of ghosts, thinking she had to get the advice of her best girlfriend, she reached for the phone, but couldn't make a move. She stood like a mute thing, hesitating. For several minutes, she stood there, her ear cocked to catch the smallest sound: the creak of the house settling, the swish of the breeze through the open window, the buzz of a fly. Above it all that could be heard was the majestic chiming of the antique grandfather clock in the foyer, which sounded a particularly sweet melody to invade her heart and bring gladness to the world. Splinters of filaments from the chandelier carved rainbows from the sunlight that streamed through the skylight and expansive front windows, further lifting her spirits, but the phone sat motionless in the air, suspended in her hand. Petrified with indecision, she was unable to text or call. Too many questions percolated. As much as they confided in each other, certain things might be too juicy for Mattie to keep to herself. Shelli could just imagine Mattie's active imagination going haywire, making it impossible for her to talk to their friends without finding out that they had heard all. And she had no doubt Mattie would tell her husband, and if she did, Rick would blab about it to everyone. Shelli knew she had to be careful.

Shelli threw on her raincoat. She knew Mattie would be working at home that day, and it didn't matter when Shelli showed up at work. She drove uphill along a rain-soaked road to Mattie's house, and once parked, went around to the back, stepping into Mattie's light airy kitchen, leaving a trail of puddles behind her. She took in the rich, earthy smell of coffee mixing with the scent of lavender from the garden outside. Bleached wood held everything in place, the drapes hand-painted in bold classic designs. Mattie greeted her dressed in a pink camisole and floppy flannels, having temporarily abandoned an industrial-looking coffee maker on the thick slab of white granite, steam issuing forth, to give Shelli a hug that cut her breath for a second. Mattie poured both of them a cup of coffee and brought out the half and half to her kitchen table, a custom finished maple.

"Hey, before I forget, are you two going to be around next weekend?"

Turned out a friend who owned a lot of investment properties in Maine, an Orthodox Jew who happened to be gay planned to visit Mattie and Rick. "And because he doesn't violate Halakhah, Jewish law and tradition, he never engages in sexual intercourse with a man. I'd love for you to meet him."

Shelli cupped her hand to her mouth as if engulfing an imaginary banana.

"That's right—he only has oral sex," Mattie breathed, her green eyes widening. "He never breaks a commandment."

"Last night I stepped out of my comfort zone," Shelli said, sipping the coffee, a French roast, "and used the dildo and vibrator together."

"That's big."

Shelli only intended to poke around the subject, not wanting to reveal much, just enough to get a sense what Mattie would think of any sort of sexual experimentation. Uppermost on her mind, would such goings-on be good for her marriage? But she couldn't ask directly, and risk disfavor or outright rejection.

"How did it work out?" Mattie said encouragingly.

"Stefan said he had the best orgasm ever," Shelli said. "But this morning when he was walking out to his car—it was out parked at the end of the driveway, don't ask—two pretty girls about eighteen were walking by. He called out to them."

"Are you kidding? What a bozo."

"He kept saying he wouldn't bite."

"That's rich." Mattie's voice sounded raspy and raw, like an engine that needed a tune-up. "You know what I do when Rick ogles teenage hotties?"

"What?" I asked.

"I look at the guys. I point out the ones I like," Mattie said. "When they smile at me, he starts spouting trash." She drank from her coffee.

Placing her elbows squarely on the table Shelli lifted her cup with reverence as if offering it to the gods, and asked, "What does he say exactly?" She sipped her coffee, breathing in its earthy aroma.

"He says they could never love me like he does." Mattie lifted an eyebrow.

"Love that."

"Me too."

"Have you ever talked about doing it with other people?" Sweat trickled down her sides. It was not what she meant to say, but there it stood. "Remember the dinner at our house, and you mentioned that couple with the lovers, now Stefan can't talk about anything else."

"Of course." Her face was inscrutable. She looked like the psychotherapist she was, gathering information. "But your relationship is on solid ground, yes?"

"I don't know… sometimes we seem to connect, and we do have fun occasionally, but other times we're throwing lamps at each other."

"Likely his interest has nothing to do with how he feels about you or your relationship. He's indulging in a common male fantasy."

Shelli sipped from the refill on the coffee that Mattie put in front of her, wondering how much to reveal, feeling this secret like a bag of sand weighing her down.

"Well?" Mattie looked worried.

"He likes to kid around," Shelli said.

"Stefan's all talk. The last time you two were over, you were talking with someone else, and I told Stefan not to worry if he was too drunk to drive, I had beds made up. And knowing how much he likes hot tubs, I said we could go into the hot tub, but he said no, he wanted to be in his own bed."

"Sounds like Stefan."

"Rick has some monster fantasies," Mattie said, her voice sounding like the sweet tinkle of silvery bells. "He likes to make-believe that we've hired a drop-dead gorgeous teenager to help me around the house, he says she'd be my sex slave. He's very careful to include me as a full participant, telling me in graphic detail how she'd work me over before she does anything for him."

Above all, Shelli admired how Rick treated his wife, and Mattie telling this fantasy of his sparked Shelli's interest in how this couple interacted with each other. Whenever she saw them, he was always very polite, very considerate—something Shelli couldn't always say about her husband. Stefan meant well, and sometimes he remembered to do things for her, like the occasional opening of doors, but he never volunteered to help with the cooking or cleaning, he said it never occurred to him. Sometimes he was there for the boys, but just as often he said he was too busy.

Was Rick the same way in bed? Shelli wanted to know how much Rick went out of his way to take her there, but she felt strange asking Mattie to reveal intimate details about what she and Rick did together when no one else was around, undressing them in her mind's eye. She blamed her mother who confiscated novels alluding to sex and ripped off book and magazine covers depicting scantily clothed women. Nor did she allow movies that showed physical affection, including a simple kiss between opposite sexes. Gunfire she tolerated as part of the fabric of life. Growing up in that environment, Shelli felt that she had absorbed some of her mom's squeamishness concerning sex, and as a result, she had no idea what constituted acceptable behavior, and where to draw the line.

Shelli stopped her musing and listened to what Mattie had to say.

"It's good to joke about it," Mattie said. Her lovely skin glowed, and the way she breathed—a seductive grasping of air, quickly exhaled, as if her admission was the most bewitching thing—had Shelli riveted. "Make it fun," she added, as if having great sex were as easy and carefree as eating the icing off a cake. "And don't worry it overly much."

Relieved by the positive message Mattie was bent on delivering, Shelli hugged her tight. Some people might consider it strange that Shelli was ready to tell Mattie her innermost fears knowing how much Stefan lusted after her, but Stefan lusted after every smart, good looking woman, did that mean Shelli would be wise to befriend only plain women? The truth was that she felt more comfortable around Mattie than with the other women he flirted with, attractive or not. At the core, Shelli had a lot of trust in Mattie. Overriding all else, with Mattie, there was no concern whether Shelli met some unspoken criteria. Mattie seemed to understand whatever Shelli said, however she said it.

A call came that Mattie had to take. Shelli got up and put away the coffee cups, grabbed her work things, happy that she hadn't said anything she might regret. Heading to work past massive ferns and flowering hydrangea bushes fighting for space among statuesque evergreens, pines and spruces. The very air pulsated with energy, turning grass and leaves into a vibrant shimmering green. *Wild Thing* by the Troggs played on the radio. Amid all this joy, images of multiple women kissing Stefan popped up, getting her in a heat, pummeled by lust and jealousy both in equal measure, turning her restless arms and fingers into a clicking orchestra of bracelets and rings, torso dancing.

Walking through the yard of the magazine's offices, she was reminded of the house she thought of as her home as a child, although she had lived in several homes, but none as beautiful as this. Her favorite childhood home had a wraparound porch in front, and a huge patio in back backed by a warren of corrals surrounding big old-fashioned stables built in the 1920s. Pasture stretched into the hills where horses sauntered about, nibbling grass, something they could do for hours without getting bored. Chewing grass for a horse has a pacifier affect, calming and soothing, the animals don't feel as compelled to rub themselves on fence posts if there's something succulent to chew and miles to walk. One of the pastures ran along the patio where her father liked to hang out with Louie, a professional horseman Shelli had trained with, many an afternoon they would watch the sun set over the hills, drinking and telling stories. Louie ran horses year-round over her father's three hundred acres of wild grasses and scrub in the foothills of the Gabilan Mountains in California. John Steinbeck in *East of Eden* called them "light gay mountains full of fun and loveliness and a kind of invitation…" Living in foothills along the boot of the Gabilan range afforded views sweeping across the San Joaquin Valley, looking over to the Sierra Nevada Mountains rising like brown elephants to the east.

Summer months were lush but rarely green, buck brush mixed freely with the peppergrass, and California poppies and bush poppies were everywhere. The few trees hardy enough to make it in that arid land remained isolated from one another, even the scrubbiest oak required a wide reach to leach moisture it needed from the soil. The trees bore an abundance of Spanish moss hanging like delicate lace from their stunted, twisted limbs. As a child Shelli rode horseback through these yellow hills sprinkled with the occasional tree like confetti, sometime riding sideways as she had seen pictures of the American Indians do to avoid being shot by cavalry, holding on to the horse's mane to stabilize their bodies, in a delicate balancing act over the ribs of the horse. She did this because she thought it was cool, imagining she was an Indian warrior back in the day riding with minimal equipment, depending only on her agility and instincts to navigate the terrain.

She played cowboys and Indians on horseback with several of her brothers. They'd take each other captive and tie each other up. If they could undo the ropes that bound them, they were free; Shelli became an expert at untying ropes. An early memory popped up of her father bouncing all of them at the same time crowding the length of his leg, sometimes riding his ankle, and giggling uncontrollably, especially when he bounced his leg rough and high. When he got tired, he shooed them off, and they wrestled each other down, jumping on the piled-up bodies.

She went inside, said hello to a few co-workers, and climbed the stairs to her office on the second floor. Once seated, she looked out the window at the large dogwood tree, coffee to her lips savoring the earthy taste, and briefly evaluated Stefan's desire for a threesome. The idea seemed outlandish. Where would he find a woman who wanted this? Would the women do lesbian things together? Lick and rub each other? Why did that prospect excite her?

Although she couldn't see anything other than bright shiny leaves and the bit of lawn outside, it was enough to satisfy, so much better than the space she inhabited in her previous job, smack dab in the inner catacombs of the glass tower she inhabited as a high powered broker. She felt worlds away from Manhattan, although its tentacles reached everywhere. Then she remembered an ex-boyfriend who expressed the desire for a threesome with her mother and herself, not just once, but several times. She thought, oh sure, he probably fantasied about making it with his mother, too.

With a flip of her wrist, she fired up her computer and started her day speaking to an environmentalist she had met at a rally. The facts were unsettling: When Governor Katherine Todd Wickham, known affectionately as "Kat" took office in 1994, the state had more Superfund sites than any other state, and more were being discovered. Two years later, to make good on her promise to cut taxes, she ordered budget cuts on virtually every environmental program. Efficiencies nosedived. Air pollution inspections declined by more than 40 percent, fish inspections for PCBs simply weren't happening and 85 percent of the state's waterways were deemed unsafe for fishing or swimming.

Shelli heard a knock at her door. The door was open, and if she craned her head, she could see Beth, the food editor, looking at her with imploring eyes. She removed her headphones.

"There's a new place I want to try," she said. "Come with me?"

Shelli hesitated, usually she loved these invitations, it would be a working lunch, i.e. paid for by the magazine, but it also entailed at least two hours, maybe more, and she would have to reschedule interviews.

"Can we do next week instead?" Shelli said.

"For you, yes."

Shelli turned back to her computer and put her headphones back on. This was the kind of story that Shelli lived for. She was making life better for people by exposing the inequities. That day she didn't leave her desk, recording her conversations with environmentalists and urban planners, many of whom were calling Wickham's open market emission trading program a travesty, along with everything else. The idea of threesomes was still resident in her mind but had taken a back seat, never completely erased; waiting for the moment she could return to it when she had the leisure. This part of her life she could keep separate.

She spent some of the day typing up her notes not wanting to wait, thinking she might forget something important that someone said including the smallest inflection, feeling her way through the enormity of the story. She wasn't going to depend solely on the phone for her research, she made an exception for the people who truly had a bead on the things that couldn't easily be transmitted over the phone, and sometimes there was something to see visibly or trust to be gained. If she thought she would gain something by it, she would meet face-to-face, but often meeting people wasn't worth the bother.

She stopped by her editor's office at the day's end, approaching his door gingerly, ready to vamoose if necessary. With a great measure of timidity she knocked on his door jamb, having ascertained that Fred wasn't busy with someone else. But she didn't want to irritate this man who appeared at times unknowable, in his quiet way not an easy read. She wanted to let him that the governor's office hadn't returned her calls, and to ask Fred, who had connections everywhere, if he would intercede for her.

Fred looked up at her knock, nodding at her and gesturing with his good arm, his narrow shoulders bunched. His face was delicate for a man, suggesting sensitivity to the plight of others.

"How's the story going?" The light from the desk lamp threw funny shadows on Fred's face, elongating his nose and pitting his eyes into deep troughs.

"The conservation people are happy we're doing a story on this, and Senator Bradley agreed to talk to me." Bill Bradley was the Princeton and Oxford educated ex-basketball player who always returned her calls and played by the rules. He was courteous to a fault, everyone liked him, but he fought an uphill battle. He had been on the Senate Energy and National Resources Committee, and instrumental in crafting key environmental laws, but he left Congress when they needed him most in 1997 just as Wickham was taking her scissors to the EPA, leaving the agency a bloody hulk and everyone including Robert Kennedy resented him for it. Bradley had famously said politics was broken, and he was going home. Those words buried him in the minds of career environmentalists.

"I can't get anyone in Wickham's press office to return my calls. I'm working on Senator Lautenberg; he agreed to talk to me at the end of the week. We have yet to pin down a time. Right now Lautenberg's meeting with his committee to update laws on toxic chemicals and can't be disturbed for anything short of nuclear war."

"Lautenberg has been an amazing resource, he's a natural leader and has the democrat vote but he has yet to persuade the republicans to jump on board anything he's done. So far, most of his bills have ended up in the dust heap." Fred shook his head at Shelli as if it was her fault.

"He's working for the people." Shelli said. She liked Lautenberg. But knowing she would soon have the chance to get back to her ruminations made her want to get the conversation over with, but she stilled her impatience.

"Take a deep breath and focus on giving both sides a fair shake; remember there's often an element of truth in what everyone has to say."

"The crazy thing about it, Lautenberg's working on updating the law on toxic substances—what's it called, the Toxic Substances Control Act—something that Gore wouldn't touch with a ten-foot pole."

"It's tough when your daddy's money is tied in oil," Fred said.

"Well, I, for one, applaud Lautenberg's efforts."

"Sounds fishy to me," Fred said.

The boys rocked the car with raucous laughter as they described in gory detail the soccer they played, boasting of how they kneed and elbowed their way to the goal several times without getting killed. Inevitable that they would start arguing over whom was the better player. Shelli's good cheer quickly turned into a wince at the way her lovely sons fought, teeth bared, and claws sharpened, it took all her persuasive powers to break them up. She had too much on her mind to care about their silly fights. Halfway home, Seth remembered that he left his new jacket at the soccer field. Shelli turned the SUV around to go back and inadvertently plowed into a hydrant partially hidden by a profusion of plants. There was a loud smacking sound.

Wordlessly, Shelli got out and contemplated the damage. She felt hot and sweaty in the pudding air. By the time she slid back behind the wheel, her hands were shaking. The boys must have understood because they quieted down and began drawing letters with their fingers on the steamed windows, leaving her to her musings. She thought about her mother who, on a regular basis, scratched her big boat of a car, a blushing pink 1959 Chrysler Imperial Crown Coupe with the big fins and stepped up chrome. Growing up she thought her mother's car ugly and misshapen, but now she thought it a classic, a gorgeous car, something she would want for herself. But that car had been sold long ago. Did her mother smash her car because she was beside herself (not thinking responsibly, crazed even) at the discovery that Shelli's father wasn't the religious zealot she had assumed from the way he talked before marriage? Gabrielle complained to Shelli that Larry, her father, promised to accompany her to church, but somewhere along the line, during that first year of marriage, he stopped going, saying it interfered with his work. She wanted him to go every day; it was too much for him. After a time, he stopped going altogether. She claimed he mislead her, and held it against him, and vowed her revenge. Revenge consisted of opposing everything he wanted, which begs the question: Does religious zealotry wake the destructive gene, and ferment a desire to smash favorite things?

Growing up, Shelli thought it unfair that her father could bow out of going and she couldn't. When her mother wasn't looking, Shelli snuck away when her brothers piled into the car to go to services, knowing her mother couldn't keep track in the mayhem of bodies. She thought God would strike her down dead as her mother had threatened, but she lived, not even a scratch, no verbal remand from above. That's when it dawned on her that her mother was wrong about a lot of things. She took a walk with her father down their driveway to the creek that bisected their property and asked about the ancient Sceptics, who counseled a general suspension of judgement about the world, and which Husserl referred to as an phenomenological reduction—the idea being that you investigate religious beliefs like anything else, without the so-called "faith" and with a great degree of skepticism. Her father agreed, and said he was of like mind, but there was no negotiating with her mother.

"Before marriage, I thought she was exaggerating when she said this is what she wanted," he said. "I tried to soften her, but she won't budge. She might calm down if she thinks you're on her side."

"But her side is untenable."

As Galileo once said, "I do not feel obliged to believe that the same god who has endowed us with senses, reason and intellect intended us to forgo their use." Darwin on the same subject: "The impossibility of conceiving that this grand and wondrous universe, with our conscious selves, rose through chance seems the chief argument of real value for the existence of God; but whether this is an argument of real value, I have never able to decide." Shelli was of like mind and liked that Judaism doesn't require a belief in the existence of a supreme being. The individual decides for himself, which is the intelligent way to approach a question that has no absolute answers. The individual abides by a moral code even so, god or no god.

Shelli vowed she would never compromise, but on this matter Shelli's mother was a strict disciplinarian, she turned religion into a cudgel and beat her children with it, forcing them on their knees every night, making them recite endless prayers until their knees bled. They lived in perpetual fear of a clip around the ear, a slap, or beatings with wooden brushes, belts, or hangers if they mumbled the words, or forgot the words of a hymn—not from her father but her mother. They would be hit for talking, or sitting incorrectly, maybe this is what her mother thought was the way to show love, but Shelli didn't feel this was love. As a character-building exercise when not in school she was given chores that took hours to finish: washing floors, dishes and the out-of-control laundry, while her brothers ran free. Having to work harder than her brothers rankled and Shelli vowed revenge, someday, somehow. When she complained, her mother said, "What it is to be a woman." That's when she realized her mother confused discipline with love.

A thin reedy child's voice interpreted her thoughts.

"Can we put some music on?" Seth said. "The Eminem CD?"

"Sure," Shelli said.

The lyrics from the *Slim Shady* LP filled the car:

Y'all act like you never seen a white person before
Jaws all on the floor like Pam and Tommy just burst in the
    door

Shelli liked Eminem better than those other hip-hop artists the boys liked, he didn't just sing about seducing girls, his interests were wide ranging, his core themes: revenge, resentment and heartbreak. And he sang with a raw passion. He sang of the kind of hurt that time doesn't heal. Shelli felt a kinship with the singer, a sense that they had parallel lives. As a child, music saved her from utter despair and had come though time and time again. Shelli had an early memory of a trip to France to hear the Gregorian chant at the church of St Pierre des Chartreux in Toulouse sung by the monks. The church was said to have finest classical organ in France, built for convent of Les Jacobins in Toulouse in 1683, and completely restored in the 1980s. Shelli found herself drawn by the ethereal beauty of the music. At home she listened to the recordings of operas on her father's eight-track as often as she could, and on the car radio, jazz, country, and bluegrass. Her paterfamilias took her to operas and musicals, she preferred Shakespeare.

As Shelli passed the Medical Art Center on Route 35, an old rusted car passed her, the driver leaning on his horn for some unknown reason bringing her crashing down to earth. Remembered at the last minute to turn at the Middletown Township City Hall, happy she hadn't overshot the turn, as she tended to do when ruminating on the past, getting all cranked up. She turned again toward the shore onto Kings Highway East at Dunkin' Donuts, driving into the forested canopy where slender white birches dominated the landscape, new housing kept to a minimum thanks to strict zoning laws. And then flew up the hill to Coquette Lane.

Shelli's therapist had been invaluable, particularly in the beginning when she had converted to Judaism, which admittedly she had done lightly and not because she had an aversion to Jesus. It had nothing to do with the music, or maybe it did. Her favorite musicians growing up happened to be Bob Dylan, Paul Simon, and Billy Joel, all Jewish singers displaying a heady dose of caustic wit. Her mother's upset when John Lennon said the Beatles were more popular than Jesus and claimed rock music would outlast Christianity stayed with her. And now Eminem calling himself a Rap God, Shelli wished her mother was still alive so she could tell her about it.

Shelli thought personal choice should be paramount, who cares if you fudged the rules? When she met Stefan he didn't belong to a shul, she assumed he didn't ascribe to the organized religion aspect of it, that's how she interpreted his talk about his dad's refusal to step inside a synagogue. It seemed to Shelli that organized prayer of any stripe is a response to the generalized fear that people have of the future, the not knowing, coupled with a feeble attempt to ward off evil, as if there was a guy up in the cosmos that cared about the petty things that occupy humans. Something Emile Durkheim wrote *in The Elementary Forms of*

Religious Life, hit her: that religion, at its roots, does not try to explain what is mysterious and unknown, but rather to explain what is ordinary and commonplace. "For religious conceptions have as their object, before everything else, to express and explain, not that which is exceptional and abnormal in things, but, on the contrary, that which is constant and regular." Like death. His sense that the cosmos is mysterious, that it contains unfathomable enigmas, is something that comes about once the intellect has broken through to the more complex, higher-order functions: "It is science and not religion which has taught men that things are complex and difficult to understand."

She believed what propelled Stefan to take up religion was simply an excuse to get people together. He liked to be with people to observe Shabbat, the high holy days and Passover, which she enjoyed as well, along with the food: the bagels, kugel, and the like. The social context was invaluable; meals combined with prayer conducted in people's homes. She didn't mind that prayers were thrown in, essentially reminders to be good to one another, and assumed that Stefan wouldn't want to go to synagogue because his father didn't go, not even for the high holy days. Henrik said he didn't attend in protest that God allowed the Holocaust to happen. But when their sons started elementary school, Stefan wanted to join a synagogue. At first she put aside her own qualms about institutionalized religion and worked on a committee through the synagogue to work on the behalf of families struggling to make ends meet, the ones with big families and both parents worked multiple jobs and still in arrears. Shelli and Stefan and their boys made things easier on the poor by painting and cleaning their houses and bringing them meals. But when these activities took over more of their lives, and Shelli found herself being asked to do more things that took her way from her family, and work, and people had these expectations that she'd show up to this or that meeting, she felt that she wanted to get her life back, yet she felt powerless to do anything about it. She didn't even try to broach the subject with Stefan though his religious stance worried her with its suggestion of intolerance and rigidity of thought.

Shelli parked in the garage and the boys bounced out of the car and into the kitchen. Their dad was drinking coffee and talking on the phone. The boys ran screaming by with a speed that made her wonder aloud if they were being chased by packs of vicious dogs, and she recalled Stefan saying earlier that he had picked up a new video game, which probably accounted for their excitement. Must be radar imbedded in children's brains that detects the presence of toys, she thought.

What grabbed Shelli's attention was Stefan's expressive face; he never could hide what he was feeling, the sudden shift of emotion around his cratered eyes and wide mouth conveyed his surprise at seeing her. But was he happy to see her? She wasn't sure, but the surprise was real.

"Sweetheart," she said softly, and reached on her tippy toes for a kiss, lightly dusting his proffered cheek with her lips.

"Back already? I didn't expect you for another hour. I believe me; I know how those meetings go."

"The meeting ran a couple hours overtime."

"I took a peek at this website," he said, his face conveying a tremor of excitement. He looked like a boy who was caught taking all the cookies. "I'll have to show you later—and damn, the phone rang."

After dinner of spaghelli and meatballs, and toasted garlic bread which all the males scarfed down as if there was no eating ever again, eating seconds and thirds and probably would have eaten more if there was anything left. They complimented her cooking, and her spirits bounced back as if her moods poised dancer-like on a trampoline. They pulled out a game of Monopoly and played for a while, but then it dragged on and no one wanted to finish it. The boys kept stirring up the heat, getting on her nerves. Out of desperation, she directed them toward the family room, where they could comfortably play their gaming machines. Stefan got a call and went to his office to take it.

Shelli with them to the den and to watch a rerun of "Family Guy," their new favorite show. They seemed to know exactly where to find the best new offerings as if they had special sensors that detected the most risqué. They watched "The Trap" with the family playing out the Return of the Jedi. Shelli laughed with them, a rare occurrence; most of the jokes on television bored her, playing to the common dominator.

There were plenty of South Park jokes: Seth liked that the mom on Family Guy, Lois, played by Alex Borstein, unfreezes Han, at which time he releases a long fart. Luke played the clueless teenager on Family Guy, and falls into a pit where he battles and kills the bad guy, voice supplied by Rush Limbaugh, which delighted Shelli. (Shelli happened to like Rush Limbaugh. She was attracted to smart people and wasn't a knee-jerk anything.) Following Yoda's advice, Luke surrenders to Vader in order to confront him. Vader tries to convince Luke to turn to the dark side. Luke refuses, learns that it's taco night, and is content. The two meet the Emperor, who reveals that Luke's friends are walking into a trap on the forest moon. When this revelation fails to anger Luke, the Emperor begins to mock actor Seth Green, the voice of Chris. The boys liked Green, having seen him in "Buffy the Vampire Slayer" and to a man, they cheered when Luke defended Green saying that he's been in successful projects, only to have the Emperor remarking on the negative side of Green's roles. Luke began dueling with Vader.

By the time their bedtime rolled around they were both in too good of a mood for sleep. She hoped that for once they would tire without delay, but she knew that she could wish all she wanted, they needed to wind down first. As a way of getting their spirits to calm, Shelli told them that she read that Seth MacFarlane, the creator of Family Guy, had to go to George Lucus to get permission to do the parody of Star Wars. Lucus's only condition was to ensure that the characters look exactly as they did in the movies, and except for the mesh shirts, they did everything to Lucus's specifications. She told her boys that now MacFarlane and Lucas are buddies. She knew that piece of information would make her boys happy, and it did.

When she got back to their bedroom, Shelli noted Stefan hastily putting away a Playboy magazine.

"You don't want to read that in front of me?" she said.

"No. I don't want you watching me."

"You want two women tending to you," she whispered.

"Don't you ever fantasize about having two sets of hands on your body, or kissing someone else's lips at the same time I'm going down on you?"

"The truth? I dream of your mouth on me everywhere at once." She looked into his eyes but nothing stirred there.

"That's what I'm talking about, filling in the empty spaces." He rubbed her shoulders. "I can't be everywhere at once."

"Why not?"

"Good question, maybe I'm too focused on myself."

"I think maybe so."

Twelve years before their boys were born, they met on the job. She got up to get a refill on her coffee, and bumped into Stefan, the freewheeling maestro of the sell. He was always getting refills on coffee, and stopping by people's desks, saying funny one-liners, filling the office with laughter. He stood out in an office where most people were more interested in getting ahead than getting to know each other. Besides his good looks—athletic with broad shoulders and a pleasing face, thick eyebrows and piercing hazel eyes over a square jaw—he had a big personality, liked to laugh, and laughed often. It wasn't so much what he said as how he said it, as if he genuinely wanted to connect.

Stefan gestured like a manic, making fun of the way their colleague, Vinny, combed his hair that morning straight back in the Wolf of Wall Street style, plastering his own fine hair back with water from the tap, even so, his hair refused to lie flat. Vinny made monkeyfaces.

"I could just die," Shelli said, "from laughing, I mean."

"Why don't you, then?" he replied.

She gave him a horrified look.

"You opened yourself up for that one," he said, chuckling.

Shelli looked across the trading floor, a vast enterprise that inspired awe with its nonstop action from about nine-thirty in the morning to dusk, the gyrating silhouettes of her fellow traders jumping up and checking their monitors at all hours, talking on their phones in an agitated manner and sweating and shouting to each other. They had these crazy hand signals that made her think of the kids in the movie Ferris Bueller's Day Off. Everything appeared to be undergoing turmoil. The Chetniks were demonstrating on the behalf of their co-religious, with the intent of leaving everything in chaos, hoping to upend the work of Yeltsin. And the Serbian Orthodox in Kosovo had been quelling the separatist movement of the Islamic Albanians with gut-wrenching brutality until the US stepped in. The volatility in the Asian markets and political turmoil in South America paled by comparison. But nothing seemed likely to derail the IPO market, bulging with backlog of companies itching to go public. The world had already tried war and impeachment; maybe there were a few plagues left. No matter, just a month on the job and the money was pouring in; the valve couldn't be shut off.

The mood was electric, upbeat, sophomoric, the energy kinetic. This she was used to, growing up in a family of nine brothers. Her heart sang in the same way mice are said to sing, by default.

Right at the that moment they were filing into the conference room of the managing director, Matt Mnuchin, to hear the latest in a dizzying array of pre-IPO road shows that had gone through their offices of late. The firm was situated on the sixtieth floor of a skyscraper that took up half of a block in lower Manhattan not far from the ferry building. It made Shelli dizzy to contemplate the enormity of it. Matt looked his usual disarming self, a plaid jacket with no tie announcing to the world that he didn't need to bow to convention and looking like a bookish academic with his John Lennon styled oval glasses. Matt had the iron gut, street smarts and unblinking discipline of a sharp businessman that he hid under a veneer of affability and sharp wit. He was a good listener, too. Before he joined the firm, he led the group that bought failed subprime lender DinkyMac for pennies on the dollar, and negotiated terms with the FDIC, convincing regulators that it was in the best interest of taxpayers that the government assume 75 percent losses of the losses as part of the sale. Matt renamed the bank Far West and soon had the feds on his tail for robo-signings that gave no quarter to homeowners in default. He got pilloried for that in the media, but as he explained to anyone who would lend him an ear, it wasn't AI, and somewhere along the line he had to start making money.

Edward Haddad, tanned, trim, and impatient, looking much younger than his 55 years, entered the room squaring his shoulders like the space wasn't big enough to hold his bulk. The very floor seethed under him as he covered ground. He looked like a man with an agenda, shaking hands in a crushing grip with a nervous energy that missed no one. And went up to a hand-carved mahogany conference table stood in the middle of the room facing a wall of plate glass, revealing a garish display of the gleaming Hudson River and rotting piers of New Jersey stretching into infinity. Shelli watched from her perch near the window.

Just a month before, Haddad had stepped down from his role at the world's top advisory firm, Andreasen Consulting, which he had transformed and guided through a string of five consecutive years of over 20 percent growth to take the helm of a new startup grocery that dispensed with storefronts to offer online order fulfillment and delivery, FreshGrub.com. Richard Bashir, who at one time ran End of the World Books with his brother and sold to J Mart in 1992 for $215 million when they had just 21 stores, was credited for originating the concept for FreshGrub.com. Both were Lebanese Christian; their parents had come as refugees to the U.S. to avoid religious persecution. Then, as now, Muslims were killing Christians right and left, as if the Middle Ages never ended. And this from the fastest growing religion on the planet. Guess it pays to eliminate one's enemies.

"What made you decide to leave Andreasen?" Stefan said.

"A chance like this, to really soar, doesn't come along often."

"Some people would say you were already at the top of the pinnacle," Matt said.

"I wasn't really running the show, and I couldn't split Andreasen Consulting off. There was a tricky matter of a poison pill in the partnership agreement."

Shelli understood that to mean the parent company made it too expensive for any of the majority shareholders to acquire enough shares to take control of the consulting arm of the business.

"What I want to talk to you is e-commerce," Ed said, and turned to the whiteboard next to a projector and a screen. "What is FreshGrub.com?" he scribbled.

Ed began speaking: "What can't we live without? Why do we start with groceries? I was at the DLJ conference a week ago, and Jeff Bezos spoke before I did. He made a comment that Amazon tackled the tough item first, selling books on the Internet. Well, I've to tell you, I sat in the back of the room thinking about eggs and milk and ice cream and all this. And, so when I got up there I said I didn't think that Amazon tackled the tough thing first. I think its groceries. Everyone eats and eats quite frequently; this gives us scale. It gives us an opportunity to have very frequent contact with our customers. Once you have a large group of customers, you can do a lot with that relationship."

"How important is it that groceries are perishable," Matt said.

"That's where our robots come in. I developed—we developed—FreshGrub.com developed—huge Frisbee-shaped robots guided by a grid of floor magnets to pick up customer orders. The robots deliver the items to the operator, who then verifies that the bar codes are correct, puts the items in the box with the customer's name on it—a process that takes a matter of seconds. The operator can fill 16 orders simultaneously. No human can do that."

"It's brilliant," Matt said.

In Stefan's ear, Shelli whispered, "Can the robot detect rotted fruit?"

"Shhh," Stefan said.

If Matt liked you, he was your biggest cheerleader. Shelli learned from Matt that empathy drives better performance. She saw it in her own performance, but she did not have the smooth style of a good salesman. As a matter of principle, she wouldn't drink the Kool Aide. Her ruminations were cut short by Stefan nudging her with his elbow. Shelli snapped back to the present and gave Ed a listen.

"We know profit margins in this business are razor thin, but by leveraging technology, it's not unconceivable that we capture three percent of the soccer mom market. If that happens, we'll squeeze out an eight percent profit margin."

Keeping in mind that marketers bend over backwards to entice them into their stores, the question she wanted to ask Ed was this: Would enough women cede control over the selection of their fresh produce to a robot?

But Stefan frowned at her when he saw that she was preparing to ask that very question. And while she wasn't surprised he looked at her in that way, after all, he was never one to pose the difficult questions, but he would stand by his good friends as long things went well, and if they got in any trouble, Stefan would disavow any knowledge. It was the one aspect of Stefan's personality that gave her pause, but she told herself everyone has faults, and it seemed to her that there were far worse traits, like ongoing bitterness or hostility. Stefan seemed more interested in getting along; he was all about consensus building. He reminded her of her father, they seemed a lot alike, even to the way their smiles never left their faces.

She heard people clapping and forced herself to pay attention.

"We're going to work closely with our suppliers," Ed replied. "We'll be spotting trends. And we won't have slotting fees. No diverting. Just sell us the products our customers want at your best price and we'll work with you. Our couriers, the men and women who come into your home, get paid an attractive salary with benefits and stock options, unlike the Postal Service, which doesn't have a workforce that's incented or built around customer service. Our method is straightforward and because of that, the market is going to explode."

The meeting concluded. Shelli told Stefan that she admired Ed's confidence, his quick grasp of the facts on the ground and his ability to wiggle out of the thorniest questions, but there was something about his eagerness to wave away criticism that made her think his plans hadn't been well thought out. Stefan maintained that despite everything, FreshGrub.com would be an easy sell. Shelli shook her head: When it comes to fruit and vegetables, women are browsers; it's the prehistoric way, written in their genes. Vinny agreed, saying he'd seen how fussy his Italian mother was about selecting produce.

Shelli grew up in an unconventional household. Her dad did most of the food shopping; she made it her business to accompany him to the grocery store because most of the time he forgot things and refused to make a list, part of his frontier mentality, so she came along with her list to remind him. He taught her the important stuff, like how to check for ripeness, having learned from his Irish mother. Her own mother did none of grocery shopping, though she also grew up in a farming family she was too busy with the cooking and cleaning, although she did have a French girl to help her a few days a week that hugged and dressed Shelli like a doll and combed her hair incessantly.

Her father hired a southern woman from Arkansas black as coal who walked into the house dressed in crisp nurse's whites and heavy stockings and wearing two-tone saddle shoes. Her name was Charlotte, but everyone called her Charlie, and she had the sweetest disposition of anyone Shelli had the privilege to meet. Most afternoons she whipped up dinners of collard greens and black-eyed peas, BBQ chicken and pecan pie, providing a wonderful and earthy change from the French girl's cassoulets. The memory of the two women trying to outcook her mother, one with her chocolate mousse, and crème brûlée, alternating with Charlie's masterpiece salted-caramel pecan pie, had Shelli dancing in the hallway. But her favorite was Charlie's limeade made fresh from the limes in their backyard.

Back on the trading floor the pranksters were at it again; someone had taped a piece of paper on the rear of one of the new interns with the words "kick me" scrawled in red ink. Whenever that kid passed by, people did a tribal dance and chanted his name, very sophomoric, but even visitors had to laugh. Several of the guys wore old ticker tape clinging to the backs of their shirts, and someone was busy scraping off the gum stuck to the bottoms of their shoes, likely flicked on the floor for some unsuspecting yahoo to step on. Most of them had graduated from prestigious universities, but no one cared about your GPA if you couldn't laugh a little, then haul ass and get the work done. The place was a zoo.

People were shouting at each other:

"Someone pick up the phone!"

"Check out those numbers, you couldn't ask for better numbers."

"Step up to the fucking plate…Qualcomm is up 2000 percent."

The room looked a lot like a newspaper city room in that it had no partitions and no signs of visible rank. Everyone sat at the same gunmetal gray desks crowded with large terminals, the screens blinking at them in green-diode, with graphs, news stories, and rows of numbers skidding across, updates in real time on important news as it happened minute-by-minute in tandem with the reactions of financial markets in London, Tokyo, Shanghai, Hong Kong, Frankfurt, and others— conferring a degree of power to the select few who knew how to interpret events and act quickly. Behind the monitors, wires and technological wizardry took up the narrow aisle between the rows of desk facing each other, tucked away, but not invisible, and why should it be?

She listened to the roar of the chosen; all of whom had been handpicked to lead the charge in the trading of financial instruments—these were traders from all over the world, but the nexus of Wall Street in the heel of Manhattan, still the most powerful place on earth. Their managers had high expectations, the pressure to perform a steady and unrelenting drumbeat, quickening every heart. Shelli smelled the fear and greed emanating from the pores of her compatriots, and she liked it well enough, but now that Stefan came into her world, she liked her job a great deal more, and could take more of the rankness of raw sweat; everything took on a glittery patina, even sweat, even her battered desk took on a shine. She liked that she could see Stefan several rows in front of her, with Vinny alongside, a comic duo not exactly like Mutt and Jeff, Stefan was tall but Vinny wasn't short, average more like, but they bounced off each other like they were born to it.

"Did you see what happened to Globe.com," Vinny said. "After posting the largest first day gain in history."

"What you saying?" Stefan cupped his hand over the receiver of his phone, his voice tinged with an exuberant tremor of joy that seemed to reside there, waiting to explode in laughter. "What happened to Globe is a fluke. I'm telling them to buy, buy, buy…Check out the Yahoo acquisition of Broadcast.com. It's going be big, baby." He went back to his phone calls, speaking with great urgency.

A woman came by, one of those women blessed with full breast and small waist curving into slim hips. Shelli had seen her around but never met. They got into a conversation which Shelli heard snatches of what he said: "Watch where you're grabbing; be careful with the family jewels," or "The best way to get me to ask you out for a drink is to say I'm too old to do that." It wasn't so much what he said, but how he said it, with the friendliest smile, as if the person speaking was the most important in his life. She looked totally charmed. His jokes seemed to touch on sex while flashing his interloper a suggestive look, followed by a little laugh, as if to say, we're adults here, we can joke about this.

Occasionally they talked about deeper things, but Stefan tended to skirt anything that hinted at anything serious, and for a long time, she preferred it. The main thing they agreed on: people were more important than profits, but lately she wondered if either of them still believed that anymore.

"Everyone's saying to dump Apple," Stefan said in a soft, soothing voice into the mouthpiece of his phone. "Now it looks like Microsoft and Compaq are having Apple for dinner. But Jobs has been doing some behind the scenes tinkering—I've been keeping an eye on him. He's giving away Macs to elementary schools. Its brilliant marketing: all these kids learning on Macs, and when they get out of school, guess whose computers they'll be buying?' Stefan said a few jokes, made his goodbyes after his customer told him to make the buy, clicking off the phone before the dude could change his mind.

"I like that you back the underdog," Shelli said.

"I'm also banking on Microsoft," Stefan said.

After work they decided to hit the bars, something their team did on a weekly basis. Outside the ocean breeze had cooled. The briny smell of the ocean blew from the south, stirring her hair and painting a glow on her cheeks. Seagulls appeared over the bit of Battery Park that could be glimpsed between the tall buildings, looking like white paint smudges in the darkening sky. They passed Hanover Bank, the first major home of the New York Cotton Exchange, and the Anglo-Italianate India House, another New York landmark.

From force of habit they gravitated over to Stone Street, which was said to be the first paved street in New York. It was about as long as a football field and packed with more restaurants and bars than most small cities have. The humble and weather-beaten buildings, a rare surviving cluster of early nineteenth century commercial structures built on the heels of the Great Fire of 1835 that had leveled the greater part of lower Manhattan south of Wall Street, looked imposing framed by skyscrapers bristling like daggers poking holes into the velvet sky.

Hit by the realization that she was in the beating heart of one of the greatest cities in the world, and knowing it had its dangers, part of its draw, made her pull her breath in as if she had been shoved into the street without warning.

Suddenly a man's voice intruded. She immediately recognized Stefan's deep bass buzzing in her ear. She asked him to repeat what he had said.

"New York at its best," Stefan said.

And indeed it was. The atmosphere was festive; bunting, flags and colorful parasols hung above their heads. Knots of good-looking young people passed them by. She watched him check out the women indulgently, not caring, liking that he was comfortable enough to do that in her presence, she also enjoyed scanning the beauties in high heels and halter tops, tight little skirts riding bared thighs, flirting with men in suits with loose ties and loose lips, most of them new to New York, their accents many and varied. The multitude of conversations sounded like the tittering of birds and had to rank as one of the most pleasant sounds she had ever heard.

"Yo, speak for yourself," Vinny said, "but yea, it's the best pickup scene."

Shelli didn't doubt Vinny's boast, she figured in New York there had to be plenty of girls who liked his look. Vinny pulled out a comb and ran it through his hair—worn swept up in a pompadour aka James Dean.

"Such a Guido, always stylin,'" Stefan said.

Shelli marveled that these men turned ethnic slurs into terms of endearment, making them sound like caresses.

Vinny's good-humored smile disappeared into his equally impressive five o'clock shadow; he was one of those guys who constantly look like they need a shave.

"Hey, Cafone," Stefan said. "Wanna take this table?" He gestured at one of the austere Greek revival shopfronts where one empty table gleamed amid a cluster of tables filled with people from all corners of the globe, drinks in hand.

They sat near tourists with hearty Irish accents drinking Guinness. The owner of the joint came by, wiping his hands on a rag, a look of concern on his face. "Hawereya," he said, speaking in thick brogue. "WhatcanIdayafor?" He was short man with a narrow face out of which shone the light blue eyes that looked like they were lit from within.

"Hey Danny," Stefan roared. "I'm delirious with happiness so I'm feeling generous today." He ordered a pitcher of the lager to share around. 'What about you?"

"Grand altagether."

"He gets like that when the market goes crazy," Vinny said, and ordered a Remy Martin at $30 a shot as a chaser.

"Righteeo."

Their waiter was in good spirits, and why not when most of his clientele were stockbrokers, salesmen at heart with a gift for gab, and magnificent tippers. Danny moved over to a table filled with tourists from Ireland. In an accent that became almost unrecognizable—having thickened it up considerably—roared he was born in Ireland as if daring them to refute him. Someone at the table dodged that bullet, with a question about the history of the street.

"At one time it was a hangout for druggies and a garbage dump," Danny said with a ready smile.

"Have you checked the numbers on Microsoft today?" Vinny asked, turning to Stefan.

"If I was a betting man, I'd say Microsoft has Apple beat," Stefan said. "But Jobs could surprise us. What he did with the Mac is simply astonishing. He totally changed the face of computing. He's a visionary…but so is Bill Gates. I love watching the two of them go at it."

"Gates won this round," Shelli said. "He's got the enterprise market locked up solid."

"It may take Jobs a few years to turn things around, but if anyone can do it, he can," Stefan said. "I still have faith in the dude."

"I'd love to think your right, but…who knows, Jobs may surprise us," Shelli said, thinking to herself that if there is one thing she learned watching her mother: don't beat people with a metaphorical club.

Danny came by with their beer and frosty glasses.

"I'll drink to your mama," Vinny lifted his beer.

Later she realized that Stefan had a history of ignoring others—something about his character that slowly dawned on her as time went on. And yes, she didn't look too deeply into his motivations in the early days of their love, she didn't want to face the hard questions either, not until much later, when she saw firsthand how this sort of avoidance truncates dreams and shrivels souls, and causes the best of lovers to turn cannibalistically on each other.

If anyone would have suggested that a mutual reluctance to discuss difficult subjects could fray even the strongest love, would that have changed anything? Now, looking back, she became more of a believer in predestination, in the sense that our characters lead us to act this or that way, regardless of what is happening around us.

At the time she was all innocence and ignorance, easily swayed by his handsome face, sweet smile, easygoing ways, and the fact that, even with clothes on, his attention to fitness was obvious. All muscle and brawn with a head for books, put simply, he made it easy for her to fall for him. All she could think about that night was how impressed she was with his knowledge.

They downed their glasses. He moved slowly, so slowly she heard the floor creaking underfoot. When he reached for her, she felt a blood rush, a sensation akin to a thousand little needles pricking her skin all over, scalding every nerve.

The most difficult aspect for her was not body image; it was more about loosening the stranglehold her mother had placed on sex. In those days, when she met a guy she had the hots for, she had a hard time getting past her mother's admonishments, her metaphorical finger wagging, telling her men were beasts. She wasn't thrilled with the few experiences she had, which seemed to bear out what her mother said about it.

Growing up, Shelli's mother quoted the Bible at great length, mostly indictments from God concerning just about anything she thought Shelli might be guilty of, often pinning her to the wall for wearing a sleeveless dress or the miniskirts she viewed as the devil's tool. With her large brown eyes raised in a martyr's pantomime to the ceiling, and a look of doom stretched across her angelic features, she'd reprimand Shelli, citing biblical stories, many and varied—restraints to curtail the natural tendencies in human nature. She'd slap Shelli's hands and threaten her with eternal damnation if she touched her body, even to banning mirrors in the house to prevent vanity and ripping off suggestive covers.

That first night that they slept together in the same bed, she told him she had never orgasmed. He asked if she masturbated and she said she had never touched herself that way. He talked her into going to a therapist. But it was not until she got stoned on pot that she began to loosen up, thanks to the therapist, who suggested smoking pot to help her lose her inhibitions. With pot as the nutrient and sex as the water, their love kept growing as if it were a well-tended flower. Each voluptuous evening spent together was filled with laughter and sensuous delight, beginning with their version of a highball—a pipe filled with pot smoked on the veranda. They added slight variations to enhance and titillate: a glass of wine, sometimes both pot and wine. After a time, she didn't think she needed the pot anymore, but she welcomed the greater sensitivity it afforded.

Three

Stefan's parents promised not to smoke inside when Shelli and Stefan visited, but it hardly mattered if his parents smoked or not; the smell was the same. It smelled as if the windows hadn't been opened for weeks, if not years. The stink of cigarettes overwhelmed all else; the odor clung to the walls, drapery, and furniture as if the very molecules had fused together. For double good measure, a double helix of curtain and blinds had been drawn against the lurid noonday sun in that tiny living space, leaving Shelli feeling claustrophobic. The doctors had asked Stefan's mother to stop smoking, but she couldn't stop, not on her own. She smoked out of necessity, to loosen the hold of circumstances she couldn't control. She didn't hide how she felt, the bitterness came through. Shelli wanted to shield her sons from Lois, knowing a pessimistic attitude is easily absorbed.

Lois sat back against the hard surface of her chair, all lumps in her shapeless housedress, her jowls fanning her collar like the wax on a candle, her hand wrapped around a coffee cup, saying in that scratchy voice that she would have liked to have plastic surgery on her jowls but the doctors had said they would not touch her, because of the smoking. On the shelf above her head, a figurine of a ballerina stood in lonely splendor. A few feet away, past a yawning emptiness, the prancing figurines of two poodles came into view. The dancer looked lonely.

Shelli wanted to ask how it felt to be unwilling to do the one thing that would change it all, then, if changing her jowls mattered that much to her, but Lois replied that she couldn't consider stopping. Then she said that she had a stroke, but hadn't even known it happened until the doctor insisted it had. He found evidence of a blood clot that had exploded in her brain. She said she had wondered at her confusion.

Yet Shelli's heart filled with tenderness for this poor woman who never had it easy. As different as they were, Shelli was drawn to Lois. She was the polar opposite of her mother for whom appearances were everything. Lois didn't put on airs. Shelli liked the older woman's bluntness, her acerbic wit. When Lois wanted to step out to have a smoke, the other women said they would come, too. It was a good excuse to get some air. They went outside to sit on the porch. The street was quiet at that time of day. No words exchanged; only curious stares across their fortresses, a divide of brick and wrought iron. A few children played stoop ball against garage doors. Shelli mused on this scene, thinking this is how Stefan grew up; he described in it in detail. Otherwise, there was nothing remarkable about a street lined with identical two-story brick row houses topped by antennas that looked like shorn trees. On the surface, there was nothing to make one want to hit the panic button, although Lois seemed to withdraw inside herself as if she felt naked without the four walls to protect her. Shelli asked her about neighborhood. Lois said that she had only a few friends left, her mouth downcast, most of them moving out of state, some to be near their kids, some to retire in Florida.

Tom Petty came the radio.

"Whenever I hear Tom Petty on the TV I switch stations," Lois said. "Looking at him turns my stomach."

Shelli couldn't understand how Lois could find a singer's looks so abhorrent that she would refuse to listen to him. And thought there was no use trying to change ingrown bias. People often have certain ideas about things that aren't rational and most of the time, they're immune to rational arguments, no matter how well the facts are marshalled.

"I'm too old to change," Lois said, her hand stroking her chin where the skin had become loose and wrinkly. Her mouth formed an inverted half-circle. "After the hard childhood I had," Lois said, "orphaned; bounced around from relative to relative." She lowered her voice to a whisper, saying her father died when she was five—he was a printer, poisoned by the ink he used—her mother died a few years later of tuberculosis. Lois was shunted between uncles and aunts, never in one place for long. "It would mean a lot to have work done on my face, but the doctors refuse to do anything for me, no matter how much I say I'll pay whatever they ask," she added, her vowels blurring into the consonants. Lois's strong, sad face looked even more masculine, her man's haircut adding a severe edge. Her breath smelled of coffee and cigarettes.

Shelli wanted to say she understood what a lack of familial love can do, but she didn't want to talk about her parents. She didn't think Lois would understand a father who worked all sorts of hours (many times he had the night shift at the hospital), and drank himself to the point of oblivion, and a mother who spent her days sifting through thrift shops and attending religious services, and once home she'd throw her purchases into a spare room and not look at it again. After her parents died within a week of each other, her brother told her he found the room stuffed to the ceiling with unopened packages. Shelli's parents had tried to love her, but when the love between the parents is rarely in evidence, and when all a child hears is verbal putdowns and sparring, a child sees what a child sees, it colors everything with an ugly tint—she refused to cry about it.

Only a few minutes passed it seemed before Henrik's wine-red Falcon pulled into the drive, and Stefan and David trailed by Micah, Seth and Nate, leapt out carrying multiple bags of food, enough to feed an army. Lois was all over the place, reaching for Henrik's jacket and to dig up the latest newspaper so he could do his crossword puzzles, then rushing to get him coffee. Henrik was just as tall as Stefan but he looked sickly, rail thin, not broad and robust like his son. Henrik bent over the table, dark eyes roaming the room with a worried expression. But it was his look of despair that had Lois reaching for every little thing. Henrik's threadbare shirt and pants he must have bought years ago at J.C. Penny's now looked like a disaster, hanging loose on his thin frame like curtains. Everything about him had that same lack of attention to detail. Stefan told Shelli once that he couldn't remember his dad ever caring about how he looked. He spent his whole career hiding out as a low-level functionary in the byzantine New York City administration, never attempting to start his own company, which was a dream he had, one that he openly and repeatedly talked about, telling his family he shoulda, woulda. Shelli imagined him in meetings with other city employees, bringing up minutiae that only he cared about, and if the response was negative, he'd go to the bathroom afterwards and smash his hand against the wall. Stefan said that's what he did at home when something frustrated him, but he never talked about it. Thinking about that made Shelli feel sorry for Lois, never being able to talk things out with Henrik, always dodging the issues, never coming to any resolution.

The boys went into the living room to play their Gameboys.

Lois clapped her hand to her forehead. "Oy, I've got to call a meeting," she called out of nowhere. "We've got to start rehearsals. They're counting on me."

"My God, Ma, you just suffered a stroke," David said.

"You can't keep doing things like you done," Stefan said.

"The doctor put me on meds," Lois said.

"You need to take this seriously," David said.

Lois, her children, and all her women friends and their kids got together a few times a week for months on end to rehearse famous Broadway musicals. Then for a week each spring they would act and sing the best songs and moments taken from these musicals in front of sold-out houses as fund-raisers for the adult retarded. All of Canarsie would attend. They raised roughly half a million dollars each year which gave Lois an exalted status in the community. People went out of their way to thank her, she got freebies everywhere. Afterwards, pizza and Coke would be brought in for volunteers who put on the show. Shelli sensed that's why Stefan preferred to socialize in groups. The look of bliss on his face when he recited lines from his favorite musicals, as he was doing right that minute:

> When you're a Jet,
> You're the top cat in town,
> You're the gold medal kid
> With the heavyweight crown!

Stefan pointed to his watch: "Remember we have to keep an eye on the time," he said.

He had spoken to Phyllis, Lois's best girlfriend, who was planning a surprise for later that afternoon, but Lois wasn't to know about it. Henrik worked his puzzles, mouthing "Don't say a word," and placing his finger over his lips assuming a look of mystery.

Turning to his mother, Stefan said he had paid for the takeout out of his "Jewish bank roll" and to demonstrate what he meant by that, he pulled out a wad of bills with a twenty visible on top, shuffling through ten one dollar bills that lay underneath giving the wad heft.

"Drum roll," Lois said drily.

"Don't thank me," Stefan said. "Dad taught me everything I know."

Henrik looked like he hadn't heard a thing. Busily he worked on his puzzles, filling in the squares without pausing to take a sip from his instant coffee. Shelli guessed he did everything to prevent new information getting in, allowing his hair to grow around his ears like thick tufts of dandelion grass, likely a measure to prevent him from hearing what other people had to say. Stefan often complained about it, saying that Henrik should get his hearing checked, and lately he started saying that same thing to Shelli, a frightening development, making her think her husband was confusing her with his father, something it seemed Lois was doing as well, saying one time that neither Henrik nor Shelli could tell a story without boring people to tears.

"Do you remember the race riots, back in 1972-73?" Stefan said, "Kids swiping tools from workshop to beat each other up on the basketball courts."

"That happened here in Brooklyn?" Carmen said.

"Mostly between the Italians and the blacks," Stefan said. "The Jews stayed out of it."

"That's why you have so many black friends," Shelli said.

"I go out of my way to be nice," Stefan said.

"There was a lot of hostility back then," Lois said, "but some of us tried to defuse it. But the Limousine Liberals, the people who rule New York's outer boroughs from Manhattan, were trying to tell us what to do. It was a case of upper middle class patronizing the labor classes. They didn't realize that we were dealing with entrenched bias, unshakeable even with all the mounting evidence to the contrary."

Back in the day Canarsie was looked down by the rest of New York for its alleged frontier-like toughness.

"Mom was a precinct chair for the Democrat Party in the mid-70s," Stefan said.

"Back then Canarsie voted Reagan, after voting Carter in 1980 and Mondale in 1984," Lois said.

"Whites in Canarsie abandoned their liberal attitudes when they felt threatened, but reverted back when the things simmered down," Stefan said.

Henrik turned to Lois. "Did you check with the doctor," he asked.

"I forgot," Lois fussed.

"Take my phone." Stefan reached out with his cell phone in his hand.

"She's never going to use one of those new-fangled things," Henrik said.

"You're a secret Luddite," Stefan said, with a shake of his head.

"I'm more comfortable with the rotary phone," Henrik said. "It's simple to understand, it works the first time, and it doesn't break if I drop it."

Stefan put his cell phone down.

"It's a solid piece of metal I can grip in my hand and the voice comes out ringing," Henrik continued. "It's not some tinny sound I can barely hear."

Henrik kept up a running commentary on everything he hated about cellphones that reminded Shelli of the extreme edge of talk show hosts, all Sturm und Drang, despite Stefan's attempts to break into his monologue. But it didn't matter how much Stefan explained about the mobile device, Henrik refused to look at it. He walked away from Stefan in a huff and stood in front of the television set. Stefan followed. Together, father and son ruminated about all the possible things that might go wrong with the country and, by extension, Stefan's mother, which translated into hair-raising possibilities like heart stoppages and frigid fingers. Shelli moved around them, busy with dishes, listening, reminded of her own philosopher-father, who, despite his redneck background, quoted Livy and Plutarch as bespoke his Ivy League education, sounding nothing like the working man's polemic from the lips of Henrik, but underneath it all they voiced the same viewpoint. Despite Shelli's father being a surgeon, he identified with the laboring classes; he knew what it was to be poor. Same with Stefan, when Stefan and his parents got together, Stefan devolved; mouthing opinions that mostly came out sounding like swear words.

"What they're doing is criminal! They should be arrested! Aren't there laws in this country?"

"What kind of shit is that?" Stefan said. "You can't arrest someone for sharing his opinion, for Christsakes."

"Stefan should go into politics," Shelli said.

"Yeah, right," Stefan said.

"He'd get assassinated," Henrik said.

"You're so pessimistic," Shelli countered.

Unlike Henrik, who only read the dailies, Stefan read the complete works of modern historians, including Barbara Tuchman and Paul Johnson, both of whom explained history in light of its personal impact on people's lives, but rarely quoted when he talked to his father. It was like he never read anything other than the tabloids when they got together.

Shelli and Carmen helped Lois navigate between the phad thai noodles and the cashew chicken, served with dinner rolls. Shelli knew from eating with Stefan's parents that Henrik didn't eat much else. He had a thing about dinner rolls. He said it had to do with his childhood memories of walking by bakeries in Dusseldorf, made more poignant by his stomach hurting from hunger, his stomach on fire. Lois would eat only Chinese take-out noodles and Jewish deli.

"The kids at school took turns beating me up," Henrik said matter-of-factly. "Sometimes on the playground, sometimes ambushing me on my way home from the bakery, my arms filled with challah for Shabbat."

"Were they like that all the time?" Shelli said. Her German grandfather left long before Hitler rose to power, but did that absolve him, or Shelli, for that matter?

"No," Henrik said. "Hot and cold."

"Did you ever refuse to go for the challah?"

"Never."

A few weeks before Kristallnacht Celia and Henrik and his sister left Germany, helped along by a Hungarian diplomat who took a shine to Celia. Tensions were high and Henrik was glad to leave all the bad memories behind. Once on US soil, he lied about his age so he could join the US Marines and help defeat Hitler. Henrik was thirteen, and said he constantly pinches himself to think that he is living here in the United States and that Brooklyn is his home, and no one refuses to serve him because he's Jewish.

"Do you ever worry that anti-Semitism could take hold here?" Shelli said.

"My mother says every day: 'Thank God for George Washington," Henrik said. "There is a reason for that. To the people who attended the first synagogue on U.S. soil he promised: 'the government gives to bigotry no sanction, and to persecution no assistance.'"

"And the framers of the constitution made it very difficult for a demagogue to take over," Stefan said. "That's the main reason for the Electoral College. Part of the checks and balances."

Spoons flew, and for a short while, everyone was too busy chewing to say another word. After a while the conversation at the other end of the table started up again. Henrik was telling

Stefan that he had just talked to a doctor earlier that day and heard that Lois continued to have every kind of disturbance. Even the smallest thing had to be analyzed lest it led to something worse. Lois had more than her fair share of throat and stomach problems, but now that the doctors knew of her smoking and her love of junk food her intake of medication would be more strictly monitored. As they spoke, Shelli couldn't stop looking at Henrik, sitting at Stefan's right. She was fascinated by his manner of scattering bits of bread on the floor like birdseed as he chewed and rocking in his chair as if he was davening. Lois had promised not to smoke inside and kept running out of the room to have a smoke, which Shelli enjoyed for the fresh air she brought in each time she returned to the table. The boys at the other end of the table appeared delighted when Lois came back into the room with dessert, a pound cake with icing. She asked Carmen to bring out more coffee, or sodas if people wanted that instead. Their world revolved around drinking Coke and Sanka rather than alcohol. Stefan drank alcohol sparingly and his parents only on special occasions. Neither of Shelli's parents smoked or drank sugary sodas, and her mother never drank spirits, but her father certainly loved his whiskey. It made Shelli wonder about the whys of cultural differences.

Shelli found a few bottles of purified water in a closet and took one. There was Dr. Brown's soda, both cream and black cherry. Shelli asked Stefan how he could stand the taste of diet Coke. He shrugged and said he hated diet but he liked the regular, it reminded him of going to the ballgames with his dad. That led to a discussion with the men outdoing each other defending the NY Giants as the best team in the league and proving yet again why Lawrence Taylor was the best linebacker ever.

"Why don't you guys ever have wine on the table?" Shelli said. "The only time I've seen you drink wine is on Passover."

"Jews don't drink," Stefan said. "It'd interfere with our suffering."

Though it surprised Shelli when they started dating, as time went on, she grew to accept his temperance; he got her to drastically cut down. She wished, however, that instead of outlawing alcohol consumption, his parents would cut the smoking, but even so, she was proud of her flexibility in this matter of libations. It made her think they could overcome all the other issues. Plenty of Jews marry gentiles and made it work. But it seemed every time they rounded a corner, she stepped on a landmine. Her faux pas started the day he brought her home to meet his family. His grandmother Celia who was pushing ninety-nine but still spry and her mind totally intact was visiting that day. Celia told Shelli that Henrik was born in Germany, but she grew up in Lwow, Galicia, when it was part of Poland; now part of the Ukraine. Shelli told Celia that her father's grandfather had emigrated from Germany. Shelli could see in Celia's eyes that painful memories were stirred by Shelli's words. She didn't need to say it, her expression made it clear: she held Shelli's people responsible for everything that happened to the Jews. It was nothing she said directly, she communicated what she felt in other, more subtle ways. That's when Shelli learned that Stefan's grandfather, who came from Kiev in the Ukraine stopped in Lwow on his way to Germany and stayed long enough to marry Celia. He planned to stay in Germany for a few months to bankroll a trip for them to the United States. He found a job and started saving his money. Before he had a chance to find passage to the States—he had to first find a sponsor and that took some time to arrange—he was forced into a slave labor camp, tortured, and beaten to death. This was before the era of concentration camps when Hitler was experimenting to see how much he could get away with.

Celia called Shelli a "balaboosta," Yiddish for perfect housewife. Shelli knew this was a compliment and her heart swelled with pride. Shelli's therapist had been invaluable, particularly in the beginning when she had converted to Judaism, which admittedly she did lightly and not because she had an aversion to Jesus. The idea of Jesus being simply a prophet and not a god made more sense, anyway, and Shelli liked the common-sense approach that Judaism fostered. Prodded by her therapist, she told Stefan that she liked the emphasis Jews placed on action as opposed to the pious insincerity she encountered among most of Christians she knew. And then there was the shock value. Her mother never recovered. They couldn't say two words to each other without her mother carrying on. Gabrielle believed in Jesus with a faith so blind it caused a sort of mental scar tissue to form between them. Shelli stopped answering her mother's reflexive question, dished out like so much leftover oatmeal the rare times they saw each other: "How could you blaspheme Him?" After a few similar confrontations she stopped talking altogether. Even on her deathbed she refused to talk to Shelli, saying she was holding out until Shelli repented and went back to Jesus. But now Shelli wasn't so sure she could navigate successfully around her in-laws' fear of a second coming of Hitler. Suffice it to say that she felt somehow suspect for having been born of a vagina that had not been blessed by a rabbi. It was not so much what anyone said as much as what they did not say. Even so she was determined to make things better between them. Celia and Lois shopped TJ Maxx and made a wide berth around high-priced stores. Shelli didn't mention she shopped the sales at the fancy stores. But somehow, they knew. And their cultural differences bled into the texture of their relationship, underlying everything else. And as much as she tried to skirt these issues, it seemed that whatever she said on that score made the older women uneasy. The same could be said of Shelli; she didn't always relish their comments, and constantly wondered if she was misinterpreting things. After Celia died, Stefan and Shelli and the kids went to Brooklyn countless times and sat with his parents for hours at a stretch, and the constant exposure didn't help anyone gain more understanding, yet every now and then his mother made references to Shelli's 'Guido' style of dress, and complimented Carmen for her frugality, wearing the same polyester dress everywhere.

Shelli looked up and noticed that no one at the table was talking. Usually Stefan kept things going, no one knew more about sports or collected more arcane trivia about Hollywood stars than him. Lois fretted with Stefan in the bathroom. But, just like always, every time she visited with Stefan's folks, the ghost of Celia would shake her finger at Shelli. Reflectively she looked up at the ballerina posed above Lois's head. The ballerina looked happier, magically the dogs moved closer. Shelli wondered who moved them. Looking at all the faces of the humans in the room, she couldn't tell, no one giving clues.

On his return he went up to his mother and ran his hands along her shoulders, kneading her gently, and saying, "Ma, I worry that you don't take care of yourself."

"I can't eat the vegetables," she said.

"So, what else is new?"

They sat listening to David dredging up doomsday scenarios, citing what could go wrong, chilling statistics, like eighty percent of stroke victims will suffer another stroke in the same year, along with other arcane information, such as stokes have edged out chronic obstructive lung disease as the leading cause of the death in the world. (In the US, heart disease is still the number one killer.)

It was plain that she rejected the healthy diet and exercise regime and had no plans to alter her lifestyle. Her arteries were beyond calcified; the blood sluggish. Difficult to turn back the hands of time—she on a blood clotting medicine but that merely delayed the inevitable.

Stefan looked at his watch, changing the subject. "Phyllis asked me if you're going to move to Florida with them. She's hoping you'll say yes."

"Florida might be fun," David said.

"I told her we'd think about it," Lois said. "I have misgivings."

"Ok, so you're not moving, what else is new?" Stefan said.

"Like I said to Phyllis 'what do we know from Florida?' And then as if I had never spoken, Phyllis bought airplane tickets and made hotel reservations for us to come for the weekend. She said it's her treat."

"You'll love Miami," David said.

"I really don't want to upset our lives in this way, but Phyllis insists we go," Lois said. "Phyllis said her good friend was mugged on the way to shul. And then another friend had her car stolen. Now she's afraid for me."

"It just takes one *meshugge*," David said.

I'm so sick over this, you can't imagine," Lois said. "Such *tsuris*. I told her we were married in this house and you children were born here. This house has seen many good times…parties… friendships…I can't imagine leaving this house."

"It won't be the same without Phyllis," Henrik said.

Lois ignored Henrik and continued: "So you know what she said? We're moving, and the rest of your friends are moving."

"No one to talk to," Shelli heard Henrik say. "The days stretch out, no one calls, and no one comes by. Besides your visits, we have nothing else to look forward to."

"What about the three stooges, Marv, Irv, and Rubin?" David said.

"Marv and Irv are gone." Henrik's mouth drooped into jowls that looked to be covered with a fine coat of prickly sandpaper that disappeared into his frayed collar. "I heard Rubin started an herb farm in his backyard."

"He's leaving, too," Lois said.

Listening to them talk made Shelli drowsy. Through half-shuttered eyes against the lurid June sun that managed to come though the blinds, Shelli daydreamed of sugary beaches lulled by warm breezes. There was a beach only a few blocks away, admittedly not tropical, but a beach nonetheless, and she knew the boys would have liked to go to there, but Stefan's parents weren't fond of beaches, so she squelched the thought. But if they moved to Miami, maybe they could get them to a beach.

On Wednesday mornings Shelli worked as a parent volunteer in one of seventh grade classes leading book discussions. The class had been assigned the first chapter of *The Hobbit* by J.R.R. Tolkien by the teacher. Some of them hadn't read it or forgot what it was about, so she had the kids take turns reading the chapter out loud before she attempted a discussion. It seemed that children needed to translate the words first and then hear it again and then again for a third time before they wrapped their minds around it. She was amazed to discover how few of the kids recalled basic things that they read just minutes ago, and it seemed that many didn't know the meanings of words. Shelli asked them to tell her which ones they didn't know, like "immovably" and "blundering." She told them what the words meant, and hoped this would facilitate discussion, but found only a few brave souls wanted to talk. In desperation, thinking they might loosen up if she entertained them by reading one line from one of her favorite James Joyce's short stories to illustrate how alliteration can used. She read only the last sentence of the story that critic and writer Seamus Deane opined, 'surrenders to lyricism,' hoping this would inspire them to see reading as something beautiful.

The last sentence of *The Dead*: "His soul swooned slowly as he heard the snow falling faintly through the universe and faintly falling, like the second of their last end, upon all the living and the dead."

She asked them to repeat the words slowly and chew the words like candy on the tongue. One of the girls giggled when she said that.

The children seemed to warm up to this. They repeated the words and tried to make their own attempts at alliteration, mostly silly ones, but at least they were trying, and interested. She went back to the novel they had been reading, and asked them to use their imagination in another way, to describe what they thought hobbits looked like, and their hobbit holes, again with the hope that when they went home and opened their books, they would be interested in paying attention to the details of what they were reading. The kids liked this sort of thing, and most of them participated, which was gratifying, and she listened to all the wild things they said, much of it preposterous, and smiled her approval. She made sure her own children read every day, and she was proud of their reading ability, and thought it was the enthusiastic readers who made great parents and created the right environment for learning. Secretly she thought Seth and Micah grasped things more quickly than most of their children in their class, but she also realized the kids might be less inhibited at home.

Shelli left the class and walked out to the parking lot. Her thoughts wandered to Stefan and his repeated suggestions about having a threesome, what was that about? She had no desire for another man, and personally liked their sex life, even the porn that they occasionally indulged. She remembered what Stefan said the other day. They were walking down the street heading to a festival in Freehold, and he tried to explain the intensity of emotion he experienced when passing teenage girls looking succulent as all hell, and his desire would engulf him completely, his hunger obliterating everything else, and he insisted that it had nothing to do with her. He asked if that was something she could understand and she told him she knew that feeling, but only experienced at odd times. Stefan said that kind of feeling happened constantly for guys whether they had a steady companion, even if the sex was really good. A new woman appears, and a guy must talk himself down.

She continued to mull it over, with no new insights, on the drive to Allaire State Park. It was Governor Kat Todd Wickham's plan to speak to environmentalists and journalists here in the park in a bid to prop up her flagging reputation. She was known colloquially as the most anti-environmental governor in the history of the state, and still had a loyal following. The governor commanded respect by virtue of her height, over six feet, and striking good looks. Likely she expected her physical attributes would go far in ameliorating a bad situation in the environmental mess she inherited, getting worse with no end in sight. But what Shelli suspected, the woman planned to do nothing about it except talk about her good intentions, let people know she cared, and flash her award-winning smile. Later in that afternoon the governor planned to spend the afternoon cycling the perimeter of the park. She had on a plain tee shirt under a tech vest with the Op brand emblazoned on the shoulders, paired with black padded cycling pants.

"I promised to cut taxes when I campaigned for governor and I don't like breaking my promises. If we ask for voluntary compliance then we don't have to spend the taxpayer's hard-earned dollars on monitoring these companies, and we can offer more services." For decades General Electric used to dump old chemicals around New Jersey's waterways, although GE said at one time that the company was not responsible, and then they said it was not harmful. Nobody could convince them to do anything about it, but then the new governor changed his mind. "I told Jack the public was demanding action, and the state of New Jersey doesn't have the funds. He'd not prepared to spend as much as people would like, but he's said he's going to do it."

For a few miles they rode on a broad boardwalk made of planks over a peat swamp bog, essentially soggy marsh in a forest of white cedar trees fed by tiny streams, and in some areas composed of a spongy, wet organic material that looked like something people could walk on. The places with standing water were filled with floating plants. An intense earthy smell greeted them on both sides.

"Right now we're committing all our resources to cleaning up the state's beaches," the governor's soft voice broke the stillness. "The first thing on our agenda is the medical waste. Some of it has been found to be contaminated with HIV and hepatitis B viruses, and people are in an uproar about it. We're diverting EPA personal from the interior to do the testing."

"People won't go to the beach if they get sick from it."

"It's our number one priority," Kat said. "The shore generates $36 billion to the state's economy and employs over 470,000 people."

At the end of their ride amid handshakes and well wishes, the governor invited Shelli and Stefan to the family farm for lunch later that month.

Shelli listened to Stefan with half an ear when she got home, too preoccupied with the boys' shenanigans to pay much mind to anything else, calling each other 'stinky' and challenging each other's gaming skills. Micah asked for a new game. At the mention, the other boy's head jerked up, as if an invisible cord had been yanked.

"I want a new game, too," Seth shouted.

"Me too," Micah seconded.

"You're breaking my eardrums," Shelli grumbled.

"If he gets a game, so do I," Micah said, his voice piercing.

"Of course," Shelli said.

"Good," Micah shouted before diving back to his hand-held entertainment center.

"How do we know you're not just saying that?" Seth said.

"I always follow through on my promises," Shelli said.

"No, you don't."

They kept on like that until she threatened to take their gaming machines away. Most of the time, they listened when they sensed she was at the breaking point, and this time was no exception. Thankfully they forgot about their concern for a new toy and got busy again manipulating the technological gizmos that filled their days. With his earphones on, Micah turned into a shadow of himself, seemingly in another world, staring aimlessly with a dreamy expression while the other merry prankster worked his handheld game machine full throttle, his eyes shooting sparks, drilling holes into the screen. An avalanche could descend, and they would not notice.

Later that night, after the boys settled down to sleep, Shelli came to the room she shared with Stefan and fell on the bed. Her eyes roamed the antique dresser, couch, and the small library table she had carefully chosen on forays to Maine antique stores and felt a profound sense of satisfaction. She noted that the huge spider plant hanging in one of the windows that Stefan made his pet project was growing new shoots.

"Your plant," she said. "A dozen new shoots at least."

"Yea, I saw that."

She gazed out the window at the velvet sky, drinking the view in. Behind him, through the big wall of windows that ran on one side of their bedroom, past the blackness of ocean below, the jeweled crescent of New York City blazed with a fierce brilliance, as if the cool gray of thrusting towers were covered in diamonds.

"I'm getting some porn on."

She sat back on the pillows, hoping she looked in need of succor, thinking if only he could accommodate her wishes occasionally things would ease up between them.

But Stefan was too busy turning on the television to see. She humored him, knowing how much he liked it, but the frequency of him reaching for that particular crutch bothered her. The thought nagged her, couldn't she, some of the time, be enough of a stimulus? She also knew that men were more visual, and they liked variety, so she supposed that she had to make allowances.

"Okay I get that you're not interested in having a threesome," he said, his face lightning up as if inspiration has just struck. "Look here, I've got a better idea" he pulled out his laptop and typed in "interactive sex" and then clicked on the first link that came up, a website for swingers. "What do you think of this?" he asked. "Doesn't this look like fun?" The opening screen suggested that onlookers set up a profile. It was the only way to see anything inside the site.

Shelli stared wide-eyed. The cruciform of hairs on his exposed chest glinted like live wires in the stark bluish light from the computer, his excitement visible in the way he leaned in and focused right then on the sinuous parade of bodies parading across the screen.

"It looks like the same old porn to me."

"Let me put it to you this way: do you really want to go through the next fifty years or however long we live having sex with just me? Doesn't that sound boring as all hell?" He took his eyes off the screen and stroked her breasts softly.

"I never thought about it in that way."

"We only have one life. Don't you want to live it to the fullest?"

"That's a given," she said slowly, thinking she had an idea where this was going, and felt a mix of trepidation and ambivalence. She hoped he wasn't suggesting that she screw perfect strangers.

"There is no greater pleasure than sex," he said.

"Doing this doesn't necessarily have to lead to intercourse with other people." His voice purred in that cat-like way he affected when tickled. "We could stop at flirting and foreplay. The rules of engagement are ours to make."

"Sounds like a Playboy fantasy."

"Why don't we try it? Anytime you don't like something, we stop." He had a playful look on his face. "For one thing, I don't think our marriage will last if we didn't do something like this."

"You want a divorce." Shelli had a hard time believing that if he wanted other women, he would want her to stick around. Why, so she could cook and clean for him?

"I'm not saying I want a divorce, I'm saying you've been buying lots of expensive clothes, and furniture, and having a great time doing it, which does nothing for me, in fact it's the exact opposite, I've asked you to return those items and you refused—"

"I told you some of them weren't returnable. I returned the ones that were."

"Well, now it's time I have some fun, too. It's not just about you."

"I'm not buying any more stuff." She felt a cold shudder invade her heart. It was anything but pleasurable to hear him go on like this.

"In any case, eventually our sex life will hit the skids if we don't do something to make it exciting. Do we want to be one of these couples who never screw? We need to change things up now and then." That purr again.

He said something else, but she couldn't absorb what he was saying, whatever he said escaped her. She could hear the mouth smack around the formation of the words, the click of teeth. Running below the words there was his breath, the audible pauses, difficult to hear them, the words, and when she did hear them there was so much space around them that she thought, perhaps she hadn't heard them, and later, she realized that she was in shock. She had not let the words into her body. She had a dizzy spell when she heard the words. It was only later that his words began to enter her: she tasted them, gagged as they went down, and felt them course though her bloodstream, leaving a chill in her fingers.

"Repeat what you just said," Shelli blurted.

"You heard me."

"Why don't you have an affair? Just don't tell me about it."

"I don't want to sneak around. I want you to be part of it," He said, pulling her to him, enclosing her in his arms. "That way, there's no jealousy."

She pulled her head back from him to look at his face; she knew he could never hide what he was feeling, and she needed to read what was going on, now more than ever. Uppermost in her mind, did he love her? A man who loves his woman, would he be so quick to share her around? But on the other hand, she knew from all her reading in psychology that human beings, especially men, are happiest with multiple simultaneous sexual relationships, and suffer a steady decrease in libido that has everything to do with biology and hormones regardless of how wonderful the woman in their lives when faced with long-term monogamy. But even as she understood how this worked on an intellectual level, she couldn't help but feel jilted. Doesn't matter how long they've been together, women like their men to prefer them above all others. It's a problem unique to the modern marriage with increasing life spans.

"What makes you think there won't be jealousy if I'm part of it?" Shelli said, voicing her surprise. "You're okay with me fucking another guy?"

It was only later, on reflection that she realized that he said: "Only if he has an equally beautiful woman for me, otherwise, no."

It took a lot to admit that monogamy might not be the answer, at least not for them as a couple, and agree to negotiate this. She felt strongly that to make a good marriage, both parties must be willing to adapt to each other's needs. If she showed flexibility here maybe he would loosen up his tightwad ways.

"What? You talk casually about it as if it's no big deal." She said this in a bid to have him flesh out how he thought this would work on a day-to-day level.

"A friend at work has done this and says he would never go back to the old way. He says he knows a lot of married people who do it."

"What if I hate it?"

"We can stop anytime."

"You'll have to convince me that if I do this, you'll pay more attention to me at social functions. I don't want to be the invisible wife."

"Okay, I can do that." His voice sounded a strong note, but she didn't put much faith in what he said until she saw visible change.

And yet she was eager to get along and see it from all sides. On the positive side, he was giving her the final say, which made her think the idea a workable one, if he stuck to his promises. She had met people in California with open marriages, but she didn't know them well and had no idea if playing around improved their relationship. Or did it do the opposite? What it would be like to meet another hot couple and flirt like they meant it? If either of them fell for other people, what would it be like to love more than one person? She suspected that for all his kidding, he had never screwed anyone but her from the day they met. He said she could put the brakes on if she wanted, and in her defense, she had a voice that could freeze entire solar systems if she worked it. Stefan paid attention when she got crazy on him, it didn't happen often, and only when she was really scared, like the time he rode his bike down a twisting mountain road at breakneck speed, while she trundled behind, full stop on the brakes. He laughed at her fear. It certainly didn't help when she heard from a good friend that her father who was an avid cyclist misjudged the sharpness of a turn and went off a cliff. Parts of his mangled body and bicycle were found scattered on the rocks 50 feet below. So understandably she looked askance at Stefan when he said he had a book for Shelli to read, *The Ethical Slut* written by marriage therapist Dossie Easton. Easton claims other lovers can enhance a marriage provided each partner assumes that the other will remain the main attachment and believes it can work if both parties are open emotionally to each other. Honesty and transparency rather than fidelity become the guiding principles. After reading the book, she thought her fear was probably unreasonable. Then Stefan pounced, asking if this might qualify as an opportunity she couldn't pass up, the thrill of playing a sexual Russian roulette. How many married people can say they've had such experiences? He added that he had checked popular dating site OkCupid, and found that couples seeking other partners can link to each other's profiles; he found as many as 20 percent of users listed themselves as "non-monogamous."

"It's an underground revolution," Stefan said. There was a thrill in his voice.

Shelli thought long and hard, why was she resisting this? What was she trying to protect? He didn't want to have an affair; that must count for something. And if the transgression is known to both parties, and they have each other's consent, and are together when it's happening, how can that be wrong? Maybe sex shouldn't be held up as this sacred thing in a marriage. What was so bad about men getting into her pants anyways, in this age of the birth control, if they were attractive and kind in their ministrations, and provided she liked it?

The next time they spoke about it, Shelli's defenses toppled like a crème puff in a high wind.

"We can't go after anyone in our group." Shelli let out a big sigh.

"Don't you think I know that?"

"How do we set up a profile?"

"We're going to have fun with this." His eyes lit up like fire-crackers.

Against her better instincts she told him she was willing to work with him though he had a history of ignoring her in his quest to charm the multitudes. Part of her was drawn to this game, part of it scared her. At the present, she had no desire for another man, except that perhaps gorgeous hunk she saw occasionally in the gym; she certainly had fantasies about him.

She asked Stefan to pick out a woman from the profiles that flooded their screen that he liked best and show her picture next to her man. A big, strapping guy with abs like a washboard, arms corded and lean, popped up. She couldn't help but stare. She couldn't see his face, just his beach-perfect body. The photos had obviously been taken by an amateur photographer. Stefan told her that faces were averted or cut to protect identities. Okay, she nodded, that made sense, not everyone would look kindly on this sort of hobby and without comment watched Stefan drool over the pictures of a pretty girl with a model-thin body and big bazookas, his thick eyebrows bumping his nose. The kind of guy she fell for varied. Sometimes she hankered for the Harley look, with leather breeches, shaved head, and tats on basketball-sized biceps. Other times, she preferred a man she would want to date, someone like herself, educated, with knowledge of finance, literature, and the arts, someone she could talk to. That's what scared her—how close this came to singles dating—but she brushed that thought away. She was drawn in by a powerful force beyond her control, Jell-O in the website god's hands.

When Stefan and Shelli ran across people they liked the looks of, they checked with each other for approval before adding that couple to their list. Some profiles they lingered over a few extra minutes so she could read the copy; sometimes he joined her, although most of the time he didn't budge from the pictures. In the middle of all this, out of nowhere, he reiterated his desire to keep their philandering to strangers. She was relieved to hear him state this so emphatically, without prompting. Good. Their friends were off-limits.

"We won't be bringing any of this into the house," Shelli said. "I don't want the boys to have any clue what their parents are up to." She thought he was too permissive with what they saw on the telly; well, she wanted to make damn sure this was one part of adult life they wouldn't be seeing from their parents.

"You won't be getting any pushback from me."

"I wouldn't put it past you, sometimes you're that clueless."

"Not true."

"Ha! You're the one who let them get into your Playboys. You know when you insisted on putting your stash under our bed?"

"I found a better hiding place…back of the closet."

They had no pictures to put in their profile, never having taken anything that could be considered remotely sexy. Without pictures they had no chance of attracting another couple. Stefan suggested they take some. Shelli posed in tasteful lingerie. Posing like that and knowing they would be posting these pictures, made her feel like a teenager out on a first date, her palms sweaty and her heart palpating. She took a few of him in boxer shorts. Posting them on the website, knowing it had worldwide reach and over 34 million members, brought up a mix of emotions, alternating between extreme excitement and nervousness.

"Shelli, you look great in this picture," Stefan exclaimed. He pointed out one of her prancing in bra and panties.

She was shocked to see she looked that good. "You look amazing too," she immediately offered. She couldn't stop staring at herself, never having any man take pictures of her in lingerie. The image gratified her lust to see how others saw her. And she meant what she said about Stefan, although she secretly thought she looked better. His chest was well developed, not sunken in like those namby-pamby math geeks that roam the streets of Manhattan, guys who can't turn off the mental calculator even on weekends, but he had the beginnings of a paunch, which wasn't obvious when he sucked it all in. She angled the camera artfully so no one could tell.

"I love you, honeybunch," he crooned, stroking and kissing her. "You've got an adventurous spirit. You don't freak out when I say we need something to lift us out of our same old. How many wives would be this accommodating?"

The thought that she was being too accommodating did worry her, but then she could simply refuse when anything felt wrong and she couldn't imagine he'd back out of his agreement.

"I'm going to be very, very picky, I want you to know that upfront."

"That's a given."

He tackled this business of finding the perfect couple for them with unbridled enthusiasm. "I love looking at the hot females," he said. "I get a secret thrill knowing we might possibly end up in bed together."

"If I were you, I wouldn't presume anything's going to happen."

"Can't you joke about anything? Must everything be so serious?"

Suddenly, in her mind's eye, she saw how Agamemnon must have looked when he made the sign to his servants signaling the time had come to sacrifice his daughter Iphigenia. Whatever love he had for his daughter was overshadowed by his impatience with the long, windless calm preventing the Achaean ships from leaving Sparta. The oracle said the only way was to offer Iphigenia as a sacrifice to Artemis. Agamemnon was certain Artemis was mad at him for killing one of her sacred deer. With the death of Iphigenia he thought the goddess would relent and let the winds blow again. Achilles tried to oppose the sacrifice; Iphigenia was one he wanted to marry. Iphigenia was brought to the altar and Achilles was out of luck, never to see her again. And eventually the winds did pick up again. But what is curious about this story: At the end of the Trojan War, Agamemnon again decides to sacrifice another virgin to coax steady winds allowing the return of the Achaean ships home. Apparently he believed sacrificing a beautiful young woman would sway the gods. In that vein, he chooses the Trojan Polyxena, whom Achilles said he wanted to marry. Achilles seems to have bad luck in picking women to wed. Agamemnon gave the order for Polyxana to be killed, and ordered Neoptolemus, Achilles' son, to plunge the knife into her throat. But it seems a weird way to reward your best warrior; is it possible Agamemnon perceived Achilles as a threat? After her death, the warriors scattered leaves on the girl. "They throw leaves over Polyxena, as if she had won an event at the games: for this was the way they congratulated the winners." Woe to the winner! Why must the most beautiful girls be thus sacrificed?

The Israelites had a different response when it came to appeals to divine entities: In the Torah it says that Abraham was tested by his god, who tells him to sacrifice his only son as a burnt offering. Just as Abraham is about to do the deed, his god tells him he's passed the test and not to kill his son, Abraham instead makes a sacrifice of a ram. The Israelites rarely performed human sacrifice, the only instance (other than Abraham; and that was never completed) was Ahaz, King of Judah of his son to Baal, but he was defeated by the Assyrians anyway, and had to live under their rule. Christianity offered Jesus as a sacrifice to atone for any perceived wrongdoing by humankind, an absolving of sorts, hugely popular with the hoi polloi. The communicants murder their god, this symbolic father combined with the son to reclaim and re-incorporate the surrendered potency in the cannibalism implicit in the act of eating the flesh and blood of Jesus as re-imagined in the wafer. Shelli thought that the ancient myths were likely meant as teaching tools embodying timeless truths, and like many myths the world over there was plenty of hyperbole and fiction woven in. Then there was the sacrifice she was making, maybe it would turn out not to be so much of a sacrifice. It didn't make her angry: she felt a sense of inevitability.

They sat like that for several minutes, silently taken with their own private thoughts, gazing at the pictures as if they held a celestial power, safely encircled by the warm night. Stefan lit the bong, sucking in the smoke and holding it in as if he was going to dive very deep, and released it slowly, his eyes contemplative.

"Too many of the women look out-of-shape," he said after a pause, his voice lifting a notch as if he had discovered a weed that needed rooting out. "Maybe their women feel there's no need to exercise. Do they think that they'll get laid regardless?"

Up popped a guy on the screen built like a horse, his biceps tensed, fist clenched, abs like punched steel. The woman was a scrawny kind of high school beauty, leggy and angular with large breasts. Shelli's palms sank into the silk duvet they rested upon. She noticed every woman he lingered over had large breasts. It made her wonder if he thought her own breasts were too small. She caught her breath.

Swingers in Bombay made them their favorites, and a couple in Dubai sent them a nice note. Another pair, from Hong Kong, said they wanted to meet on their next trip to the States. To think that all these people were slobbering over her pictures made her giddy. Stefan moved to another screen, this one of a beautiful girl with the most perfectly rounded body. He pursed his lips. In a voice trembling with excitement, he asked Shelli to look at what he had found. The woman was a knockout. She clicked on the picture, enlarging it.

"She's nice," Shelli said casually.

He snuggled her, his skin hot to the touch. "Breasts like melons, and those legs, umm, nearly as shapely as yours. And check out the guy. You think he's hot?"

"You want to meet this couple?"

They agreed to email out this message: "Your pictures are hot. We're an athletic, fit couple, and we love to cap off a day of cycling, tennis, horseback riding, or golf with erotic adventures. We're new at this, hoping to meet other compatible couples for an occasional evening of banter, flirting, and possibly more. If you're interested, drop us a line."

Passing the bong back and forth, Shelli felt her head lighten as if it was a balloon filled with helium having smoked a lungful. Her body felt languid, the pot had turned her into a jelly. They emailed a handful of couples and laughed over the wording. Shelli suggested that "athletic" was the term that fat people use to hide behind. Stefan told her that was bonkers. She imagined she would have liked joining the ancient Greek women in their erotic festivals, and asked Stefan if the ancient Israelites had similar type of festivals. He said Moses put a stop to that. Coughing as if something had lodged deep in her throat, but it was only her body announcing that it had enough, she couldn't get any higher. A quiet rain had begun, drumming at the windows, sealing them in. She passed the bong to Stefan, watching him pull it in and hold it, his face reddening. He hiccupped and they started to laugh about nothing at all. A draft from the windows washed over her and she felt the night beyond her hunched shoulders, an extensiveness pressing against the confines of the house, a blackness filled with rustling leaves and hooting owl. He put the bong down and reached for her. He asked if they had plans for Saturday night. "Nope," she said, shaking her head.

"I can see it now," she said, "dozens of beautiful chicks jumping on you..." She grabbed the cat and began stoking him, feeling the nerve endings in her fingertips and palm sizzle. Bubbles purred like a twin engine. She wasn't ready to put her hands on Stefan, not yet.

"What, you think I'd send them packing? I don't think so."

"Let's call Hugh Hefner," she said, thinking the whole thing struck her as surreal.

"You won't see me suckin' some guy, no matter how he's hung. But a pair of tits—that's another matter." Then he backpedaled. "What if we run into someone we know?"

"They can't say a word." She couldn't imagine anyone she knew doing this.

"They could destroy our reputation in the community."

Her mouth went dry. "Everyone would know they were doing it, too." She licked her chapped lips. Why was she so sure that people they knew wouldn't have secret lives like this? Just the other day, at work she heard about a guy who had two wives. Neither one knew about the other, this went on for years. How cultures change, at one time centuries ago, having several wives was something to aspire to, now it can get you arrested. But the wise among men have evolved with the times, now they have a wife and several mistresses, or they swing. When you think about it, how much has really changed? At least now women have choices."

"I dunno." He combed his hair back with his hand the way he did when mulling over a new concept he found thrilling, but then he reconsidered. "This whole thing seems weird, us as a couple trying to seduce hotties. Are we perverts?"

"Well, we know you are," she said.

Four

"Mom look," Seth said, demonstrating a swift front kick, leg lifted chin high hitting empty air, causing the very molecules to vibrate across the den, shattering Shelli's tranquilly. "This is what I'd do if someone tried to attack me." Flushed with his athleticism, he jumped again, as if to underscore his achievement.

Micah moved quickly into the breach. "Look at me," he urged, his face mirroring his brother's excitement. "I can do that, too." He aimed his kick higher than Seth's at a considerable effort, evident by the grunting that accompanied it.

They looked almost identical in every way, though Seth's stance was more assertive.

"I got a red stripe," Seth said.

Stefan came into the room. "You guys are amazing," Stefan said. "I never took karate, looks like fun."

"Look Dad," Seth said.

He positioned in a karate stance and kicked sideways in the direction of Shelli's leg. He did this artfully without touching her leg. "Like that."

"I can do kicks, too," Micah said. He demonstrated the same kick, his eyes widening into large saucers.

The boys squared off, going into the pose.

Seth did a side blade kick, the leg forming a blade shape with the pinky edge of the foot, executed to the side of his body and pointed at Micah. Shelli marveled at the strength of Seth's, quads and glutes, and how well his kicking leg rotated with his flexed toes aiming down on a diagonal. When Seth's side kick landed in front of him, Micah raised his front knee and dropped his elbow onto Seth's extended ankle thus delivering two destructive attacks to Seth's attacking leg. When Seth did it again, Micah employed a low line sweeping deflection, with his rear leg coming up and thrusting a kick to Seth's supporting knee. Seth fell both times.

"You guys are good," Shelli said.

Micah then delivered a roundhouse kick and Seth went on the defense. He blitzed inside and opened with hand speed and caught the kick, and then he dropped into cover mode, laying a kick of his own; feinting a front snap kick to the groin.

"That's just one way to defend," Seth said. "Let's do it again and show Mom some other ways."

Micah delivered his kick again. The kick came in, and Seth shuffled to the side and slightly in, allowing the kick to come past his body. And just then with the outside arm, he did a downward block at the ankle. And with the forearm executed a block, and quickly swapping arm positions (the downward block came up into a forearm block and vice versa) he trapped the Micah's leg at the ankle and knee. He followed that up with a knee lock and pantomimed taking Micah down to the ground.

Seth delivered another kick, one that glanced off Micah's shoulder and threw his brother off balance. Shelli wanted to rush in and ask Seth not to kick Micah so hard, but she had heard from the school counsellor that it was better not to interfere in normal adolescence exuberance, if the other party was in no danger. It was the most difficult thing, to let the boys tussle, holding her breath, mentally wishing to gird this more conciliatory son with a stronger backbone. It wasn't that she considered Micah weak but he was more accommodating and peace loving, in that way might be considered the less strong of the two. But then Micah knocked his head against a chair and immediately started to pummel Seth with his fists. The sleeping giant had woken.

"I'm hoping the furniture can take the abuse," Shelli said to Stefan.

"Wanna come outside and play some baseball?" Stefan said. "Or basketball?"

"I'm fighting for my life here," Seth said, between gasps. Micah had him in a chokehold.

"I thought you liked ball sports," Stefan said in an injured tone.

"I like karate better," Seth said.

Shelli found it difficult to listen to this.

"Dad he hit me," Micah said.

"Hit him back," Stefan said. "Hey both of you might want to take it outside or to the playroom where you're not breaking Mom's best furniture."

"Nothing's broken," Seth said. "See?" He gestured at the overturned Stickley chair, "No damage."

Shelli could see that Seth's aggression upset Micah, and she tried to make it up to him, but he would have none of it, shooing her away. She thought she could detect sadness in Micah's eyes whenever Seth lorded it over him, but she tried to stay out of it. When Seth refused to play games that Micah suggested, and then later put out the same ideas as if they came from Seth, she let that ride, thinking that happens to everyone, Micah better get used to it. Right then they liked each other, likely because Micah had let Seth win. And together they stood tall, proud to be wearing the Karategi, their karate uniforms, their faces reflecting their outsize enthusiasm bursting with joy to be learning karate.

Seth lifted the ends of the red belt that the instructor had given him as if presenting an offering to the gods. Micah took his red belt off, flashing it around, keeping time with his parody of karate moves. Shelli felt her heart quicken. As a child, Shelli had played with her brothers like this, although she had never taken karate, mostly she had played the same sports as they. She had done the soccer and loved how fit she became, the energy and the feeling of raw power that it gave her. But it came at a cost. One time she'd been hit in the face by a soccer ball at age eleven and had suffered a numbed cheek, her eyes stinging so she could barely see, and had to sit out the game during second half, just when her team began scoring big, so she had an inkling what her kids' were going through. Shelli wanted Stefan to feel the same pride that she had, so they could *kvell* together, and experience the great feeling that rendered her speechless, seeing her children learning survival skills. She was delighted with virtually everything her precious darlings did, from the most mundane like enjoying food she made special for them to drawing clever pictures and saying clever things.

"When was the first time you felt that special sense of achievement?' Shelli said to Stefan, hoping to engage him in a conversation about the coolness of favorite sports. She wanted to add, if it can be said that some sports are more important for survival, this one might be a better one to master. Karate is about discipline and control; life is much the same. But she didn't want to look like she was casting aspersions on a sport Stefan loved, it didn't really matter if baseball didn't help fight off attackers, if they enjoyed it, that counts for a lot, and she knew Stefan put a lot of his ego into the sports he followed. She would have been just as happy if they liked baseball, but they didn't. And she was sorry for Stefan that they didn't, she was afraid he would take it badly.

"My first strikeout as a pitcher," Stefan said, "but I was playing baseball every day, so I got really good."

"But you're good at every sport," Shelli said.

"They never stick with anything," Stefan said.

"Give them a chance," Shelli said, wishing Stefan wasn't so contentious about sports, and so eager to play the bully.

"I hate quitters," he muttered, glowering, folding his arms as if he was making a last stand. Shelli thought this is what Leonidas I, warrior king of the Greek city-state of Sparta must have looked like when holding off Xerxes and the Persian imperial army at Thermopylae.

Shelli followed her sons downstairs. They raced the stairs two at a time with the boisterousness of young puppies, while she plodded along behind, listening to their thudding feet, and realizing that the simple pleasures in life are really the best: such as seeing her boys master that first real achievement, the one they'll remember forever. They'd learn much more than kicking and punching, although it was the kicking and punching that captivated them. They'd learn what it means to be disciplined, respectful, patient, and controlled. And they'd learn what it means to be men in this modern world.

"Would you like to do something else," Shelli said. "I mean, give the karate a rest?"

"Okay," Seth said. "Let's play Tomb Raider."

She went upstairs to prepare dinner. Preparing tacos didn't take much analysis, she could chop vegetables on remote control—yet several times she had to remind herself where she was, reveling in carnal thoughts, and just as quickly brushing her sense of guilt that she could have a secret life apart from her sons like so much fairy dust. She carefully selected the onion she planned to slice—a purple one that was smaller than average and rounded; its flesh hard to the touch, its skin multifarious and tissue thin, and sliced, its juices spraying the counter, which called to mind her classical Greek class with Professor Giannopoulos, who looked like he stepped out of a sarcophagus, and by far the most interesting teacher on campus, full of interesting information, such as the ancients' use of onions to heighten sexual desire. Americans view the onion as a lowly condiment, but the ancient Egyptians, Greeks, Romans, and even Druids used onions as a sexual aid. Even today, the French still follow an old tradition of serving newlyweds onion soup the morning after their wedding night to restore their libido. More to the point, she realized that she had it better as a married woman—she could fantasize not from starvation, but from greed.

Stefan came into the kitchen impatient for his dinner. While she was getting things ready, they talked the practicalities that ruled their lives. Then out of nowhere, he said repeated what he said earlier in the day, that he was upset about the boys not wanting to play baseball anymore. She counseled him to encourage them in the sport of their choice, but he would have none of it.

"They started this thing," he said, and then repeated his comment from earlier in the day: "I don't like quitters."

"Let them choose," Shelli said. "As long as they're doing a sport, what do you care?"

"Yeah, but it hurts that they don't like baseball."

"You'll get over it."

After dinner Stefan went to a meeting for one of the charity organizations he belonged to, so the rest of night was hers to do what she liked. With some prodding she got the boys to do their homework, promising television as their reward for finishing it, and then it came time to put them to bed, she stayed with them until they had fallen asleep.

For the next two hours, she combed the web pages, seeing if she could find a picture of the guy she kissed in at the nightclub, reasoning away her obsession as a pressing need to fortify what was good about her marriage rather than as a psychological thing to watch out for, as counterintuitive as that sounds. Their shared obsession had quickly taken over their free time and set their collective imaginations on fire—more than any other thing they had together—it was like someone had lit a match in a parched forest. Shelli knew now that she was hooked, maybe not as badly as Stefan, but looking at these people engaged in ways normally considered taboo in public was one of the most thrilling things she had ever done. Having sexual contact with random strangers might turn out to be something entirely different, but this peek-a-boo stuff was highly tantalizing, she could no more put an end to this then she could stop breathing.

Later that night, as was their usual habit, they looked at emails together. Stefan said something about having a possible date that weekend. "Hey, that couple finally replied to our e-mail." He stroked her hand like she was the kitty. "They want to get together but can't for another week or so. They're waiting for the weekend when they won't have their kids."

"Oh." Shelli tried to control her breathing. Her desire was easily pricked. Viewing sex websites had awakened a monster. Bubbles jumped on her lap and Shelli stroked her fur, marveling that her sexual desire stayed with her all the time, growing in intensity though the day, a combustive force that demanded constant release.

Apparently, the woman Stefan had been emailing worked as a doctor and her husband a lawyer. Just what we need, she thought, someone to sue us, and the other one to stitch us up.

Noting the way Stefan's eyes darted back to the computer when a close-up of the women's breasts came on the screen Shelli put the cat down on the bed, placed her arms around his shoulders and, breathing in the musky smell of him, hoped the other men would smell this good. But she didn't want those men, the search was titillating but for her the fantasy was enough. Though she had qualms about how he would behave if a new woman came into the picture. Feeling the boundaries shifting in real time made her stomach queasy.

He bent his head like he could not get close enough, his nose practically on top of the picture of the woman's bountiful breasts. Had he never seen a pair of mammary glands before? Shelli was surprised to see him fetishize the breast like this, making love to it with his eyes, ah, was he licking the screen, or was she imagining it? She caught his eye and he moved his hand up her legs, causing her nerve endings to sizzle.

"They're both hot," she said, keeping her voice deliberately low and running her fingers through his mass of hair, a dense jungle, and thought how quickly their world had become bifurcated with platonic friends from the neighborhood getting increasingly shorter shrift in favor of their secret internet playpen.

Stefan sent an email saying they were interested in meeting. The other couple returned his e-mail promptly, saying that they had been burned too many times by flakes and liked to go slow, asking questions like, "Are you beer drinkers or do you fancy quality wines?" They attached a photo of themselves doing bicep curls with the message: "Daily visits to the gym."

Stefan sent an email asking if they could meet that weekend and received a reply in the affirmative. Shelli did a happy dance but only because she had Stefan, if she was doing this on her own, she wouldn't care for this sort of game. Stefan sent another e-mail, suggesting a time and place of meeting, saying, "We look forward to having our collective cherry broken."

Years before she met Stefan, Shelli had been invited to a massage workshop held in a refurbished warehouse in Sausalito, led by a yoga master and masseur extraordinaire who incorporated dolphin sounds as part of the experience. She never suspected that the workshop would turn into this sexually charged thing, with guys pressuring girls to go home with them. That sort of insistence turned her off, but when it was happened organically, mutual attraction, then she was fine ending up in bed together. She viewed the swinging as a way of controlling Stefan's wandering eye, actively seeking to have sex with another couple was not something that she could imagine doing for an indefinite length of time, but she didn't want to put a time limit on it yet, not when they were just getting started. At that moment, she wasn't sure she wanted to do anything sexual with anyone else, not unless she was hot for that someone. Lately Stefan became obsessed with working out, claiming he needed washer board abs, spending untold hours doing crunches. Shelli told him he looked fine, he just needed to suck it in, though she liked him working out.

"Tell me the truth. Is my penis big enough?"

Shelli was taken aback. "It's big enough for me," she said, carefully parsing her words. "You know me; I would have let you know early on if there was a problem." After a pause, she asked: "What about me? If you could, would you change the size of my breasts?"

"More than a handful is a waste." He said with a kiss.

She was grateful for that answer, although she didn't believe him. But it really didn't matter, she was happy with her breasts; she thought they were nicely curved and hung beautifully on her torso.

But all that fantasizing made Shelli feel terribly excited and nervous, and anticipatory, hugging and kissing Stefan endlessly and getting him excited at odd times. She thought the boys were getting off on all that hugging and kissing, too, they seemed to thrive on the energy. Stefan would say suggestive remarks, nothing too overt when the boys were with them, and when they were alone, he could talk of nothing else, casting them in different scenarios. The guy would boff her from behind and Stefan would take the woman sitting down. In their imaginings, Shelli told Stefan that she wanted him to stay close, just in case the other guy was a dud. If the guy failed her, Shelli asked Stefan to step in, saying that if his intent was to make this all about him and not about her too, well, then. What's good for the gander sort of thing; he promised to do everything she said.

Now that they finally had a couple in their sights, she hoped they would turn out to be a sensuous delight, warm and caring. And she prayed they'd both like her, she didn't really think she'd jump in bed with a strange man, but it was fun to speculate what that would be like if the guy was too wonderful to pass up. Her sexual desire was like a drum beat loud and obnoxious, drowning out everything else; she shivered to think what the male half of their date would be like in bed. At the moment, she could care less about the pollution story. She knew it wasn't going away so fast; it would still be there when she was ready for it.

Alastair's curvy better half sat like her chair had turned into a springboard, jumping and gesturing excitedly about everything that came up, shutting people down in the middle of sentences and swinging her arms like battering rams, her voice rising. Several people at neighboring tables looked her way. Her energy infected everyone and lent a note of hilarity to the proceedings. Shelli completely forget her jangly nerves and imagined that the four of them would go out on dates and the women would go on shopping trips together and be besties and fill the spaces their spouses refused to go. It would be like friends with benefits only better. When the talk veered to skiing, Tequila butted in, shamelessly switching everyone to hiking, and when the conversation flowed to vacation hotspots, she promptly hit the manual override and had them dredging up air travel horror stories. Alastair began describing his wife's sexual proclivities, getting only a couple of words in before Tequila took over again, running the conversation as if she couldn't share the podium, least of all, with him.

"She likes you to dress up," Alastair said, looking at Stefan. "Black satin tighties."

The pictures of Alastair on the website showed a shirtless, muscular body, and from what could be glimpsed under his jacket that evening, that was an honest portrayal. But what the pictures didn't show: a face androgynous like Mick Jagger with strawberry-blond hair and pale Scottish skin. She found his delicate features and full lips attractive. He was fair skinned like her, a change of scenery from Stefan's Mediterranean looks and appeared to be the quiet one, yen to his wife's yang; the type who takes pains to get along with people, and like Stefan, didn't come off as overly aggressive. Shelli thought that maybe the two men might hit it off. Although everything felt strange, she liked these people; they appeared to be intelligent, college-educated, and witty. What more could she ask for?

The waitress came by and asked for their drink orders. The girl was young and wholesome, with a bright cheery face and big smile, and wore a white tee shirt that said "get them while they're hot."

They ordered a pitcher of handcrafted beer. They waited until the girl had gone out of earshot to speak, but they needn't have bothered. People around them spoke loudly, filling the tables around them. It was not even a question whether anyone could hear them, rather who'd care?

"She's into kink," Alasdair said. "Spankings, handcuffs..."

"*Cabrón*, it's his fault."

"What?" Stefan looked confused.

"I was an innocent when I met him—didn't know my way around a man's body at all." Tequila took over the story with aplomb. "One day, we were watching the crazy lesbian fights on Jerry Springer together. I was giving him the massage of his life, better than any bacchanalian feast—and he starts talking orgies."

Stefan was riveted. His eyes gave him away. Each time Tequila spoke, Stefan's eyes swept right past her thick shoulder-length hair, a tapestry of shimmering ebony, and those pouty lips, which hung slightly open, as if inviting a wet, sloppy kiss. He headed straight for Tequila's voluptuous chest and lingered there. Alasdair seemed pleased at the attention his wife was getting. Apparently, Stefan had forgotten his wife sitting next to him, his eyes fixed on his new conquest. Most of the time, Shelli didn't care, as long as she enjoyed her conversation with the woman's husband, but every so often, she wanted Stefan to connect with her, and pass her a loving look letting her know that she mattered to him. It irked her that he didn't do this, wasn't this supposed to be about them, not just him? Did he forget his manners in the excitement of the chase?

"I give very good massages," Tequila said, staring directly at Stefan with eyes the color of blackest night, complementing her glowing brown skin.

They were meeting in a deserted section of Red Bank along the Navesink River in what looked like an abandoned building;

it seemed the perfect meeting place for an assignation. Out of big windows looking on the river, the many points of light from the sun's rays looked like dancing silver coins topping the crescents of teeming blue-black water. Candles had been placed on each table, creating little worlds where diners looked to be cozily ensconced. It was tailor made for people seeking privacy, with muted colors and dark wooded furnishings, and plenty of space between tables. They could have been planning a major heist and no one would have had a clue. Shelli could see why their dates had picked this peculiar restaurant. No one could hear anything they said, even if they yelled their faces off.

Scuttlebutt had it that several people in the lifestyle had been blackmailed (someone had hoped to make money by outing a politician and his wife who participated in orgies, and it went on from there), so everyone was super cautious. No surprise that this couple would claim fake screen names, but this didn't bother Shelli; all she cared about is that the pictures didn't lie. They learned later that these names were indeed camouflage.

"I bet you do," Stefan purred.

With eyebrows raised and hands lifted, the diva detailed how she came to be a masseuse extraordinaire. She described, in excruciating minutiae, classes and books devoured on massage practice and theory, followed by a year traveling through Asia where she learned how to ply a man's muscles until he became putty in her hands. At that point in her narrative, she stared intently at Stefan as if she were about to perform surgery on him. Tequila was smart and charming, like Medea, who conspired to have Theseus poisoned so she could install her son as king of Athens. In mythology, those kinds of people get turned into monsters; in real life, they get laid. Being nobody's *pendaja* (her words) and from her talk, a thoughtful soul, the type who when anyone in her family falls sick, she writes letters to nuns in

Puerto Rico, and asks the holy ones to pray for her relatives' health.

Tequila and Alasdair excused themselves to go to the bathroom. Shelli couldn't think of anything to say, having mulled a series of depressing thoughts freezing her brain so she couldn't think straight without sounding malicious and unkind. An uneasy silence descended.

"I like that she's a professional," Stefan said, coming to Shelli's rescue. "I prefer intelligent women with looks."

"Honey, you only go after the best." Shelli decided to take his comment at face value. She kept her tone light, teasing, affecting the light-hearted romp that she knew he preferred. She didn't want to bleed in front of him and ruin his favorite Billy Joel tee-shirt. It was too soon for that.

"Of course, I picked you, didn't I?" Stefan said.

She could easily have fallen into a state-of-suspicion trap, especially since they were contemplating having carnal relations with these people, but she understood what he meant when he said he found the woman attractive.

"She's on fire," Shelli said, tongue firmly in cheek.

"Remember, I'm the best husband you ever had, and don't you forget it."

"Oh, sweetie, of course you are." She kissed his cheek, thinking if women were this touchy, few relationships would ever make it past the first spilled coffee. And if she took her fears out of the equation, it felt sinfully delicious to talk openly of sex with people she didn't know but found attractive, swilling beer in mouth. The other couple returned.

Alasdair turned to Shelli. "Do you have any toys we can play with?"

Shelli was about to say something about dildos, pausing to absorb the strange way Alasdair's right eye went out of kilter, straying off as if he was looking at two objects. She tried to ignore the lazy eye and was about to speak but then stopped at the black look she received from Tequila, who had massages covered and wanted to own the sex toys market too, apparently. Alasdair shrugged his shoulders, smiling at Shelli. Tequila sat like a black widow, ready to pounce and deliver the death rattle, her penetrating gaze declaring that she was not happy to see everyone's attention diverted.

"I took a class from the top oral sex instructor in New York," Shelli said. "I have an incredibly complex skill set that takes weeks to learn. I'd love to show you what I know." After all, Stefan did make clear that he preferred strong women. Shelli decided to show Alasdair and Stefan that she had it in her, too.

"What you have is nothing compared to years of medical training, and along the way, acquiring an encyclopedic knowledge of how the body works, inside and out," Tequila affected her most scathing tone, her onyx eyes shining with a ghostly transparence. "To say that my training is evident in the way I work a dildo, or the way I give a massage, is to understate the point." Tequila claimed she could pry anyone's muscles free from physical and emotional scars, something no one else at the table could do. Shelli doubted she knew how to give a decent massage. Tequila would soon learn that she was up to the challenge. The outsized female entertainment center sitting on the other end of the table was full of hot air, and Shelli was certain she could outmaneuver the other woman without breaking a sweat.

"We'll each take turns giving head. The guys will judge," Shelli said. Stefan would get a ringside seat. They would have it out woman-to-woman. "We'll see who has the most feckless mouth."

"No, *jamás, never,*" Tequila breathed.

Shelli was starting to talk as loud as Tequila in order to be heard above the cacophony in the room. People were looking their way in an inquisitive fashion. A couple waiting for a table glanced at them as if they would have liked to pull up chairs. Another passerby, a woman, came within inches of Shelli, slowing down as she got closer, on her face wide-open curiosity and longing. All around, it seemed to Shelli as if a groundswell of approval and admiration appeared.

Stefan gave her a pleased look.

"You're on," Tequila said.

"What the hell," Alasdair's voice sounded raspy, his stiff upper lip trembling with excitement, both eyes locked on Tequila.

It appeared that his right eye didn't stray all the time, just when he was tired, having had imperfect vision in that eye when young, which was corrected later, but still leaving a lingering effect. All this he explained to Shelli later as they were leaving the restaurant, at a time Tequila and Stefan had stepped out of earshot. For some reason, Shelli sensed he was able to speak more candidly when they couldn't be overheard.

"Honey, I'm not done talking," Tequila said, "We have yet to discuss the rules of the game."

Tequila visibly brightened when everyone—including the table behind them—turned to her with rapt expressions as if their only joy was to listen to her expound about her job as a gynecologist. And why she decided to speak about her work, Shelli could only guess, maybe the sneers and raised eyebrows had an effect.

Her voice rose as she went on to explain that climbing health care costs led her take time with her patients, time that she was not compensated to for, to talk up better diet and exercise even though she knew that her efforts were about likely about as effective as those of a tiny ant trying to stop a tidal wave with a blade of grass. "I used to be one of them, the people on diets that don't work, starving myself instead of eliminating carbs, and doing the sort of exercise that made me fatter."

Stefan smiled at Tequila, said agreeable things, nodding at nearly everything she said. His body appeared to vibrate with friendliness. His eyes were kind, generous, flirty, glowing with passion. It was the kind of look she had seen before, that's what he looked like when he was interested in a woman. That was the look he wore the day he met Shelli. She recalled telling him something, she couldn't remember what she said, but she remembered the expression he had on his face when he looked at her, like he rode on a surfeit of endorphins. It was that same look that drew her like a song. How could he look at Tequila like that when everything that came out of her mouth was banal, easily forgotten? Still, she saw that look reappear again. There was no mistaking it. But rather than give into the impulse to cause a scene, which would likely backfire in the long run, she consoled herself with the thought that likely Tequila wasn't interested in Stefan for the long haul. Tequila had children; no way would Stefan want a woman with children. He had his own children to worry about. She couldn't imagine Stefan wanting to take on someone else's children. Shelli knew with a certainty that Stefan was gaga over his sons. Nor was Tequila the kind of woman Shelli had seen Stefan go for. He usually liked them skinny and built.

Shelli relaxed her fingers on the chair she had been griping, and asked Alasdair what led him to try partner swapping. "I was married for six years," Alasdair said. "After the divorce I realized how much I liked having sex with more than one woman. But I also craved a relationship with just one woman. I need both."

"And you found that woman," Shelli said, happy to point out this out to the table at large, hoping to remind Stefan that he had a beautiful relationship not easily replaced, and lovely sons who would be heartbroken if he messed things up with their mom.

"When you do it together as a couple it takes out the fear," Alasdair said, "and the feeling that one of you doesn't know what's going on with the other. Or that the other has secrets that can't be shared. Luckily for me, Tequila was open-minded enough to try it, which speaks volumes about her." He drained his beer, his eye behaving for once.

The waitress came by with food. Tequila had ordered lobster mac and cheese. Stefan and Alasdair both went with hamburgers and fries. Shelli ordered eggplant parmesan.

"When he met me, he didn't want to give up dating," Tequila said with a shrug.

"For people to expect men to be monogamous, this is relatively new," Alasdair said.

The music and singing made the place feel cozy, layered over the chatter of multiple conversations, amid the spray of laughter.

"In ancient matrilineal societies," Tequila picked up the conversation with a hooded glance in Shelli's direction. "Everyone played around. Men forced monogamy on women, not wanting to raise someone else's kid, and the men continued to have multiple partners. It's easier for men to get away with it; they don't have the babies."

"My mother tried to eradicate sex as if it were a vicious weed to be killed," Shelli said. "She was an old-fashioned Latin Mass sort of Catholic."

"Mine was the Spanish version," Tequila said. "But everyone had sex, even *el cura*. Except my *madre*. Funny, huh, that you and I meet."

"You ever hear of the Oneida Community?" Alasdair said. "Sometime in the mid-1800s in upstate New York there were

300 of them. Each of the women was married to each of the men. But they could only have sex when John Noyes, the head of the community said, and he'd choose whom they could bed, and when they could have children."

"The group disbanded when their leader, was arrested for statutory rape and fled the country," Tequila said.

"Noyes was a strange dude," Alasdair said, his weaker eye doing a slight shimmer of a dance.

"Then he took the kids away from their parents as soon as they could walk," Tequila said.

"We're not advocating any of that," Alasdair said.

"Kinsey researchers swapped spouses," Shelli said.

The waitress showed up and stood there waiting, her ears pricked, waiting for an opening. Stefan ordered another round.

"Swapping partners became wildly popular in the sixties," Tequila said. "The first organized swingers clubs were in the Bay Area, Berkeley actually."

"Your guys are into swapping partners?" the waitress asked. "But you look so normal."

"What did you expect?"

"Oh, I don't know," the waitress said. "Women with fake breasts and lots of makeup and skin showing."

"Funny," Tequila said. "I'm wearing a turtleneck and very little makeup. And my *tetas* may be big, but they're real."

"What I'm wearing," Shelli said, "No cleavage showing."

The waitress took off, shaking her head in wonderment.

"I dress this way so people know that although we've agreed to meet," Tequila said, "it doesn't mean anything is going happen. It puts things in the proper perspective."

"Wow," Stefan said. "He ain't heavy, he's my brother."

"Remember the Doors," Shelli said. "Love was sex, and sex was death, and therein lay salvation."

"What do the Doors have to do with anything?" Stefan asked.

"The Doors were the missionaries of apocalyptic sex," Shelli said.

"Yeah, but the Doors lived in LA."

"They reflected the ethos."

"The California sun melted your brain," Stefan said.

"Remember," Tequila said. "That picture you said you liked of my *tetas*?" She batted her kitten eyes at Stefan as if he was the only one in the room.

"You do have nice jugs," Stefan said. "I'd love to give them a squeeze."

Shelli looked around. No one was looking at them; everyone appeared to be engaged in their own conversations. Their table was seemingly invisible to everyone else. The noise level so high, it was doubtful that anyone overheard even if they had shouted "fire" to the skies.

"You have a tight body," Alasdair said. "Do you lift?"

"I do a lot of things," Shelli said. "Yoga, jogging, tennis, the whole schmear."

"I work out too," Alasdair said. "But I have yet to meet someone as fit as me. I'm t-h-r-r-i-l-l-e-d to pieces. Please, please, say you want to get together with us." Both eyes drilling down.

It was no ordinary smile, the way Tequila spread those big, juicy lips between succulent cheeks, twisting one thick, luscious strand of hair between her fingers. No, that was a major come-on smile.

"You're a lucky man to have found someone like Tequila," Shelli hastened to say, smiling at her to let her know that she had no desire to have her man for keeps, hoping to avoid any rumbles. "And we're lucky to find such a smart, good-looking couple for our first rendezvous," and though she was nervous about the prospect, Shelli wanted Alasdair to understand that she was as hot for him as Stefan was for Tequila, but she had to couch her words, she didn't want to frighten his girl off. Alasdair was good looking, and fit. Shelli had no problem with his looks, and he wasn't demented or crazy.

"I wanted a guy who was sexually open, and I got him," Tequila said.

On their first date, Tequila got drunk and threw up all over his bed. He did not get mad or disgusted; rather, he cleaned up the vomit without a word, and continued where they left off. In return, Tequila said yes to swinging, and they got married two weeks later before a justice of the peace. As might be expected, they left out the monogamy part in their oath to each other. All's well that ends well, Stefan said in response.

"It's interesting that we get along," Tequila said, with a warm look at Shelli, apparently happy with her for the moment. "You wouldn't think to look at us. We're such different types. I grew up dirt poor in Puerto Rico. My parents were uneducated and underemployed and rarely had money to buy us things. Thank God they moved to New York, or medical school would have been totally out of the picture. I went through on scholarships. To think a poor, fat Latino is living the American dream. Alasdair had it a lot easier. His parents migrated from Scotland, made money here. Early on, he developed a thing for Latino women. The darker the better, he says."

"My ex is Puerto Rican too," Alasdair said. His right eye twitched. "She's way darker than you. You're the whitest Puerto Rican I've ever met. You sure you're Puerto Rican?"

Tequila ignored his comment. "His ex's ability to earn money is limited," she said. "Her English is poor, and she has no skills. She spends all her time trying to figure out how to get more support from Alasdair. Oh, yes, and she hates me with a passion. Funny, huh, when I'm such a good role model for the child she had with Alasdair. The first time we met, she wouldn't talk to me. We nearly came to blows at the door. She got so mad she nearly left without picking up her son."

"Perfectly understandable," Shelli said, smiling at Tequila.

Tequila was vivacious, smart, and beautiful, someone Shelli thought she could like as a friend, if she could hold her jealousy in check. What would that be like, to be fuck friends? And how often would she get the opportunity to borrow this woman's spouse for a few hours? And was that something she wanted?

"A month ago, she asked me about birth control. That's when the ice melted. Now there's grudging acceptance."

"A lot of people say I look Spanish," Shelli said, cupping her chin in one hand, waiting to be admired.

"You're striking," Alasdair said. "And yes, you do look Spanish. From Europe."

Tequila shot him a look that said, watch it.

"I don't think you want to get involved with this one," Stefan said. "When I met her, she lied about her birthday. Can you believe that she told me the wrong day? She led me to believe she was born on the second when really she was born on the twenty-ninth."

"You heard me wrong, and then you invited all these people, and I meant to tell you, but I forgot." There he goes, Shelli thought, undercutting me. Nice.

"Yeah, right—I learned months later."

"I forget things all the time," Alasdair said.

"What does it matter?" Shelli said, holding back her desire to slap Stefan.

But it tickled Shelli that he was jealous, although she would have preferred that he not criticize her to make his point, but she also knew she couldn't ask him about it, he would say he had been joking, and where was her sense of humor. She would have to soothe his feathers later, but maybe not; the man never admitted when he misspoke.

Alasdair preferred to dish out silly witticisms as if vying for a prize, laughing nonstop over his own acerbic political commentary. He must have hit a nerve with Stefan, who agreed hands down that President Bush had been something of a patrician, the kind who tends to follow Rudyard Kipling's advice to treat triumph and disaster as impostors both. Stefan pointed out that Bush Senior flew fifty-eight combat missions by the time he was twenty, and lost his cojones in the White House, refusing to engage Saddam Hussein when American forces overran Kuwait. Stefan maintained he must have known they had nerve gas, a gift from President Reagan for use in their war against the Iranians. Turned out Saddam used that gas against the Kurds for their support of the Americans.

"You know your politics," Tequila noted.

"Right you are," Alasdair said with great enthusiasm, squinting as he raised his glass.

"You guys are a lot of fun," Tequila said, her pretty mouth bathed in smiles. "Most of the people we've met from the website have been incredibly boring."

"We'd love you to come by our house," Alasdair said. "On a Saturday night when we don't have kids."

Tequila echoed her husband's offer. "Please, please!" Her voice fell soft as rain on Shelli's ears.

"Up to you, honey," Stefan said.

Shelli looked at Stefan's eager fingers dancing an Irish jig on the table, his expression naughty like a boy whose been told to stay away from dessert before dinner and got caught with frosting all over his face. Shelli knew he was dreaming of those breasts. But if they were doing it together, maybe she would find it interesting, maybe even pleasurable? The thought of the two of them suckling Tequila's tits together—one on each teat—sent shivers up her spine. She was amazed she was thinking like this. It was the weirdest thing, she had to pinch herself.

"Definitely," Shelli said. "The sooner the better." She tried to slow her breathing. She was trembling.

"How about next Saturday?" Alasdair asked, looking at Shelli with a smile.

"We'd love to," Shelli said, her words sounding hollow to her ears.

My God, Shelli thought, it's really happening. They were going to the house of a couple they had just met for sex. The idea of it seemed so unreal. Her heart beat faster. She looked at Alasdair's crotch and tried to guess how big his package was, wondering at the trembling in her thighs. The intensity of her curiosity to experience what another man would feel like made her head spin. It had been ages since she had been with anyone else. Far too long.

Friday afternoon Shelli picked up the boys from the bus stop near their home, thinking how unreal; one more night to go. Seth was in high form, bouncing around the back seat, saying the teachers beat him with sticks and starved him. She was used to this kind of talk from Seth and tended to ignore the most extreme of his claims when delivered in a jocular tone. She thought if this was really the case, he would be sounding stressed, and minus the chuckles.

"Any idiots out today, mom?" Seth said.

"Fuckin' cars," Micah said. "What are all those fuckin' cars doing here?"

"Where did you hear that word?" Shelli asked. "I don't talk like that."

"Yes you do."

"When?" Shelli said.

"I forget," Seth said.

"I heard a joke at school," Micah said, "but I don't get it."

"Tell me the joke," Shelli said.

What comes after 69?" Micah said, bouncing on the seat.

"Seventy," Shelli said.

"No, mouthwash," Micah said.

"What's funny about that?" Seth said.

"Mouthwash?" Shelli said. "Maybe they shower in mouth-wash?"

What?" Seth said.

"Maybe it's a thing," Shelli said.

She took them with her to the tennis club, a cavernous affair resembling the inside of an airport hangar, to which the serious tennis players in town belonged. The club also had a pool and day care with pool privileges for members. Shelli had signed the boys up for tennis lessons in another area of the club and watched them scamper off, marveling that these beautiful creatures came out of her body, and went to the court reserved for her group, an old-fashioned design with a clay foundation, and sat on the bench to wait for the others, lulled by the sounds of the birds tittering in the trees that surrounded the compound.

She recalled the trying time of their birth, nothing Stefan could understand. Having a C-section unmoored her, sent her reeling. Weakened by the physical necessities of birth, the raw, barbaric blood and ooze, the hurt where the staples nailed her stomach incision together—she couldn't even cough or draw a deep breath without her stitches causing her pain. And she had no help at home, the hospital stay was her vacation; she found it physically difficult to care for her newborn twins by herself, with that wound still smarting in her lower abdomen although she did what she had to do, cradling one, than the other, in a continual nonstop lovefest. It was exhausting. But the worst was the continual, non-stop crying. They were born premature, a month early, so their sucking reflex never developed, and yet they needed to eat all the time. She had to express her milk and couldn't manage the pump easily—it was the type that pulled at the breast and made her nipples sore. That's when her marriage suffered some cracks. She had done and said hurtful things back then, things she'd like to take back. She blanched at the memory. Uppermost in her mind, both crying and she asked Stefan at 3 a.m. to help her and he said he'd rather not; he had an early morning meeting. She blurted out, "I'd have been happy with just one."

He looked at her like she was the weakest thing. Hurtful words were exchanged, something from her about him having no empathy, and him calling her a terrible mom. No help for that now. Nothing she could take back, nothing he could forget. His attitude toward her changed after that, a subtle shift, barely decipherable in a look or a gesture, nothing she could pin down, visible, nonetheless. His mother, Lois, stayed with them for the second month, but she turned out to be more of a hindrance than a help. She kept pressing Shelli to feed them store-bought formula. They argued about that, and more. Lois didn't think Shelli should hold them so much, she was a fan of the school of letting them cry their hearts out. Shelli told her mother-in-law that theory had been debunked. But the worse was feeding time. Feeding them at the same time took the skills of a juggler and fortitude of a saint. Multiply that by a two dozen feedings a day and it becomes apparent how quickly her life turned into an exorable march of Kafkaesque incidents revolving around the feeding and cleaning of her new charges that didn't end until they could hold a cup, a year and a half later. Their father never understood the strain she went through. He gained forty pounds, too, when she was pregnant, but then she removed all treats from their cupboards until she lost most of it, but a decade and half later he still carried the vestiges of a tire, like a pimple that won't go away. And now she had these big, boisterous boys tearing around the house, trailed by circle of friends, spilling sticky cereal and marshmallows that gets caught in the carpet. It's enough to make a grown woman cry. Like Joan Rivers says, can we talk? And yes, they're extraordinarily handsome and a pleasure to gaze upon, thanks for asking. They're everything to her. She asked them in her sweetest voice to cool it with the cereal and to help her clean it up, meanwhile she's bending over and scrapping the sticky mess out of the carpet, vowing to herself never to have Lucky Charms in the house again, not until they're much, much older, and wiser. But did they help her? An attempt was made, and then they were off again on some wild chase. She had to hunt them down and cajole with a promise of a reward to help her finish the job. She would give her life for them, but the prospect of going rogue on a Saturday night when the boys were occupied elsewhere appealed to her. It seemed there was always work to do, and it never got easier, the problems just changed. She needed more breaks, not less. If she took off the way she wanted to, she reasoned, likely she would be a better parent, even if it was to have sex with other people. She just couldn't bring it into the home, that's where she drew the line.

To laugh at the idea of it: a prissy virgin afraid of sex for the longest time. It wasn't until Shelli was almost out of high school that she had her first sexual experience, although like many of her contemporaries in the San Francisco Bay Area she tried pot at thirteen and acid a couple years later, and went to parties where people openly made out. A lot of her friends screwed around. Not her. She found few boys interesting enough to want to bed and was celibate for long periods. Thinking about those times when she found herself hungering for a lover to ease her loneliness, someone who, like a good musician, would know how to tease out the singular sensual note, and would be flexible enough to segue into new arrangements when the timing was right put her into a strange disquiet. Ideally, he would keep adding to the build until both parties hit their climactic moment but few fit the bill. She had one steady boyfriend in college and had only been with a few other guys when she met Stefan. He came from a very traditional background, so taking it slow made sense for them.

Shelli spotted Mattie looking long and lean in her short tennis skirt, topped by blonde hair that never frizzed or lost its shine. Julia was right behind her, looking worried, shaking her head, as if to say it was too much on her shoulders. Her lustrous red hair was perfect combed, not a stray curl.

"Did you bring the triplets?" Shelli said.

Julian, Riley, and Shaw, two boys and a girl, were five years old and terribly cute, but a handful. The tennis club's day care was one of best, stocked with plenty of F.A.O. Schwarz-style toys, a jungle gym and swing set, and a high ratio of teenaged childcare support on hand.

Shelli's mind kept returning to their plans for the weekend. Were they were really going to the house of strangers to have sex the next evening?

Four women moved into the court next to them and started to lob balls at each other. One of them, a tall blonde, was wearing an Adidas by Stella McCartney dress in fiery red and hot pink. She had the body for it. Another leggy blonde had on a retro color-blocked dress designed by Pharrell Williams that looked designed specifically for her, it fit that good. The other two were dressed more conservatively in their tennis whites, reflecting muted tones befitting the establishment. Shelli felt intimidated by all that beauty, and watched them in hushed silence, thinking she was sorely tempted to blurt her secret to everyone. Shout it to the skies. A part of her thought, if she talked about this, it might free her of the insecurities that plagued her on a daily basis. Her most fervent desire: to be taller, more graceful, her hair easier to control, and to have more of a grip on her emotions. And most of all, she longed to lose the fear of exposing her inner self. The depraved self that wanted so much, a greedy thing, presenting a hungry maw that was connected to some great unhinging like a snake's jaw and swallowing its prey whole.

The strongest of these voices spoke of love and acceptance, and of losing the fear body, consigning it to the past along with hairy legs. Another voice, the cautious one, said that no human being could be trusted with this information, or any information that might possibly be used against her. That voice said other things, too, such as: Shelli was mistaken to think that Stefan, if he had a choice, would choose her consistently over and over, over all other women out there, and that she was bonkers to think that over time his interest would not degrade. She was not one to disregard that voice. That voice spoke to her in deepest night, telling her emphatically that swinging would be the end of her marriage if she persisted. These two voices warred inside, tearing her up, keeping her awake at night. Yet she didn't know how to stop what had been started. How do you say, 'I know we just dipped our toes in, and the water feels delicious, but it might be the worst thing ever?' And then to say, 'I have no evidence, only a premonition.' And then to stop everything, stop the sexy emails and the texting, and go back to the same old. She had a sick feeling that they couldn't go back to the same old.

Mattie served first. She whacked the tennis ball hard with a spirally spin on it that had Shelli galloping across the court, straining the muscles on her arms, and smashing the ball with a savage blow. Mattie returned with a wallop, her lips drawn tight, most of her lipstick licked off. Shelli delivered a strong backswing. For the next couple of hours, they played like they were out to kill each other, concentrating solely on anticipating each other's moves and hitting the ball as hard and as accurately as possible. Each of them had trained well and knew how to prepare a specific place for the ball to land, turning the game into who could outthink the other and react more quickly to the instinctual kind of analysis they knew to level at each other.

With a practiced air they took their places on opposite sides of the court and got into the stance, body bent in a semi-squat, racquet held in front with both hands on the handle, ready to move in either direction, a slight bounce to the feet. They both played nearly every day and had gotten quite good. It was a competitive thing; neither stopped playing for any length of time, so their forearms had built a measure of inner resiliency, confident they could whack the ball with precision to any corner of the court.

Several times she found herself flashing on the ramped-up sex she and Stefan had been enjoying of late making everything new and interesting again and lost her concentration. That cost her a few games. Shelli knew that if she allowed anything else to wander in, she'd lose the deep concentration that was so vital to her play and refused to think about anything unrelated to the game. She turned ferocious, delivering a series of hard-hitting balls barely skimming the net, landing too far in front of Mattie to reach, despite her wild scramble. Shelli won the next two.

Mattie won the next round with several well-placed backhands, whacking a series of balls into far corners; Shelli couldn't cover them all. But it didn't really matter who won. What mattered was how the game was played, and they both were excellent players. Julia and Suzie weren't as skilled as Mattie and Shelli. After all of them had exhausted themselves, they strung their racquets across their backs and walked arm-in-arm down the narrow breezeway, on one side a brick wall, and on the other a dark green tarp across the back of the courts as a catchall for errant balls. They passed the section for doubles play, where young suburban moms in groups of four squared off. Some of these players looked like they had never lifted anything heavier than their pocketbooks. These were the rank beginners. Many of them held their racquets awkwardly, as if they were not used to moving their jelly-filled arms past the refrigerator door. They would learn soon enough. Some of players did cardio other than tennis, or lifted weights. Taking their cues from the coaches, they also spent time at the tennis court daily. For this rarified breed, tennis was more than a lifestyle, it was a religion and treasured lover all rolled into one.

Julia went to the day care on the premises and free to members to fetch her little ones while Shelli and Mattie went the area reserved for youth lessons to pick the older children. They came running, tossing their rackets in the air and complaining of hunger, hair tousled and cheeks rouged from the athleticism of their play.

Mattie's daughter, Hannah, a tall lanky girl with the long legs of a gazelle, and long blonde hair to her waist that she kept flicking back over her shoulders, looked dewy, as fresh as spring rain. Her brother looked equally striking, a blond Adonis.

"How was class?" Mattie said.

"The boys were being silly," Hannah said to her mother. The two looked much alike. "They got on my nerves."

"She's making that up," Chase said. "We didn't fight once."

"Can I have a twizzle?" Micah said, looking slender and coltish next to the older boy.

"That's not real food," Shelli said. "Can you wait until we get home?"

"Please," Seth said. "Can't we have something from the snack bar?"

"Let's see what they have."

Shelli gave her boys a choice between mozzarella sticks, popcorn, corn chips, or granola bars, and successfully steered them away from the candy. They seemed pleased with their selections. Seth had the corn chips and Micah a granola bar filled with nuts and chocolate chips. Hannah took corn chips and Chase wanted a hot dog.

Shelli told Mattie that although their dentist told Shelli that even these food items were suspect, Shelli didn't want to go so hardcore with their food choices, making food rules more important than the people in her life, or nor did she want to take the joy out of eating. Mattie said she felt the same way.

The smaller children held on to their mothers, the older children raced past the adults to the lawn where they ran around in circles, playing a tag or some facsimile. Behind them, the building that housed the courts provided a distinctive backdrop, a heavy, low-slung affair that resembled a military installation, its utilitarian design partially softened by the abundance of flowers and exotic plants artfully arrayed.

"What are you and Stefan up to these days? You guys are never around."

"We'd love to do something with you guys."

"I have been calling, but you're always busy." Mattie made a loud tsk-tsk.

"Darling, Stefan's mother has been sick, and we've been going to Brooklyn to take care of things, everything a mad scramble."

"Just pick up the phone, that's all I ask," Mattie said.

"You never said anything," Julia said. "What are we, strangers?"

"I didn't mean to dis you guys, you know I love you both to pieces," Shelli said, opening her hands wide.

"Well you have a strange way of showing it," Mattie said, her frown deepening, "If you rebuff our overtures, what are we supposed to think?"

"What are you guys doing weekend after next," Shelli said. "Let's make plans."

"Call tomorrow, we'll talk?" Mattie said, and called her children to the car. Hannah went into the front seat and clipped on her seat belt, and immediately looked out the window, seemingly lost in a daydream. Chase lounged in the back, his hands raised in a pantomime of flight, his mouth making the putt-putt sound of an engine.

Mattie threw her arms around Shelli, saying, "Love you." Shelli returned the hug and held her friend for a few minutes. The hug felt wonderfully satisfying. Then she opened the front door for Mattie who settled herself in the front against rich vanilla upholstery of her sedan gleaming in the pale, watery sun. "We'll make plans," she said. Raising her face to the sky and putting her shades on, she looked like an advertisement for an expensive line of European clothing, mysterious and beguiling.

"Enough of this Jewish farewell." Mattie started her engine and, in a whir of sparks, drove off. She was referring to the extended farewells that were the cultural mainstay of many tribal groups, as the old saying goes: WASPS leave and don't say goodbye, Jews say goodbye and don't leave.

Shelli walked away twirling her racquet, her head pivoting the yard looking for any sign of her boys. "Micah? Seth?"

Five

Giddy with anticipation, Stefan quickened his step. His hunger, mixing with the ache of deferred pleasure, and longing, showed on his face at the sight of Tequila, lighting up as if someone had bequeathed him a great treasure. Behind her, Alasdair's mouth hung slightly ajar, as though she were a goddess and he merely thankful to worship at her feet. In her presence he seemed to shrink, sliding into the background like a table or a chair. Shelli disappeared from his consciousness. There was no one in the world besides Tequila. He was drawn to her beautiful, pouty mouth, as bloody red as her nails and the kimono around her body that he wanted to rip off her like the wrapping on a present. Her mocha skin glowed with health. At his look she fell back against the couch, the blue-black of her hair spreading out like multiple fans, her moist mouth opening for a kiss. Stefan's eyes moved to her bountiful chest, his blood surging. He had never fucked a pair like those; none of the girls had chests big enough. This was an opportunity not to be missed.

With a smart click of his heels, Alasdair rudely interrupted Stefan's chain of thought. He came abreast of Stefan and made an about-face in front of his wife as if preparing to say "Sieg Heil," or at least bow deeply. Tequila's eyes remained fixed on Stefan. Shelli and Alasdair might have well been on another planet. Stefan looked at Alasdair but couldn't catch his eye. Alasdair was gazing at Tequila like he was enjoying seeing her looking seductive.

Tequila patted the couch next to her and looked at Stefan as if she wanted to swallow him up alive. In a fluty voice that sounded as sticky as a bonbon, the temptress commanded, "Sit." Stefan was her newest in a long line of drones, he harbored no illusions. Promptly he fell on the couch as he had been commanded, and looked to Tequila for further instructions, making no demands, merely thankful to be in her presence. It was Deja vu, all over again, and with his brain in the deep freeze, he couldn't think what to say, he was at a loss for words. This always happened when he got excited, especially when gazing into the large, expressive eyes on a gorgeous woman. With this one he had a sense that she remained the unknowable, an enigma, throwing to a stranger a single spark from a fathomless sea for him to puzzle over. He found himself in a row of mirrors with endless reflection and counter-reflections. She seemed terribly experienced and worldly wise, possessing vast knowledge. He understood the difficulty of scaling her walls; it's nearly impossible to know and possess a labyrinth. Stefan had known only a handful of women before he met Shelli, and had a history of falling for the strong ones, from the first girl he had bedded, a redhead who would fly into the kitchen of the restaurant in the Catskills where he worked as a dishwasher one summer teasing him in her black miniskirt on the pretext of filling an order, and laughing at his discomfort as she flaunted her bouncing bite-sized cupcakes adorned with large aureoles looking like newly ripened cherries.

He didn't know what the problem was; he found it difficult to talk them into going to bed with him for whatever reason, and as a consequence felt that he had not lived at all. He'd just begun to realize that he had been hibernating, doing the things that are expected of him but that are boring, innocuous, and gives him no pleasure. He looked to Tequila to tell him what it is to be alive. But as much as he yearned to fulfill his lustful desires, he realized that always there was inherent risk. Could he please such a woman? The thought that he might not rise to the task (pardon the pun) made his blood run cold.

Stefan didn't hear Alasdair and Shelli leave the room, but he heard Alasdair coming back, saying he had a bottle of Partida Reposado Tequila that he had been saving for an occasion like this. The patter of heels was followed by Shelli wearing a tight minidress exposing long luscious legs and carrying a large cutting board bearing a mound of drawn and quartered limes, and jiggers of salt. She was laughing over something Alasdair said, and looking beautiful. Amazing how quickly this woman acclimated to a new man. It made him feel superfluous. Alasdair handed Tequila a shot glass filled with tequila with salt on the rim and in her other hand, a cut lime. Stefan downed his drink with relish and promptly bit into the lime but instead of feeling his spirits expand like a bellows, a vague discontent settled into his bones. Overriding everything else, he would have preferred not to see Shelli's putting on the charm for this guy. He would have preferred her to be angry that he forced her into this, or at least act unsettled about it.

Stefan shook his head morosely, then pulled himself together and focused his attention on Tequila. "You're saving me from the very jaws of death," he said.

"What do you mean?"

"You make me feel alive. On the other side of the divide lies boredom and monotony."

"But cariño, your wife is so pretty, she has that amazing body, she must work out like, six hours a day." The queen bee opened her eyes wide.

"You'd have a body like her if you cycled hills like we do," Stefan said, his throat thick with mucus. He glanced at Shelli to see how she was taking this, but she was filling her shot glass and talking to Alasdair and didn't appear to be listening to what Stefan was saying. He tamped down his annoyance and put on his happy face. "I get tired of the same body, day in and day out, as beautiful as it might be."

"That's why we're meeting, isn't it? But I can't help comparing …I'm not as fit as I'd like to be."

"You have amazing breasts."

"*Muchas gracias*…but if I lost weight, I'd lose my beautiful *tatas*."

"We all have our insecurities," Stefan said, allowing himself to gaze upon the tatas in question.

"It didn't bother me so much until this afternoon and then I had to have a drink to fortify myself."

"No harm in that," Stefan said, and stole a sideways look at Shelli. He wanted to see jealousy out of Shelli and but Shelli didn't react, too busy talking to Alasdair.

Alasdair had the great idea of starting things off with a card game. They settled around the coffee table, while he recited the rules for five-card poker with a truth or dare component, passing out three cards and five chips to each person with a nod and a wink. A sense of mischievousness lurked behind the Scotsman's professional air. Players with the worst hand had to belt a shot and remove an article of clothing if they wanted to continue playing. Anyone wanting to buy back in had to remove something. They started to play. Shelli lost a hand and took off her dress, leaving on a red lace bra and panties. Tequila had to remove something too; she took the belt from her kimono. Stefan peeked inside her kimono to the black tulle bra underneath. Titillated, he wondered what the night might bring, and flashed on an image of him kneading her breasts and her moaning under him.

"Girls looking delectable," Stefan said. But he kept his hands to himself, wanting to show his manners.

Tequila pressed her plush, full lips together like little pillows, and he thought he detected a smile, buoying his feeling that things were working out. A few hands later, Tequila lost again. She removed her kimono, exposing her voluptuous flesh. Stefan was mesmerized. Feeling inhibited around his wife, he questioned his desire to do this together. How far he could take things with her watching? It seemed they were both trapped in their own spheres, an invisible wall separated them. He noticed Alasdair stealing looks at Tequila, but Shelli seemed to be pointedly not looking at him.

"Can't we move things along?" Stefan asked.

"Upstairs," Alasdair said with a sideways glance at the stairs.

Stefan gave Tequila his hand to help her up and put his arm around her shoulders protectively to steady her, but not because she needed it, but because he wanted to touch her. A floral scent rose from her hair. In the light, strands of it looked dark blue. He placed one hand on her moon-shaped rump, squeezing gently, and began steering her gently toward the stairs. He didn't see what Shelli and Alasdair were doing. On the way, Tequila said that Alasdair had taken her to a famous sex club in Amsterdam. She said swinging was widely accepted in Europe and there were clubs and nude beaches everywhere, and everyone knew how to find them, there wasn't a stigma, no one judged you. And they found playing around invigorated their relationship. Her husband no longer took her for granted, she said with a smile.

He had trouble making it down the hall, his anticipation threatening to unmoor him. On the margins of his consciousness he could hear Shelli behind him laughing at something Alasdair said. Double doors on the landing upstairs led to the master suite. At first Stefan saw nothing, just whirling blackness. Heavy dark blinds, solid walnut furniture, and glossy black sheets made the room seem darker still even after his eyes had adjusted to the flickering black light next to the bed. A wall-mounted TV was on with the volume off. On the screen, a woman struggled against her bindings. A man stood above her flicking a whip.

Alasdair filled jiggers full of tequila. Stefan downed his glass and set it down. Alasdair poured him another. Stefan downed that too.

"Stefan grew up in a teetotaler household," Shelli said. "Now he drinks everything, except whisky and bourbon."

"Yeah, well, my parents were lushes, but *mierda*, do I care?" Tequila said and reached for a jigger, promptly downing her drink and pouring another. "Look, I want to take a shower." She looked at Stefan as she said this. "It's a big shower. Come with?"

"Sure," he said, his eyes on her retreating back. There was the sound of running water.

Alasdair poured himself another shot. "Better to be crocked," he said, turning to Shelli, his brow knit in a series of ridges, dark and brooding. In the purple sheen from the black light, his reddish-blond hair and face looked unearthly.

"Do you want some, Stefan," Shelli said over the splashing liquid.

"Sure." His response was automatic. He couldn't think coherently, his mind a blur of cascading sensations as if the reptilian side of his brain had completely taken over.

She went to the table and filled two glasses and handed one to Stefan. He drank the amber liquid.

"I'm heading into the bathroom," Stefan croaked, but the words didn't flow easily, his throat felt constricted.

The bathroom was large and excessively lavish, with a settee in a corner next to an ornate dressing table and bay windows around the jetted tub. His emotions were a seething jumble, nothing he could resolve on his own. He wondered if he had screwed this up. He certainly looked forward to having sex with another woman, but he couldn't quiet the insistent voice that cried foul, a nasty creature to spoil his dreams. He seesawed between wanting a life of sexual adventurism and on the other hand keeping things as they were, even though he found sex with his wife boring. Part of him wondered if they could survive it, but there also was a part of him that wondered if he cared. He took off his clothes with trembling hands. Taking this action, his head felt strange, lightheaded and giddy, his stomach in knots. He couldn't believe what was happening; perhaps he was dreaming. The excitement was killing him; he knew he could never forgive himself if he didn't go ahead with it. He was happy to see in the steamy mirror that his body looked relatively good. His arms and abs could use some work, but he didn't know how to lift weights effectively and was impatient with the time and discipline it took to develop muscles. His legs and ass were his crowning achievement honed on the road from the massive amount of cycling he did; his torso was a little soft, but nothing to be ashamed of. He sucked in his stomach. Tequila stood on the other side of the steamed door, her eyes at half mast, rubbing her nipples into fine hard points. Stefan watched, feeling like a voyeur who has stumbled into a stranger's bathroom by mistake. He stroked his aching pole, delaying his entry into the shower to contemplate how delicious she looked. The shower was roomy, with multiple shower heads; *there would be no issue with others hogging the water flow. He turned her around to admire her shapely body. She moved readily to his touch. A smattering of dark hair between her legs which he felt necessary to probe with his fingers before* stepping back to watch her massaging her breasts, better than any wet dream. He took the soap away from her and plied her breasts and teased her clit with it, and with the other hand, stroked his hard-on before *nestling himself flat into the meeting of her buttocks. He scrubbed her back. He was sure his hard-on would never disappear.* His energy kept climbing; he was in a light-filled space walking on air.

"El amante, we join the others?" she said.

They stepped out of the shower and he toweled her off, paying special attention to her nipples. She sucked him like a Popsicle and seemed to be enjoying it. And noticed her lashes were lush, longer and thicker than he had ever seen on a woman. "Stop," he cried a few minutes later. "I don't want to come yet." He had to take her mouth off him, it felt too good. She said she was wearing permanent makeup and lash extensions, augmented with natural mink mixed in with her own. He marveled at the artifice—the things women will do for beauty. They entered the bedroom. He looked at Alasdair laughing about something with Shelli. He thought if she truly loved him, she wouldn't enjoy sex with these other men, no matter how good looking, or how well hung they were, nor would she be able to orgasm with them, at the least, they wouldn't be able to do it for her like he could, no matter how well they're hung. Stefan went to Shelli and she kissed him, lightly, but the kiss felt awkward, hurried, and led Stefan to wonder what Shelli was thinking, did she prefer the other guy. He noted concern on Shelli's face, her brow etched tight.

"Honey, are you alright?"

"Yah." But he wasn't, not really.

What an irony, he thought, just when he was finally shrugging off his insecurities and his fears, and allowing himself to have a great time with another woman, and then this, the minute he sees his woman flirting with another man he felt unsettled, his stomach nauseous. During that moment, the hot breath of jealousy petrified him, and he couldn't move. He tried to squash all thoughts of betrayal aside, yet he couldn't help but think that he was in fact betrayed by his urges, doomed by his longing for the flesh of strangers. Things were so much easier when their love was new, and he didn't want anyone else. At a loss, he watched Shelli go back to her conversation with Alasdair, and then as if controlled by automation, an external force, he plastered a smile on and turned to Tequila, gratified that she came readily to him, and led him to her magnificent California-sized bed. In one fluid movement she slipped out of her robe and arranged herself on pillows, opening her legs and lifting her arms to receive him. In the corner of his eye, he saw Alasdair and Shelli *playacting drunk and laughing. He forced himself not to look at Shelli, but he couldn't take his eyes off her and kept glancing over, shifting his eyes quickly as if the teacher was going to punish him if she caught him taking his eyes off the blackboard.*

Tequila stopped what she was doing and looked over, too, mirroring Stefan's affect and manner. They both turned to watch Alasdair and Shelli fondling each other as if totally mesmerized. Alasdair's penis was huge, big as a yam. He wondered what Tequila thought of his package, but she gave no indication. Stefan drew his breath sharply, noting the hands that Shelli ran down Alasdair's brawny back, her eyes wide and shiny like pennies, and his heart fell to his feet when Alasdair kissed her breasts with the reverence that people usually reserve for special friends. Stefan blinked several times and shook his head, but the image of Shelli having sex with this stranger assaulted him, pinging behind his eyeballs like badly scored film. The guy was good looking, but still it shook him to the core that she would give in so easily. It made him question her love for him. He had no idea that she was such a slut.

Gradually his mind cleared and he got busy with the woman spread before him, moving down her beautiful legs, but he couldn't totally rid himself of what was happening on the other side of the bed, pausing every so often to lift his head and gaze upon t*ight calves, Shelli's legs lifting, the rounded curve of Alasdair's ass, Shelli's hair splayed. That* little scene played out in front of him beat anything he'd ever seen on screen, nothing like real action to stimulate the juices. He heard Tequila call out to him and his *hands moved all over, ending at her inner thigh inching slowly to where the legs meet.* Her bounteous curves held his attention. Before he knew what was happening, having managed a mere thrust, if anyone was counting, he came, which embarrassed him to no end, knowing she couldn't possibly have had an orgasm in that short of time. He hoped he could get hard again, and apologized, told her it was because she was so incredibly hot. She told him she was fine, but he knew that the rhythm had already been set and they were moving at a different pace.

Stefan asked Tequila if she liked sports. Tequila said she and Alasdair watched football together. Stefan and Tequila talked about the prospects for their preferred teams. It turned out they both liked the Jets. But he couldn't keep his mind on football, which was the weirdest thing, knowing how much he loved the sport. His mind kept coming back to the old saw: How was it that Shelli had connected so smoothly with the first guy who came along, a total stranger, and to rub salt on the wound, they didn't stop fucking, not for another half-hour, not until Stefan crawled up to their entwined bodies, shook Shelli by the shoulder and said, "Enough," in a rough voice and giving the evil eye to Alasdair.

Shelli turned to Stefan. "Come join us?" Shelli said.

When Stefan said "No" in a ringing tone, Alasdair pulled out, eyes carefully averted as if to avoid being singed—and muttered, "Sorry." Stefan could see that Shelli looked disappointed, her mouth tightening, but she said nothing.

Sunday morning Shelli woke shivering in the artificially chilly air. Stefan was sleeping, his broad back facing her. He liked it colder than Shelli could tolerate which often caused some friction between the two, with Shelli pleading with him to lift it out of the Frigid Zone, sometimes he'd agree, and sometimes not. The cold triggered her Raynaud's syndrome, forcing the arteries in her fingers and toes to constrict in their overzealous monitoring of heat loss, causing the passageways to slam nearly shut, resulting in a numb sensation to flood her extremities. She tried to explain this to him, but he said she was overreacting, and couldn't understand the problem, even when she showed him her purple-tinged fingers, and rubbed her hands and feet to return their color to a natural state to show him the difference. He had the opposite problem; he sweated easily and was often too hot. His side of the bed typically was wet from sweat every morning, even when he slept with just a sheet over him.

She stood up and felt her head throbbing as if a hammer had been applied to it. She wished she hadn't drunk so much from the night before, knowing she couldn't handle the hard liquor. She downed some aspirin with the glass of water sitting on her dresser and put on a long-sleeved tee and pajama bottoms before closing the bedroom door and heading downstairs. Sounds from the television wafted from below.

The boys were sitting on the pale buttercream leather couch in an alcove off the kitchen watching Spongebob Squarepants. Shelli stayed a minute to watch the show with them.

On the screen, a horde of anchovies rushed the casher's station, tossing it about like a boat on rough seas until it splintered into fragments. Mr. Krabs shouted, "Batten the hatches, Mister

Squidward!...We're taking on water, Mister Squidward!...I WANT MY MOMMY, MISTER SQUIDWARD!"

Mister Squidward imitated Mr. Krabs, proprietor of the Krusty Krab. Mr. Krabs was not amused.

"It wasn't an insult, Mr. Krabs, it was a tribute," Mister Squidward says, leaning at an extreme angle away from Mr. Krabs' anger and sweating copiously, big drops leaving no doubt he was frightened. "Have you ever heard that imitation is the sincerest form of flattery?"

"You're telling me that was a compliment?" Mr Krabs said.

"Exactly! My homage to you and your love of money!" Mister Squidward said.

The boys started tussling, their energy coursing through their bodies like an electric current. Seth had on his red Star Wars pajamas, Micah the blue one. Shelli liked to dress them in different colors so she could more easily tell them apart. She couldn't get enough of watching them, not only because they were so beautiful, but from sheer amazement that all she had to do was incubate, and feed on spinach and Brussels sprouts for the folate acid, and grass-fed steak for the iron, and drink lots of yogurt smoothies, all of which turned out to be quite pleasurable. As her reward, she had let their hair grow thick and shiny, she couldn't bear to cut it completely off. They still looked like boys, but with a lot of hair.

"Hungry?" Shelli asked, stroking their beautiful blond locks, and thinking women who chose not to have children miss out on the pleasure of seeing this gorgeousness, a display that for a mother is akin to viewing porn, although modestly dressed they still looked virginal and chaste and incredibly delicate; the finest art that nature could devise. And when she touched their skin or hair, her nerve endings vibrated with a joy that was deeper than anything she had known before.

They had bagels with lox and cream cheese. While they were eating, the friends Seth had invited to play at their house came over: Max, who looked like a young Groucho Marx complete with the glasses and wild hair, and was funny besides, and Ben, smaller than the others and spunky, with a head full of science trivia thanks to his dad the PhD who ran a biotech startup. Shelli offered them bagels. They ate a few bites and raced off, saying they wanted to play hide and seek. Shelli went into the big home office she shared with Stefan, leaving the door open. She sat at her desk near the window and turned on her computer, thinking she would rework some of the short items she had been working on for the front of the magazine, and get a start on the week. She heard the patter of the childish feet and a gurgled laugh then silence. She wondered if she should check on them and then remembered, duh, this was supposed to be a game of hide and seek. Stefan came in yawning and sat at his desk in his sweats and a Grateful Dead tee shirt checking his emails and nursing his coffee. "Sweetheart, could you come here for a moment? We got an email from those guys."

Shelli left her desk and sat in the chair adjacent to his desk looking at his screen. Alasdair had sent an email saying they wanted to meet again—as soon as possible. Stefan argued against getting too cozy right off the bat, pointing out that Alasdair and Tequila lived an hour away.

"All those back roads, and no streetlights. It was so bad I couldn't tell the road from the curb without flipping on full beam headlights. The whole thing was a huge nuisance—I had to constantly switch the main lights off to accommodate oncoming traffic and then flip them on again or risk a crash. It was nerve-wracking."

Shelli wanted to say, "That drive is no further than your parents' house, and you make that drive all the time." But she said nothing, looking instead past him to the credenza which bristled with grown-up toys: 4-LOM and Jar Jar Blinks from Star Wars, assorted vintage cycling helmets and a windup Sandy Kaufax. At the rear of the room, crouching in the shadows, sat the long, slender lines of an Italian leather sofa which Shelli lined with plushy, damask cushions.

"It looked to me that you were watching me more than you were paying attention to her," Shelli said, and felt a trace of bitterness leak into her voice. She wanted to say, "Look at the complexities you opened us up to." But she didn't want to sound accusatory, not when she enjoyed her time with Alasdair. Or talk about how depressed she felt after Stefan put the brakes in that propriety way as if he owned her without any regard to her feelings just as she was having her moment, never mind how it affected Alasdair.

"I had never seen you with anyone else," Stefan sighed. "I was amazed at how good you looked." In the tensed muscles of his face, he betrayed his unsettled emotions. "Watching you, part of me felt this great sadness."

"Same for me."

"I couldn't stand watching any more of that."

"I had to watch you do the private things we do with someone else."

"It seemed to me that you were totally into that guy."

"It was a zipless fuck. Just like yours was. And I must remind you, I didn't interrupt what you were doing. You were rude all by yourself."

"Are you going to go on and on about it?" Stefan said.

Shelli didn't reply, thinking it better not to antagonize him further. No doubt he thought he was right on this. Perhaps like many men, he thought when he was finished it didn't matter about the woman. His response was a way of coping out, he never admitted fault when he was shown to have behaved boorishly. At least she made him aware that she was not happy with how it played out, and that it wasn't enough for her. She didn't require his apology, although it would have been nice.

Stefan went ahead and sent an email to Alasdair saying that he was travelling, and promised when he returned, they would figure out a time to meet again. Stefan had a pensive look as he wrote this; part of her was relieved that he wanted to back away. The more adventurous side of her enjoyed what they did, but the more sober side looked askance and questioned what it meant for their relationship. She would have liked it better if Stefan and Tequila had gone out of the room so Alasdair and she could have finished up on a more positive note. She thought she'd give Stefan time to calm down before bringing up that possibility apropos of their next assignation.

Shelli went downstairs to check on the boys, hearing nothing she looked around the white couches arrayed around the coffee table in the living room and the big leather chairs by the windows. She saw no one. Down in the basement, Seth's face was clearly visible, not just a part of his face but his whole head. He looked terribly intent it was obvious he thought no one could see him. She came up to him quietly with her finger braced against her lips and suggested he put his entire head below the chair he was hiding behind and let little of his face show. He ducked, and she quickly went away from him, not wanting to reveal his whereabouts. Her love for her sons filled her heart to the breaking point, so much that she ached. How cute he looked behind the chair, thinking no one could see him.

Shelli went back upstairs and finished what she had set out to do. A howling heralded the end of the boys' game. Apparently, no one could find Micah. They yelled 'ollie oxen free' and out of the laundry room came Micah wearing a big smile, announcing he had found the best hiding place of all: the dryer. Shelli asked him what he would have done if he couldn't open the door from the inside of the dryer on his own. He said he hadn't fully closed it, and he had the good sense to hold his breath when someone went into the laundry room, and of course he just about croaked, but as luck would have it they looked in the closet and not the dryer, which had Micah laughing to the point of tears.

Shelli laid out homemade fruit salad, celery and crackers with peanut butter, and fruit juice as a snack. The boys gathered around, scarfing the food.

A long-drawn-out fart sounded: Brrraaapp! Followed by vreeeeeeeeeeeeeew.

"Awww…" Matt said.

It turned out Matt had brought a fart bag and placed it on Seth's chair just before Seth sat down. Each of the boys had to sit on it. Multiple times. Their laughter grew more strident.

"Mom, why do people fart?" Seth said.

"Stomach bacteria breaks down sugars and starches you can't digest," Shelli said. "Farts are the release of these indigestible gasses."

"My dad can light his farts on fire," Matt said.

"Methane is flammable," Ben said, "but not everyone's farts contain high levels of methane. Does your dad eat a lot of red meat?"

"Yeah," Matt said.

"Prunes make me fart," Seth said.

"Beans make me fart," Ben said.

"Cole slaw makes me fart," Matt said.

"What makes you fart, Micah," Shelli said.

"Everything," Micah said.

"You guys watch South Park?" Seth said.

"My favorite show," Matt said.

"I've got Spontaneous Combustion CD," Seth said.

"I love when they're outside and they meet the preacher and he says: 'If the lord hadn't wanted us to fart he wouldn't have given us asses,' Matt said.

The guys got together to play basketball every Thursday night at the Y. Stefan had always been a natural, one of the star players in high school and college basketball, adept at the pivot, jump, and set, but he never had been good at fending off the aggressive players, his play was polite at best, if not on the defensive side. But he had always been quick, and when the offense was weak, he was able to shine. Just now, bouncing the basketball, Stefan's hands and fingertips trembled with elation, glorying in the natural feel of the basketball, the feeling that he was in his element. He faked a pass—something he was good at—and buffeted by the grind of bone and socket, the copious sweat running into his eyes momentarily blinding him, he stumbled, but he didn't care about that. Now he glides toward the net, and an image of a steep downhill on his bicycle pops up, wind in his hair, he's singing *pick and roll* to himself and it sounds as musical as ever. The other men give him room, but Rick attempted to block him, with a smile that said 'I love you man, but I've gotta do this,' but his effort was ineffectual, and Stefan moved sideways without taking any missteps, gliding on a blessing, knowing just what to do. He knew how to parry and feint. The sweat in his eyebrows multiplied and he couldn't see so well but he felt good and cool and free.

The ball seemed to ride up of its own accord and came off his shoulder as his knees dipped in one fluid motion. And looked like he missed shot, thought he came at it from an angle where it appeared that the ball was not going toward the backboard. But it was not aimed there. The guys must have thought he was going way off, because they reacted slowly, as if they thought nothing would come of it. But then a wind come up and a glass saber of muted light hit the backboard and boys rose up in the men, wings sprouting at their backs. The ball spun in the darkening air in increasingly tighter spirals in front of a hushed audience before dropping into the circle of the rim, whipping against the metal of the rim before heading down. They stopped—men after all with the aches and pains of the deskbound unused to heavy physical exercise—and clapped each other's backs, wheezing and winded. Stefan wasn't as fit as he used to be, in the days when he played all the time—that was centuries ago—and his breath came short and scratchy, his lungs feeling like they might burst into tiny bits. He quit readily although he wasn't happy about ending the evening's fun. But then Stefan got this idea that they could hit a topless bar after their game. Everyone was down with that.

This was not their first visit to a strip joint. The guys often went to clubs in SoHo and Tribeca, a way to blow off steam on a weekday night. His biggest gripe, there always seemed to be strings attached to sex unless money was exchanged, and that wasn't Stefan's thing, and he didn't pick up women in bars, which left few options for a guy wanting to play around. Swinging had seemed a good option at first, but now appeared to have its problems, too. His thoughts about swinging caromed in crazy zigzags. Surrounded by his best buddies, he could marshal his scattered feelings. He was all for this adventure, the possibility of having other women was tantalizing, but he was ashamed of his performance with Tequila and hoped he'd get his bearings and become the ladies' man that he had always envisioned. He was impatient for the dream to materialize.

Rick's eyelids scrunched down and he assumed his trademark smile with that little head nod that indicted his good will, his signal that he wanted you to know he meant no offense to anyone—and said, "Looking for the next best thing to having sex with someone other than your wife?"

"The next best thing would be having sex with someone other than my wife," Stefan said. "Anything else is a tease."

"Couldn't pull the wool over your eyes," Rick said. "Would you be able to handle going to a topless bar in Matawan? It's half an hour east of here. Just for a tease."

"It'll make sex tonight more interesting," Stefan said.

"Definitely," Daniel said. "I could use the inspiration."

"Its south of Perth Amboy," Rick said, "near a former submarine factory, interesting neighborhood."

The area was away from Stefan's usual haunts and like most of the Jersey Shore dated from the revolutionary war with 18th century mansions and cute little capes. Most of the assembled dressed in t-shirts and hoodies, certainly not the usual garb for a slick Manhattan club. They would be welcome however they dressed in along Matawan's back roads. The seediness appealed to everyone, there were far fewer chances they'd bump into people they knew there. The guys readily piled into Rick's car kidding Rick that he must be a regular visitor to be so familiar with the streets of Matawan. Rick took it good naturedly; telling them it was his second home. Stefan had yet to see Rick get mad about anything; he was always the first to excuse anyone's behavior, even the most egregious. Stefan imagined that's why Rick and Mattie got along so well. But then he had this thought: if he had a babe like Mattie to go home to, he would gladly put his aside his small irritations, his feeble protests against the implacability of things? Then the realization hit him that the pressure he was under at work to meet an impossible quota was causing him to gain weight. That knowledge hit him hard. He had acquired a lot of things, now he realized that in fact ownership of personal property had enslaved him. He was responsible for a mortgage that he felt burdened by. And the cars; and the myriad investments that need constant tending, like a garden, otherwise the weeds would choke new growth. He used to think that acquisition put him in the position of the absolute dominion over inanimate things, but then he learned that is not in fact true. Too late he learned that each of his things have opposing exit strategies. It's as if they're aware they will outlive him, and that they will have the last laugh.

Stefan wasn't driving, so he took the opportunity afforded him to look around. The summer was over, the early breath of hoary winter could be felt in the wind tickling his neck making him shiver, but he didn't mind leaving the stickiness behind like a bad dream. The glorious autumn all red and gold and the leaves more gorgeous than ever; already several floating down, amber and golden in the low slanting sun's rays energized him. It was his first look around his neighborhood, having rarely ventured out the Jersey Shore area. He didn't know the rest of the state except for what he could see from the highway, most of it viewed from the hard, narrow seat of an Italian touring bicycle. He liked to joke to Shelli that the blood keeping his balls alive was in serious jeopardy of being truncated. He wasn't entirely kidding. Sometimes when he got off his bike, he found his groin had gone numb. One time, he had been ridden through the corn fields to reach Cape May on a century ride in the worst of the summer heat (he didn't want to repeat the experience) and when they reached the midpoint of the ride where they would have an hour to relax, he couldn't walk; his thighs had been rubbed raw, exacerbated by the action on his legs. They learned that the Cape May township still had the blue laws on the books, and they left town without getting any beer (the laws have since been changed). Stefan attached band-aides to his thighs to prevent further chaffing. This was after having ridden in and around Princeton, skirting the cranberry bogs around Cranberry and stopping for ice cream along the way, and then riding his bike along the entire section of the Delaware River that ran along New Jersey's border with Pennsylvania.

An old glass factory abandoned since 1996 looked like a ghostly hulk in the waning light, neglected and forlorn, choked by weeds and covered in peeling paint. Other buildings looked equally run down, a haven for mice and owls. Abandoned factories and warehouses, the kind of forlorn places where people disappear in the thick of the night. The fields between the buildings glistened as if covered in cloaks of various colors: amethyst, pearl, silver, rose, and smoky blue. And there was such a heaping of leaves rustling in the hollows of the trees, and bunches of them moving across the road. He thought about his sons, and his heart melted into an ode to sentimentality. His father had impressed on him the value of saving his pennies for the proverbial rainy day, that inexorable time of great need, and he felt aggrieved about the family finances. He sensed that Shelli thought he went overboard with this sense of things, but Shelli had no idea, she was too much the kind of person who allows money to disappear down a black hole, and not know what happened to it, and be aghast when she runs out of money. And now Shelli implied it was his fault that he couldn't get it up after an episode of coming too fast, and her demanding that he get it up again the minute they got home when all he wanted to do was crawl in a hole. And then the hubris of telling him if he relaxed and took it slow his problems would vanish, like she's the expert. What made think Shelli think she could lay claim to the mantle of authority? Where did that come from? He couldn't convince her that she was beautiful (a few inches taller and she'd look like a topflight model). It would be one thing if she would simply ask what he thought of this or that dress or give his unvarnished opinion of how her butt looked, and then drop it. But she had to milk it to death, challenging his opinions and if she didn't like what he said, telling him he was lying to her. Periodically he was required to recite steady stream of carefully calibrated and worded compliments to smooth her prickly ego. Her constant need of stroking of this sort, the lofty and many splendored affirmations of her beauty, were taking a toll. On one hand she was totally unsecure and on the other, she was the most elitist stuck up narcissistic bitch Stefan had ever met, acting so superior because she went to a big-name college.

This latest thing Stefan had to deal with, he couldn't believe how unsympathetic Shelli was; saying he could have entertained Tequila in other ways to give Shelli more time with Alasdair. It irritated him that she had gotten cozy right off with someone she had never met, as if Stefan didn't matter to her in the least, and that bothered him big time, like a wound that would never heal, he knew he'd just pick at that scab until it bled. What pissed him off the most: Shelli made it all about her. And then to top it off, she got mad at him for not wanting to fuck her the minute they got home, saying that Stefan had stopped Alasdair when she was about to come, which made her incredibly horny, and he owed her. Like he was a dog doing tricks for his master. Stefan had always shown her consideration, but whatever he did, it was never enough. If he didn't have sex with her every other day, she claimed neglect. Why was she so demanding? Women were always hard to read. The girls he dated in college would make similar claims that he dissed them in some way, and they'd stop talking to him, he never knew what drove them to such lengths. Perhaps females suffered from periodic bouts of hysteria, like the early Greeks would have it. He couldn't say this, otherwise he was in trouble with the feminists, but this is what he truly believed. His first real girlfriend was the best, no problems with her. She lived five blocks from him in a brick walkup with a stoop identical to Stefan's which made things so convenient. They had the same postage-stamp front yard that had been painted green to look like the real thing. When Debbie's parents weren't home, she'd invite him over and they've have sex as soon as he closed the front door to her house, right in the foyer. He routinely had her clothes off before she could close the door. Afterwards he'd sing to her a few lines of that song by Foreigner:

> Just you wait and see
> How urgent our love can be

They met at the commuter college they both attended and from that day on, he struggled to keep his mind on his lessons, his mind would wander to the sensual, the smell of her skin, akin to fresh cotton, and smooth as silk. After six glorious months they had a fight about nothing, he couldn't remember what it was about, something about her wanting to go steady while he objected on the grounds that he was happy the way things were. Secretly he didn't like the idea of being tied down to one girl. He hadn't dated others and he wanted to see how it would go before getting official about their union. He thought it was a reasonable request and then she started crying and got all mopey on him, and sullen. She wanted to talk about it, and he was okay with that at first, but then they started arguing when she kept repeating that she wasn't a slut. He agreed, but she thought he was mocking her and slapped his face, he walked out. The slap really galled him, especially when she wouldn't answer his calls.

A few days later he saw her at school with another guy, his hand on her tushe as if he owned her. He never got over it. It still smarted to this day. And then there were other girls, getting all hissy when he tried to cop a feel, like they were such prizes. He thought to himself, if this is what feminism has wrought, he'd had enough.

He preferred the company of guys. They were easy to please. He didn't have to be careful what he said nor did, a guy could make fun of a guy friend and no one's feelings were hurt.

The car jolted to a stop. Stefan looked up and surveyed the dreary parking lot full of battered cars tucked behind a car wash and gas station. They got out and followed Rick to a vault-like door where an affable bouncer in a suit made light conversation and checked their IDs. As they passed through the doorway, the unmistakable electronic notes of Nicki Minaj's "Truffle Butter" washed over them:

Uh, thinkin' out loud
I must have a quarter million on me right now
Hard to make a song 'bout somethin' other than the money
Two things I'm 'bout is talkin' blunt and staying blunted
Pretty women, are you here? Are you here right now, huh?

He paid a cashier the fifteen dollar cover fee and followed the others into the main room, a seedy place that had seen better days, where hot women milled about in tight skirts and stilettos that shook like trees in a high wind. The crowd of loud, raucous men emitted a rank smell that mixed uneasily with the perfumed scent of the women and only added to the sense that sex clubs are the new normal in an culture saturated with sexuality, where porn is available at the click of a mouse, and hip-hop videos are far raunchier than the racy moves playing on the soft-core cable

171

channels. Sex clubs function as a refuge of sorts, where a man can step outside the anxiety-fraught dating scene, and express his sexuality without being met with a sexual harassment lawsuit and where women parade around nude or nearly so and nobody gets arrested or elicits gasps. Everything is out in the open, sex simply another appetite.

Stefan told the guys there was no way he'd bring his wife to a place like this. Shelli would be jealous of any attention he paid to the girls and forget about having a conversation with anyone with a vagina. Rick agreed. He said wives were way too possessive. If Mattie was there, nothing would be allowed. The problem was not that male sexual fantasies were too complex, but that they were frequently politically incorrect and directly opposed to the female fantasy of being loved above all others. But Stefan knew that if the reverse was true he would not like seeing Shelli getting involved emotionally with another man, but the reason he gave himself, women don't have casual sex, they fall in love. A guy can separate the two.

A fit looking Asian girl with incredible hair, long and unfettered to her waist, came up to their table and looked directly at him, sending shockwaves through his intestines. She asked if he wanted a lap dance. He looked down at her bouncy tits and croaked "Yes," as if he had a relay of frogs residing in his throat. She looked only at him, making him feel like he was the only man at their table, leading him to a sectioned-off space, and motioned him to a comfortable chair. With grave formality, she bowed slightly, and positioned herself above him, not touching, her thick hair a veil she arranged over them. She was the hottest woman he'd ever seen, with legs that never ended and a body that he couldn't quite trust was real even though he could see it in front of him, so close, and which she said he couldn't touch.

She came off as if she really liked him although he couldn't quite trust he was good-looking enough to attract someone like her without a fat bank account, but he was okay buying into the illusion. He loved being close to a beautiful woman whether something came of it, and enjoyed her erotic dancing, it didn't matter that she didn't know him. He thought if she were to get to know him, she'd like him.

"I need a drink to loosen up," Stefan said. "What about you?"

She agreed wholeheartedly, giving thumbs up gesture. He bought a bottle of champagne because she said she liked it and told her that it was his first time in a strip club, hoping to score some points.

"Are you married?" she asked.

"I love her dearly, but I need to temporarily escape the shackles from time to time."

"I feel the same way about my boyfriend."

"I wish she had her own friends and a life independent of me, but she doesn't. What about you? How did you end up here?"

"Working my way through college. I'm Vietnamese; I came here with my family. Boat people."

She moved her hands around her body in a slow sensual way, as if she were rubbing bubbly soap all over herself. Then she turned all the way around and in the dim light she became a blur, spinning in a flurry of motion, and started shaking her ass like she was filled with a combustible energy that couldn't be contained, not unless she was in a steel box.

The more alcohol he drank the more sexed up he felt. They finished the champagne and started an expensive whiskey that he knew was watered down, but she said it took the edge off and made it easier to do her job, which, when it came down to it, basically consisted of grinding on a stranger's hard dick through the thinnest cloth. Her jiggly tits were driving him crazy.

He asked if he could squeeze them and called them juicy. She said 'no touching' when he asked if she'd let him fuck them. He told her it was a special fantasy of his and that he that he'd never done it before. He told her he was a virgin as regards titty fucking. She said she would love it, too, but the rules were no touching. He had to be content with being masturbated through cloth.

He composed his face to look the portrait of pathetic want, the kind of impotence that reminded him of a dog's desperate pant and furrowed brow as it waits for table scraps that never come.

She suggested more drinks. He couldn't say nor did he think he could handle his mounting excitement. He wanted to get down with her right there.

Stefan could see she liked him. He looked at her pouty lips, her luscious hair sparking a thousand points of light, totally awed by the delicacy of her body, so strong and yet so frail. He told her he had a physical need to touch her, called it a sexual emergency but she counseled against it, there were hidden cameras in the rooms. A couple more drinks later, he couldn't stop himself, he came in his underwear. He asked her if she could meet on her break, or maybe after work, but she said no.

It turned out she couldn't let Stefan fuck her tits because of her boyfriend. He'd kill her if she did. He barely tolerated her working at the club, and if he knew how much she was letting Stefan get away with, well, he'd be super-pissed. That was his one rule and she wasn't about to disobey, she wasn't good at keeping secrets, and was deadly afraid if she did anything that he'd object to, the boyfriend would kill both of them. If it was him in the role of the boyfriend, he'd do the same, the girl was that hot. He loved the coy way she teased him, but not so much when they told him he had purchased $200 worth of booze and they wouldn't take a credit card; luckily he had the cash.

In the parking lot, Stefan told the guys he would have fucked her if she let him, and that he tried all his persuasive powers. The guys ribbed him about it. Rick claimed he never screwed anyone other than Mattie, that he had been a model husband; Daniel said the same thing, and Joe, too. Stefan said he never had either (okay he lied), but not for a lack of trying, and bemoaned this. What to do to change it? The guys suggested a prostitute, but Stefan said he wouldn't pay for it and claimed it was the principal of the matter.

"Getting it free is a problem," Rick said. "You'd have to make promises you might not want to keep."

That's true my man," Stefan said, clapping Rick on the back with a hearty guffaw.

When Stefan got home, he told Shelli about the sex club, and blamed it on Rick, saying he had insisted, and the guys made it uncomfortable for Stefan, calling him prissy, so he gave in. She asked him if he enjoyed it, he replied that it boiled down to a big tease. He didn't tell her about the lap dance. He said none of the women were as beautiful or sexy as Shelli, and that he was happy to be leaving those women and coming home to her.

Shelli said she understood what he meant. In the world of sexual freedom, she felt as if she had been reborn. Stefan agreed. Speaking freely and engaging in fantasies they couldn't talk about openly anywhere else, illuminated the trajectory of their own meandering search of self. He felt he had gained a new understanding of the role religion often plays in social discourse. His sense was that divine worship started as a joyful celebration that embraced sensual pleasure, but somewhere along the line, it became rigid and unyielding, and through the centuries, fear and ignorance snuffed out the sensual, stratifying and hardening.

After all, Shelli told Stefan, her all-time favorite woman author, Simone de Beauvoir, remained unmarried and free to engage openly in any number of relationships while Jean Paul Sartre did the same. Many of these affairs involved students of theirs. Bianca Bienenfeld, a 17-year-old student at the Lycée Molière in Paris where Simone de Beauvoir taught philosophy, dazzled by the beauty and "brilliant, piercing, bold intelligence" of her teacher, developed a passionate attachment for her. For almost a year, Bianca did not meet Sartre, about whom she was curious and not a little jealous. When they did meet, he seduced her into a short affair, as was his wont with de Beauvoir's young friends. In her book, Bianca accuses de Beauvoir of pimping for Sartre, yet at the same time she describes their affair as a love triangle. Bianca had some grounds for believing that they had formed a threesome because the two writers already had that kind of a relationship with another of de Beauvoir's students, Olga Kosakiewicz. Olga was part of a coterie of young followers they called 'the Family,' and for a time took the role of surrogate for the children they had decided to forgo. Bianca sought the same prerogative, perhaps, for her part, unconsciously seeking parent substitutes. Bianca's affair with Sartre lasted less than a year, and despite knowing that he was having concurrent affairs with several other young women, she wrote in a book that the end was traumatic, and that she couldn't let it go for years. For de Beauvoir, Bianca's obsession with the affair was tiresome, yet they remained in contact and on friendly terms until Bianca married Bernard Lamblin, one of Sartre's students. Shelli couldn't imagine having to compete for Stefan's attentions, or surviving that sort of onslaught on a continual basis. And while there was no one Shelli felt understood her quite like Sartre and Beauvoir did each other—there was no finely honed rapport with Stefan, nor did she expect there to be, sometimes she laughed at his jokes, and that's all she could expect from him and she was okay with that—but there was no true meeting of the minds, she despaired ever getting that close with anyone— still she liked the idea of meeting people who knew what they were doing, people who could instruct them in the finer points of foursomes. She told herself that she would never become jealous of these women, as long as there was another guy in the picture whom she enjoyed being with, she thought they could offset any of the dangers by keeping their passions in check, and act the proverbial adults.

The pictures of a gorgeous woman appeared on the computer screen. Stefan disrobed Shelli, all the while his eyes on the screen. He was doing this expertly like a man so familiar with the ins and outs of women's clothing that he could be doing this blind. The woman had a face like a cherub, a pale complexion stretched over high cheekbones, framed by bright waves of blond to the point of whiteness that fell to her shoulders. And surprise, surprise, the male half of this couple had a nice smile and a well-maintained body. As soon as Shelli saw the man, she stopped Stefan's hands and sat down at the computer to send off an e-mail. She received a response within minutes. Both were longtime swingers.

The couple they planned to meet did not live together. Both were divorced, with children. Some of the couples they met would have passed on these two—the ones who said they only played with other married couples. Shelli told Stefan she didn't feel it was important to date only married couples. He agreed. Just because they're married, doesn't mean they are committed to each other and would never do anything to mess that up. It was chancy, but Shelli thought that trying to preserve a marriage by staying away from people who hooked up to have group sex wasn't the solution, if only it was that simple.

The night of their date, Shelli waited with the children downstairs for the babysitter to show up and put on *where in the World is Carmen Sandiego?* Seth changed the channel to a wild, shoot-em up show and both boys moved to the edge of their seats, listening eagerly.

"All I wanna do is find me a beautiful chick and smoke a big fatty," the actor said in a husky voice.

The boys started chuckling. Did they understand what they were hearing?

"Yeah, smoke that big fatty all the wwaayyyy down…"

Shelli switched the station to SpongeBob. Shelli welcomed their attempt to pull her into the story, and laughed with them, happy to see their joyful exuberance. Seth started wrestling with Micah. All of a sudden, they had become all legs, looking more coltish by the day, two beautiful youths, she loved the way they looked, big eyes with these incredible lashes, their faces losing some of the baby fat, exposing high cheekbones, and Mick Jagger lips. Most people couldn't tell them apart. Shelli often had trouble; sometimes only when emotion passed over their faces and they expressed themselves verbally that their personalities came through.

Micah tended to be quieter, more introverted, but when you got him talking, he wouldn't shut up, like right now, telling Shelli about a recent show they had seen involving a vampire with huge fangs. Even so Seth was the leader. Regardless of their differences, whenever he got into anything, Micah invariably followed.

Shelli had to leave to answer the phone, to get away from these boys with their overly vociferous laughter, trying to act like they understood the world of adults. Their gaiety reminded Shelli of her own childhood when out of boredom, she would watch pro wrestling on television, but only because her brothers loved watching this sort of performance art, the kind of bone-crunching theater that passes for wrestling in which the players put their bodies and sometimes their lives on the line. It was a highly choreographed story line with a simple premise that even a child can understand: one guy is good and the other one evil, but no kid thinks grown men resolve disputes with body slams and piledrivers. But Shelli and her brothers enjoyed booing the antics of Killer Kowalski who with Big John Studd called themselves the masked Executioners in tag team titles, and they'd sit that the edge of their chairs holding their breath watching the big guys slam each other down and do crazy flips and acrobatics. That was before they were defeated by Tony Garea and Haystacks Calhoun in one of the longest reigns ever. But Shelli and her brothers were fickle in their allegiance, their attention was easily diverted. En masse, they defected to Hulk Hogan when he squared off against Andre the Giant in Wrestlemania III, cementing Hogan's place as an immortal the day he slammed the Giant and got the pinfall.

One of her brothers had the idea of staging a wrestling match in the barn, creating a ring out of mattresses and rope, with Shelli as referee, saying she would be the best judge. Shelli readily agreed. Until they turned thirteen, Shelli could beat them in one-to-one combat, she had learned all the tricks, but not any longer, they gained too much in the arms and shoulders as they got older. And again, she had never liked the fighting, she did it to maintain her position in the pecking order, and yet, she liked that they could derive so much pleasure out of their tussling, continual energy outputs, like puppies.

Her dad came in, telling them that the whole thing was staged. "It's all a show," he said, "the outcome fixed from the start; they're pretending to hate each other." After that her dad set the rules for any fighting: no choking, no hard punches, no slamming down on the opponent's back while he's facing down on the floor and pulling his legs into a leg lock (known as the Walls of Jericho). None of Shelli's brothers wanted to hear that indictment on their favorite sport. They sparred like Power Rangers—like her sons decades later—the muscles flexing, but not doing anything substantive, not really, more growling then actual display of male ferocity.

Shelli told Stefan about this. He said he and his brother, David, fought over everything, including the seats they sat on and the food on the table. She didn't think much of it, until she spoke to David who said that Stefan had knocked a couple of his teeth out during one of their fights, but Stefan laughed it off.

"It figures that you would be really hard on your brother," Shelli said.

"What do you mean? Just normal fighting between brothers. I can't help that I'm bigger than him."

"My oldest brother was like that. I didn't like it much. Neither did David, apparently."

"So you have that in common."

Shelli told Stefan about the rodeo bronc that totally shattered five of her teeth beyond any hope of repair requiring two implants to anchor a bridge; most of her other teeth so badly chipped they required crowns. He looked at her in disbelief.

"A rodeo bronc?"

"Yep. I was trying to gentle him on a bet."

"And you accuse me of making up stories."

"It fucking happened, ask my brothers. They were there, yuking it up."

In a blink of an eye, Shelli was brought back to that day, her brain spinning in a cauldron of emotion. She could smell her fear mixed with her sweat as her father jumped away from the horse, a pale Irishman with skin scorched a deep red, almost the same color as the cayuse she rode on. She gripped the horn so tight that her knuckles turned white. But in all her imaginings she never anticipated the force or the violence of his bucking, the bronc moving as if a tiger had landed on his back, sunfishing and windmilling, and the likes of which she had never experienced before or since. The impact shattered her teeth and vibrated her skull, her mouth filling with sharp tooth fragments that crunched like gritty sand. She crawled on her hands and knees, making haste to get out from under the hooves, scrambling for the fence.

She imagined she was a Kentauroi, a centaur, her animal spirit joined as one with the horse. She had an innate gift; having practiced the concept of gentle training, or "horse whispering" as it's now known. Gentle methods were praised by the Greek philosopher Xenophon, reached cult status among 19th century Scots horsemen. Shelli's father raised her on the myths and legend of the Wild West but this was the first time she tried to tame a wild horse, and of course she had to pick a rodeo reject. It was her dream, but the reality turned out to be a nightmare. She hadn't realized that rodeo stock was something entirely different from your average run-of-the-mill mustang. Neither did her father, or his best friend, Louie, who knew horses better than anyone alive. She loved horses with a passion verging on the maniacal since she was small, drawn by the freedom, grace and strength they embody, the raw instinct and purity of spirit. (She still loved them, but couldn't fit them in, and then there was the expense.) Until that day riding the bronc, she felt invincible on the back of any horse, and felt protected from harm by her love for these animals.

Roused out of her musings by Micah, who appeared out of nowhere sobbing as if his heart would break, lifting her mood from a black place, and in a rush of emotion, Shelli hugged her son, happy to let go of her sadness, thinking of her dad, whom she had loved, and wishing he was still alive so he could experience her sons growing up. It would have been a thrill for him. Seth came out into the hallway and joined them. When Seth saw the impact Micah's tears had on Shelli—how effusive her kisses and hugs—he started crying, too, big alligator tears. She opened her arms and hugged both children with equal passion, quelling their cries. The kids meant a lot to her, called up a mix of emotions, never one sentiment isolated from another. The fact that they loved their mother, that's all that she could think about.

They started fighting again. Shelli quizzed Micah and started piecing the puzzle together. It all started when they were sitting in front of the television. They had been playing a game. Seth hit Micah, and Micah hit him back. They pulled each other's hair. Seth chased Micah around the house, knocking over a lamp. Shelli tried to get them to sit down and play a game of cards with her, but they wouldn't sit still, kept hitting each other, making her despair of ever quieting them down. Dodging their flailing limbs, she brought them into her arms wrapping them up into a group catharsis and asked them to apologize to each other.

When they settled down, she sat with them in the playroom while they played with Legos.

"My nails are too long for this sort of thing," Shelli said to the boys when they asked her to help with some miniaturized pieces. Ruefully, she added, "If I get called upon to do this again, I may have to cut them down."

"No," Seth said. "Keep them long like a vampire."

"You like my nails, huh?"

"Sure," Seth said. "They're sick."

Seth jumped up, waving an airplane he built, a grin splitting his face, his merry eyes gleaming. Something sticky had gotten clumped into his hair, giving him a slightly disheveled look and his shirt had a new rip in it. He looked happy his cheeks reddened from the athleticism of his play. Micah was putting the finishing touches on his airplane, adding wings with a massive reach. He looked intent, focused, a budding engineer. He had more interest than his brother in building things. Seth tended to be more the lawyerly type, arguing everything to death.

"Hey, that's a great plane, Micah," Shelli said, pulling at her tangled hair so it wouldn't fall into her eyes.

"Mom," Seth cried. "Look what I made!" He held up a strange, spacey, ship-like contraption with wings sticking out of it at odd places, Star Wars gone amuck.

"It's beautiful, sweetie," Shelli said.

He swiped at his face when she gave him a big kiss on his cheek. "Ewww," he said, but she knew he was just saving face, his grin seemed genuinely happy.

The babysitter walked in and Shelli got up. She stood in front of children and the babysitter; hands impatiently squared on her hips. "Be good to Emily, ya' hear?"

They didn't say anything, too busy showing Emily what they had made. Shelli turned to go and the children who sprang from her loins did not even look at her, too busy flying their airplanes and driving the trucks they had built out of Legos at speeds that made her tremble. Their father came in. They looked up briefly and said "Bye," they had no qualms about their parents leaving for the night. Stefan closed the front door, and stepped outside, a big grin on his face.

Shelli felt a big hole in her heart thinking about the last time they visited her parents, a few months before they died.

Her children were small then. She took comfort in the words of Julian Barnes: "The fact that someone is dead may mean that they are not alive, but it doesn't mean that they don't exist." The only way to give meaning to sorrow howl at the moon that otherwise might have sounded merely a stubbed-toe cry.

Six

They met at a waterfront bar near the old part of town on a street that looked deserted of anything friendly, only a few old cars and broken-down dogs visible between rundown buildings. From the outside, the place looked like was about to fall apart, but inside it had the look of a charming Parisian bistro with only a dozen or so tables. The place was filled to overflowing, and the bar jammed solid. Into the din, Stefan was saying something meant to disarm: "You're the veterans," and chortling, his body vibrating the way it did when he wanted to please. After making these social niceties, Stefan talked only to Camila, Wilhelm's date. Shelli didn't feel jealous of the other woman, she was pretty but not a knockout and more to the point, her bust was average, not the full melons Stefan fantasized about. Most of her weight appeared to be lodged in her ass. But the rest of her was beautiful. Her hair was so blonde it sparkled in the light, and her eyes so blue they appeared to be filled with starlight. And she looked like a trembling opal, dressed in a gauzy number that refracted light from all directions mirroring her hair and lighting up the bar. She seemed like a mirage, a harem girl that Shelli had dreamed up to make love to her husband, and then she would magically disappear.

She studied Wilhelm's pale face in the large mirror behind the bar. She had questions about him, he didn't reveal himself readily. Around him as if a halo has formed, the deep blue of the sky faded to a shimmer. A rising excitement, similar to her single days when she would happen into a really hunky guy and desire would flood her consciousness to the point of obliterating all else, sweeping her up in a rush of endorphins. Only now she had more of a sense of who she was and how much she could get away with.

She liked that Wilhelm took control of the conversation, larding his talk with compliments, and asking her what she thought of this or that. Such a smooth operator, stroking her leg with erotic precision as if he did this on an hourly basis with strangers who piqued his interest, she imagined him quizzing them with great thoroughness afterward, as if he was bent on improving the quality of the meet and greet for potential lovers everywhere. He appeared to be the rare guy bent on refining his technique, desiring nothing more than to see his lovers— as temporary as they might be—derive maximum enjoyment. His voice waxed low and passionate as he imagined out loud how and where they'd do it, yet his manner remained respectful. He wanted her outside in the garden and the kitchen, turning those areas into erotic landscapes—but never would he entertain doing it in the marital bed.

She had on an ivory bustier by Dolce, pushing her breasts into jiggly cupcake-shaped mounds, making her super conscious of how she looked, and willed Stefan out of her consciousness. Shelli liked that Wilhelm looked unstudied and casual in torn jeans and tee shirt with his broad shoulders and nicely modulated biceps, not in the least bit fussy or mussed up. He gave her a hug, as if they were old friends. Shelli immediately warmed to him, liking that this man stood out from the crowd of lumps with big bellies and narrow shoulders and arms; the difference quite stark.

"I'd love to do you without a condom," he said in his exotic accent, his words laced with rolling 'r's and hard 'o's and his 'om' as in 'come' coming out as 'ow.' His hand lightly caressed her thigh until it glowed incandescent. "But I'm afraid I'll have to use one," he added as if it was an afterthought.

"I appreciate your concern," Shelli said, her head swimming as if newly deprived of oxygen, her breath coming quick. "But you must admit, I've got more to worry about in that department than you do, seeing as I have only screwed one other person other than my husband for nearly ten years. You, by your own admission, have been around."

"Do you think I'm diseased?" he asked, leaning forward, his lips twitching. "Wouldn't I tell you if I was?"

"Because you're so incredibly good-looking, I should consider you trustworthy?" Shelli wrapped her finger around a strand of her hair, twisting it, liking this flirting not caring about the outcome. She would deal with it when the time came.

"Maybe I won't use a condom," he replied.

"I demand you wear one." She snuggled closer, she feeling like she was on fire from the inside out.

But then her mouth suddenly dried up. "Let's get drinks," she said.

Wilhelm signaled the bartender.

"Two daiquiris," he said crisply, "the classic way, no simple syrup, a few strawberries as sweetener and muddle don't blend, then shake everything over ice."

For one wild minute, Shelli thought she might throw all convention aside, and lay her hot lips on his right here in this bar for all to see, and after feeling the heat of his skin until she could take no more, and rip off his clothes. Then she'd drag him into a corner and hump him silly. She imagined all the men in the place would watch while maintaining a respectful distance. She licked her lips and wondered what was happening to her. She didn't usually think like this when talking to good looking men. It wasn't just his hard body. He appeared kindhearted too, and full of humor, as well as being an experienced lover. She wanted to touch him like she rarely wanted to touch anyone.

She could see he was enjoying her discomfort.

"What kind of body turns you on?"

"I like all sizes," he said. "I like variety."

Partially to staunch her excitement, she looked over at Stefan, which usually tended to bring her back to earth. He sat on other side of Camila, looking stiff, very much like the corporate executive who put on the wrong clothes and entered this bar by mistake. He looked like he was enjoying himself—he loved meeting new people—but it was hard to see if he wanted anything more than the chance to talk. His demeanor puzzled her. Wasn't their meeting primarily about seeing if they wanted to have sex with these other people? His elbows were planted on the thick wood counter and he spoke with animation to Camila—about what, she could only guess. But judging by his standoffish demeanor, he probably was talking to her about politics or sports, or maybe he had just learned that Camila was a Nazi. She could only think that sexual attraction was convoluted, and its workings—the whys and wherefores—were not readily visible. Camila had a gorgeous, peaches-and-cream face out of which shone big gumdrop eyes batting a million miles a minute over a little button nose, and square jaw. Shelli imagined that if she were a man, she would have been all over Camila in a second. If anything turned Stefan off, Camila's breasts looked to be on the small side. Shelli's spirits sank.

"You don't want to talk to me anymore," Wilhelm said, gently nudging Shelli's shoulder.

"You must have women falling all over you," Shelli said, turning her attention back to Wilhelm. "You must be pushing away the women."

Out of the corner of her eye, she saw a blonde head spin on its axis. Camila had her ear cocked in Wilhelm's direction, her head listing to one side, her shimmering strands falling over her face, her lips pensive. She appeared to be listening intently for Wilhelm's answer.

"No," Wilhelm said, shaking his head. "Men need women more than women need men. Women want children. And once they have them, they develop a stronger physical connection with their children than they do with their men. The divorced ones see something sexy on television and they masturbate, but they don't go out to meet men."

"Is this what they tell you? Is it really like that? Your girlfriend has kids, and she's with you. How did you meet?"

"I saw her in a parking lot, and I said something to her."

"You saw my big thighs, and you wanted to fuck me," Camila said.

Stefan's eyes widened.

"That's right," Wilhelm said. "I wanted to fuck you."

"You heard what he said about women not actively looking for dates?" Shelli said.

"Sure," Camila said, and after a pause added, "Women get tired of the bullshit."

She could understand why Camila would make an exception for Wilhelm. He stood out in a field littered with overweight, tired-looking people. That's not to say that being in shape was the end all, but a life of sexual hedonism and decadence was not possible without a decent body. While it's true that attraction depends on more, something elusive, a level of connection and congeniality can't be pinned down easily, it has to start with a body that's at least acceptable. And Shelli and Stefan's standards were high; Stefan's perhaps more than Shelli's. Although it could also be said that physical attraction isn't always easy to understand: an ugly face could be terribly sexy, and a plump body, too, but Stefan clung unwavering to ideals formed in his adolescence—a few times, he confided that his heartthrob as a teenager was Terri Garr in the movie *Young Frankenstein* by Mel Brooks, you know that scene when Gene Wilder says "What knockers!" and she replies, "Oh, thank you doctor." And then later that night Wilder says, "Elevate me." A lot of young males lusting on Garr after that. Stefan had been one of those lusting youths.

"What do you do," Shelli said. "For work, I mean."

"Investments…my passion…photography…I'd love to take some pictures of you, but mostly I'm into capturing moments, catching the light in the way of Ansel Adams, or William Klein. Lately I've been obsessing over Klein's use of natural lighting, blurred effects and wide-angle lens."

"Susan Sontag said: "The picture may distort, but there's always a presumption that something exists, or did exist, like what's in the picture."

""Photographs fiddle with the scale of the world and can be doctored and tricked out. That's my specialty."

"Ah, so you are a trickster?"

"Stieglitz especially had a singular gift."

"I love his photo of the young Georgia O'Keeffe robed, hair unbound," Shelli said. And tried to contain her mounting excitement wanting to have the appearance of not caring.

"I'd like sometime to spend the day with you and take pictures of you lounging in silk."

"Perhaps that can be arranged."

After their feast of appetizers and drinks, they strolled out of the restaurant into the cool lavender air. An unusually nice day had turned into a spectacular evening. Along the wharf, the gray, low-slung buildings crouched like big rocks, exuding warmth collected from the day, a heat that rose out of those hard places and the swell of sidewalk they walked on, enveloping them in a hot stench, Vulcan's gulph smelling something like laundry exhaust, but the odor was quickly swept away by a breeze, and the further they walked, the cooler the breeze got. Closer to the wharf, she breathed deeply of the tart of salt water and rotting wood, a potent combination that cleared the nostrils. They stopped at a grassy knoll to look over the water heavy with the scent of flowers—rose and jasmine mixing with lilies, sweet pea, and chrysanthemums. She stood rooted to the spot, her spirits unaccountably rising with the continued application of sweet floral essence, mesmerized by the sparks cast by the moonlight dancing over the corrugated crests, the liquid energy mirroring her optimism about their prospects for the night.

"Why did you marry him?" her erstwhile companion asked, nodding at Stefan. "He's a cold fish, and you're as passionate as they come, if you'll pardon the pun."

Shelli fell silent for a minute and listened to Stefan discoursing with Wilhelm's girlfriend on such sexy topics as the ins and outs of youth soccer. Her two sons, it turned out, played varsity soccer.

"He can be fun."

They stopped walking.

Wilhelm gazed into Shelli's eyes. "And the sex is good?" he asked slowly.

"Like every married couple, over the years the passion cools."

"I know exactly what you mean," he said with a knowing nod, "It's the same for us."

They stopped by a stone water fountain. Camila turned to Wilhelm and said, "Let's go to a nightclub." Ah, so that explained her glittery dress, which did seem overmuch for a casual bar.

"What do you think?" Wilhelm said.

"Doesn't appeal to me," Stefan said.

Shelli would have been surprised if he had agreed, she had never known him to go to nightclubs with her to dance, except that one time they went to a swing club hoping to pick up someone, and then once, at a company party held in a nightclub in SoHo made famous by Yoko Ono's frequent presence. Stefan never wanted to go to nightclubs on a date with Shelli, he preferred a good restaurant. Stefan liked going to strip clubs, but not with her, only with guys.

"Well, we can't go to our house," Shelli said: "We have children at home."

"My children aren't home," Camila said. "Even so, my house is in Long Island. It'd take us an hour to drive there."

Her date refused to offer his place, saying simply, "Can't."

"What about a hotel?" Shelli suggested.

"I say we end the evening," Stefan said. "Did you notice the time? Its past midnight. I have to work tomorrow. I know it's the weekend, but this in my busy time. Let's do this next weekend… we'll get together at a nice hotel, my treat."

Shelli knew that the real reason he wanted to cut the evening short was that he had no interest in Camila. She suspected that Camila knew it too. All they talked about was politics and soccer, not the sort of talk Stefan engaged in when he was interested in more. And Camila was so beautiful, with the face of an angel. Yet he didn't fall for Camila and behave like the Lothario he had always fancied himself. Perhaps his lack of interest had more to do with Shelli than with Camila? How would he have reacted if Shelli had not acted gaga over Wilhelm?

Perhaps when it came down to it, he couldn't stomach seeing her with someone else unless he had someone fabulous. But Shelli knew he'd never tell her exactly what went on in his head, he never fully revealed himself. Each of the faces he presented to her was a chimera meant to obscure or reinvent the truth. She rarely saw the real man, occasionally a frightened, lost soul peered out, and only when under duress and never for more than a few minutes. Like a bolt of electricity, it hit her that they lacked the essential trust and understanding to pull off this swinging thing. She knew they needed to talk about it and tease this thing out. Why did he want to do this if he was so jealous? But Shelli also knew that if he said he didn't want to swing anymore she might have a problem. Shelli had changed; her universe expanding to include handpicked others, the last thing she wanted was to stifle her newly awakened sexual self. It seemed unjust to stop just when she felt she had been freed of the shackles of convention. It would be just like him, she thought, to get her worked up over something good and when he realized she liked it, he'd take it away.

On the drive home, she asked him what he thought of Wilhelm. "I don't know," Stefan said. "I couldn't put my finger to on it." He called Wilhelm a 'poseur.'

"What about the shiksa?"

"She was nice enough, but she didn't interest me in that way."

"Oy, they're the first decent couple," Shelli said clapping her hands to her face.

"Not with that fat rump," Stefan said.

"But her tits were okay, weren't they?"

"You're not a man, what do you know."

"You're picky." Shelli stared at him, her eyes filling.

She wanted to say that Mattie wasn't the only sexy woman out there. But she knew saying such a thing would get her nowhere. He might even take it as a challenge, or worse, shut her off entirely. Couldn't he see, without her repeating it, that she couldn't handle him having Mattie, who was born Jewish

(Shelli knew that meant something to him), very beautiful, and blessed with that large personality. It would tear her apart to see those two together—anyone but her. But Shelli was happy to see him with Tequila—Stefan would never run away with a fat girl, didn't matter how big her bosom was—and she wondered why he never mentioned her. At home in bed, she finally got up the courage to ask.

What about Tequila?"

"I want to get together with a few other women first, before we meet them again. I was so nervous I couldn't hold off. Maybe I just need a little practice? It's ironic; I can last forever with you."

Shelli relented, put her arms around him, and gave him a big kiss. They broke apart and she asked, "Do you love me, mishege?"

"Yes, shelemiel." He gave her quick buss on the cheek.

"No really," Shelli asked, thinking just a few months ago, she wouldn't have felt the need to ask. But she was glad she did, meantime he acted like he was being court martialed, which led her to think something was going on.

"Yes really," he said evenly, his eyes searching hers.

"If I told you this new game didn't make me happy, and we need to stop doing it, would you?"

"So much kvetching." He paled.

"Mishege, I need to know that if I insisted, you would."

Right then he devolved into a temperamental child who had been reprimanded, and pouting like his favorite teddy bear had been taken from him. "Sure," he said, but he looked distraught. "I'd do anything for you."

"Spoken like a mensch," Shelli said in a light tone, knowing just how the conversation should go, knowing that a tease worked better on him than anything else she could come up with. "No worries, you're off the hook for now." She said nothing more, but she remained in mourning for the things that didn't happen and could have if only Stefan could go more than skin deep. How much he loved her was still debatable. And she worried that sexual performance with strangers had become too important in their lives.

She fell asleep that night dreaming that they were returning from a date with yet another disappointing couple. Unable to shake it off, she had gone off by herself, hoping a stroll would help her relax. She ended up walking down a narrow, rutted road along the cliff below their house. On either side, houses were scattered among the thick cropping of trees like confetti. A full moon overhead and the ocean shimmering like cut glass below had her singing a soulful song, something passionate and heartfelt. She heard the clip-clop of metal horseshoes striking against pavement and turned to see a muscular white horse with a long mane and tail.

The horse snorted several times in quick succession and flexed his powerful neck. His balls swung heavily as he walked. He came up to Shelli and nudged her with his head, breathing hard. She pushed him away, but he kept coming back, pecking at her shirt with his lips, pulling the cloth away from her body. She turned to face him, and he placed his head between her breasts. His lips brushed her nipples, rousing them to high, hard, reddened points. She looked again and saw that he had become a man. Below, he was larger than most, even when flaccid. As she gazed upon him, his penis became a prehensile thing, swelling and enlarging until it was bigger than an elephant tusk. Her eyes widened, and her lips went slack with desire. She wanted to put her hand on him, and her mouth.

She asked him to go into a barbershop and cut his mane, which he did. When he came out, he still looked like a man, except he had a horse's hoofs instead of feet and a horse's face.

He came closer to her, looking at her suggestively, his hand wrapped around the base of his still-growing circumference. She didn't remember what happened after that. All she could remember was how beautiful and soft his skin was, and how exquisite his hair.

Shelli entered the packed auditorium in the Pompton Lakes community center as quietly as her clacking heels allowed. A member of the Sierra Club, who introduced himself as Jeff Tittel, stood at the podium saying he wanted to comment on a report claiming the state of New Jersey had higher incidents of cancer than any other state. He wanted to point out that, when incidents were broken down by locality, Pompton Lakes held the dubious distinction of heading that list.

Tittel read from a prepared statement:

"Department of Health and Senior Service found pollution in the sediment of Pompton Lake and Passaic River to be at toxic levels. The researchers traced the pollution to a creek that runs through the DuPont property and empties into the lake. DuPont (formally known as E.I. DuPont De Nemours & Company) operated a munitions facility on 570 acres from 1902 through 1994 and made blasting caps, metal wires, and aluminum and copper ammunition shells."

Tittel stopped reading from the prepared script and said. "And I'm here to tell you: there's something very wrong here. They were told to clean it up. The study found that the company's efforts to date have been inadequate. This is a matter of great urgency for the entire region. Time to write your representatives in Congress."

"What if we have cancer?" a voice called out from the audience. "Will DuPont pay our hospital bills?"

Around the room, a groundswell of assent rose from the crowd, a singularly aware audience composed of people who go to meetings and picket Congress, but sometimes forgets to recycle, or throws full coffee cups in the trash. The same hopes and concerns appeared on every face, registering an amalgam of shock and dismay having learned that there were significantly elevated rates of kidney cancer in women and non-Hodgkin's lymphoma in men living in this area. At one time Shelli and Stefan had lived in Pompton Lakes, so she was more than a little concerned, though they never swam or fished the lake. But she knew people who had. She thought putting their stories out there would create a groundswell of sympathy, and if the outcry was vociferous enough, the polluters would be shamed into doing something about it so taxpayers wouldn't have to. On the drive back home, driving in heavy traffic dodging three-wheelers and trucks hauling large loads, Shelli had a lot of time to mull over what she had learned that day. Governor Kat maintained that the CEOs she knew would do right by the people, particularly if not doing so would reflect poorly on them, which made sense, didn't it? But from what everything Shelli had heard, the environmental cleanups that weren't on the public radar were being shelved for lack of manpower and funds, thanks to the governor's cuts, and the new information that kept washing up on Shelli's doorstep that made her wonder if the CEOs would come though. But the numbers being floated, upward to $43 million (and that was just for starters) was said to be a conservative estimate of the true costs. People said anything less would be simply a cosmetic fix. The quoted figure covered for the cost of removing only a single layer of the contaminated sediment, about 130,000 cubic yards of muck that would have to be carted away—10,600 dump trucks' worth, leaving open the possibility that the mercury could migrate farther downstream, potentially putting Pompton Lake's drinking water well system at risk. Shelli thought about the immense cost of removing the toxins that had been around since the time of the revolutionary war when munitions factories were set up all around New Jersey.

First day Rivka Ackerman, a well-known activist in the Jewish community stood in front of the class of Jewish converts to teach about Jewish rituals she was dressed in a flowered cotton midi dress with short sleeves that covered her collarbone exposing very little flesh, other than her forearms, which were supple and beguiling, and talked about the proper way for a married woman to dress when out in public, quoting sections of Jewish law known as "Tznius," which translates from Hebrew to mean "modesty." Rivka's favorite place to buy clothes: A franchise called Chico's. She mentioned a clothing outlet in Newark that sold off the rack, hastening to add that she never bought anything at the full price, only shopped the sales. "Only goyim shop retail," she quipped. If anyone wanted to sign up to be on a list to be notified when clothing discounts were happening at stores in the tri-state area, sample sales also, she'd pass out a sheet. And she promised she would have a few personal shoppers on hand to offer fashion advice on selections at these events. Stefan would soon have nothing to laugh at. She imagined Stefan bowing with respect, struck dumb with wonder.

Shelli wrote a quick one-line on her notepad: "So many rules."

"Yes," Julia wrote underneath Shelli's scribble, "but the sales will be fun."

Rivka had a beautiful classically shaped face and delicate features, her real hair covered with a luxurious chestnut colored wig. Shelli had taken classes from Rivka before, and would have liked to know her better but didn't know how to change the dynamic of their relationship. Rivka looked utterly content with her lot, not at all bowed by birthing five children, and saying she wanted more. Nothing was too much, her love spread around the room like the ocean, she had infinite capacity. Shelli thought that Rivka seemed fulfilled sexually as well. And in case anyone had any doubt, Rivka announced to the class that even though she was forbidden to touch her husband during her time of month, and then only after she had immersed herself in the mitzvah, a ritual bath the size of a small wading pool, even with those constraints they had an active sex life, and their desire for each other was growing stronger, not less. She suggested perhaps the answer was withholding sex and living as a frum, the nickname for Jews that have turned exceedingly devout and ritualize everything, including bathing in the mitzvah, with a string of prayers to mark the moment before and after. With only a week or so when screwing was allowed, Stefan's desire for her might grow. She had to smile at the idea of her dressing frum, (as frumpy as possible), and beginning a life following all the religious laws regarding food, and loads of prayer to accompany each meal, but would Stefan enjoy this sort of life? He would have to give up pizza and cheeseburgers, the foods he lived on most of his life. Shelli couldn't imagine it.

Rivka was teaching about the Jewish holidays from a cultural point of view, specifically the etiquette and manner of the rituals and the food. "I'm here to tell you that the main thing to remember in Judaism is to eat," Rivka said to the room of twenty women sitting at long wood tables. "Food is central in creating a Jewish home. I would say the most important, after prayer. You don't want to scrimp on the food, prepare it wrong, or leave anyone wanting more. You see me, look at my body, obviously I love to eat, I'm plump, and I'm also a good cook. I spend a lot of time in the kitchen; I'm not one of your feminists who do not prize their role as a balesboste. I come from a long line of Polish Rebbes and can trace my ancestry as far back as the 16th century. This is not a requirement, but I'd say if you really want to embrace Jewish culture, you will familiarize yourself with the best Jewish cookbooks. I happen to love Joan Nathan and Mimi Sheraton, and Claudia Roden for the Sephardic, but there are others."

Rivka sketched out the lesson plan and talked about the classes on cooking that would meet at Sur La Table, with guest chefs teaching the staples for the major holidays, dishes like blintz and kugel. They would all have a chance to participate in cooking a part of the meal, and they would eat together. Shelli and Julia exchanged excited glances, and the other people in the class perked up as well. Cooking meals as a class would be fun.

Back at home, Shelli was all fired up to make a pot roast. She knew how to follow a recipe and decided to experiment on her own. Stefan was aghast, and said not to make his mother's pot roast, hers were always terrible. Shelli told him she was confident she could make this dish taste as good as a five-star restaurant, and promised she'd have an alternate meat on hand in case. She postulated that Stefan's mom didn't add enough braising liquid or use a Le Creuset cast iron pot with its trademark tight-fitting lid.

"Of course not," Stefan said, "You've seen what she cooks with, whatever she can get on sale at TJ Maxx."

Shelli took the time to research recipes, looking first at the Jewish cookbooks, and comparing the recipes by the French chefs. She found one in *Bon Appetit* that she preferred by Jenny Rosenstrach and Andy Ward that was actually for bone-in short ribs but Shelli thought it looked more interesting, calling for more herbs than any of the other recipes, which she knew would impart a stronger, more intense flavor to the meat. She thought the problem with the classic Jewish recipes was not enough herbs: the typical pot roast called for four cloves of garlic, one sprig of rosemary and one bay leaf, and no red wine. Joan Nathan's version called for one clove of garlic, a sprig each of thyme, rosemary, and a one-fourth cup of parsley, two times the amount of carrots, celery, and two cups of red wine. But what Shelli liked about the Rosenstrach/Ward recipe was the ratio of herbs: eight sprigs of thyme, four of oregano, two sprigs rosemary and a whole head of garlic halved crosswise, plus a whole bottle of Cabernet. At first Shelli kept it conservative, keeping the wine to two cups, and then adding a can of whole tomatoes (the next time she threw in a whole bottle of wine with the tomatoes, and an overkill of herbs, and garlic). It turned out it didn't matter the amount of wine, but two cups turned out to be the minimum needed, depending on how much intensity of flavor she wanted. Adding an ox bone, along with extra vegetables—one or two zucchini, a handful of mushrooms and two onions instead of one—as well as additional wine and tomatoes turned into an incredibly flavorful sauce, coupled with an increase of the time allocated to braising. By lowering the temperature to 300 degrees for four hours, the meat turned out divine. Stefan stuffed himself, going back for seconds and thirds.

There was no escape from the relentless sun other than the barn that had been upgraded with every modern convenience, including a state of the art heating and cooling system that smelled like no barn Shelli had been in: no musk of animal fur, no stank of dung, not a speck of dust anywhere, every molecule immaculately groomed. The governor just now pointed out her daughter's horse grazing in a pasture visible out one of the windows, saying that she often looked out that window for inspiration. And that endeared Shelli, but she could never copy Kat's style or confident air, the sort that comes with the security of a comfortable upbringing, a cloak of invincibility that said louder than words: 'None of what you say matters; none of you plebes can hurt me where it counts.' When asked about the opposition of the teacher's union for her support of Jersey City's school-choice voucher program, Kat said, with unfeigned indifference, "They hate me anyway."

"Everyone is still amazed that you were able to cut income tax by 30 percent over three years," Shelli said. "Something every pundit ridiculed and said it couldn't be done. To fly in the face of all that criticism must have been the scariest thing."

"I didn't just say 'Read My Lips.' Kat said. "I'm doing it.' Oozing sincerity, looking directly into Shelli's eyes, displaying one of her best attributes—her warmth—had Shelli swooning. She was a patrician with a populist touch; people often compared her to Bill Clinton. "But the credit goes to John. He encouraged me to run, and he brought in Larry and Steve to the house to help me put together a platform."

She was referring to Lawrence Kudlow, chief economist at Bear Stearns, a former advisor to Reagan, and economic guru of Jack Kemp, all of whom bought the Art Laffer's supply-side theory. Steve Forbes Jr., publisher of *Forbes,* was also part of the circle, along with Tom Kean, a former governor of New Jersey who, like Kat and her husband John had come from an impressive line of the *historire ancienne* ruling class around the New York-New Jersey axis. Kean's mother the former Elizabeth Stuyvesant Howard–was related to Peter Stuyvesant, the Dutch colonial governor of Nieuw Amsterdam. His grandmother, Katharine Winthrop, was a direct descendant of John Winthrop, the first governor of the Massachusetts Bay Colony. They would have been considered part of the entrenched aristocracy if America, like Britain, favored the descendants of the ruling elite above all others. As things stood, even in America, special favors are granted people with storied lineages, such as invites to the A-list parties, and who knows what else.

"You've heard of the Laffer Curve," John said, his eyes glinting behind his horn rims. "Essentially the formula shows that lower taxes accompanied by cuts to nonproductive government spending stimulate economic growth. This is in lieu of the high-tax rate progressive income tax systems like Nixon had in the 1970s."

"You know the old joke, why did God create stock analysts?" Stefan said. "To make weather forecasters look good." He leaned back, smiling as if he said the most interesting thing. Everyone in the room responded the joy he got from sharing the jokes that he saved up like chits when strapped for something meaningful to say.

"No guarantees, just good analysis," John said, lifting his coffee mug. His eyes, calculating, analytical, hung like two moons over a straight nose and decisive mouth. A purposeful aura clung to him like a second skin, all adding up to one thing: this was a man who got things done. Stefan wasn't surprised to learn that he ran a startup worth $20 million.

"Why wasn't Jesus born in the USA?" Stefan interrupted.

"Don't know," John said.

"Seems God couldn't find three wise men and a virgin anywhere on American soil," Stefan said with a roar of laughter.

"Can you stop with the Jesus's jokes already?" Shelli said, a little of the irritation she was feeling at his constant harking to religious themes when meeting people descended from the Visigoths, a snappish quality coming through.

"He missed his calling as a comic," John said.

"I could have been a contender," Stefan said.

"In any case, we're proving it can be done," Kat said, her mouth resolute, eyes on John.

"You cut government spending in part by lowering the cost of funding the pension obligation by pushing out most of the cost for 20 years," Shelli said into the neutral and affectless silence. "Now someone else will have that headache," she paused for a moment to allow this fact to sink in before continuing, "then you raised the sales and property taxes because there was still a shortfall. Doesn't that seem gimmicky?"

Stefan threw Shelli a sharp look. This was one of Stefan's pet peeves about Shelli; he didn't like her confrontational style. He only confronted people when their backs were turned. The air in the room took on a hostile quality.

"What I did was no different from the others who came before me," Kat didn't sound defensive, but rather like a teacher explaining a difficult concept to a slow student, and as time went on, appeared to relish the question, leaning forward, her eyes glowing. "I handled payments to the pension fund no differently than a host of other New Jersey governors, including Florio. Florio relied on one-time, non-recurring revenues in his budget, I did that too. There isn't much difference in our outlook; I hold the same beliefs on social issues." Her voice was calm, nonjudgmental. The mood in the room relaxed, even Stefan was smiling.

"So now you're outing yourself...as closet democrat?" Stefan interjected, and flashed his slippery salesman's smile.

"Not much difference between my views and Bill Clinton's," Kat said.

"Not much difference between the two parties, actually," John said, "when you get down to it."

"I was able to hold to these deep income tax cuts," Kat said, speaking in that breezy, disaffected way of hers as of Shelli had never broached that question about sales and property taxes, "and the corporate tax rate for small business—right now, it's lowest it's ever been."

Shelli picked up her coffee from where she had laid it on a side table, tasting the sweet black nectar liberally laced with half and half and drank the liquid deeply.

John took Stefan outside to point out the solar-powered system affixed to the roof. As he spoke, Stefan noticed how distinguished looking he looked, with his open, square face marked by strong features, particularly his jaw—its width making him look like the kind of guy who could date Barbie or pop out of a wedding cake. Shelli stayed behind with Kat in the large breezeway at the front of the barn, where the air conditioning sucked out the stickiness even at the double front doors, making the air feel as light and frothy as a whipped confection, the machinery whirling behind it completely undetectable. Stepping of her lethargy and constant drowsiness from the humidity was out proving hard to do. Her skin merely served as the container for water left simmering in the center of a vast oven that is the whole perceived world. The heat as thick as pudding. She wanted to stay longer, she knew that was greedy but she didn't care, but was forced to follow Kat into one of the stalls to pet the dappled face of a horse smelling of soap, nostrils flaring, fur dancing under her fingers like satin. The air conditioning made everything perfectly delicious.

"My kids would have loved this," Shelli said.

"Why didn't you bring them?" Kat said.

"When I heard your kids were in camp," Shelli said, "I thought not to bring mine so we could talk like adults and not bore them. They'll be leaving for camp in Maine in a few days, so it's no biggie that they will miss this outing."

"My daughter begged me to send her to camp," Kat said, "and my son said I was too busy these days and wanted to travel, too. That's the price I have to pay."

"For Kat's sake, we scared off the handlers," John said. "Gave them the afternoon. So now we're free to do whatever."

More questions bubbled. She wanted to ask why Kat had gutted the environmental task force and allowed it to tank, when she paid so much lip service to land conservation. They were not the same thing but linked in some way. To her mind, picking up the trash, recycling, and keeping the rivers clean were part and parcel. But it takes a concerned citizenry, and too many people don't give a shit. Even if God laid down the law. Thinking this way made her blood boil. But she held back and willed herself to listen to what the others had to say; knowing it would be best if she waited for the proper moment to pose this question, if at all.

Shelli glanced at Kat and flashed on an image of Kat and John naked in bed, two good-looking people, him sightless without his glasses, nothing overtly fetish, conducted mostly in the dark and in the missionary position. They might not go as far as putting a sheet between them, but Shelli wouldn't have been surprised to hear this was so. To erase this image from her mind, she hastened to steer the conversation away from taxes, which tended to be a quagmire.

"The Tea Party has called you one of the lunatic fringe," Shelli said. "They're desperately trying to marginalize you."

"I'm the *bête noire* of the pro-life movement," Kat said.

"Remember when Bill Clinton repudiated Sister Soulijah's remark that blacks should kill white people, and compared her to KKK's David Duke?" John broke in, his hands sawing at the air.

"People tell me I have Bill's charisma."

"You have Ann Richards' spunk," Shelli said, with a glance at Stefan, hoping he noticed that she was buttering the governor up, not tearing her down.

"You've met?" Kat said, smoothing back her hair.

"In the Federal Capitol Building some years ago," Shelli said, "when she was at the height of her power. I observed her in action."

"In politics, the truth often gets twisted beyond recognition," John said. "Yet it's the perception that matters. Remember Goebbels who said, *"If you tell a lie big enough and keep repeating it, people will eventually come to believe it."*

"Kind of like how Gore opened up the Elk Hills Oil Reserve in California for Occidental Petroleum, after Nixon and Reagan tried and failed," Shelli said.

"Showing how smart you are," Stefan said, his mouth inching up to form shadow of a smile.

"She happens to be right on that one," John said smoothly, with a wink at Shelli. "It's all about knowing the right people. Gore's dad was the chairman of Occidental's coal subsidiary, Island Creek."

"On Al Senior's watch," Shelli said. "Island Creek committed a slew of environmental violations, some of them involving strip mining—a practice his son as a congressman campaigned against. But neither did Al Jr. turn down the half a mill in campaign contributions from Occidental when he decided to run for president."

"Business is business, as they say," Kat said.

"Mouthing slogans and promises that you never intend to honor?" Shelli said.

"I went in with the best intentions," Kat said, "Now there's no money in my till even if I wanted to do something about it."

"Spinning your wheels, sweetheart," Stefan said, with a smirk in Shelli's direction.

A cloud descended on Shelli's good mood. Why did he always trivialize and mock her?

A few days later Shelli drove down to Brick, one of the many coastal towns south of Sandy Hook, to interview a business analyst and tech whiz. His office was close to the highway in a suburban office park near a sandy stretch of beach where the few trees that spanned the horizon appeared to be dehydrated, limp and anemic, lending a desolately air, in direct rebuttal of the glowing orange marmalade sun riding herd on all things living. Shelli got out of her car and entered the soupy heat. The building turned out to be a frigid zone where she had to don a sweater just to make it down the hallway. Shivering in the chair and asking about some of the things he thought might change in the next few years, specifically why it was that no one was modernizing the phone. The technology hadn't changed in fifty years; this was a big topic among the phone people she knew servicing the financial district. Fiber optics was just starting to take hold with its promise of greater speed and more complex data streaming. Her interloper echoed her questions but had no answers. This seemed strange coming from someone who had a history of accurately predicting computer trends, such as the demise of the mainframe, the rise of the personal computer, and the miniaturization of all things electronic.

They concluded the interview. Shelli shook his hand, disappointed that she hadn't learned anything earthshaking, and went outside, took off the sweater, happy to be wearing a linen shift. Thinking about her boys, hoping they were having fun with their dad; he was picking them up that day. The weather had changed and not for the better. The closer she got to the parking lot the more intense the humidity. The prickling of dusk blurred the light of the sun so gradually that there was just a slight darkening in the sky, then everything shifted on a dime and Shelli couldn't find her way without stumbling.

At her car she fumbled for her car keys, her cell phone buzzing. She pulled everything out of her purse, and still couldn't find her phone. It kept ringing, rudely invading her thoughts. She wondered if it was Stefan with an update about his mom, and thought back to his irritability towards her at the Wickhams the other day, saying to herself that he never appreciated her even though she tried to do little things like cooking and cleaning for his mother when she lived in Brooklyn and who had never been kind to her. But even so, the fact that he derided her like that in public in front of people she admired and wanted to impress grated on her. If anything could drive a wedge between them that would be it. The one time she asked him not to say things like that in public anymore, he said nothing, but later, at home, he said he would continue to say whatever he wanted, and didn't care what she thought of it. He repeated several times that he had nothing apologize for, and heckled her to the point she ended up apologizing to him for bringing it up at all, just to end his tirade, the memory of which rankled like a burr buried deep in her hair.

Finding the phone, she stood listening as the warmth of her caller's voice enveloped her, plying her with old-style European romance in a way no American man ever would do. The voice didn't register at first, slowly penetrating within the foggy detritus that swirled her brain. "Baby, I forgot to tell you how ravishing you were the other night," Wilhelm oozed. "I can't stop thinking about you. Umm, I wanted to run my hands all over your perfect body at that bar. I just love slender, shapely women. Not many out there like you."

Shelli lapped his words like a hungry thing, feeling greedy, but so what? It wasn't cheating when your husband was the one encouraging this to happen. But then she had a sudden thought. She and Stefan had a fancy address and drove expensive cars; perhaps Wilhelm thought they were ripe for plunder? She flashed on her sons, everything she did impacted them in some way; it wasn't just about her and Stefan anymore, they had two young sons who depended on them for sustenance and love. As he spoke, her mood turned as dark as the sky, her spirits plummeting at the thought that he was stringing her along, thinking her a woman starved for love. She flashed on Wilhelm's symmetrical features, dominated by that strong jaw. Through clumps of trees looming darkly mystical, the last of the sun's rays sparkled like shards of brittle light piercing the fragile silk of the ocean.

"I wanted you too," Shelli said. "Could you not tell?"

"But your husband's not into Camila."

"We know a woman who isn't any more beautiful than Camila, and he's antsy as all get-out to fuck her. I think the difference here is he can see I'm attracted to you. And that ruins it for him."

"I see."

Shelli strolled down the narrow street away from her car, into the night toward the beach, feeling the cool ocean breeze brush her hair, her spirits ascending as the rich tones of Wilhelm's voice swelled like the notes of a violin through the phone, her heartbeat quickening with desire. It wasn't just his looks; there was something about the way he spoke that showed intelligence and good breeding. Inside, she was all quivering need. Having hunted sex partners like wine connoisseurs chasing after a good bottle of wine, and now that they had found a great couple, her lust grew tenfold. She longed to be loved by someone new. She felt she was being teased, first with Alasdair and now with Wilhelm, and recalled that Stefan said that he had tried to get in touch, and wondered if Stefan had been bald face lying. If this was a tactic meant to bring them closer as a couple—keeping her starved to the point of affliction so she would gladly gobble up any crumbs—it wasn't working. The breeze picked up, but Shelli didn't notice it—that's how far gone she was. She shivered, teeth chattering, even though the air continued its oven-like temperature. To the west, the sky loomed expansive, cloudless, a deep purple with pinks and lavenders lingering along the horizon meeting the dark purple of the sea. But she was blind to the beauty, focusing only on Wilhelm's voice, catching her breath when he started speaking again, her limbs trembling as his voice stirred her skin feathery soft. She took a deep breath and the sweet lemony scent from the abundance of evening primrose filled her nostrils.

"Come here now and have sex with me," he said.

"My husband and children are expecting me. I told him five minutes ago I'd be heading home around now. I can't tell him that I made other plans."

"Tell him you had a flat."

"I don't think he'd believe that. Not when I just bought these amazing Michelin tires."

"Even the best tires get flats."

To her ears, her voice sounded a plaintive longing as she demurred, her days of impetuosity long gone. But she couldn't stop these raw feelings of physical want that kept rising like liquid nitrogen, dangerous if confined in a small space, along with the desire to be adored by someone so squeaky new, he would try extra hard to please her. She walked back to the car and got in, her mind fallow of all thought, turned the ignition, and started driving north along the road hugging the shore, her ears cocked to that wonderful Dutch accent of his. Around her the new butted up against the old—tennis courts and horse corrals ringed by flowering gardens, crowding farmland buried under the scythe—a subtle manifestation of the cultural change sweeping the area.

One time, Stefan said that what they did in bed was boring and wished that Shelli had more skills sexually. Shelli said she was sorry she didn't have a penis, so she could pleasure herself whenever. His response: "Wish all you want."

"Oh, baby, I need you more than he does," Wilhelm crooned.

"I feel the same way." Her desire was in mortal danger of spilling over and causing some mishap. "But I'm married with two young children. I can't sneak around, not even when we're not getting along, like now."

"They're more important than your happiness?" He sounded animated.

"At the moment…yes." Couldn't he see she couldn't just take off—that she had a family to care for; she couldn't just take off on a whim.

She told him good-bye as firmly as possible and clicked off. She was driving her car with a mile to go when her cell phone rang again like a five-alarm fire. She fumbled for it, picking it up at the last ring, idly wondering if it was Stefan calling to grumble at her for being late. He and the children were probably hungry, filling up on celery and hummus, or tortilla chips and salsa, take your pick, waiting for her to cook for them. She floored the accelerator. With hooded eyes, she glanced at the velvet ocean darkening at the edges and felt her heart lurch.

"I'm nearly there," she said without listening for Stefan's scold.

"Without my help?" A breathless, deeply masculine voice carried through the airwaves, invading the inner recesses of her car. "Without me...?"

"Who's this?" She stalled, although she instantly recognized that singular voice. She felt a prickle of heat warming her insides.

"You sound luscious when you're uncertain...makes me want to kiss you."

"Ah, I've missed you," she teased, her eyes roaming the verdant countryside, calling him "my telephone lover" in a tone of endearment.

"And I've missed you too." His clipped tones caressed her ear. "I can't stop thinking about you. I want you to come over and allow me to take sexy pictures of you."

"Can I tell you the truth?"

"Of course. You can tell me anything," he said. "I don't judge."

"I've only been with one other man other than my husband," she began, and then changed direction. "It started with Stefan wanting to add people to our sex life. Back then I wasn't sure I wanted to do this, but now I'm dying to rip my cherry as wide open as possible. I'm starved for the kind of flirting we're doing. It's not about him anymore. It's about me." The more she explained that after meeting Wilhelm her desire to flirt and maybe more with someone other than her husband had infiltrated her thoughts, making it impossible for her to focus on anything else for any length of time, the more sympathetic he became.

"I've been in the lifestyle for years. I'm European. I'm not the best person to be giving advice."

"I don't want advice; I just want to vent."

"Why not just come over and have sex with me then?"

"Impossible..."

"You're putting up walls where there should be none."

"Tonight?" Shelli said, but right away she dismissed that idea. She did not believe Stefan would simply let her go and screw another guy, not unless the guy had an equally beautiful female for Stefan, and only if she didn't like the guy. But she didn't want him to lose hope, so she added: "Maybe we can figure something out. Let me think about it."

She drove into her driveway. What would have happened if she had immediately turned around and headed to Wilhelm's? He had intimated that he lived north of the Highlands, but that designation could include any one of a dozen places. She imagined being in the darkness lost along the dunes, calling his name and no one answering, hearing nothing but the muted wind and soft unfolding of ocean spray as waves hit the sand. Her husband's gray Boxster blended into the darkness of the furred trees around the back of the house. Its distinctive outline became visible when she drove in closer.

She spotted below the trees the muted glitter of the night blooming tropical water lily floating in the pond, its brilliant reds blending into the darkening night. She stayed there awhile, not stirring, not wanting to end the spell, nor did she wish to end her conversation with Wilhelm just yet. She killed the engine. Then she tarried outside, moving away from the house out into forest. The last thing she wanted was Stefan standing over her listening to this sort of lustful talk.

"Stefan is expecting me home."

"Then, grit your teeth, come over here, and let me have my way with you. Every woman likes the idea of being forcibly seduced. I'll make it romantic. I promise. Then you can tell him to shove it."

"Look, I have to go. The kids have discovered me. Kisses. I'll talk to you later." She clicked off the phone abruptly, thinking that he must be used to this type of shattered ending.

Hoping to quiet her mind, Shelli entered the house and went into the den, drawn there by the trio of male voices screaming joyously. She felt a burst of pride in the carefully cultivated man-cave atmosphere that she had created there with posters from famous sci-fi movies that Stefan liked, and the kind of furniture that would suit both. It took some time to find the right sofa, something comfortable for Stefan that would look fashionable but also last, handling spills and other mishaps, and she hoped that Stefan appreciated how cozy she made it for him. Outside the window, the yellowish gloom of an impending storm made the darkness of the night appear eerier still. She couldn't dispel a nagging concern that she shouldn't be spilling her heart to Wilhelm, and she wished fervently that Alasdair and Tequila would come back into our lives. They had seemed safer, somehow, less mysterious.

All that occurred to her and more as she stood at the entrance of the room and contemplated Stefan and the boys sitting on the couch squealing like apes stumbling on a trove of ripe bananas. "It's nice to be inside," she said and stooped to give Stefan a kiss.

"You should have seen Larry Johnson's miracle play," Stefan said loudly making her wince. "We're going to the finals, despite Patrick Ewing out with a ripped Achilles, thanks to a four-point play by Larry Johnson."

"Larry, Larry, Larry!" the boys called in unison.

She passed out hugs, stepping back when they wiggled out of her arms and then jumping like she had been electrocuted when Stefan yelled for her to get out of the way of the TV.

She reconsidered her decision to go home. Would she have sounded convincing if she had said she had another interview that popped up at the last minute? She felt deflated after Wilhelm's call, conflicted over her decision to take the virtuous route. But also knowing she couldn't have lied with any plausibility.

"Mommy, can we go to the beach tomorrow?" Seth asked, pushing back long blond hair that had grown past his ears, which he refused to have cut. "I wanna see seals."

"You have karate tomorrow," Shelli said. "Maybe on the weekend, we'll see what the weather is like."

"I wanna go to the beach." Seth stuck his lower lip out in an exaggerated pout. "And see the lightning storms. You promised."

"We have to wait for a storm to happen," Shelli said.

"Plenty of time to go to the beach," Stefan said.

"You guys work on your homework, we'll find time to go to the beach, okay?" Shelli said, "But I can't promise you storms."

Shelli went into the kitchen and flicked on the small TV set mounted underneath the cupboard, switching to the news. Earlier that day a small plane with John F. Kennedy Jr. at the controls crashed into the ocean off the coast of Martha's Vineyard. Radar data showed the plane plummeting from 2,200 feet to 1,100 feet, and then disappearing from the radar screen. Shelli was stunned by the news. The young Kennedy, a dead ringer for his dad, and Carolyn, his beautiful blonde leggy wife, and her sister, Lauren, were presumed dead. Shelli had simply adored JFK's son. He had sex appeal, and Carolyn evoked everything Shelli wanted to be, taller, certainly, and a fashion icon, someone all the guys would fall for. And she had an abundance of hair like her boys. John Jr. was equally gorgeous, and had just started George, an eagerly awaited new magazine, which led to talk among Washington pundits that John Jr. had planned to write highly embarrassing political exposés, an ambitious plan cut short.

She ran into the den on light feet to tell Stefan what she had heard.

"Yeah," he said. "It's incredibly tragic. I heard about it on the car radio coming home. John-John had just gotten his license—it wasn't a full license—he hadn't learned how to fly using the instrument panel. Yet he made the decision to fly on a moonless night. An experienced pilot friend offered to accompany him but he said he wanted to do it alone."

And then he said after a pause, as if this thought had just occurred to him: "You know the Kennedys, from the Paterfamilias Joe on down lived along the blade of a knife. The only problem, when a Kennedy runs a stop sign, there always seems to be an 18-weheeler truck coming from the other direction."

"Not lucky."

"That's why I leave the flying to the experts," he said.

Talking of John-John's death made her heart sick. She went back to the kitchen and sniffled back her tears, patted her eyes, and with her Kleenex to her nose turned the volume of the TV way down. Crazy how the news made her feel depressed, like somehow the misfortunes of the Kennedys impacted her own life. She sought to banish those thoughts of impending disaster and kept getting lost in her task of organizing the ingredients for the sliders she was planning to make. She concentrated on slicing the tomato, onion, cheese, lettuce and avocado, before putting the meat in the broiler, almost forgetting to put cheese on each miniature patty, which she knew would cause a major upset at the table.

At the last minute she remembered to place the tiny buns in the toaster oven, just as her thoughts left the Kennedys and slipped back to Wilhelm. She flashed on that unbelievably romantic conversation she had in the car and she felt her knees buckle. The dam had been opened, her desire for that kind of banter, unsullied by misunderstandings that plagued conversations she had with Stefan washed over her like the incoming tide.

Trying to imagine what kind of life included him as a lover, she assembled the side dishes: a green salad drizzled with vinaigrette and a basket of French fries. Realizing with a start that despite her qualms, she was drawn to Wilhelm like a fish to water, thinking that he offered the kind of sweet interlude that she always yearned for but in the past had found beyond her grasp. He was the kind of man she had often admired from afar but who always belonged to another woman. His good manners and unpremeditated simplicity of dress, whether he wore his gray chinos and a button-down or jeans and his Harvard tee shirt, put him in a class way above her and Stefan. Or so she thought. And that made her pause, was she fooling herself, thinking she had a chance with this guy? She stopped working on the food and stood looking out the kitchen window at the evening sky. Pausing ever so often to check the time, but whenever she looked, she could not see what the clock said; it didn't register in her brain. Her strange disconnect stayed with her, even when consumed with little things, like selecting a chardonnay for dinner, she kept getting lost. She had to stop several times to reorient herself.

After dinner, she raced to finish the cleaning—Stefan rarely helped, and when he did, he was excessively sloppy; she had to re-clean everything, plus his carping about her attention to recycling drove her crazy. And then she joined the boys to sit with them while they did their homework. Afterward they watched TV and Shelli came up with them to their room and supervised the brushing of their teeth. In bed, they played a rhyming game that Shelli knew and tried to come up with one of their own. Seth did an outstanding job, coming up with:

Yucky Chucky was smelly
never took a bath and hardly ever brushed his teeth
Everywhere he went he left an odor in the air
And never combed his hair.

Micah cried that he couldn't think of anything. "Am I stupid," he said.

"No," Shelli said. "Your brain processes information differently. Seth likes to jump in without thinking much about it, and you need more time to work things out perfectly. Dream about what is funny to you and you'll come up with something for tomorrow, ok?"

After the boys fell asleep, she went to find Stefan. He was doing the bills. He saw the charge for the Balenciaga jacket she had just purchased and surveyed it with a look of thunder, eyebrows forming an impermeable berm.

"I want you to return this," he said.

"I've already worn it," she said. "And the tags are ripped off."

"Your salary is half what you used to make," he said. "But you've been spending as if you had gotten a raise."

"I lost my head. I apologize for that. I'm going to stay away from the stores until I pay it off."

"Good to hear. A little fiscal responsibility goes a long way."

That conversation shook her. Shopping was her weakness. She loved clothes, loved trying things on to see how great she looked. It was in front of the mirror that she fought her biggest battles. She knew that once she tried anything on, and it looked good, she'd have to fight the overwhelming urge to buy the garment, most of the time she felt that she couldn't live without that particular dress, or jacket, sometimes it was the shoes that held her captive, and in all of these cases, it took a huge effort to drag herself away. While working at the brokerage house and showered with money, she had become obsessed with labels. And at parties, and even at the fundraising dinners for the charities they favored, she felt inadequate if she didn't have the perfect thing, that piece of fluff that made men's heads swivel. More than once she felt vindicated when a grand dame of the charity circuit came up to her and said, "If you've got it, might as well flaunt it." Part of it was driven by her desire to be admired by her husband, to have girlfriends think her sexy, and to get the attention of men they met on dates. But acquiring these special items became a vicious circle. The more she shopped the more the things she thought she needed to have. Her purchases turned into pressing necessities, as vital to her survival as breathing air; she had become a slave to the chase. And the more she chased, the more she needed the chase. She was hooked on the adrenaline rush, or maybe it was dopamine?

They went upstairs together not speaking. He broke the silence, asking if she had been sulking, and her bridling at the question, thinking his question sarcastic, saying, "Of course not; why would I be?" He said nothing, looking as if he was hiding a smirk, and then leaping the rest of the stairs, quick on his feet, acting on a jolt of energy that she didn't feel, she dragging after, relieved when she hit the flat of the floor. Her gaze on the dense blackness pressing against the window didn't break the glass, amazing her, and then feeling her pensiveness return, silently got ready for bed, and went to the bathroom after him to brush her teeth and wash her face. By the time she slid into bed, she felt that the one with the problem was her. Watching Stefan shed his clothes, dropping them on the floor with complete abandon, she realized he had the power. Her job was to please him, not the other way around. Guys leave their debris for their women to pick up. Women have won the right to work, vote, and use contraceptives, but in the home, she still shoulders most of the burden for the grunt work of cooking and cleaning, and picking the trail of clothes men leave in their wake. But she knew enough not to complain, it was a tradeoff, he made most of the money and it was thanks to him that they could afford their beautiful home, and he did participate in many facets of the boys' lives—she had to give him allowances, given his commute and demanding work schedule. She closed her eyes, thinking she didn't feel like talking and likely he didn't either. Neither did they perform their nightly good night kiss—she remembered but made no move to initiate physical contact—if he had done so, she would have gloried in the gesture, but as she was always the one to do it, she felt it had lost its meaning. But even she had to acknowledge it wasn't as weird as being in bed with one man and dreaming about another.

The next day Wilhelm called her again and said so many naughty things she couldn't concentrate on the two interviews for the magazine she had scheduled. It was good she had all her questions written out beforehand. Nor could she keep her mind on the vultures feeding on secondary markets for a short piece she was doing. The rest of that day she felt alternatively frightened and brazen, although she had done nothing except think wicked thoughts, and yet treading on new (and possibility dangerous) territory made her feel timid. She resolved to take baby steps—her children coming to mind their welfare in her hands. Her marriage might be falling apart, but it was better for her sons to smooth things over.

That evening, Stefan told her he had lunch with John Wickham, and got offered a job with more money at a more senior level position. He told John he needed to discuss it first with his wife, and John heartily approved.

Seven

Shelli and Stefan brought their boys to the JCC around noon to meet the busses to take them to summer camp in Maine. Both appeared to be excited to be with their friends on an adventure away from the parents. Shelli talked to the other mothers and made plans to see the boys on visitors' day. Stefan helped them with their bags and made inquiries to make sure they were on the proper bus.

On the way home, the boys having left on the bus, she didn't know how they got on the topic of breasts.

"Is it so bad that I want to experience someone different? Don't you have fantasies? I've always wanted to screw someone with huge jugs. Doesn't mean I don't love you."

And yet when pressed, she had to admit she was also drawn to the idea of having new bedpartners, and pointed out that there was no one in the queue, but didn't he find it frustrating to be always on the hunt? Wouldn't it be better to have a few steady girlfriends and boyfriends to choose between?

"I love the hunt," he said.

"Sometimes I think it's the weirdest thing, us trying to find new sex partners together, as if we're frat brothers or something."

"It's not any weirder than anything else we do together."

Shelli thought that finding two people they both considered adequate would prove impossible, and was it a good idea to pursue this angle? She would have preferred that they wouldn't be doing it with new people each time, not unless the new people were too wonderful to miss out on, but Stefan seemed mystified by her remark.

"I've been enjoying this hugely," Stefan said. "I no longer care about finding perfect couple. I just want to be turned on for a couple hours."

It was a novel concept, to view men primarily as meat, their function to service her most primal urges. But most of the guys they met didn't turn her on, nor did she want to engage in stupid conversations with people she didn't care for, yet she agreed to join Stefan in meeting a few more random couples to humor him, and minimize the flak.

The rest of the day she worked in her home office and started piecing together a story from her notes, but her mind strayed. She would have liked to call her boys at their camp, but calls were forbidden, she would have to wait for the letters the counsellors had promised that the kids would write. She longed to hug them and kiss their sweet faces, experiencing a monetary twinge remembering their expressions as they hugged her goodbye, Seth telling her he and his friend Matt were planning to ride together on the bus, which had Micah looking like he wanted to cry, his eyes narrowing and mouth turned down—but Shelli quickly asked Micah to buddy up with someone else not his brother. Micah put on a brave front and said he would pair up Ben, the friend who knew the names of many obscure diseases. It was cute to see the kids so excited to be on a trip together. Off and on, she thought about Wilhelm, reflecting on the flash of sunlight on his pale hair as he turned to talk to her, and the way his eyes crinkled when amused.

Midafternoon, Wilhelm called. She picked up the phone, feeling a sudden burst of energy and paced the floor, talking. It was the perfect opportunity to get some answers to the questions crowding her brain. They talked for about an hour, touching mostly on his yen for showy cars and flashy boats, subjects that delighted her as much as she knew her husband would have been turned off by their mention. She loved having someone she could talk to about all kinds of frivolities, with an emphasis on what was in and what was out. Their conversation had nothing to do with lust. Or maybe it did. She needed to know where the mask ended, and the real person began—just how much of his story should she believe. Why this mattered right then she couldn't say, except that truth and integrity were important to her. She went past the bathroom and stopped there to study her image in the bathroom mirror. Gleaming back at her, two shining ecstatic eyes had established dominance in her visage, her naughtiness exposed for all to see. She was not so timid anymore, something else stirred her blood. She was breaking all the norms of good behavior that she had been raised to be. She didn't know how or when the change began, but she realized that her thoughts no longer revolved solely around her children and Stefan. Somewhere along the line, her attention became bifurcated—although her boys were still her top priority—with Alasdair, and then Wilhelm, and now Stefan was simply another guy she bedded, although she still felt love for him, she was more aware of his shortcomings, and less tolerant of his game playing. And these days she didn't anguish over the trials and tribulations of her children in the same way she used to, when she had no one else to think about.

Was this how the Europeans did it? She had heard that they have a revolving door of lovers, marriage more of a business than a love affair. Children handed off to nursemaids and governesses. Would she care for her children as much if other people were raising them? In any case, she had gotten used to having someone new to think about. She decided she had to see more of Wilhelm in different situations. The question was how long before he let his guard down, and the real person emerged, even the flaws.

Through the window, the heat of the sun in an iridescent summer sky bore down and warmed her with a meteor's intensity, causing her thoughts to spin lazily like dust circling the air. This room was her signature piece, her pride and joy, the outcome of months traipsing New England and upstate New York to shop for antiques, playing the role of interior decorator. She surveyed the rich color palette that she had put together in the room, taking pleasure in her exquisite taste, pausing over the period pieces, the Edwardian hall seat, and the wooden Mahogany sideboard.

Wilhelm boasted that he could give her an experience few other men were capable of. "I'm the new man," he whispered. "I know how to seduce a woman. I hold her hand, I touch her, and I tell her sexy things. And I ask questions: do you like this, do you like that? Men in Holland, they know how to do this. In America, men don't know how to approach women. They're too stiff and macho to put themselves out."

He liked watching other men fuck Camila, and it turned him on to take her afterward, still reeling from the man she had just been with. He said he was on the lookout for big cocks for his woman, cocks measuring at least as long as his eight inches. Shelli had never heard anything like this before. When she told him this, he backtracked, saying he wasn't just a sex junkie, oh, no. He let slip that he liked to see the latest theatre, equally happy with opera as with burlesque. He talked Pinter and Ibsen too.

He asked her if she would see him soon, he was dying inside. He said the truth was that Camila had never satisfied him, she was just a woman to date, no one special, someone to have orgies with, nothing like Shelli had turned out to be. She wavered; doing so would entail sneaking around and wouldn't qualify as swinging—Stefan would never approve of Shelli going solo to meet Wilhelm—rather that would constitute an affair in the old time-honored way. She was sorely tempted to simplify things and simply have an affair, but she hesitated to do that right off. Keeping an affair secret would take some doing, and she wasn't sure she could handle the stress. At no time did she back away from her plan to keep her marriage and children her top priorities.

It wasn't a moral or religious code that stopped her. Shelli suspected that many of her beliefs have been mandated by the powers-that-be, whether it was government or religion, both of which tend to condone behavior that doesn't make a person happy, but helps hold society together. Society doesn't care how this suits the individual, as John Stuart Mill says in *On Liberty.* Social progress can only take place if limits are placed on individual liberties, but Mill also believes a well-run society would necessitate the freeing of the individual from such limits, particularly if these individual freedoms aren't hurting anyone and nets the individual a measure of happiness. Mill advocates individual initiative over social control, and asserts that things done by the individual do much to advance the mental education of that individual, something that government action cannot ever do, for government action always poses a threat to liberty and must be carefully watched. Shelli would say the same thing goes for religion, which often stands in for government, and has often wielded the same kind of blind power.

Meanwhile, her platonic lover displayed a knack for observation and analysis, reserving his emotional outbursts for what he considered to be the mercenary nature of modern art, a subject that didn't interest Stefan. She masturbated, listening to Wilhelm's sexy voice, feeling the heat in her groin while listening to Wilhelm talk about the current practice of blurring commercial fashion sensibility with a fine art aesthetic which had become way too popular, citing Juergen Teller's rich glamorization of the vulgar, the strange, and the disturbing, something Wilhelm called the new iconic. His favorite examples were the photograph of Bjork devouring or upchucking black spaghetti (depending on your point of view) and Teller's sandwich shot of former Spice Girl Victoria Beckham's legs hanging out of a Marc Jacobs bag. The idea of it stirred her.

A flash in the shadows outside as a furry thing lunged through the bushes and shook everything around. Then all fell still, as if all the forest creatures had been playing a game of hide and seek. Looking past the roses—strangely wilted in the humid air—Shelli heard Wilhelm mention his boat again. She didn't like this direction, thinking she wouldn't like being away from land for the hours that he required, but perhaps boating would be more fun than watching basketball with Stefan. The biggest drawback: it would take at least one hour to get out and one to get back at a minimum.

Still, for all her brave talk, she wasn't entirely comfortable with her situation. Everything seemed too much. All she could think about was having a bern so intense it made every cell of her body scream with pleasure. The thought nagged at her that she was one of those women who fall for any good-looking guy who says he wants her. She let off her playing with herself to ponder this new idea. Was she looking for more punishment, a masochist? Why did the desire for illicit sex follow her everywhere, invading her home, chasing her in her dreams? She wondered would she have enjoyed their tête-à-tête as much if they hadn't met under the auspices of group sex, with the corresponding tension that underlay all their communication.

Wilhelm said something about meeting up later for coffee. She talked more often to him, it seemed, than she spoke to any of her friends, including Mattie. She dealt with her momentary prick of concern of what this implied by telling him she couldn't meet for coffee that day. They'd have to put it off. She had too much to do before nightfall. And in the back of her mind, there lurked the fear that if they did meet alone and had sex, it would be the end for her and Stefan. And that would be too heavy a weight to bear.

A few days later Stefan texted his supervisor, reminding him that Stefan would be late to work, he had an appointment with his dentist, and wasn't sure when he'd be in, providing him with a cover for his plans to get together with an exceedingly buxom woman he and Shelli had met earlier that week at a meet and greet. Though her husband Ecuador was a strange one, always gracing sentences with statements like "Holy Guacamole!" but otherwise not interesting, just another socially inept scientist to neutralize with his wit. He didn't understand how Ecuador ended up with a woman like that. Someone so va-va-boom, lighting all his fuses. Not a typical pin up, more like what Marilyn Monroe might have looked like had she reached her fortieth year: a soft blonde, going heavy in her haunches and waist, but what drew Stefan, her creased, kindly eyes. Stefan had gotten Kay's phone number after learning from Kay that Kay's husband, Ecuador (the screen name he used), traveled for work often, and right then decided he would have an affair with Kay, but he had a different story for Shelli, telling her that he'd handle arranging for the four of them to hook up upon Ecuador's return. And to be fair, Stefan had planned for them to get together—all four of them—but it turned out Ecuador was leaving in a few days and they would have to wait at least a month to schedule anything. Then Stefan called and learned that Ecuador was on his way to Mexico. Since then Stefan was in such in a lather to see Kay, he hadn't been able to sleep, and deluged her with text after text, and countless emails, saying that he had no patience with waiting, and to have pity on him. Ecuador was planning to spend a month doing marine research in international waters with a team of graduate students, leaving Kay at home alone with their elementary age child. Kay said she would meet him for coffee to discuss getting together as a foursome, during the hours her daughter would be away at summer day camp between 9 and 3 o'clock.

Stefan texted Rick at the last minute to say he overslept and had to board a later ferry. Usually they rode the same ferry, but Stefan preferred to do this trip alone on this day, knowing he couldn't hide anything from his best friend. He had a habit of revealing too much, his face an emotional roadmap, neon signs posted everywhere. He couldn't escape a vision that kept invading his thoughts: the two of them joking about sex, because of course his mind would be on sex, and he'd start telling sexual jokes, or laugh too much, or blurt out the truth and have to cover it up, causing Rick to guess what was going on.

Kay said they could meet at a coffee shop near her building, but Stefan asked if they could meet at her place first. She readily agreed and said there were only two condos at the penthouse level, so privacy wasn't an issue, and met him at the penthouse on Fifth and 79th that she shared with Ecuador and their young child.

Approaching her in the doorway it was if his eyes were being controlled remotely, his will power erased. He felt flushed all over, his hands shook in his effort to stop himself from reaching for her breasts.

"You're magnificent," he said, sobbing his desire.

"Woo cowboy," Kay said. "So eager. Come inside." She closed the door and said, "You like some pot?"

"Now you're talking," Stefan said, his voice dropping to a purr, his face pricked by a humorous greed, a wordless question.

Stefan caught a whiff of her perfume, a heady floral, and stared at her luxuriant rear end, reveling in the sway of her hips. It was all he could do to suppress the desire to caress that curvature of flesh, and place him between those trembling globes. He never dated a woman this heavy, never held a woman of such abundant proportions, the heavy tits and thighs that curved out like a fertility goddess, nothing linear. In the past, he preferred to go out with slim women for myriad culturally embedded reasons that if he teased them out, he would find shame in the practice. Chiefly he liked how they looked on his arm, craving the approval of his friends, and hoping to elicit envious looks from his father, but he didn't acknowledge that until now he felt more comfortable with heavy women. It was a revelation, born of Kay's beauty. His mother at one time had been heavy, and his sister early on had a thing for pasta and sweets, her weight riding a trampoline.

The room they had entered, rectangular, furnished simply, a couple of couches and chairs around a round coffee table near a large window overlooking Central Park. Childish toys scattered throughout. A faint rumble of traffic could be heard below.

"I would offer you a drink but it's too early for that."

"I'll stick with coffee."

"How about a shot of Bailey's in your coffee?"

"Sure, with cream." He moved to the fireplace, and idly looked at the pictures on the mantel. The mantel was crowded with them, mostly pictures of their kid. She came back and handed him a mug of coffee.

"You never told me what you do," Stefan said.

"I did, don't you remember, we joked about that? I'm responsible for the online classes at the university. We have quite a roster these days, amazing how many people do their studies online."

"Right, I guess my head was too muddled to remember." He sipped his drink.

She filled a small handheld pipe that looked like a piece of hand-blown glass artwork striped in primary colors. With a practiced hand, she handed it to him with a lighter.

He took a long draught from the pipe and held it in. Kay pulled down his pants and proceeded to blow him.

"Stop," Stefan said. "That feels too good. Have some of this pot."

She sat up and took the pipe. The smoke swirled around them in lazy arcs. The smell of skunk filled the air.

Time stood still; sounds from the outside seemed to recede, he couldn't hear anything but the sound of his breath, and hers. She took his hand and said 'Come' and led him to what she said was the guest bedroom. It was obviously not lived in, nothing on top of the dresser, the closets were bare, but the queen-sized bed was made up with fancy pillows sporting elaborate, highly erotic embroidery, mostly scenes taken from the Kamasutra. The shutters were discreetly closed. She fell on the bed.

"You've fucked others here." His interest briefly checked by this discovery, and then realizing, what did it matter.

"I always change the sheets afterwards and scrub everything with Lysol."

"Including your pussy?"

"Of course."

He moved on top of her and began toying with her nipples, playing and teasing, the sensations growing more intense the higher he floated in the heavy, dampening, euphoric cloud that engulfed him. They fell into a sixty-nine. Stefan was amazed the amount of flesh he held in his hands, this woman had no bones, soft as a down pillow, yet a tiny element of fear wormed its way into his consciousness. He hoped he could satisfy her. He had never met a married woman who openly professed to fucking guys in this fashion, so free and easy, as if sex were merely something to be enjoyed like an ice cream cone.

Stefan thought back to one of the wives he met at a holiday party at the firm, having introduced himself to the husband who happened to be a new hire, and the enjoyment of getting the man to laugh at his jokes while he checked out the wife, Stefan showing appreciation with nods and winks, all the while wearing an idiotic smile. The woman wore the most revealing top, the shape of her erect nipples poking through the thin fabric. A lot of wives that way just begging for someone to satisfy their most lustful urge, husbands not capable.

After a pause, Stefan asked: "Does your husband know?"

"We both play around when he's away, but we rarely talk about it."

"I didn't tell my wife that I'm meeting you today. She can't handle it."

"You didn't tell her that we're meeting to fine-tune you mojo? Tell her it's strictly in a professional capacity; tell her I'm your therapist."

"She's jealous of shapely women. She knows I secretly prefer them."

"That could spell trouble down the road."

"I'll tell her when you tell your hubby."

The air was heavy, smelling of Kay. The temperature inside felt like a tropical heat, or perhaps a better description: a heater on overdrive. Outside the building the normal traffic sounds had receded, they must have been in the back of the building. But the sounds of a bus making a p-p-ssss sound as the automatic bypass safety valves went to work to maintain the air pressure sounded magnified. Stefan moved over Kay's magnificent body in a delirium. He felt privileged to be at that moment suspended in air above her.

Mostly Stefan liked Shelli's athletic body and her ability to last forever, she was inexhaustible, but there were small things that grated on his nerves. He had complained to Shelli many times about her pubic bone grinding into him during intercourse. Stefan felt none of that with Kay—she was like an ocean liner, there was no point that he felt bumps or imperfections anywhere, her legs meaty hams between which he had to strain to get inside, a couple of times he slipped out. He couldn't throw her around, and she wanted him off almost immediately, but curiously, neither could he continue it. Yet he liked the change, he was certain it was not possible to feel anything but pleasure with this woman.

In the back of his mind, there was the thought that soon he would have to shower and dress, and head downtown, and that put a damper on his mood. He tried to hurry things along, perhaps not the best policy when you're trying to make nice, but he also wrestling with a certain amount of anxiety, which made him less solicitous of her needs than he might otherwise have been.

He looked out a window that faced 79th Street, and she said casually, "You know Michael Bloomberg? He lives over there in that perfectly exquisite Beau-Arts limestone."

"The white one?"

"His place is bigger than Rupert Murdoch up from us on Fifth."

"That's exactly why I moved out of Manhattan," Stefan said. "I could afford this neighborhood if I took the job I was offered yesterday—I'm thinking to do it—but not if it means giving up my free time to be with my children."

That night, Shelli served roast chicken, mashed potatoes and peas. And listened to her husband ask questions of the boys, but her mind kept slipping to the last conversation she had with Wilhelm, despite her efforts at trying (and failing) to get a conversation going with Stefan, the King of Conversationalists. It did not seem to matter that her mind was elsewhere; Stefan seemed equally preoccupied. After dinner, she saw a text from Wilhelm notifying her that he wanted to call. Overhead, a heavy, dense blanket of clouds cast a bleak pallor over the entire known world, completely obscuring Mount Mitchell. The oppressive gray led her to wonder if there had been a mountain there once, or had she imagined it. Her eyes traveled to the trees rearing up below the house and to the thin layer of fog that lay on top of the bowl of the water like granular whipped cream. At times, especially at night, the fog got so thick the Indians used to say that at night Ellis Island disappeared below the waterline. On reflection, she could understand why they'd say that. To the right, below the clouds, a dense growth of dark green thrust skyward, their tips disappearing into the gray marbling, her silent friends calming and soothing her fears, making things seem less bleak. But it wasn't just the trees that made her feel this way. She looked down at the yard to see how the roses were faring; they looked droopy, their petals gone. Seeing that put her in a bleak mood.

Frequent conversations with Wilhelm had become a compulsion, a driving need. And when she was not speaking with him, she was thinking about what she would say to him when they did speak again. Most of the people she knew did not talk so frankly about everything—not even Mattie. And she was careful not to tell Wilhelm the exact nature of their relationship, or how she and Stefan got along, nothing outside of sex. No reason to give Wilhelm false hope.

To avoid any awkwardness, if Stefan was around she wouldn't pick up the phone, preferring to wait until she could find a hidden place somewhere to return the call. As she did so, her heart would beat a thousand miles a minute, and as soon as their calls would end, and she would start looking forward to the next one. When she was not on the phone with him, she was thinking about their last conversation and brooding about what he looked like, musing on the square jaw, the tousled flaxen hair, that little smirk in the corner of his mouth when he spoke. The more he called, the more her desire for him grew. Mostly the temptations roiling her nerve endings sprang from her fevered imagination, even so, all around her, good-looking men popped up, tantalizing her. She only had to poke her head outside to see Trevor, the neighborhood hunk, mowing his lawn, for a slow burn to move over her body. Several times a week, he was out there dressed in cutoffs, his beautiful torso exposed. Just then, right after she got off the phone with Wilhelm, she spotted Trevor making his way across his lawn, which fired her up as if she had been struck by a thunderbolt. For a mad moment, she fought the impulse to cozy up to her neighbor across the way as he puttered around his yard and run her hands down his taut chest and those cut thighs. At old moments, in the middle of her feverish imaginings, she thought about her boys and felt guilty, almost like she was not being a good mother thinking like this, and in an effort to snuff her uneasiness, she ran to her office and looked for the camp website for photos, and saw a couple of photos that showed several shots of both of them in a game of dodgeball, and that reassured her somewhat, seeing that her motherly instincts came up like a geyser, threatening to bury her in hot tears. But even with her continual thoughts of gorgeous men, the unseen presence of her children was never far from her mind.

Inside the restaurant, its interior aglow in pastels, the smells of fragrant cooking stirred the air. Shelli spotted Wilhelm waving furiously near a bank of windows fronting the ocean, his smile warm and inviting. She liked the way he stood, angular and loose, a man in tune with his body. At their approach, his face loomed up, craggy and lean. He hugged them in turn as if they were old friends. Camila was just as open. Shelli breathed in the sweet floral scent Camila wore and took her to her bosom, enveloping her in a big hug. They were meeting because Wilhelm had posted new pictures of Camila, which Shelli had been grateful for, pictures that made her look ultra-sleek her sumptuous ass breathtaking. Stefan said he might have been wrong about her. Shelli felt victorious having talked Stefan into meeting them again to see if they might click.

Camila brushed her platinum hair back from her forehead; feathery wisps that fell back into her beautiful baby blues marked by thick lines of kohl. She wore a diaphanous dress of pale shimmer and on her feet, delicate gold sandals, her legs moving as she were keeping time with an invisible melody, reinforcing the sense that she was something extraordinary, a nymph, perhaps, sent by the gods to entertain them. Shelli thought this time Stefan had to succumb, how could he not?

Wilhelm complimented Shelli effusively, calling her beautiful and sexy. She'd always been a sucker for compliments, and preened like a prom queen being fussed over by her minions, but she took care not to look overly long at Wilhelm, or look like she wanted him, she didn't want Stefan to feel that Wilhelm was any threat, focusing her attentions instead on Camila.

"I'm glad you consented to be with us this evening," Wilhelm said.

"We're very picky," Stefan said.

"We're the same," Wilhelm said. "We need to connect mentally and emotionally as well as physically."

Shelli's heart swelled she didn't trust herself to say anything. Camila seemed equally interested in Wilhelm's call to friendship, nodding vigorously when he said they wanted to be with people they could spend time with, and not just in the bedroom.

"We want to be friends as well as fuck mates," she said.

Although Camila spoke rarely, when she did, her bell-like voice rang with conviction, compelling those around her to listen. Her warmth and humor drew Shelli in, and it looked like Stefan felt the same way.

They shared some appetizers—garlic shrimp and calamari—and a round of martinis. Wilhelm suggested they leave as soon as they finished the appetizers, and Stefan seemed particularly eager, bolting a few shrimps and his drink in one gulp, and urging the others to do the same. On the way out, Stefan pulled Camila along, making her laugh.

Outside the restaurant, stopping to watch a troubadour dressed in black tails set up with his cello in the middle of a crowded sidewalk, waiting through a rendition of a plaintive folk song, while dodging vendors pushing everything from falsely labeled purses to hijacked porn movies, and working their way through the crowd. Around them, groups of teenagers sat, paper and charcoals scattered around, trying to sell their sketches of passersby. Some were busily drawing; others simply chattered the day away. It did not seem to matter what time it was; there were always people thronging the streets. Shelli took mental note of a young man with dark, curly hair posing as a dancer, his arm wrapped around a woman as skinny as a telephone pole, the two intertwined like they couldn't get enough of each other. She looked at them longingly, thinking she wanted more of that in her life. That part of her relationship with Stefan had quieted to a low murmur and now they no longer felt that raw passion born of hunger. They no longer clung to each other like lovers do in that *amour fou* stage. And when she thought about it, she realized that he had always been somewhat aloof, she had never aroused him to the point where lust is secondary to a genuine meeting of the minds, their understanding of each other had always been superficial; there was never a deep understanding. She realized that now. And like most relationships, somewhere along the way, that sense of want had been replaced by something else, the feeling that their bodies had become too familiar, and sex became more about finding ways to deflect the sameness of it, the monotony. In fact it seemed to have evolved into soft core adversarial.

Wilhelm offered his house half an hour south of them, not far from the Deal Ocean Club on Monmouth Drive. The exterior of his dwelling was undistinguishable from the run of tastefully landscaped houses around him, plain and understated. The windows fronting the house faced the ocean, and at the back, facing east, a garden spanned the property with high hedges all around. Inside Shelli breathed deeply as if to absorb into her lungs the twelve-foot ceilings and high windows, along with the scent of roses which came in from somewhere. On walls painted a muted array of colors yellows, lavenders, reds, and pinks she tried to make sense of the array of artwork blazing brilliantly like a parade of peacocks—memorabilia from other lands, tribal masks, and primitive carvings.

They crowded into his kitchen to prepare drinks, laughing and talking comfortably. Wilhelm kissed Camila. Shelli and Stefan looked on. Not to be outdone, Stefan lifted Camila's skirt and ran his hands along her thighs. Shelli kept busy filling everyone's glasses with ice, vodka, *limoncello*, and a slice of lime to each. The air crackled with electricity. Wilhelm and Stefan led the way to the living room and out to the deck looking over the water. Shelli and Camila put their arms around each other and danced together, while the men whistled and hooted. The women looked great together, both in full sexual bloom bursting with life.

The men sat balancing their drinks on the wide arms of their chairs facing the Atlantic. Shelli sat down in Wilhelm's seat, squeezing between him and the edge of the chair, saying there was ample room. Her thigh rubbed his, sending electric currents up her body. He ran his hand along the inside of her leg, adding to the prickly sensations. She didn't know why she felt so nervous; she hid behind a dense curtain of eyelashes and surreptitiously admired Wilhelm's strong, fit body and those defined arms.

"Is that new?" Stefan asked. His eyes settled on her dress, his eyebrows forming a cement-like berm.

"Yes," Shelli said somewhat frostily, and turned her back on Stefan, wishing he'd disappear. Her leg continued to radiate heat under Wilhelm's palm.

"Didn't I tell you to stop buying clothes?" Stefan said.

"Can you please argue about this at home?" Wilhelm said.

"It cost $50 on sale," Shelli said.

"I bet," Stefan said.

"I was with her, and I can verify it was $50," Camila said.

"What were we talking about before Stefan rudely interrupted?" Shelli said, trying to stop the trembling in her voice, her underarms heating up like geysers, determined to put this fracas in a back cupboard of her mind somewhere, and return to the topic at hand. "You met where?" In trying to keep her voice calm she felt the edges cracking like parchment paper that had been in the oven too long. She wished Stefan would stop embarrassing her in public like that.

"After I'd been with Wilhelm, I couldn't stand the way my husband made love," Camila said quietly from her perch on Stefan's lap. "He was a terrible kisser and didn't like foreplay, and he was only comfortable doing it doggy style. I didn't realize how disconnected and passionless that was until Wilhelm showed me what was possible. Sex with him has been magical."

Stefan began lightly stoking Camila's arm.

"We stayed in that room for three hours, talking and fucking. Being with him felt so intimate and wonderful and close, I knew that was what I'd been missing all my life. But there came a time when everyone else had gone, except my husband and the hosts. We had to part, and I went home with my husband."

Stefan continued to slowly stroke Camila's arm, his eyes unfocused, mouth slightly ajar.

Shelli didn't know what possessed her. The hand holding her drink was shaking; she tried to relax and not to appear disconcerted by what she saw happening in Stefan and Camila's chair.

"I liked my husband, but I felt no passion for him."

"You couldn't fix what was broken between you and your husband?" Shelli said.

In the corner of her eye she saw the flicker of a frown on Stefan's face and wanted to get down on her knees and beg him to relent. Couldn't they backtrack and make it right?

"He's a chef. It's his whole life; it's all he thinks about. I worked at the restaurant as many hours as he did, keeping the books and waiting tables. But to me it was a job, to him it was everything. The restaurant wasn't enough to hold me to him. A few months after I met Wilhelm, I told my husband I couldn't live with him. He didn't like what I had to say, but he was quite nice about it. He didn't yell or try to stop me. I packed my things, took the dog without any interference from him, found my own place, and filed for divorce."

The shock of that word "divorce" hit Shelli with the force of jackhammers. Something was wrong between them it was hard to imagine it was only her spending habits. What happened through the years to change his opinion about her? Was it her leaving Wall Street? They used to be friends, but no more. She looked at his face and knew if she asked about it later he would call her weak and say she was playing the victim card. When they should be making each other delirious with happiness, and making their children feel loved and secure. But there was nothing she could say to counter Stefan's assault on the worst of her female tendencies. She had no choice but to follow out this script.

"Are you ready to go inside?" Wilhelm interrupted, adding crisply, "Stefan and Camila can have my bedroom." He looked at Shelli. "We get the spare room. It's quite comfortable."

With a sideways look at Wilhelm. "I'm game," she said, her heart quickening.

At this moment looking at the hard face Stefan presented her in passing she knew that it was possible that he planned to throw her under the bus. Likely they were falling apart and headed for a split unless she did something, it was up to her. Likely it didn't matter how many kugels she made or the nature of the blintz she made for the family. At her first attempt to prepare the dough (the chief difference between crepe and blintz dough is simply a ratio of eggs to flour) the dough had been too thick because she forgot to add more butter. He said that goys can't get it right it doesn't matter how hard they try. And then he got on the phone with his mother to decry the way she massacred the blintz, making Shelli out be this blundering oaf. In his defense, the next attempt was perfect, and he said so. Shelli was gratified to hear him acknowledge that she had the recipe down, but the memory of what seemed to her a mean-spirited hazing that mother and son foisted continued to fester. She had to work herself back to a pleasant mood. She thought about how men like the ancient Greek god Heracles who could rape and impregnate fifty in a single night as he did with Thespius' daughters, and become their slave as he did with Omphale, but he could never absorb a woman's wisdom. The combination of force and intellect isn't enough for a man to get to the higher level of consciousness. He needs a woman's help, and empathy would go a long way to resolving this bugaboo about her love of costumes and bring harmony to their lives. And now Shelli needed to erase memory. She asked Wilhelm if she could have another drink and calmly noted Stefan's dancing eyes and his appreciative smile directed at Camila as he ushered her upstairs. Stefan was leaving with Camila and that soon they would fuck. Everything about that seemed natural and right. The way was clear; Stefan and Shelli would both have fun separately, and whatever happened as a result of their newfound freedom would have to be okay. Life was unpredictable. She could only hope that Stefan would treat the kids well whatever happened. This was as good a time as any to get used to it.

"Sounds good to me," Stefan purred.

Camila ran her hands through her hair, making her blonde strands stand on end. Stefan touched Camila's arm and they disappeared upstairs in the blink of an eye.

Shelli went with Wilhelm into his light-filled kitchen to stand at the wide granite countertop and watched him make two stiff drinks. They shared a joint.

"Don't let him rattle you," Wilhelm said. "Clearly that's what he intends."

"He's dragging me though this swinging thing to prove a point. He wants to see me suffer."

"You've got to rise above it. Otherwise this wouldn't work. Otherwise I probably should drive you home. I'll do whatever you want."

Wilhelm stared at Shelli, his eyes openly questioning, his brow furrowed. She met his glance, and remained as still as he, barely breathing.

"I want to be with you," she said, and drank from the watery confection.

He lifted his drink, clinked it against hers. "Good." He took a long drink and nearly emptied his glass.

Seconds ticked by, but she didn't hear anything other than her blood rushing through her veins and the pounding in her ears. When it came to sex, she had always been shy around strangers. This realization wasn't a surprise for her, but she hadn't expected to be overcome with stage fright in this intense way. She had hoped to be over this sort of thing, but there it was, a visible presence, stopping her from taking control. Not knowing where to look. Maybe it was the heat of her eyes on him that caused him to flex his muscles unconsciously, without conceit, moving involuntarily like a puppy would do. Should she strip with her hips flashing the rumba, or rush over and kiss him madly? Maybe he liked his girls demure, looking innocent and virginal rather than on active display. He did not move or say anything to indicate what he wanted. He just stood there, his eyes twinkling, a small smile playing at the corners of his mouth, as patient as a mountain. His smile emboldened her red-tipped fingers. She took off her dress, feeling the soft air kissing her skin and smelling the heavy scent of the flowers growing outside in abundance below the deck, and worked the bra she wore as if guided by a puppeteer, first playing with snaps, then moving the top back and forth as if the cloth had been wound too tightly and the puppeteer was afraid to rip it. Wilhelm's smile widened, giving her courage. She brushed aside her sadness and took a deep breath and plunged ahead, pulling everything off but her panties off.

Naked, they drew together. She liked the way he placed his beautifully shaped arms around her, protectively, like her father used to do, and the way he kissed her gently, not at all like her father. Wilhelm explored the inner reaches of her mouth with a practiced tongue. Soon they were touching each other all over, their fingers and the palms gently rousing the faint hairs on arms and legs, lips brushing skin, body temperature rising, her mind numbed from the sensual pleasure of touching, the prickly sensation from the heat of his skin warming her very essence. She tried not to let the sadness she felt overwhelm her.

"You feel toasty," she said.

"You too," he whispered.

She tried to go down on him, but he stopped her, something that Stefan would never do.

"Let me lead," he said. "I like to be the dom."

She puzzled over his need to claim this title. Wasn't the guy always the dom? She certainly preferred the submissive role, so no problems there. When it came to foreplay, she liked to initiate moves some of the time, other times taking a passive role, and all the while helping to further and heighten her pleasure, and hopefully his. For the ancient Greeks, more used to the pleasures of male bonding, and leading separate lives the passive role was suspect, concealing a malignancy. She began to stoke Wilhelm with abandon not caring about what he said about being the dom. Then an image of her husband intruded for some unexplainable reason—something about the way Wilhelm turned to her, leading to thoughts about her sons and suddenly she felt strange about what she was doing with this man and what this meant for the stability of her marriage and was she playing with fire. A sorry outcome indeed if she did anything to upset her sons' security and their feeling of being loved by both parents. Thinking about them ruined her pleasure, and she stopped thinking about her sons. It was something to ponder for another day, as she didn't want to let her thoughts about her children ruin her good time or screw things up for everyone— pining for them wouldn't advance her children's happiness, or make things better with Stefan. And where's the harm in lying with a lover that's already been spoken for? It's her choice, or his, or theirs. Some creatures crave the full palette of love on a temporary basis and she was merely there providing it. She turned into the rainbow, the shapeshifter, or the doppelgänger of their desire, and tried to make an effort to placate the brute in them. At some point, she did not know how long they'd been lying together; it could have been hours, or even days, in the midst of all this joy, she felt a fragile touch on her arm and heard a scraping near her ear. She turned her head to see Camila kneeling next to her with Stefan right behind her.

"Can we join you?" Camila asked. Streams of mascara ran down her flushed cheeks, and her tangled hair rose around her face in pleasing disarray.

Shelli stifled the urge to tell Camila to bug off. "Sure," Shelli said, her mood sinking down to the pit of her stomach, knowing that Camila wanted to get back with Wilhelm, and thinking that Wilhelm was, after all, Camila's man.

"Get your strap-on, honey," Wilhelm said.

Camila pulled out a long, dangling, black silicone affair affixed to a leather apparatus that she placed around her middle, buckling the strap with a practiced hand in one uninterrupted flow. The phallus looked ridiculously long, like it had been designed for Greek comedy. The little vixen moved toward Shelli, wagging her hips, the silicone bouncing roguishly, her eyes glowing fluorescent like a tropical noontime sky.

"What do you want me to do?" Shelli asked, curious about this device she had read about in Stefan's *Playboy* magazines but never seen before.

"Just lie there," Camila said. "I'll do everything."

The blonde kitten bent down and placed her small, delicate lips on Shelli's mouth. Shelli felt like she was kissing a mirror image of herself. The other woman's body felt nearly identical to Shelli's, just leaner and more petite. Although Camila was shorter by nearly three inches, the women shared the same angular features and muscular frame, physically similar in so many respects. Shelli ran her fingers along the other woman's cheek and down her swan neck to her beautiful sloping shoulders, marveling at the incongruity of this delicate creature hoisting a simulacrum of a male's appendage and affixing it to herself like a barbaric sword. What thoughts ran through this woman's mind as she inserted that wickedly huge dildo inside Shelli? It didn't look comfortable at all, but Camila insisted she was getting pleasure out of it.

Together they moved like two fluttering birds, lighter than air. Wilhelm and Stefan watched silently. The two men didn't acknowledge each other, but there wasn't any visible tension. Wilhelm's cock was still hard and listing to one side, oozing pre-come, but Stefan's cock had shriveled up like a prune, and that made Shelli lose some of her enthusiasm, but she decided to ignore Stefan and just have fun.

Shelli squeezed Camila's hand. What if they become lovers—she could still feel the press of Camila's delicious lips, the full softness. But as much as Shelli liked Camila, she longed to return to Wilhelm. It was obvious that Stefan was not interested in sex at the moment, he looked bored; his eyes were elsewhere, and she felt she had been dissed by him, and stung by his lack of enthusiasm. As soon as Camila was finished with Shelli, Wilhelm jumped on Camila and started fucking her, madly, passionately, with great abandon. No more slow stuff. All the constraints had been lifted.

Shelli tried to hide her dismay, but she couldn't completely wipe away the sorrow that splattered her face. It was visible, she knew, in the clamp of her downturned mouth.

"You look so miserable," Stefan said. "Guess he didn't do it for you, huh?" There was triumph in his eyes.

"Stefan, honey…" Shelli wanted more. She would have liked to have Stefan's arms around her.

"Let's go home."

Shelli stared at Stefan, dumbstruck. Her disappointment eclipsed everything else. "Really?" she said, pausing to steady her voice, "Maybe I can revive you. I've worked a similar magic before." She went down on her knees.

Stefan covered his groin. "I've had enough, I'm tired." His eyes, muddy pools, tightened into pinpricks. "Get off your knees, unless your intention is to scrub the floor." His voice had a clipped edge to it.

Obviously, Stefan didn't care about her needs. She went to gather her clothes. She wondered what was happening to them. She felt that she was finally getting a taste of what swinging was about, and her hunger knew no bounds, but Stefan didn't care what she wanted, it was all about him. She forced herself to push that thought out of her mind; she didn't want to be the woman who is never satisfied, always complaining. She had something invested, like Stefan, in not thinking deeply about what they were doing. The thought popped in her head that she was the one who was being selfish. She had had ample time with Wilhelm and had come more often than she had in a long time. And yet her lust had grown like a tumor to monstrous proportions and would be as difficult to eradicate. She also thought if Stefan had shown her a little attention and had shown her some love, maybe she wouldn't feel so needy.

On the way home, they sat in the darkness, entombed by the car, neither one saying anything. Stefan turned on the radio. They learned that navy divers recovered the bodies of JFK Jr., his wife, and sister-in-law from the wreckage of the plane, crushed under 116 feet of water about eight miles off the Vineyard's shores. Shelli silently mourned the loss of America's crown prince, an especially poignant sadness given the relentless string of tragedies that have haunted the Kennedy family over the years.

"So sad," Shelli said her voice breaking.

Stefan turned the channel.

After a time, she found the words she needed: "Couldn't you tell I needed more attention?"

"I didn't want to say anything in front of Wilhelm," Stefan said in a timbre befitting a funeral. In the dimness, she searched his face and saw consternation etched in his knotted brow. "But I couldn't for the life of me hold off. I came a few minutes of entering her. But she was a trooper. She worked me over, and got me hard again, even as I kept wilting. But I was so ashamed; I couldn't hold my head up. That's why I didn't want to stay."

'Oh, sweetheart, I had no idea."

There was one hitch: she realized she didn't want to stop being with Wilhelm, not when things were starting to get interesting. Part of her was happy that Stefan was experiencing this difficulty; likely women wouldn't be all in a lather to steal him away if he was like this with others. But on the other hand, she felt sorry for him. Men are expected to perform. It's all on their shoulders.

A silence fell.

And then she thought, say he learns to relax and can last as long as he wants, how does that change anything? But whether she spent money or not, the likelihood of him fucking her after having had someone else seemed as remote as her winning the lottery—she remembered how he was after Tequila. And if he performed well, he'd be more in demand, and how did that help her? In either case she'd have to forgo sex with him, unless he got a boost from somewhere. Perhaps if Stefan stepped up his workouts his body might start producing more testosterone, and then not only would he be able to last longer, but his desire would rise, too, and maybe he would want her right after being with another woman. And maybe he wouldn't get as irritated as often. But even if she could get Stefan to sign on, it would be a multi-year project. He'd have to grow new muscle first. There were no quick fixes outside of a pill.

"There's always Viagra."

"I don't look forward to having a hard-on lasting four hours. Guys tell me it's uncomfortable. There's got to be another solution."

At home she went into their office and instant-messaged Wilhelm.

Shelli: You were distracted, so we didn't say goodbye. We didn't think you'd mind.

Wilhelm: Your guy wasn't into it?

Shelli: No.

Wilhelm: I don't see what you see in the guy.

Shelli: You haven't seen his sweet side.

Wilhelm: I guess you want to raise your kids together.

Shelli went upstairs to change and bumped into Stefan stepping out of the shower, water still clinging to his hair, smelling of toothpaste and spring rain. She went up to him and sought his lips. Their contact was brief, cursory, not the passionate embrace she had hoped for.

"Remember at Wilhelm's house you got mad at me for buying that new dress? What made you bring that up?"

"Don't you have enough dresses?"

"Even if it's true, why do you talk about me like that with our new friends?" Shelli allowed her irritation to come through. "Why set up these meetings, if you're going to ruin everyone's mood?"

"I don't know…I got annoyed all of a sudden."

"Well, I'm staying away from the stores."

"Good."

Filled with nostalgia for the time when things seemed to flow so much easier, the time the boys were young and they both were so full with the joy of learning all about these small persons, at a time Stefan didn't seem to care for any other woman but her, those days when he would say that when she was on her period he didn't want sex, his libido had taken a nosedive, he fell in with her cycles. Tears in her eyes, she went to the computer and looked at the camp website. She found several more photos of their boys, and called Stefan over to see, hoping they could reconnect through their mutual love for these beautiful people they made together. Stefan gazed upon the photos, mutely overcome, seeing their happy faces, flushed with their athleticism. The photos showed Micah playing goalie in a game of soccer, and Seth as an attacker, sliding in to take the ball away from another player.

Stefan was in a good mood all week, although they didn't have sex that week or the next. He kept saying that he was too tired from Camila. Shelli called this their second honeymoon phase. She didn't go into any stores or look at the women's magazines, even avoiding the fashion section of *The New York Times* lest it enticed her to want new things. All that week she became uncharacteristically attentive, asking if he was hungry or thirsty, bringing his treats and drinks unbidden. He responded by buttering her up: "You have a sexier body than Camila. But I like having a new woman occasionally, do you mind?" He asked Shelli to step up the search for more hotties for him to screw. She told him she was on it. In any case, she wanted to see Wilhelm again and soon. Or perhaps any number of men with personalities and brains like that. The train had departed from the station, and there was no way could she stop what they had started.

Stefan found a spot to stand in the middle of a subway car, heading on an uptown express, literally wall-to-wall people, every inch occupied. He remained aware of the people around him; there were pickpockets, some of them blending in with the office workers, everyone a suspect. A man shorter than five feet with narrow shoulders like a child but with an old face came up, Stefan recognized him instantly as the man posing as a living statue who did his performance art at the park at Union Square; he stood out in a town filled with interesting characters, his act, a combination of mime and dance, was not to be believed. The little man was dressed in white paint with a greenish tint to resemble statues long exposed to the elements, with a layer of baby powder to create the texture of a sculpture, his body wrapped in a grey cloth. Stefan gave him a passing glance, trying not to stare. New York people respect the privacy of anyone whether well-known or not. Yet people gave him space. The air felt like a pressure cooker, hot and dense, permeated by the faint smell of urine overlaid by the temporary and intense presence of cologne and perfume whiffing by. Bankers' trim haircuts and long grave withholding faces over thin well-cut gabardine suits, mostly gray or navy, and women in tasteful short sleeve dresses of all colors and the occasional suit, their faces preoccupied, hair coifed, heading for skyscrapers of midtown and downtown. The occasional grafter appeared, mixing with short order cooks and back office people, street people who lived by what they could sell on the street or the drugs they delivered to the office workers. He imagined scores of messenger boys carrying packages filled with cocaine for the office parties later that afternoon.

He looked forward to seeing Kay but had it with Kay and her excuses. He asked her to give him a time that worked for her, so they could make their usual once a week, but Kay told him one thing, and then another, and then she had to break her date with him, saying she couldn't miss that much work. He didn't object, wishing to be considerate of her needs and act new man, although he had been terribly disappointed both times. He hated getting the runaround. They made another date. He texted the day before to make sure she was into it, planning to be totally accepting if she wasn't, mentally preparing himself for her to change her mind yet again. It's a woman's prerogative, he said to himself. But the next time he asked her, his heart wedged tightly in his throat, she didn't postpone, oh no, she assured him that everything was on, and he couldn't stop his heart from swelling, his spirits shooting to the moon and back. In his text, he said he couldn't wait, thinking that would be a safe thing to say, conveying his excitement in a nonaggressive way, demonstrating his desire to play nice. His fingers trembled as he typed a message to her in his phone to be posted when he got above ground, and his breathing grew raspy in his throat. He pictured her breasts swinging in his face, nipples at attention, and wrote that he wanted to play for hours with them the next time he visited, but he didn't forget her words warning him against falling in love, that first time, when he kissed her in a frenzy of emotion, saying "I love you," that she blurted out: "I will never leave Ecuador, so disavow yourself of that notion."

He got off the subway, his brain a mishmash of conflicting emotions mostly positive. To take his mind off his mounting excitement he stopped at a news stand below ground and scanned the headlines, but the news didn't engage him; he had a passing interest in Waco, and then there was the bomb that exploded in Moscow, Russia, killing roughly 119 people. He paused over the story reflecting the aftermath of the discovery off the coast of Martha's Vineyard of the bodies of JFK Jr., Caroline, and her sister, what that might have been like at the exact moment of death trapped in fuselage, plunging into the ocean. The horror of it impacted him, and yet paled next to the images crowding his brain, seductive images of Kay's rump. He got so mesmerized in his imaginings that on the concrete steps leading up from the underground, he almost lost his balance, and a tremor lighted up his forearms, a feeling akin to pins and needles. He turned to look down into the abyss, shuddering to think he could have broken his skull. His giddiness vanished, and he forced himself to pay attention to what he was doing.

Waiting for the light, he posted his comments on the phone and she immediately responded texting that she was looking forward—reading this was like a jolt of electricity to his brain.

The cooler air outside refreshed his sweaty skin. In his excitement he ran all the way to her building, only a few blocks. Yet his exertion made him sweat profusely despite a chill in the breeze, rivers of sweat collected everywhere, his brow, his sternum, and spinal cord. The front door kept opening letting in people and gallons of hot air. The amount of foot traffic that day astonished him. He asked the doorman if it was always like that. The doorman said it was typical, always people and more people. It turned out Key asked the doorman to have him wait, saying she had gone out on a quick errand that turned out to be quite a long time, at least twenty minutes. In middling heat he lifted his arms up as if he was stretching and yawning, wanting to air out his armpits. He would have liked a shower. He sat helplessly on a couch in the lobby looking out the window at passersby, thinking he was wasting time doing nothing when he could be doing all sorts of other things, not all of them sexual. And when Kay finally came in, Stefan felt irritable, ready to explode. He had been so accommodating, but if there was one thing he hated, it was to be kept waiting. She ran up to him, all apologies, and gave him a hug, saying she had run out of several toilettes including toothpaste, so she went around the corner but there were people in line, and had to dodge people on the street walking slow. He looked at her heaving breasts and pressed himself against their soft mass, and accepted her kiss, but inside he remained disgruntled. He had come a long way, and he felt running off to the store was inconsiderate. He told her he didn't mind her sour breath. He after all was a sweaty mess. At the very least, she could make up for it by falling to her knees and give him head in the elevator. But a totally unappetizing woman stepped into the elevator and put the kibosh on that idea.

Stefan recalled what the yogi master had told him in the tantric arts class: "Breathe slowly," the wise one counseled, "Your body will calm." He found it difficult to slow his breathing, having never tried. He felt that to do so was a monumental task, too big for one person, it took a village. He needed someone to guide him along the way. Kay's disappointment was etched in the slant of her eyes and crumpled mouth. How mortifying. How deflating. How reduced. He knew he came too quickly with everyone, except Shelli, the outcome of being extremely bored, and which explained a lot, and infuriated Stefan. What was it with him? He wanted to give himself a stern scold. He had to admit that he was a slave to his emotions. His dick looked laughable, like a wizened root vegetable that had been left out too long. Kay said not a word of complaint; she got to work on his sorry excuse of a sexual tool, laboring over it for many moons until slowly, lugubriously. It began to show signs of life, but to grow big and stiff enough to do the job took some doing. He surmised that Kay was not enjoying their time together as fully as he would have liked. He thought she was just doing humoring him because she felt she should, and that made him feel crummy. But she kept telling him it was fine. And it took him much longer the second time around to come, thanks God and she said it was worth waiting for, and could he please lighten up already? He told Kay the reason he was so sensitive about it, his wife harped about it continually, and gave him a complex about it. But then he looked at the time and felt anxious that he had overstayed. He tried to calm himself, but he didn't think he was successful in masking his stress, probably transmitted that in subtle ways. Just before parting she said she couldn't meet him, coinciding with Ecuador's return, which beat all. He raced out of there, thinking he was getting sick of all her bullshit, she wasn't worth it.

He got to the office shortly after 1 p.m., thankful he could merge into the people returning from lunch, but no one remarked on his tardiness, so he didn't need to trot out any crazy stories about his fabricated dental appointment. Pandemonium reigned everywhere on the floor everyone had gathered around various computer monitors to dish on the Time

Warner proposed merger with AOL for $164 billion. There was a lot of speculation about this; everyone agreed the strategy sounded compelling. AOL was at the head of the pack as the dominant player, its sky-high stock evaluation had been bid up by investors looking for a windfall making this fledging even more valuable in market-cap terms than many blue-chips. As justification for the merger, it was said that Time Warner had tried to establish an online presence before this time and had failed. But if they completed this purchase, they would instantly have tens of millions of new subscribers. Looking at it that way, quibbling about the price might seem irrelevant, particularly when everything management ever wanted would literally be in reach. And AOL would gain access to Time Warner's cable network as well as adding a layer of user-friendly interfaces on top of the pipes. Stefan trotted out his considerable pitching skills, bringing his large personality to task, and got behind selling shares in the newly merged company, working the phones like a junkie needing his fix. But in truth, it was an easy sell. He kept quiet about the negatives: the insiders who said the cultures were not compatible. From what he heard, the Time Warner people were repulsed by the arrogance they saw displayed by the AOL people, and sabotaged the newcomers at every opportunity. And the whispers from the tech community predicted that the always-on and faster broadband, which at the time only had three percent of the market, would someday overtake the slow and cumbersome dial up service, played havoc with his pitch when he allowed himself to analyze the situation. He bet on the broadband, an obvious play.

Eight

Shelli went to her Thursday evening appointment with Dr. Weinberg in a somber mood, missing her boys and feeling neglected by Stefan. She dressed in a way that would appeal to the doctor, a pudgy man who looked like he wore the same shirt and pants every day, adopting the facade of the quintessential suburban soccer mom, donning the preppy, athletic look as if she had been born with a ball in one hand and a racquet in the other, no hint of her extracurricular activities: an innocent looking sundress to the knees, with flats, her ponytail done up like an elementary schoolgirl. She wore no makeup other than a hint of mascara. If anything, she thought she would wake up the doctor's nascent fantasies, keep his dreams wet in the wee hours of the night.

He made comforting noises, held out one arm, and bowing, ushered her into his office. Sinking into the overstuffed chair she favored, she spilled her guts out, ending with a self-accusation: "He can go a full week, sometimes more, without wanting sex with me."

The doctor leaned back in his armchair looking every inch the professor in his white button down and cream-colored khakis. "Is he under stress at work?" he asked, the shadows cast by the lamp on his desk dancing across his face, one white leather sneaker bobbing.

Shelli blinked at him, realizing that she had no idea. "It happens after he's had sex with other women," she said, and paused. At the blank look on the doctor's face, she said again, "After sex with other women…" She put the stress on the phrase *other women* while looking at him in exasperation, and then added meaningfully, "After that, he says he's too satiated to do it with me."

Dr. Weinberg looked like he was going into cardiac arrest. His face turned red and his eyes bulged a little. To give him a chance to recover, Shelli looked around beige furniture lining walls the color of vomit, pausing at each of three pictures of the seashore, among other calming elements.

"He's having sex with other women?"

"We've had sex with a few couples, yes. What they call partner swapping."

"Ah." His lips barely moved. He looked stricken. His eyebrows shot up to the ceiling.

Shelli's eyes flitted past the bronze statue of the Buddha, and over to the shelves filled with academic treatises and textbooks, (*Marriage and Longevity,* and *Marriage, Family and Relationships*; but what caught her eye, *Understanding Sexual Addiction*). After that she looked everywhere but him.

"You do this in the house with your children there?" he said, his voice flat.

"No, never in the home."

"Good."

"He says he comes too soon for the woman. He's embarrassed and wants to run out of there pronto and yanks me away leaving me wondering what we're doing there."

"Oy." He shook his head as if to clear the cobwebs there. "That makes no sense. Why is he's engaging with other women if he's suffering erectile dysfunction?"

"He thinks screwing new people will help," Shelli said. "He tells me he can't stay married without having a revolving door of new women, but he doesn't want to have affairs. He says I have to be part of it."

After a pause, Dr. Weinberg spoke in a whisper, comprehension lighting his face: "What do you think about it?"

"I'm thinking there's nothing in it for me. Nothing."

She neglected to add how much she enjoyed the hunt and loved screwing the other men she'd been with. She couldn't make this admission in front of the doctor and expose her base animal cravings. She still carried vestiges of the mother's antipathy towards the sex, the registered nurse who reluctantly after much hand wringing brought up her sexual problems with her physician and relived her mother's shame when she found she had cervical cancer. Contracting the disease was a sign of God's displeasure with her, and she redoubled the time she spent on her knees, praying. Shelli had absorbed some that reluctance. The therapist's good opinion mattered to her very much.

"I see." His shock was palpable. He looked like he had stopped breathing, the color draining out of his face, normally a rosy tint. A heavy, leaden silence descended. Seeing that Shelli had made her point, she sat back in the chair with a sigh. Eventually his life force resumed in a raspy bid for oxygen.

"Sounds like you two need to sit down together and really listen to each other, if your marriage is going to work."

"That's what I'm thinking too," Shelli said, with a rapid blink of mascara. "There's no solution, other than to stop meeting other people for sex. That's what I think in the cold light of day. But the truth is I'm hooked just as much as he is." This last sentence slipped out unawares. She wanted to take it back, but it was too late. To her relief, he didn't react.

"I'd like to see you here together." His eyes flicked at the clock on the wall. "Time's up. I'll be at a conference all next week. Does two weeks from now work for you?"

"Sure, Doc."

She exited the doctor's office and took the elevator down from the top floor. The new glass and chrome Riverview Medical Center was surrounded by parking lots that stretched out like an asphalt desert on one side and the murky Navesink River with its odor of dead fish on the other. Shelli was used to seeing dead fish in New Jersey's rivers and wrinkled her nose in a silent protest while walked through the rows of myriad, grimy metallic and chrome vehicles, looking for her car. She felt the doctor understood the gravity of the problem, and she respected his intellect, his training, and his habit of not holding back. He told her exactly what he thought, no sugarcoating. This gave her the feeling that something wonderful would come out of the discussion that they were bound to have with the therapist as moderator. If their marriage could be saved, he would save it. Shelli raced home feeling that a burden had been lifted from her shoulders, merely by articulating the problem thoughtfully and coherently, even though so much of it had been left out, and having the therapist listen with intent—her words circulating in the cold light of day where everything is visible to the naked eye—lifted her spirits so much so she felt giddy, even though no solutions had been broached.

Stefan was out in the garden, weeding under a wide expanse of blue sky. Weeds cast to the driveway offered a plethora of the spinally and grotesque. The work of cleaning that up and packing the compost would go to her. She went up to him, breathing in the moist sweetness of flowers, their primal exhalations everywhere dancing a rumba lifting to the late afternoon sun, part of the divine molecular dance of all living things, nature's music bringing gladness to her soul. She reached for a kiss. With the imprint of his lips emblazed on hers, she knew with a certainty there remained a vestige that could be salvaged from the tattered remains of their love. But they had to be equally invested. In relationships usually the woman, rarely the man leads in this enterprise. The woman makes concessions to keep the relationship in good working order, and if necessary, she's the one to initiate repairs. The man can be adventuresome, have multiple affairs, and while his wife may not like it, but she has been told this is how men are programmed, and she may look the other way. Society will respect his fearless fickleness, his overabundance of testosterone, and lead women to see him as gifted in bed, witness Mick Jagger, who at 73 doesn't lack for dates, having left his 29 year old lover who just had his child for a 20 year old, and no one accuses him of bad behavior, although he's had eight children with five women. *In his comic opera Cosi Fan Tutti, Mozart insisted that women all do it, but a far more common belief is that men all do it: "Higgamous, hoggamous, woman's monogamous; hoggamous, higgamous, man is polygamous." In Nora Ephron's movie Heartburn, Meryl Streep's husband leaves her for another woman. She turns to her father for solace, but he dismisses her complaint as the way of all male flesh: "If you want monogamy, marry a swan."*

Women are counselled to keep their legs tightly closed; otherwise they pay a hefty price. The cockaded man is considered weak, unable to keep his wife in check. Shelli heard a therapist say that infidelity is the sine qua non of divorce, but what about when husband and wife agree to swing or indulge in open marriage?

Stefan bent back to his weeding. Shelli would have liked to see him stop his work, and continue with their embrace, but he pulled away. She hinted at this, stretching her arms out like a cat, yawning, feeling like all she wanted to do find a place to settle for the day and be petted. He looked up, frowning, like all he wanted to do was work the soil, a farmer at heart. She told him about her visit to Dr. Weinberg. He promised to go with her on her next visit to the shrink.

"Maybe he can prescribe something?" Stefan said.

"Doesn't hurt to ask."

"In the meantime, time's a wastin'." Stefan cried, rubbing his hands. "Get your gardening gloves on. And tonight, you've got a job to do, lining up more hot dates."

It dawned on Shelli that Stefan wanted sex with every female but her. She longed for the simple days when all she had to worry about was finding interesting things for them to do on Saturday nights as prelude for a night of lovemaking. Things had turned complicated lately, everything uncertain. But there was one thing she was certain about: she knew she could never give up Wilhelm, so she had to make allowances. She imagined herself living like Anais Nin, with two husbands. With a life for six months in New York and the rest of the time with the other husband in Los Angeles. The New York husband didn't know about the other one. And it seemed to work out for her, but then she didn't have children. For the next hour, they worked, side by side, not talking much, coaxing ornery roots to give up their hold on the earth, sometimes they clung so hard, Shelli had to hack at them with a garden knife and trowel. The task involved patience which she bridled at but steeled her jaw and worked it. When they were done, she gathered the pulled weeds while he went into the house to clean up. She remained behind, putting away the tools, something he never did; he always left it for her, same with the dishes and vacuuming.

On her way back into the house, her cell phone rang. The voice on the other end had her stumbling in panic, her underarms heating up like a sauna and her feet dancing a jig.

"Why don't you come tomorrow with me on the boat?" Wilhelm asked. "We'll take a little ride up the coast."

"I'll ask Stefan."

"Why'd you want to tell Stefan?"

"That's what you do when you're married."

"Can't you do anything without clearing it with him?"

In the end, she said nothing to Stefan, too rushed to get to the docks the following morning. She drove like a madwoman to the marina and ran out to the docks, straining her lungs, gasping for air on the lookout for Wilhelm. He stood tall in a heavy sweater and jeans, his pale hair glistening in the watery sun, his face suffused with the languor of indolent afternoons, and his flat Dutch cheekbones evoking a long lineage of Northern European ancestors, the Saxons and the Frisians, and the Franks, especially most pale among them, and his hazel eyes reflected the ocean and sky. Shelli jumped on board, her brain filling with images of his engorged cock, and the memory of it filling her to bursting, but didn't want to appear to crave it overly much, or be too pushy. She thought it best to appear to be on the fence with it, mildly seductive but with only the whisper of a changeling mood, and attempted to corral her libido, despite it coming out in weird ways like the way she stuck her chest out and wiggled her ass at inopportune moments, and then settling for a quick bear hug and brush of lips.

They pulled out of the dock. He had her put on a thick wool sweater much like he wore, despite it being late July, usually the hottest period of the summer, and on the docks, the heat only slightly mitigated by the breeze, telling her out on the water it would be cold and windy. He gave her a tour of his Catalina 30, which looked to be sleek and well maintained, and promised to give her a quick lesson in how to balance and showed her by example how to shift her weight at every turn and to duck the boom when it passed over the boat before they headed out of the harbor, rocking gently on steel-blue waters, moving away from the rim of dunes shining as white as elephant tusk, skirting the honed edge of ocean where it met the shore. The wind whipped her body with brute force, making her catch her footing, invading her nostrils, coating her eyelashes with a salty rim, and tangling her hair in knots.

Wilhelm asked Shelli to handle the wheel and left to do something on the other side of the boat. The wheel quickly spun out of her control. He took charge. She liked the feel of his lean frame and his lips brushing her ear, causing electrical currents to course through her veins and buzz the ends of her fingertips and toes. Her heart papoomed with love and admiration. His confidence and skill a turn-on.

On one hand, she rejoiced at his attentions, and on the other, connecting with Wilhelm scared her. She felt unsure of the boundaries; they seemed to blur and change every time she checked. Even after having had sex with Wilhelm in a past encounter, she felt uneasy about doing anything behind Stefan's back, everything seemed portentous, multi-layered. She freaked out when he tried to kiss her, and then tried to cover up her dismay by playing coy. Playing hard to get, she reasoned, isn't that what her mother had counselled her, better to string them along, so they wouldn't lose interest? He gave no indication that he saw anything amiss; his face reflected his calm and his honey flecked eyes remained bemused, although they appeared at times green reflecting the blue of the water and sky. He went back to adjusting the sail with a smile tugging at his lips. And when the wind picked up, he leaped around the boat, adjusting lines, leaving her with the wheel. Vainly she struggled to maneuver but everything she did was wrong.

Each time she tried to call him back the boat tipped and pitched, throwing her off balance, and each time, the cold wind whipped her hair around her face, stealing her words away, plugging her mouth. And when the wind died down for a moment, it was the unceasing battering of the waves against the boat that drowned her feverish outcries. It seemed that nature itself conspired against her and rendered her mute. He must have heard something, as he made haste to scramble along the length of the boat, agile as a monkey, bent on rescuing her. She watched him maneuver, unable to meet his eyes for fear he would see the lust there, uncomfortable with the feeling that she was the one doing the seducing, and all the while throbbing with desire. She was happy when Wilhelm took over the wheel giving Shelli the chance to relax and gaze upon the beauty around them and surreptitiously observe Wilhelm manage the boat. The undulations of shoreline where the trees grew dense, marked by a dark green line with sharp ragged tips, seemed far way. The shore turned mysterious, trees partially obscured waterfront estates. Above them, the enamel-blue sky stretched out like a vast bowl, pierced overhead by a white gull hanging motionless against the breeze, its feet tucked up into the translucent blue fire that seemed to go on forever. Over the roar of the waves, he took the opportunity to lecture her on the superiority of European craftsmen. She told him she had done some research on yachts for a magazine article, and while acknowledging his point, added a side note, saying that Italians were considered the best designers of yacht interiors in the world, but the man who currently holds the title as most outstanding was a Frenchman, *Rémi Tessier.*

"Are you rich?" he asked, changing the subject as if as an afterthought.

"My husband makes money." she felt her eyebrows tighten. "I make a pittance."

"So you're stuck." What next came out of his mouth was not at all what she expected: "You're stuck with the mortgage, bills, maintenance. You can't go more than three weeks anywhere before everything starts to fall apart."

She shivered, the cold air nipping at her exposed skin. Conditions on the open sea were chillier than what she had expected, and blustery. She had to hold onto a rail to avoid getting pushed around, her hair a bramble bush, stomach churning from the boisterousness of the waves, salt spray constantly misting her face. Her time out on the boat could be interrupted as ruggedly romantic, but not at all the sensuous romp she had envisioned. The wind was unremitting.

"Does that not describe your situation as well," she asked.

"Oh sure, I think for most people…Are you thirsty?"

"Yes."

They went inside. She pulled off the sweater she was wearing. It felt heavy in the closed confinement of the cabin. Her arms, newly freed, felt bare, ticklish. The pitch of the ocean sent her reeling against the counter. She ran her hand over its smooth, sensuous wood, an exotic cherry, and marveled at the galley, a miniaturized beauty. He forgot about getting her a drink, reaching instead for her breasts, brushing her nipples lightly.

"I'd like to take a couple of pictures of you to look at when I'm alone. Would that be all right?"

"Of course."

She unbuttoned her shirt.

"Leave it on."

She danced around him with her shirt flapping open, her heavy breasts bouncing. She held them up for his inspection.

"Sexy." He pulled out a camera with a zoom lens and began snapping pictures, saying, "Shake'em."

Fired up, her nipples on fire from her caressing of them, and wanting him to play with her breasts, she ran up to him and put her hands under his shirt, struck anew at his relative lack of chest hair, so different from Stefan. Besotted with memories, a sizzling hotchpotch, Shelli leaned against him. He put his arms around her. "If I start touching you now, I'll turn into a raving lunatic, and possibly eat you alive. I need a drink first."

"Yes, let's prolong the agony."

He poured them a drink he called Genever, and described it as a blend of neutral spirits, juniper and botanical infusions, with a rich, funky distillate of malted barley, rye, and other grains. He said the best way to drink is called *kop-stoot*, meaning head butt. He poured two small tulip glasses of chilled genever. Set them down with two shot glasses of beer. He drank first the genever and then the beer. Shelli followed suit. The genever had a slight aroma of juniper and malt wine, went down easily, tasting like the love child of gin and whiskey, imparting a warm glow to her chest.

"There's nothing more American than that," Wilhelm said.

"Weren't the Dutch the first to colonize America?"

"You owe us big."

Shelli asked about his life. He said he had raced sailboats in the Caribbean, and he described some of the islands he visited, and praised the biscuit air of the tropics, their warm, turquoise beaches and gleaming sands. He preferred to make love in hot, sticky climates, where the mind and body slow to a luxurious crawl.

"I'm turning up the heat in the cabin." He went to a far wall and fiddled with the instrument panel.

She asked about the other women in his life. How many women was he seeing currently? He opened a cupboard and pulled out four fat photo albums neatly stacked. He opened one and took her on a tour of its glossy interior, pointing out pictures of several beauties, saying they were all in love with him. He stopped at one, the prettiest of them all. She looked to be about twenty, but he said she was thirty, a fashion designer. "She was good for me, but she left me for another man. I've never gotten over it, not really, not until now." He turned to me. "In the past, every time I looked at her picture, I used to cry. Now I can say that without tears."

He turned several more pages, a faint smile broaching his lips, and downed the rest of his drink. Shelli did likewise. She felt a pleasant buzz. Interesting that he kept a record of his conquests. Shelli had a few pictures of past boyfriends, nothing as organized as this, a shine to past loves, immortalizing memories. She wished she had taken more pictures of the good times, not so much the headshots, but the interactions with good friends.

Shelli opened another album, one that looked frayed around the edges. The pictures were grainy, and the colors faded. He said he started taking these pictures when he was in his early teens in the Netherlands. His first was ten years older, a sexy brunette with laughing eyes.

"Women find it easy to fall in love with you. It's the way you fuck them."

"Yes, I'm the master."

"Do you do it the same way with all of us?"

"The way I use my prick is the same."

"But that's not all of it."

"Most men don't bother learning what women want. Or if they do know, they're not prepared to give it to them."

"What would you say to me if I were a man and wanted to learn how to treat a woman?"

"First, I ask them about themselves," he said. "Revealing oneself to a sympathetic listener is a basic human need. At the end of the day, everyone wants to be understood and appreciated. And I love all kinds and sizes of women. But something has changed. I don't want other women anymore; I see them and think about you."

He paused and put away the albums. Then seeming to underscore his previous remark, he placed his arms around her and brought her close holding her as if she would break. "I don't want these others any longer. All I can think of is you and my desire to be with you. I want to kiss and hold you in my arms forever…it's more than a simple case of lust. I can talk to you in a way that is very personal, and you don't make me out to be a bad guy, you accept me the way I am, including my flaws. I've never experienced this."

"What about Camila?"

"She's like the rest, a diversion, someone to enjoy for the moment, but she never mattered to me."

"You're drunk."

"Do I look drunk to you? Feel my hand, as steady as a rock. I need more than that to get toasted. And since I'm steering this boat, I'm not going to go there."

"And I matter to you?"

"So much it hurts. I could see myself married to you. I've never asked anyone to marry me, except that other woman, the fashion designer who left me. But no one else has inspired me to want marriage. Not until now."

The enormity of what he said slowly sunk in.

"But I have to tell you everything. I have a child. A son. Six years old."

"And you're a good father to him?"

"I see him whenever his mother gives me permission. She's not easy to work with."

Shelli glanced at the clock on his wall. "I need to be home in two hours."

They headed back, talking of trivial things, avoiding the subject of them as a couple. Even so, rubbing shoulders, metaphorically speaking, with this engaging, gorgeous man felt bittersweet. Her longing for things that now she knew was possible filled her to bursting. But when she drilled down to what bothered her about her situation, things became more convoluted. After hearing Wilhelm's declaration of love, her emotions seesawed from one extreme to the other. Disengaging from Stefan would be a big step. Was she ready to do that? Foremost, she had to consider her boys. She thought it best not to say anything to Stefan. She would act as everything remained as it had been, and test herself in the crucible of a real-life scenario to see what she felt about Stefan, were they truly finished or just hitting a rough spot? The sort of arrangement that she had with Stefan was difficult to maintain, since they started swinging she was always watching what she said, how she behaved around him. He seemed particularly sensitive these days, prickly even. She had never seen anyone do it successfully, although she did meet a triad at a meet-and-greet swingers' party, two women and a man who lived together and said they had this crazy thing going. The third wheel, a female, was there for the woman, a bi-sexual married to the man, although the man sometimes fucked the third wheel, too. They said both women fucked other people, a mix of both women and men, but the man only did it with his wife and her lover. They said this worked for them but didn't provide clues as to whether they were all of them truly happy with their arrangement.

At the end of their trip, when Wilhelm had tied up at the dock, erotic warmth infused their sweet, too-brief kiss and filled her with all sorts of contradictory emotions, yet she felt relieved that they hadn't done anything but kiss. She wasn't sure if she could handle going home afterwards and not give everything away. She was drawn to the idea of a double life, but she also realized that she was not ready to take on the deception that entailed. Before Shelli leapt off the boat, Wilhelm grabbed her hands, calling her smart and beautiful. They kissed again, a quick brushing of lips. She lost her footing, feeling as disoriented as if she had stepped off a conveyer belt. For a moment she didn't know where she was, it was like she was drowning in a heady brew, put out by the quartet of happy neurotransmitters: serotonin, dopamine, oxytocin and endorphins. She drove home, laughing and crying both.

At home, still feeling slightly disoriented from the Dutch cocktail, Shelli hugged Stefan in her usual fashion, enveloping him in her goodwill, and saying nothing about her day, and asking about his in the most solicitous manner. For all he knew she had worked at the office like she had originally intended. He responded with a few quips about the adman mixing up handout for a conference he was helping to orchestrate. Shelli smiled to show her appreciation and headed to the kitchen to make guacamole for chips. She folded in chopped chilies, onion and tomato and doused it with lime, and pouring the blue corn chips into a large bowl as if she was on automatic, guided by remote control, then bringing everything out to the den. She joined Stefan in watching his favorite basketball team, the New York Knicks, sitting on the other end of the couch and thinking about her boat ride and feeling changed somehow, but she fought to maintain a semblance of normality.

The Knicks had been on a winning streak and were scheduled to play the Lakers at Staples Center. She knew there was bound to be celebrities ringside: Leonardo DiCaprio, Jack Nicholson, Charlize Theron, Selena Gomez or Drew Barrymore, sometimes even David Beckham or Khloe Kardashian showed up. Often Jeffery Katzenberg and Steven Spielberg would sit together, and a couple of times she spotted Dustin Hoffman somewhere up front. But always DiCaprio and Nicholson, they were regulars. Seeing the beautiful people was an easy fix. That was one thing she and the celebrity-obsessed Stefan could agree on, though she thought he took it a bit far, memorizing all the movies each of his favorite actors had starred in, and fixing on small details of their lives, reading all the celebrity worship books he could find, and sometimes quizzing Shelli, who never knew anything about their goings-on, and then making hay out of her lack of interest, saying it proved she wasn't smart. He laughed at her when she said she didn't want to junk up her brain with that sort of useless information. She thought it was weird, this preoccupation about movie stars. But it was just one of those things she accepted about him, although it irked her that he took umbrage that she only participated in his hobby tangentially. He was unduly proud of his ability to remember all sorts of trivia. She heard him boost to friends about how much he knew of trivia concerning everything produced by Gene Roddenberry for the Star Trek TV series. For instance, he could recite "Ode to Spot" a poem by Data to his cat, Spot. Same thing for Star Wars movies, Stefan studied the plot lines and character roles like he was being tested on it.

Occasionally, she paid attention to the game, taking time out from her book when Stefan pointed out a celebrity. He was hardcore about his sports, thankful that he asked her to not to talk during the game, she was afraid if she did start to talk without restraint, the dam would break, and she might tell him what she did that day and reveal all of it, including her fears and secret desires. If she did, things would not go well, she was sure of that. She asked herself about this, and realized a soul searching might bring up questions she wasn't ready to face, such as: if she was serious about her marriage, shouldn't she tell Stefan they needed to end this experiment? That she was in danger of falling for another guy? But she quailed at the thought and put it out of her mind. She couldn't bear losing Wilhelm. So that boat ride became her little secret, along with the rest of it, but they hadn't done anything on the boat and she had broken no vows—and yet the fact that she was unwilling to tell Stefan what they talked about made her assume that its very nature was suspect.

With a start, she realized that she hadn't checked the mail that day. She went out to see what the mailman left her and yes there were two letters addressed to Mr. and Mrs. Matson in childish scrawls. She opened the letters.

Dear Mom and Dad:

I like camp. It's pretty fun. People are nice here. I'm learning sword fighting and I'm getting really good. I beat everyone except the teacher, Amit. He was in the Olympics. And at night an astrometry professor went with us at night to see stars. We saw lots of them.

I'm learning archery, too.

Oh and I like the kids here. We're having fun but I still want to come home. I'm homesick.

Seth

Mom and Dad:

It's okay here. They keep us busy doing stuff. The food is good. But I miss you. When can we come home?

Micah

A commercial introducing the Apple iPod was on the telly when Shelli entered the room. She watched. "Looks cool," she said, "they shrunk the computer, bet you they sell a lot of those," and handed the letters for Stefan to read. "Check this out," she said.

But he seemed annoyed by the interruption, like all he wanted was to get back to his game.

"The house feels empty without them, doesn't it?" Shelli said.

"A little quieter, yeah." There was a note of reluctance in his voice, as if loathe to acknowledge that he missed his own sons.

She read the letters again, and left Stefan sitting on the couch, his eyes riveted to the TV, saying she would be right back. Scurrying out of the room, clutching the letters to her breast, she went to look for a box in the garage. She thought sending a care package with a pack of cards and some treats, their favorite cookies, and corn chips, the kind of healthy snacks easily shared, might be in order. In their shared office she wrote them a long letter telling them how much she loved them and missed them, and asked that they try out the camp another week and perhaps the homesickness would pass, she said if they still felt homesick in a week's time she would come up to the camp and they'd figure out a solution that worked for them. She encouraged them to try to put a positive spin on it, be outgoing; do things to make the time more enjoyable. It made her feel better to take this action, that somehow her caring for their happiness and agonizing on the proper way to convey her message of hope would be transmitted to them telepathically even before they received their first letter from her.

Wilhelm texted saying he wanted to call. It was a nice feeling, being a married woman and juggling men like a circus performer. She laughed to herself, to think that she knew intuitively how to offer succor to all stages of manhood.

The first words out of his mouth were, "You deserve a good spanking."

Shelli decided to play along. "Why? Have I been naughty?"

"I'm going to get a whip that I will use just for you."

"You wouldn't hurt me…"

"You know what I did with another girl, not Camila? I put a belt around her waist when we were doing it doggy style, rode her like a horse. Do that with your husband. Have him put a belt around your waist."

"He doesn't like to play like that. He doesn't like whips. His dad used to beat him with his belt, and he hated that. He doesn't even like to wear belts."

"All the better. Next time I see you, I'm definitely going to spank you."

He asked her to meet him alone in a bar during the week after work, but she said she couldn't do that—she hoping to slow things down—and he put off getting together as a foursome. A few days later he asked her to have dinner alone with him. He promised not to touch her, telling her what he had to say couldn't be said on the phone. Stefan had made plans to play basketball with some friends at the local gym, so Shelli told Stefan she was fine going to a party the magazine was hosting without him, and she did go, but stayed barely ten minutes before taking off to meet Wilhelm. She felt bad that she wasn't telling Stefan about getting together with Wilhelm, but then she remembered how she felt when Stefan talked about meeting Mattie around town, and how upset she had been at the mention. She knew that Stefan couldn't handle hearing about Wilhelm, the few times she talked about him after the four of them met—she saw Stefan's eyes jump as if he had been electrocuted. She quickly changed the subject, thinking he might go crazy and kill Wilhelm, and Shelli didn't want to see Stefan in prison, or worse.

Over spring rolls and sake, in an elegant restaurant with tablecloths and fancy glassware, Wilhelm asked if he could accompany her to her house and join her and Stefan in their lovemaking. The pull of his shape-shifting potency—his ability to take on different guises and alter living bodies—was tearing her asunder.

"The three of us in a hot tub," he said. "For me this would be sheer ecstasy. Pick up the phone and ask him."

"Stefan would never agree to this. He doesn't have your capacity or imagination. I don't know if you know this, but he can't perform with other men looking on."

"Ok, then, why don't you come home with me now. You can collect your things later."

If things remained the same, would she slowly waste away? And conversely, if she went with him would she turn into something else, a beautiful creature perhaps, a fabulous horse or deer, something strong and free? Her desire to do exactly what he wanted was strong, she wanted to please him, but another voice told her she had children and for that reason she needed to put things on pause.

"I can't just up and leave my children. My commitments aren't that easily brokered. What's doing with you and Camila?"

"She's not rich enough, nor beautiful enough, and unfortunately she's imbued with those spreading thighs." He spat out the words. "I see no future with that woman." Obvious that refusing him heightened his desire.

"Really? If I gained weight, you'd be finished with me too."

"You can't gain weight," he said.

"Would you change your mind about Camila if she firmed up her thighs?"

"Um."

"Get her a personal trainer."

Shelli nibbled at her raw tuna. He drank his sake.

"Stefan had me sign a pre-nup. I get no money until the boys' graduate college."

"I have enough money for the both of us," Wilhelm whispered. "Leave your husband. You don't love him, or you wouldn't be here with me. I'll break up with Camila."

From the look on his face, what she said was completely contrary to his expectations: "I used to think I was in love with Stefan, maybe now it's more embattled, and concurrently my desire for you has grown. But that doesn't change my desire to keep my marriage going, I'm not saying that things couldn't change, they well might but I don't like rushing things, not with children in the picture."

"Stefan's a lousy fuck. That's what Camila said. She doesn't lie about things like that." A short time later he said, "Come with me," he said, and pulled her up by hand and walked with her into the plush bathroom that held a single toilet and was clean and luxurious, with a lot of exotic woods, a plush rug and loveseat. He locked the door and moving close, grabbed her by the shoulders and kissed her, and biting her lip, biting her neck and chest like he was lost in some fever, like he was going to eat her with lips that were thick and filled with blood. She felt like bird held captive, and struggled to reconcile her insurgent lust making room, the way an exploding bomb makes room, clearing things out of the way, panting that she couldn't get enough of this man, having turned into putty. Strong urges that she couldn't completely fathom. She fell into his rhythm and then they climaxed together, twin explosions within. They walked out the door, and there was a dim memory of being glued to Stefan and keeping it going all day, but Shelli wondered in a moment of weakness if that was simply memory playing tricks on her. Was it even possible with Stefan to have ramped-up orgasms, one after another, in an endless parade until she was satiated, like she had experienced with Wilhelm? And how important was it that she have that kind of sexual experience?

Amid all this joy, Shelli was hit by the thought that Wilhelm might be an opportunist, simply looking to fill his photo albums. That thought sent a cold chill through her limbs, freezing her heart.

The boys returned early August to the JCC parking lot overlooking the beach, looking the same and yet not the same, taller certainly, and happy to see their parents, racing to greet them out of the chaos of children milling about, dragging on the arms of both parents alternately, depending on which parent said something or caught their eye, or seemed more interested in listening to them. The boys were in a race to tell their stories to anyone who would listen and fighting who would talk next.

"We were on the river in a boat and they let me be captain," Seth said breathlessly, his formerly dirty blond hair having gone platinum and looking like spin silk in the sun.

"Mom, I was on a boat, too," Micah said. He was near tears.

"Ok, you guys, one at a time," Shelli said. "Seth started, so let him tell what happened and then it's your turn."

"Kathy nominated me as the boat captain," Seth said. "My job was to set the direction and the speed, and every now and then someone would fight, or they'd forget their job, and I'd get everyone working together again." Turned out Kathy was his counselor.

"So how did it work out?" Stefan said. His face had turned a deep reddish tan from all cycling.

"I stopped a couple of fights," Seth said. "Kathy said I was the best captain ever."

Seth's face glowed, deepening the freckles on his face. His coloring was pale like his mom's, his tan a light dusting compared to his father's.

"That's great," Shelli said. "Ok, Micah, what happened on your boat?"

Micah swung the hand of Shelli's that he was holding. "I was the main trimmer," Micah said. "I had to trim the main sail and the jib and trim the pole-side of the spinnaker. I was running around a lot. It was fun but it was hard."

"Did you like sailing?" Shelli said, brushing his blond bangs away from his eyes.

"Yes," Micah said.

Shelli's heart leapt with love and admiration for their adventurous spirit, qualities she nurtured much as her father nurtured it in her. Her father didn't differentiate between his children; he believed both girls and boys needed to take on challenges, and she appreciated that about him.

"I don't have the time," Stefan said. "I'm not about to buy a sailing boat either. You're talking big bucks."

"I don't really want to sail," Seth said.

"Well, I do," Shelli said. "I think it'd be fun."

David, Stefan's brother, walked over to where they stood in the middle of the parking lot surrounded by sleeping bags and luggage.

"What you doing to the poor kid now?"

"Kid wants me to buy him a sailing boat," Stefan said.

"What did you tell him?" David said.

"Like hell I would," Stefan said. He folded his arms across his front and his legs braced akimbo if he were Samson arrayed against the multitudes. The look on his face was one of disdain. "What happened to the simple pleasures, when I was a kid, I found hours of entertainment with just a basketball or baseball."

"You're missing the point, meshuggeneh," Shelli said. "Seth and Micah learned how to sail, and they found enjoyment in it."

"You're just encouraging them to spend my money," Stefan grumbled. His frown deepened.

"Hey, I hate to butt in," David said, with a rueful look at Shelli, "but you have to understand how we grew up, everything our dad bought was the cheapest on the market, never mind that it fell apart the minute you got home. You've seen the junk he drives, the crappy furniture, and the black and white TV he refuses to get rid of? You know he made us go to the free college. He never spent a dime on tuition. "

"Yeah, well, he taught us the value of a dollar," Stefan said.

"Stefan doesn't have to buy a boat," Shelli said. "He can rent one through the sailing club for bupkes."

"How long do you think renting a boat will work out?" Stefan said.

"Ok, we won't take sailing lessons, it was just an idea," Shelli said. Stefan never wanted to learn anything new if it involved money, it always the same old. Right at that moment, she hated this about him.

"You don't have to do sailing to get out on the water," David said. "What about kayaking?"

"I like kayaks," Micah said. "We went out on kayaks, too."

"Well, then, I'm glad I'm not on the basketball team anymore," Seth said, throwing his hands down.

"What?" Stefan said. "When did this happen? You used to like basketball."

"We talked about this," Seth said. "I joined the team last fall because you made me. You and mom both agreed we don't need to do basketball or baseball anymore."

"Oh, come on," Stefan said. "Don't be a quitter."

"Why can't the boys choose what sport they want to play? Why should you be the one to pick their sports?" Shelli said. "You agreed that they can do karate, remember, or did you forget?"

"I hate to butt in again," David said with a snort, "but she has a point."

"Okay," Stefan said, but he didn't look pleased, his eyes narrowed into almond slits.

"Let's put the luggage in the car," Shelli said, in her most soothing voice, thinking that the slightest thing could set him off, and she never knew quite what that might be. She picked up one of the boy's duffle bags. "I think we have a plan."

"Let the boys carry their own bags," Stefan said. "You baby them too much."

"Try lifting that bag," Shelli said.

"What are you talking about?" Seth said. "I'm stronger than you."

"Oh, I almost forgot to mention," David said. "I got a job offer I can't refuse making big bucks as head of a rehab facility in Santa Monica."

"That's like saying a kineahora," Stefan said. This expression claiming to ward off the evil eye or bad luck in general the verbal equivalent of knocking on wood was said in jest with a chuckle to emphasize.

"God," David said. "I hope not."

"What? When is this?" Shelli said.

"I'll be leaving in a couple weeks and then Carmen and Nate will follow after the house is sold."

"Oh, man," Shelli said, "Really? You're taking Nate from his cousins?"

"We'll be back a lot," David said, "probably see each other more than we do now. Isn't that the way it always is? I tell you Santa Monica is nice and the weather is awesome, the institute is prestigious and, more importantly, just a block from the beach. Maybe you'll come and visit?" David looked at his watch. "Oh geez, look at the time, I've got to run off and find Nate, he went to say good-bye to a friend, but he could be anywhere."

Shelli's mind wandered. She couldn't stop the image of Wilhelm's half lidded eyes seeking hers, his lips coming into focus. The image dissolved and she was left with the hot sun baking the top of her head. She forced herself listen to the conversation, thinking she had to use the manual override.

"Okay, man," Stefan said, reaching out to hug him. "I didn't know you cared about the beach. There's plenty beach here in New Jersey."

"It's not the same," David said. "I'll explain over dinner."

"Have my people call your people."

They hugged. "Ok my man," Stefan said, and clapped his brother on the back.

The boys jumped out of the car and ran with their duffel bags slung over their shoulders, in their exuberance inadvertently slamming their heavy encumbrances into the plants now wilting in the dog days of summer. Several of the plants looked to have been trampled. Unceremoniously they dumped their bags in their room for Shelli to sort through. Seth wanted to get on his bicycle visit Max, the budding scientist, who lived about a half mile away and Micah wanted to go with him, and while Seth told Micah not to tag along, Shelli pleaded with Seth to let join him, and the boys took off. Meanwhile, Stefan vanished, not that Shelli cared. She got busy with the things that needed mending and washing, and threw out the items that were too far gone to attempt rescue, marveling at the ripped and stained clothing, and missing socks, but she didn't care about the clothes, she was happy to have ample time to dream of Wilhelm. She took full advantage, went to the bathroom to take a shower and masturbate.

Stefan appeared just as Shelli took the pizza out of the oven. At dinner Seth took a few bites of his pizza, and looking Stefan in the eye, his cheeks lumpy with half-chewed dough, said: "I liked soccer, but now I'm going to join the lacrosse team."

"I'm happy to hear that," Stefan said. "The coach said you are the best on his team, he'd never seen such drive. You'd be great in lacrosse."

They fell to eating. The silence around the table was underscored by the deepening twilight visible out the window, the blue black of the water merging into the darkening sky.

Seth stared at Stefan, a faint smile playing the corner of his lips.

"What got you into lacrosse?" Stefan said.

"We learned it in camp," Seth said. "It's so fun."

"Don't you love how it feels when you get goose bumps before a game on the back of your neck?" Stefan said.

"Yeah, it's boss."

"Lacrosse is played in the spring and early summer," Stefan said. "What are you planning for fall?" He folded his slice, muttering, "This how it's done," and taking a huge bite.

Seth stopped chewing. "I didn't choose basketball, you made me do it," he said.

"Your dad wanted you to try it to see if you liked it," Shelli said.

She congratulated herself for sending them to camp. They had come back showing a new assertiveness, talking like they had grown in their understanding of what they liked.

"Yeah, well I don't." Seth picked up his slice and folded in a U shape before taking another bite. "I didn't know about lacrosse. It's my new favorite sport."

"What, you're not going to play a sport in the fall?" Stefan said.

"Stefan," Shelli said.

"You're always talking," Stefan said. "Let him talk."

Outraged at the absurdity of his charge, Shelli sputtered, "You talk more than I do. You always dominate the conversations." But there was a tiny sliver of doubt, a disquieting sense that perhaps he was right. Why would he say it if it wasn't true? Racked with doubt, she looked at the smooth oak of the table as if seeking the answer in its rustic nature, its shellacked self that grieves for the mighty oak it had been.

"No, you do," Stefan said again.

When he said that, Shelli realized she was being had. At this point, she had to stand up to him or face being totally manipulated. He did that with everyone, his bid to power totally transparent to anyone with half a brain.

"You're basically saying I'm not allowed to join the conversation." She looked up with dagger eyes. "You're playing dictator."

"I like skateboarding," Seth said in a small voice, gulping down his food. "And I like karate."

"Skateboarding isn't an organized sport," Stefan said.

"Why can't we do it on our own?" Seth shot back, dropping his half-eaten pizza on his plate.

"He's got a point," Shelli said, feeling that perhaps no, she wasn't speaking too much.

"What? You're talking for him now?" Stefan said.

"I'm adding my two bits like you are," she said through clenched jaw and looked at him with narrowed eyes. He might not want her to speak her mind, but she was damned if he was going to silence her.

"Adults like to boss us around for no reason," Seth said, picking his slice up again.

"It's for your own good," Stefan said.

"Oh sure," Seth said. "They into power."

"It may seem like that to you," Shelli said, thinking to be impartial, to ascertain and acknowledge the truth in both sides. "But some adults really do have your interests at heart."

"That's a laugh," Seth said, pushing away his slice.

"Right," Micah said, sounding a bitter note, his mouth full of pizza.

"I don't know what's going on here," Stefan said, having finished his slice in a couple bites, "why you have problems receiving instruction. I have fond memories of playing organized sports, most of them awesome. Mainly basketball and baseball. You could practice and practice but if you keep doing it wrong, you'll never improve."

"Stefan," Shelli said.

I'm talking," Stefan said, raising his voice an octave. "Now you listen for once in your life." He paused, and then continued in a more conversational tone. "It's the best feeling, a very different feeling when the play matters—when there's going to be a loser and a winner—that's when you feel the agony and the ecstasy."

"I don't know dad," Seth said. "I feel plenty pain when I fall off the skateboard. Remember when I scrapped my knee falling off the skateboard and got all bloody?"

"Your scrapped knee didn't result in a win, right?"

"What does it matter? Why does everything have to be about winning or losing?" Seth said. "Can't I do a sport for fun?"

"They skateboard and ride their bicycles all the time, and we know they're going to be on their snowboards when the snow comes," Shelli said.

"I'm asking nicely," Stefan said, ignoring Shelli.

"Why don't you get it over with and hit me in kishka," she said pounding her stomach.

"Can you stop, already," Stefan said, "all you do is talk."

"You're the talker," Shelli said.

"You talk all the time, you talk more than me, you're always talking," Stefan said. He sounded bitter.

"How can you say that?" Shelli said. "That's simply not true." She felt she had to defend herself. Tears sprang to her eyes. Why was he picking on her for voicing her beliefs?

The boys stared at Shelli. They looked stricken.

"Mom," Seth said in a pleading voice.

The reaction of her sons shook her. What Stefan said about her was so different from how she pictured herself. She wasn't the life of the party. Stefan was. How could he deny this to her face? From her earliest memories, she had been painfully shy having stuttered as a toddler and still to this day tripping over many words. Stefan liked to poke fun of her pronunciation, and if anything her friends told her she was too quiet. Her mother was prone to sermonizing, and wouldn't let her talk, telling her "children should be seen, but not heard." Shelli was used to not having a voice, but she didn't like it. And when she could talk, she wasn't vocal around her friends either, thinking that that she wasn't pretty enough to have a voice, or didn't know what to say. Unused to the give and take of conversations.

Shelli often questioned her perception of things, but even so, she knew she was not wrong about who dominated the conversation in their house. She suspected he didn't welcome her input unless she agreed with him. He was unable to see the problem from her perspective. She talked it out with her shrink who helped her see that she was partially responsible for his intransigence. She needed to phrase things differently, as if she was asking a question, and deferring to him to decide, rather than look like she was pulling out the big guns, meanwhile keeping her anger in check, realizing that she had a lot to learn about negotiating solutions, she needed to demonstrate her willingness to compromise.

He tended to bully people into letting him have his way. He was more controlling; she preferred to give their children wider latitude. Who was to say which way was better? When he spoke like that, like he wanted to steamroll her, while she was working on dampening her admittedly short fuse, she'd reflect on the ways she could make him feel less threatened, reassure him that she wasn't trying to take over the whole operation, she simply desired a forum to air their differences and discuss the best ways to approach the problem in an adult manner. She tried to follow the shrink's advice and reframe her objections to make them seem more like questions and less confrontational, keeping in mind that Stefan provided stability, a home life, children, history, security, family, community, and a deeply satisfying Jewish connection. Most of the time he was fun to be with, less so perhaps since meeting Wilhelm, who offered excitement, emotional escape, sexual intensity, and maybe even a raison d'être. And there was the other nut. As for how much her views meshed with Wilhelm's, that was hard to say, she thought they shared the same views on many things, but they had only known each other a few months. She needed time with Wilhelm and his son, observe them together in their habitat, and see in real terms where he was at in the childrearing department, as well as other basic issues.

She hit on an idea, realizing she didn't need to be right, and worked to let go the ego thing, more important to come up with a plan that would work for the boys and also satisfy Stefan.

"Okay," Shelli said. "You want them to do an organized sport in the fall, as well as in the spring. Will you let them pick which one?"

Clearly Stefan was caught off guard. "You gave in so easily, what gives?"

"You have to give them a choice."

Stefan had to agree to save face. She knew how important that was to him. Though the victory, if you could call it that, was hers. She found it was easier than she thought to swallow her pride and think through the problem, better to concede something if it will help deflect an argument and allow the boys to make some of the decisions.

"How about karate," Seth said. "It's organized; there are winners and losers."

"Not the same thing. It's not teamwork." Stefan lifted his eyebrows.

Shelli would have liked that Stefan not require them to play a sport through all the seasons, but if he gave them choices, then she would have to give some ground. They picked track. Stefan approved, saying it was good training for lacrosse.

A few days later, they went to the therapist together.

"How are you two getting along?" Dr. Weinberg asked.

"When we go out with other couples, Stefan says mean things about me in front of everyone."

"Oh." Dr. Weinberg batted his eyes as if to repel a swarm of mites. He stopped talking for a few minutes.

"Swinging was *his* idea, not mine," Shelli said. "Doesn't matter what I want now he's making it all about him."

"Not true," Stefan shot back.

"He promised I'd have total control over what happened, but now he's reneging on that, too," she said.

"Are you both willing to listen to each other?" the therapist asked in a kindly tone. "If you are, I can work with you."

"She refuses to see what's in front of her eyes," Stefan said.

"He tells me I'm wrong if I don't see what's obvious to him."

"Marriage is never easy," Dr. Weinberg began. "Even less so with other lovers in the mix. It demands a lot of trust and a strong sense of self. With all this going on, and your relationship already on shaky ground, you need to need to communicate, and listen to what the other has to say. I can help defuse things."

"We could use a middleman," Shelli said.

"First of all, hear each other out," Dr. Weinberg said, "without interruption."

"I've `been very flexible," Stefan said. "She's the one who won't budge."

"What?" Shelli gasped.

They went in circles until the doctor got Stefan to agree that people can have different perceptions of the same event, and all of them can be right, every image distorted by one's own predilections and biases. Shelli grudgingly agreed to listen to what Stefan had to say and to let him finish without interruption—something she had trouble with. They started with Stefan's biggest gripe: money. Dr. Weinberg had them agree that they would talk over big purchases before slapping down plastic. Then Shelli weighed in on her belief that Stefan didn't care about her feelings. The doctor suggested Stefan try to accommodate Shelli.

Shelli listened to Stefan's chatter, her thoughts drifting to their honeymoon in the Catskills, where they luxuriated between satin sheets, enjoying long, voluptuous lovemaking sessions, between bouts of reading to each other, and watching oddball comedies, mostly Woody Allen and Mel Brooks. Afternoons were devoted to exercise—tennis and cycling. Back then, their love seemed impregnable, back when there was little disagreement about anything. It dawned on her that crisis is where the real work of a relationship begins. They had started out strong, but as happens with everyone, as the years wore on, feelings quieted, and the romantic moments came less often. No more spontaneous visits to seedy borscht-belt hotels. Now, with his duties at the office crowding his private life, they rarely did anything together that didn't involve other people, even sex. Could she blame stress or should she expose ennui as the masked robber? Did he really want to say she could never be as funny or smart as he—but as soon as she thought to accuse him of this, she rammed the words back into her throat, choking them down, knowing that she couldn't come up with funny things to say as quickly as he. He pointed this sad fact too frequently for her taste; it put a pall on her heart and made her resent him.

It started to rain and Shelli thought of all those rain-soaked cars, trains, and buses, carrying people home to spouses who loved them, and felt her heart constrict as if her chest was too small to contain it. They passed the A&P on Memorial Parkway and turned north to Locust Point Road from Navesink River Road, thick green hedges on either side shielding residents from prying eyes. In the dying light, Stefan's brown hair and eyes had turned one shade verging on dusk. Gazing at him, she felt sorry that they hadn't been able to handle this swinging thing very well, but there were always winners and losers. Stefan was a poor loser. And he blamed her, which was the real problem; she was always in the wrong, never him. There must have been many moments when she tumbled short of his dreams, not always her fault, sometimes due to his own colossal need for approval, whatever inside him that needed constantly to be filled by an endless stream of agreeable newcomers. Outside, the wind grew loud and somewhere in the distance sounded the faint rumble of thunder. But she didn't regret going down this path. If they had never stepped out of their comfort zone, they might have skated along never knowing how far apart they were on some issues, and not just about sex. They got home just as the last of the light disappeared. Shelli tripped over Stefan's shoe in the dark foyer, and joked about ghastly things that go bump in the night. Stefan didn't laugh. She could hear the boys laughing downstairs with the babysitter.

"Your approach isn't playful," Stefan said. His eyes drooped. "You used to be."

"Am I awful?"

Her seemingly contrite attitude had an effect on Stefan. He visibly softened and let some of his defenses down. They joked about their past foibles, laughing about Stefan's recounting of the guys' visit to the strip club, particularly Rick's reaction to Stefan's admission about wanting sex with others, and all the other guys protesting that would be impossible, no woman would allow that without some kind of quid pro quo, and then Rick asking several times about it. But they didn't have sex, she would have to wait.

The next day Shelli sent a text to Wilhelm saying things were back to normal, sweat pricking her underarms. The day was hot and muggy, better addressed by the AC. But what she saw out there gave her pause: blue upon blue, layers of blue bursting with swallowed starlight, dazzling to the naked eye, and suddenly spiraling in front of her, two blue jays kissing under blue fire from above. Question to Wilhelm: Maybe they could spend the afternoon together? He wrote asking would it be okay if he called. She replied in the affirmative.

His lush, excitable voice bursting through the phone line like a tropical storm had her trembling like a leaf in a high wind. "I miss you babe," Wilhelm's words fell on her ears like water spraying a thirsty plant. "I miss your lips..." Her husband hadn't mentioned her lips in so long, she couldn't remember the last time.

"Tell me how much." She spoke lightly as if she had not a care in the world.

He chimed in right on cue. "Way too much." But he did not stop there, oh, no, he continued to gush through the phone like a teenager deep in the throes of puppy love, saying, "I'm crazy about you" and, "I'm dying to kiss you" multiple times with great emotion, as if he were strangling on endorphins. Shelli made contrary noises to calm him down. He countered with a profuse apology for his faux pas, begging forgiveness for anything and everything, saying sorry more times than she could count, sounding as if her approval mattered a great deal. He talked about his little boy, the sweetest kid ever, and why his wife left him. His theories that sounded as vague as fog and equally hard to work though. His responses opened up more questions; he seemed genuinely befuddled as to why their relationship went on the skids and had no simple answer. She stopped asking; knowing his cryptic answers would lead her in circles. She didn't volunteer any information about Stefan, thinking it better to keep him guessing. Rather she looked forward to revealing other parts of herself, leaving her panting, unconsummated, and reveling in her hunger. Gradually it dawned on her that he was fully prepared to wait for her as long as she wanted him to, and that she had a friend.

After school Shelli weeded the backyard and the kids took turns pushing the push-reel lawnmower, a manual. Stefan loved that clattery thing, proud to have a backyard that needed mowing. She thought of her dad, who never mowed, saying he didn't have time, or the inclination, and hired others to do it. Instead of a lawn, Stefan's family had painted the little square of pavement green to look like a lawn in front of their walkup in Brooklyn, and in the rear, weeds grew in abundance. When Shelli and Stefan moved to New Jersey, he told Shelli his dream was to have a lawn big enough to play baseball in, with real grass. The day of their move, his first order of business was to go shopping for lawnmowers. Shelli told him she was fine with that, but could he consider getting one that wasn't powered by gasoline, and he said he'd check them out. They went out together and tried a few, and decided the manual models were as easy to push as the giant carts at Target. And the sound was much quieter than the gas powered versions she tried—she could have spoken on the phone over its sound without missing anything. The soft metallic whine of the lawnmower filled her ears with pleasure, a melody that provided a lovely accompaniment for the tableau spread before her, i.e. luxuriant lawn, well fed from the abundance of rainstorms that had been falling of late. Micah wouldn't let go of the lawnmower when it was Seth's turn, and they began hitting each other, and crying until Stefan stepped between them. He surveyed their work with a calculating eye and complemented them. The impeccably manicured lawn looked less plant-like and more like a moist, green, self-propagating blanket. Shelli glanced at the gossamer threads overhead, nothing like the sooty clouds that brought rain.

"Doesn't look like a storm to me," she said.

"The clouds are moving in, take my word for it," Stefan said. "You know, what they say in Maine applies here too. You don't like the weather, wait a minute." He took off for the garage to put the lawnmower away.

"That's enough of an excuse to go inside to make cookies."

The boys raced in front of her along the raised footpath that led to their front door, the scent of flowers overpowering all else. Breathing deeply, she pulled heavy floral effervescence into her lungs, and headed inside. In the chilly air, Shelli felt a sense of satisfaction in the bracing elements, the cool breeze raising the minute hairs along her arms, and the air smelling fresh, crisp, and clean, filling her nostrils with the scents of witch hazel, persimmon trees, and fragrant magnolias. She hugged her arms close, worried that it was possible she had been overly negative in taking the side of her sons in talking with their father about fall sports. She learned they would have track on Tuesdays and Thursdays, so the question of whether they should do an organized sport turned out to be non-issue. They had time on the other days to do their own thing. Her notion that she had to defend them from an overly zealous father who lived and breathed sports might have been misplaced, but underlying everything, she thought he made it more about him than the boys. How to express that concept in a way that wasn't off putting?

Inside the spacious kitchen with its gleaming granite counters, Shelli went to the cupboards to fetch the ingredients they'd need. The clouds parted, exposing the brilliance of the sun already high above the house, bathing the kitchen with lemony light. Seth wanted chocolate chip, and Micah said he'd like that, too. Seth asked if he could measure the flour and sugar. Micah commandeered the milk and baking soda, saying he was in charge of measuring those things. There were excited exclamations over the actual placing of ingredients into the measuring cups and spoons, not all of it went where it was intended, an equal amount of the flour or salt, or whatever, ended up on the counters. Shelli brought out the eggs and butter, and when everything had been mixed to the boys' satisfaction, she spooned dabbles of the raw cookie dough on the tray, and then cleaned up the spills. While the cookies were baking, Shelli sat in the rocking chair, cat on her lap. Seth came up leaning forward against her knees.

"I was talking quietly, not disturbing anyone," Seth said. "Miss Miller yelled at me to shut me up. I was just whispering something funny to my friend." He looked like he was ready to cry.

Seth started petting the cat, making her purr like a motor that had been left running. Looking at the anguish on her son's sweet face, she was moved to say something meant to calm, "She might be one of those teachers who feel insecure, and need to feel they have your attention at all times…happens a lot to new teachers."

Micah poured himself a glass of water and said, "Bullpucky."

"Where did you learn that word?" Shelli said.

"I just knew it," Micah said.

"I don't want to go to Miss Miller's class anymore," Seth said, timing his petting strokes so he didn't bump Shelli's fingers. Shelli slowed her fingers to give room to her son.

Shelli tried to remember what class Miss Miller taught… ah…science. Seth had not complained about learning the unit on electricity, or the earth science unit, but she recalled that he had not enjoyed the section on Sandy Hook's marine life as told from the perspective of the native people. Seth said the teacher glorified the Lenape tribe, and while they might have been wonderful, she talked about the Europeans as if they were bad people—calling them the colonialists in a derogatory way— and that made him feel that he wasn't hearing the whole story. Shelli had told him that thinking like this was very smart. He was learning to be a discerning thinker. This is what education is supposed to be all about, to hear both sides before making a judgement. It shouldn't be solely one-sided. He added that the teacher made everyone learn how to braid a necklace, and use a mortar and pestle to grind corn.

He said, in the way of complaint, "I've better things to do with my time."

"Like what, throwing spitballs?" Shelli retorted. The cat began kneading Shelli's thigh, making her thigh feel prickly.

"Yes."

"Think about what would have happened if the Europeans had not discovered America," Shelli said, "which of course, is so unlikely, but let's pretend. Indian tribes in America would remain undisturbed. They would have continued their little internecine wars, and nothing would have changed."

"It's hard to imagine," Seth said. "No shopping malls. No Six Flags."

"There's also another way to look at this. Sometimes having a colonial power keeping order prevents the natives from killing each other. Gandhi started a movement to push the British out of India, and Churchill predicted that when the British left there would be civil war. This is a direct quote: 'While the Hindu elaborates his argument, the Moslem sharpens his sword.' He was right. Gangs of young Muslims started killing Hindus. To stop the bloodshed, British and Indian leaders tried to carve out a separate state called Pakistan for the Muslims and leave the rest of India for the Hindus. Today, the Muslims still go after the Hindus as it is written in the Koran, but now the Hindus have legal recourse. And in America, to carry the analogy further, only for a short time did the American Indians pose a threat; European diseases killed most of them, and the superior technology of the Europeans did the rest. The Indians weren't well organized; tribes fought each other instead of uniting against a common enemy."

Micah came to stand by Shelli and started petting the cat, too. The pale blond hairs on his moving arm loomed in front of her eyes, a million glittering filaments in the sunlight. All their hands and fingers meshed together, like spaghetti.

"Did the Europeans colonize the whole world?" Seth said.

"They tried," Shelli said. "And held on for a few centuries until 1945, the end of WWII, then they handed most of it back. Not all the colonizing powers were good for the subjugated peoples. But in the case of the British, many of the changes they instituted were good and helped the people they colonized to modernize. The British could be commended for their efforts to preserve local cultures and modernizing local education systems."

The timer went off. Shelli put the cat down and took the baking sheets out of the oven. The cookies looked beautiful, the chips having melted nicely into the baked dough. Seth piled several cookies on his plate. Micah did the same and headed to the table. Shelli brought the milk and several glasses.

"If you promise to go to class," Shelli said, "I'll talk with Miss Miller and find out why she told you that, but until then, please, go to class, and do what she says."

"Why should I?" Seth said, speaking in his soft child's voice. "She's rude."

"You have to go to class so you can hear what the teacher says," Shelli said just as softly. "Some of what she says will be on the tests. It's important to do this, even on the days you don't feel like it. If you don't, you'll only hurt yourself, not the teacher, she'll give you a bad grade, and be sorry that you're wasting your potential, but she won't spend much time thinking about it. But it'll be on your record and someday you'll want to get into a good school and that may hold you back. But I also think I should talk to the teacher, okay? Maybe I can convince her to soften her approach? She probably didn't realize how harsh she sounded."

"It's useless," Seth said with in a choked voice, sounding oddly adult, his back bowed like an old man. "She's not a nice person."

Stefan came in the door, the screen door banged behind him. The sharp report sent the cat galloping into the air, his gray fur standing on end, and in a flurry of distended nails ran out of the room. Stefan went to the table and took a handful of cookies from Seth's plate. Outside the windows, the clouds came back in a capricious dance, shutting out the sun. The room darkened.

"Hey, get your own," Seth said, his hand darting over his plate.

"Who do you think pays for all this?" Stefan said as he delicately dipped a cookie into a glass of milk and then munching, his face radiating his special brand of friendliness.

Without a word, Shelli went to the counter and bought another plate heaped with cookies and placed them next to him.

"Why do you coddle him like that?" Stefan said.

"Because you don't know how to behave," Shelli said.

"Like you do," Stefan said.

Shelli let the remark pass and tasted from cookie Stefan dunked in milk, but she didn't want the whole cookie. She took two bites, gave it back, and went to sit with the boys at the trestle table. Made from solid walnut, the table was the most beautiful furniture they owned. Shelli was proud of that table and liked that all the males in the room were at the table chomping cookies, milk dribbling down their chins, happily gathered around that slab of wood. Stefan went to join them.

"Dad, mom said I have to go to a class that's taught by a mean teacher," Seth said in his most peevish voice.

"Why is that even a question?" Stefan said.

"Because she's awful," Seth said.

"I told him I'd schmooze the teacher," Shelli said.

"You've got to be meshuggeneh to think you can schmooze a teacher," Stefan said. "He's got to learn that you can't pick your teachers."

"He could try to please the teacher, and soften her up," Shelli said.

"Now there's an idea," Stefan said, "though I doubt she's going to listen to him."

Micah and Seth took their plates and glasses to the sink. Seth said he wanted to go to the basement and finish building his robotic cars. Micah said he wanted to do the same thing. Stefan tried to talk them into throwing a baseball around, but neither boy would have any of it. Shelli suggested that if they'd promised do their homework without squabbling about it that they could build their cars out of Legos. Stefan agreed reluctantly. After dinner Stefan talked them into throwing a baseball around with him. Seth told him that they liked it better when they did it as a casual thing, didn't have to go to practice or be on a team.

Wilhelm texted that he wanted to call. She went outside and waited until she reached the bend in the road before texting him that it was okay to call.

"Don't you think it's scary?" he asked.

"What?"

"This strong attraction we feel for each other."

"You feel a strong attraction to women in general."

"You like both women and men, no?"

"I loved being with Camila."

The strong musky scent of signet marigolds that Shelli's gardener planted months ago filled the air. She felt a thick nostalgia coating her throat, and took a deep breath. Unlike regular marigolds, the leaves of this hybrid put out a pleasant lemony smell and mixed well with the scent of citrus from the plethora of firs in the woods behind their house. And they looked different too, with a rounded, billowy form about 12 inches tall. Their dime-size flowers were much smaller than the classic version and their color not as brassy. They were supposed to be eatable too, but she was reluctant to try them, though the boys used to have a pet turtle that loved flowers. He died years ago, and they never replaced him, having moved on to bearded dragons.

"These days, she's looking fat and mean. That pulled-down mouth. Horrible."

"What about the other one—the one you dated a few months back? I forgot her name."

"Not the gold digger, the woman who went out with me for my money."

"I'm that way too."

"We're in agreement. Come with me on my boat and we'll sail up the coast into Canada. It's beautiful at this time of year. We could visit the mineral spas near Quebec."

"I'd love to. Lets' bring my boys, yours too."

"We'll have to plan for that. I'll have to ask the ex."

Shadows flitted across the landscape, making her jump. Like a thief, Shelli kept looking around, moving on cat feet. The last thing she wanted was for Stefan to hear her on the phone with Wilhelm. As for her children, whatever she did to stay happy, as long as they had no inkling—having a happy mother was the most important thing. And, of course Stefan could not suspect anything or the game would be up, he was too much the jealous type. What if they invited him along? Something to ponder, but just as quickly rejected. He would be too jealous. And so she spun her web. Each moment has its belief and what some people call treachery is a freshly edited spin of that belief holding sway in another moment. It's possible to love the person you are about to betray in the very act of betrayal and to be refreshed in your love by doing so. This washing of the old love into something new, renews all the faces and customs and ideals and leaves the bars of the prison shining.

A few weeks passed and then it was the Jewish New Year, Rosh Hashanah, or literally the "head of the year" when the shofar made from a carved ram's horn is sounded in temple, followed by the casting out of one's sins in a symbolic gesture at the lakefront, which was the best part for the boys, as it involved dumping their pockets—a process they found highly entertaining as evidenced by the many giggles and shoves. Out came a couple of small rocks and wadded candy wrappers to their delight. Shelli called out "l'shanah tovah," to their friends and talked about the meaning of the holiday, and the things like beginning of the cycle of sowing, growth, and harvest; although the harvest has its own festival, but all of it appears obscure in our modern world, unconnected as we are by the seasons. The boys especially loved throwing their rocks in the water.

In the days leading up to Yom Kippur she worked on her various projects. In thinking about atonement, and thought it better to clean up her act and made sure the boys were working on their homework without fail. One of those nights she sent an email that she wanted to meet with Miss Miller, better to meet in the beginning of the school year. Just then she noticed an instant message from Wilhelm blinking at her from the computer professing his undying love. Shelli felt her head spin seeing his message appear in stark black on the white screen. Just before Shelli closed down her computer for the night, an email from the teacher hurled across, landed in her inbox saying she would be glad to meet, the sooner the better.

Nine

The meeting with Miss Miller did not go off the way she envisioned. First of all, it took her a good half hour to find Miss Miller's little office, tucked behind several other offices in the oldest part of the school where the hallways occurred organically, not easy to figure out if you didn't already know your way around. Adding to her sense of being lost in a maze, as much as she tried, she couldn't get her mind off her paramour, the man who occupied her dreams. And once she found the classroom, things didn't get any easier. While the teacher seemed sweet, not at all pushy or aggressive way her son Seth depicted her to be, and was full of praise of him, telling Shelli what she suspected, that he was a quick learner and gifted, she realized how little she knew of this teacher. Yet once she heard that all that praise, her pride in her son overwhelmed her so much that for a few moments, staring at Miss Miller dumbly, she couldn't speak and had trouble understanding some of the words spoken. The teacher's accent was charming. Shelli couldn't quite place it, possibly German? She scooted her chair closer, as if the issue was about distance. She felt like her head had been suddenly pushed underwater, and scrambled to make sense of what she heard, trying not to let on that cobwebs threatened to overwhelm her. She hoped she didn't look too absentminded, but she supposed she did.

"It's good to hear that he's making a favorable impression," Shelli said. "But I'm concerned about his attitude. Have you seen any changes, is he acting differently? I received a few pre-recorded calls from the front office that he had been tardy. Or missed class. That's why I called to set up this meeting. I'm concerned."

"He's facing detention," Miss Miller said, leaning forward over her desk, "but he doesn't seem to care. He's a good student and says some insightful things and the other students love him. At times he's a model student. And other times, he's fidgety and out of control."

"He can't be the only student who does this," Shelli said, slow and measured, sounding her alarm.

"No, of course not," Miss Miller said, reassuringly. "Many of my male students act this way. I typically have about a third of the class making crazy noises and moving around in their seats at some point in the day, usually towards the end, but that's no excuse for bad behavior." Her voice took on a snappish quality. "Now I realize that boys tend to be more rambunctious, but when it's your son, the whole classroom goes in an uproar. He's a natural leader."

"I think the problem with Seth is that he needs to move around more during school hours. And getting mad at him might be counterproductive."

"So I'm supposed to excuse it, now?"

"I brought some articles I clipped on the subject for you to read. Quickly I'll read a quote from one of them, this was written by a pediatric occupational therapist for *The Washington Post*: "Children naturally start fidgeting in order to get the movement their body so desperately needs and is not getting enough of to turn their brain on. What happens when the children start fidgeting? We ask them to sit still and pay attention; therefore, their brain goes back to sleep."

"But school is not set up that way. I can't let him walk around the classroom or the schoolyard at his leisure when he wants to. Every student would be begging for the same treatment."

"Maybe you should give it to them. Recess times have been getting shorter and shorter, and less frequent. You could be the one to spearhead change." Shelli couldn't remember the kids not paying attention when she was going to middle school, way back when, but she did remember how hardcore about discipline teachers seemed.

"As much as I might want to do what you say, I'm new here, still on probation."

"You could let the kids perform science experiments that allow them to move around more or take them on more field trips." Shelli said this in a tentative voice, not sure if she was overstepping.

"Even if I wanted to do this, class sizes are simply too large."

Shelli felt a heavy sadness fall, suffocating like a wet blanket. She sensed that Miss Miller was one of those people who tend to dig in their heels and disregard what other people say if they fear they could lose their job. All the while acknowledging that what you say is true. She wanted to wipe the smug look off the teacher's face, and threaten to pull her children out of the school and put them into a private school with a low teacher-to-pupil ratio, but when she advanced the idea a few weeks before all this occurred, Stefan said, "I didn't go to private school, and neither will they." His logic defied all reason, but Stefan often aligned his decisions to the manner in which he was raised no matter what the facts on the ground were, as if his parents did everything right; their decisions not to be trifled with. So Shelli didn't say that, instead she ended on a lame note.

"I realize large classes are the outcome of funding," Shelli said. "The finance people trying to get more bang for the buck. But that doesn't make it right."

The teacher arched her eyebrows and said nothing, compressing her lips, making Shelli think about all the times voters put measures on the ballot to limit class sizes, and vote them in, only to have the legislature rule that there isn't the budget to honor the will of the people. But Shelli didn't think mentioning this would help.

Shelli plowed on, attempting to keep her voice calm. "Read these articles I'm leaving for you and the principal. You'll see that the problem is only getting worse. Compared to children from the early 1980s, only one out of twelve children possess normal strength and balance. It's approaching a crisis in the public schools all over the country. Something needs to be done."

"I understand with what you're saying, and I sympathize, but rules are rules. I'll talk to the principal and if she agrees to take it to the board, than that's something, but so you know, the school board moves slowly."

Leaving the teacher and preoccupied with her thoughts, she went past a girl with goth clothing and hair sticking up like a porcupine's quills and tried not to stare. The hallways were filling up with students going to their next class. To complicate matters, she got lost in the centuries-old brick edifice with its mysterious hallways trying to find her way back to the main floor, winding her way through an endless parade of incredible looking kids, girls swinging their long hair, legs sailing up to the sky, delicate faces blooming like hothouse flowers, and the boys equally beautiful, descendants of Greek gods. She heard names like 'Tiffany,' 'Bunny,' and 'Justin' wafting through the air and walked straight into the maelstrom of kids that circumnavigated the heart of the school, the colossal circular walkway that led to the cafeteria and auditorium not realizing. Shelli made an effort to put herself in a better mood by dwelling on the conversation with Wilhelm the previous day, running it over and over in her mind. It excited her to be thought desirable and loved for herself. If the only thing she got out of this swinging thing—learning that she still had it, whatever that was—made all the heartache worth the trouble.

At home, Shelli found the boys at the kitchen counter chowing down on cookies. She mentioned that she had met with Miss Miller. Seth frowned.

She asked what was wrong, and he said, "Why did you talk to her? You're ruining everything the way you always do."

"That's how you get things done. You talk to people." Shelli was aghast. "You think I should ignore what's happening and just hope everything will come out alright?"

"Why can't you let it alone?" He hunched with his arms over his stomach as if he was in pain.

"I thought you'd be happy I was working on your behalf. And you know what? Miss Miller likes my idea. She's going to take it to the principal."

"Yeah, she's saying that to get you out of her face."

"Do you know that recess time has been cut almost in half from the time I was in school?"

"Really?" Seth said, his eyes searching hers.

"When she heard that, she was receptive to the idea that movement helps kids to think better."

"Hard to believe," Micah said in a tired sounding voice, looking up from his partially consumed cookie, looking like he carried all the weight of the world on his shoulders.

"I plan to write an email to the principal, telling her what we talked about today and what Miss Miller promised she'd do. I'll copy you. And then I'll follow up with Miss Miller. I'm not going to let this die, but I'll do it nicely. People will be glad I brought it to their attention."

The phone rang. She lifted the phone, only to hear Mattie's hoarse, whispery voice sounding the alarm. Apparently she had been neglecting her best friend, stuck in the logjam of work and the routine of daily life.

"You're always too busy for your best friend," Mattie scolded into her ear. The vibrations echoed through the many layered tissues in Shelli's head, separately it seemed from the air conducting the sound, making for a strange disconnect.

Micah was rummaging around the cupboards, banging doors. And then there were the scrapping noises Seth made, pushing the chair out and then adjusting it; and his chewing, taking her mind away from her conversation with Mattie. She fled out of the room and positioned herself near the window in the living room where she could look at the dense growth of trees and the gray fog sifting down through the branches like gossamer silk, feeling the tension in her muscles float away.

"I'm having problems with Seth," Shelli explained. "He doesn't like his teacher and I'm having trouble motivating him to be on time to class. And work's been a bear. I didn't think you'd want to hear my kvetching."

"Please," Mattie said. "That's what I'm here for."

"You're so sweet."

"I found something really fun for us." Sounding as excited as a gangster planning her first caper, she continued, "What would you say if I told you we could stage our own S&M show?"

"I've never been one for pain."

"This has nothing to do with pain. It's about finding that exquisite edge before pleasure turns to pain. Apparently the coursework involves tying one's spouse with velvet ropes and spanking."

"If it's spanking like my dad used to do it, no thanks."

"Of course not, silly. The whips are made of feathers."

"Sounds like something we'll want our husbands to be a part of," Shelli said.

"We'll drive there together in Rick's SUV," Mattie cried. "It'd be sooo fun."

Stefan tried to keep up his mood at a high point, humming a cheerful tune and kidding Shelli about her outfit, black leather leggings and long tank top, saying she should charge admission. She said the designer was Rick Owens, like a man is going to know who that is, or care. "Why are we always late for everything?" Stefan said, brow furrowed, reflecting on Shelli's inability to get dressed in a timely fashion. He had started a habit of nudging her two hours before they had to leave for anywhere, to no avail, she was never ready on time, always having to try everything she owned first. If anything made him irritable, that was it. What he cared about: there wasn't a cloud in the sky, the deep blue empty except for geese moving high above the car, white streaks on blue fading into evening, piercing the buoyant, crisp air with their exuberant honks, lifting his spirits. And at the door, Mattie was all smiles, making Stefan feel irresistible, thinking her smile was just for him. He wanted to run his hands over her red leather formfitting number that had his eyes popping out; her hair like spun taffy and her smile as big as the sky, instead he gave her an extra big hug, which she returned, that gave him gladness in his heart, because he had been bad, lifting her skirt on a numerous occasions, and stealing kisses, and she a married woman. Upon breaking away, she handed Stefan a drink the color of liquid methane and filled with smashed mint, ribbing him about his late entrance, saying he shouldn't have dolled up for her. Stefan grumbled that everyone else were already on their second drinks. He loved the repartee, so different from the wife.

"Now everyone can be here to greet you," Shelli said. "Admit it, you love the attention."

Like him, she quoted Seinfeld in her attempt to level the playing field, which always seemed off kilter because there was no way she could win. No one could top his delivery and sense of timing; he had trained with the best at the Player's Workshop in Chicago, where he could have been a contender, but he was derailed by his struggle for survival, no one to help him. (Let the violins play.) But he was not one to cry, he left that to the women like Shelli. Were all short women crybabies, tall women more in control of their emotions, more like men?

"Just for once, I want to make a grand entrance," Stefan said. "I never make grand entrances."

"You've made some grand exits," Mattie said.

"Hey there." Rick said, putting his arm around Shelli, and giving her quick buss.

Shelli's half-hearted response made Stefan dislike her aloofness with his best friend, like she was doing him the favor. She wasn't like that with the guys they met on the swinger's websites.

"As punishment, I should get to sleep with Mattie," Stefan said laughter undergirding his words.

When he said that, Shelli gave him a quick stare, her eyes red, puffed like bee stings. As usual, Shelli didn't get that he was joking, and later would twist his words, deflect his meaning, and then claim that he was the guilty one by ragging her about it. Part of him didn't care what Shelli thought of his flirting, but he could see she wasn't thrilled, and while he gloried in her upset, at the same time her approbation grated on his nerves. He wished she wouldn't judge him, and act the mother hen, admonishing him for every little thing. He was sick of worrying about what she thought, and decided she could shove it for all he cared.

Now that they had fucked other people, she might lay aside her vigilance, but no, she didn't seem to trust that he was joking. He protested in vain that his jokes were simply jokes, nothing to them, other than the thrill of saying something risqué. He liked to say the forbidden, as long as it made him look good. Talking like that sharpened his wit.

"That's not punishing you," Rick said. "That's punishing Mattie. And cruelly, I might add."

"It's no big deal," Stefan said. "You know they botched my vasectomy."

A look of recognition flitted across Shelli's face. Likely she knew the comedy sketch he took it from. At least she might credit him with remembering all the lines verbatim, something she could never do. And credit him for remembering this stuff. She scoffed at him when he said it conferred on him the same sort of genius he was quoting, as if it made him somehow smarter than her, that he was right and she was wrong. It did make him smarter than her. And she better not say something to screw up his special moment. He would smite her down like the weasel she was with an adroit turn of phrase, something he excelled in.

"They botched it?" Rick asked; eyebrows lifted in mock surprise.

"I'm even more potent now," Stefan said, the ends of his lips twitching.

"I wish I could joke like Stefan," Shelli said. "But I'm hampered by the fact that I was raised Catholic, and Catholics are rarely funny. Ok there's George Carlin and Jimmy Fallon. That's it. There are too many Jewish comedians to count, but converting to Judaism hasn't improved my ability to tell jokes."

"It's no use; there's too much chlorine in your gene pool," Stefan said.

Shelli had a hurt look on her face. When did she get this thin-skinned? Couldn't she take a joke? Didn't she remember the last time they had quarreled she embarrassed him in front of a group of friends, claiming that most of a story that he said was true had been fabricated. Stefan told her to bug off, and stop ruining his fun. She walked away, "Fine," she said. "At least they know now that it's not true." Like it mattered. His face burned at the memory. To her retreating back he called out "toxic." The word hung in the air like the sulfuric acid coating on ash. What had he done to merit this? To anyone who would listen he said, "Welcome to my life," the same phrase his mother used when his father said something stupid. His audience sided with him and said they didn't care if it was true or not, he made a better story by changing stuff. So why did she have a problem with that? Shelli argued with his audience, saying that Stefan had to inform people that a lot of it wasn't true otherwise they'd have the wrong impression, and think that everything happened the way he said. Stefan believed that she said that to fuck with him, and laughed when she said that there's a separation between nonfiction and fiction in the bookstores, and why was that? Her defiance got on his nerves, as if her only goal in life was to point out his faults. Thinking like this made his blood boil. How many stories that are told at parties are true anyway, probably not many.

Stefan winked at Rick. He wasn't going to let Shelli ruin his good time. Like Stefan, Rick had most of Seinfeld's jokes memorized. He had a quiet air about him, but he tended to get rowdy around the party animals, getting a boost off their bigger personalities.

"Looking on the bright side, your timing is impeccable," Rick said.

Stefan was proud of his ability to call up lines verbatim. Some people might say when someone borrows other peoples' observations on a regular basis, they're playing a charade, and are basically mere cut-outs, stand-ins for someone else, but Stefan believed that by aping his favorite comedians, he paid the ultimate compliment to the greats. In parroting the masters of comedy to whom he paid lip service, he could for a moment imagine it made him fun-loving, and helped him see the world differently, leaving a residual bright light to shine in the dark corners of his mind. But what he especially liked, people looked at him as if he was the genius who made up those words up on the fly. They didn't know that it didn't come from him, wanted to ascribe authorship to him, peg him as immortal. He loved being adored like that, and did nothing to dissuade people of that false impression. Why should he when it made him feel this good?

Mattie moved out of that triangle and started pouring more drinks—something new, she said, as she bustled around, sending live sparks around the room exclaiming over the fresh mint she had picked minutes before their arrival and the drinking glasses she had contracted to a glass blower, each individually cast. To Stefan she appeared to be the most fascinating woman in the world, he fed off her energy like a piranha. Even the other women were affected. Julia and Leah looked like they were exchanging confidences, probably the sort of nasty gossip only a woman could dream up, thinking to belittle their hostess with the moistest. Hard to say, but easy to see that someone was getting roasted, those wagging fingers spoke volumes. Shelli circled the fringes.

The aura around Mattie radiated the room, it didn't matter what she wore, she could wear tatters and she would look amazing, and even more amazing, how unselfconscious and guileless she appeared, although she dressed in the height of fashion. On her it looked natural and wonderful; her fire-engine dress seemed to crackle with energy. Without a doubt she was an A-list hostess, able to keep the party spirit alive just by breathing, having that special knack for keeping things flowing, never allowing anything to get too far out of line. With a smile that never faltered, she handed out colorful libations, insisting that her recipe trumped anything any of them had ever experienced.

Stefan complimented her skill as a bartender.

"Speaking of bars, what did the condoms say when they passed a gay bar," Mattie said. That night, she was full of wisecracks.

"Beats me."

"Wanna get shit faced?"

"Where did you get the sense of humor," Stefan said. "My ears are burning."

"That's quite the compliment from the Master of Funny," she said.

Everyone was quite soused by the time they packed into Rick's cream-colored Lexus SUV. On their way over the Verrazano-Narrows Bridge, looking out at the still, gray waters of New York Bay, a convoy of small boats bobbed like toys, and in the distance, long metal-colored container ships gleamed dully as if they were coins cast out into the setting sun, Stefan told Mattie that their cute dance teacher had invited Stefan to be her partner at a competition in Los Angeles.

"It's okay if you go without me," Shelli said.

"Not to worry, honey, the teachers only ask the students to go with them in the hopes they'll pay the teacher's expenses." It was just like Shelli to throw cold water on his fun. Well, he wouldn't let her do it. "But only the students they like, obviously."

If only Shelli would stop focusing on him and just start having fun with others. He thought it was unnerving the way she clung to him, why so unsecure? Swinging didn't do anything to change that. He had hoped it would.

"Will you pay for Rick and me, too?" Mattie said, knowing just what to say.

"Oh, sure, nothing I'd rather do."

The Center for Experimental Sex was housed in an innocuous old-fashioned brick sort of warehouse with small windows—nothing like the sumptuous Montauk mansion that housed the swingers club. Reclaimed wood and brick covered the interior, giving it a cozy downhome feel, and the high, exposed ceiling added a dishabille touch—it could have doubled as a nightclub for heavy metal enthusiasts. Were it not for the whips, the multitude of candles sitting out in orderly rows for a demonstration on waxing, and trays loaded with medical-looking devices designed to deliver electric shocks to certain sensitive parts of the anatomy, the crowd gathered in the main room chatting in low tones could have passed for any upscale new age parenting group. On whole, the women were better looking and more fashionably dressed than the females at the swinger club, which was interesting; perhaps women find they don't like swapping once they discover that most men are lousy lovers, and some of the worst were the best looking ones, too consumed by their own egos.

Julia talked on and on about her baby, which Stefan was okay with, as long as the talk was entertaining. Stefan loved to talk about his sons, but not so much about their care and feeding, since that was one area he was involved himself only the rare occasion when he happened to get home early from work, and on the weekends when he wasn't busy with board meetings and the like. In the old days he happily played baseball and basketball with them, but those times were becoming increasingly rare to his sorrow, which he told Julia about—mentioning only his sadness, not his attempts to coerce them—and boasted how good the boys were in sports, but he wasn't sure how much Julia would care to hear, so he stopped talking after a time and asked her about her children, listening to her worries over the infant's crying spells and nonstop pooping, allowing his eyes to wander the room, taking in all the sights and sounds of a noir carnival in the making.

People sat on couches and seats along one wall or stood in groups, talking. One man in a custom-made suit caught Stefan's eye. The man had considerable gravitas; perhaps he was a tax lawyer or a stockbroker. Next to him sat his no-nonsense-looking schoolteacher wife with the nice body and sensible loafers, the two of them lending a scholarly air to the proceedings. Their neighbor on the right, a ponytailed young man in skintight black leather pants lounged on an overstuffed couch with his hot date. She wore short shorts and black tights underneath, her cropped tee exposing a tight belly. Seated next to them, an earth mother with frizzy tangerine hair and a long dress looked like she was slowly collapsing under the weight of the world. Her man, a somber, mustachioed fellow in an elbow-patched blazer, held her steady with an Atlas-like grip. Stefan felt a kinship with this man, having to keep the wife in check, or focused on babysitting detail, and never able to relax. He looked at the man with sympathy. They nodded to each other.

The first of the evening's examples had been set up directly in front of him—a somber affair, everything in black. The faces around him reflected the same heightened sense of excitement, the feeling that they were about to witness something new and important. On a surgical-looking slab, a woman lay prone, alabaster skin bruised, her figure as frail as if she would blow away in a slight wind, as still as death. Blindfolded and dumb, not a sound came out of her, didn't matter what people said around her. She appeared not be breathing while a slightly built man in his early thirties with a pockmarked face ran the tip of a sharp knife lightly down her body, lining her flesh with a thin trickle of blood. He dribbled ribbons of hot candle wax carefully with methodical precision into those razor-thin red lines he made, his attitude pensive. He was the artist and the woman his canvas, and looked as ravaged as if he had gone through a similar process with a pocket knife, his face as fissured as a dry creek bed, his hair uncombed as if matters of hygiene didn't concern him, his stoicism revealing nothing beyond a clenched lip.

Stefan caught Mattie's eye. He made a face, opening his mouth as if silently screaming.

"First the hot wax," the man said. As he spoke, he applied a dildo to her clit. "And then the dildo. The combination drives her crazy."

On the opposite side of the room, against one corner of the rough softwood paneling, a woman in her late forties with waist-long purple-streaked hair and silver pins along one eyebrow, was putting the finishing touches on a display of long, slender whips made of various grades of leather, from cowhide to deerskin, and, for the more adventurous, whips made of different types of rubber and plastics, from cellulose acetate to glass-reinforced polyester, everything arrayed like souvenirs at a country fair. From one rail she selected a goose feather for light tickling, and a Davy Crockett-style fur tail to apply afterward to soothe the sting between floggings. A crowd gathered around her.

She spoke about the proper way to whip. Done correctly, whipping heightens pleasure and minimizes pain. In summary: never hit near the vital organs, and no wrapping of the whip around the body. Her most important tip? Aim for the shoulders or the sweet spot on the buns.

"How did you find out about this place?" Stefan asked.

"*Village Voice*," Mattie said.

"I thought I'd seen everything but this's a doozy."

He refrained from saying what he really thought, that pain turned him off, didn't matter how elaborately it was dressed up. He turned to walk away from that display and discovered the rest of their group following suit.

They found themselves in the next room, the door plaque proclaiming it as the surgery room. From the looks of it, wood paneled and airy, and meticulously clean, and looking as if they had walked into a hip loft, Stefan flashed on scenes with Gene Wilder in *Young Frankenstein* which seemed promising. In the middle of the room, a man with shoulder-length silvery hair and a leather vest demonstrated how to strap on a contraption doctors use to alleviate back pain, known in the medical profession as a TENS machine. Here it was used in electric play, which he called *edge play* because it carries a higher than average risk. He cautioned people to approach the whole concept with caution; use the TENS machine below the waist to prevent shocks from reaching the heart. Despite the risks, it was the most popular thing in this club, guessing by the long line of people waiting to use it. Stefan angled it so he was standing next to Mattie.

"People that jaded?" He said in an aside, with a glance at Rick.

"Apparently," Mattie said.

A tall, handsome man with dark, curly hair flourished a whip made of deerskin, swishing it over the crowd as a prelude to oohs and ahhs before he began flogging a strikingly beautiful, zaftig woman, a Lady Cunegonde with gorgeous auburn hair pulled up in a bun, a few tendrils hanging winsomely around her face like vines on a flower. She looked soft as a peach, her full, rounded breasts and hips doing this little vibrating motion each time he struck her. At no time did she look scared. He took out another whip from the rack, a longer sturdier one, arching it high and testing it a few times before bringing it down lightly on her strong shoulders with a resounding slap. Stefan flinched at each lash as if he stood in her stead, a scream lodged in his throat, but she didn't react at all, seemingly oblivious to the impact, despite angry red slash marks appearing on her skin. The lashes rang out rhythmically, elegantly, with precision, each carefully aimed and lovingly applied, punctuated with long stretches of sweet talk and caresses between applications. Some five minutes passed after the peal of the last lash had sounded before she gave her master a signal and he unbound her. She fell against him with a cry, sighing with relief. He wiped her sweaty brow with concern, yet it continued to elude Stefan why anyone would want to subject themselves to that. For him, it held zero appeal.

At the moment Lady Cunegonde looked flushed, her cheeks reddened from exertion, the ends of her hair hanging limp with beaded sweat. Seeing her like that made Stefan feel faint, adding to his sadness that men did this to women. Stefan couldn't imagine her enjoying it, but maybe she did, it was hard to tell from looking at her. The flogger covered her face in kisses, big, fruity ones, as if his lips could soothe the pain—his fingers tracing circles on her breasts. Stefan couldn't stand watching the man who had been wielding the whip putting his hands on her, but he couldn't take his eyes away either. She looked like she was turned on by the flogger's touch. Stefan wondered about a woman who needed to be whipped to feel passion. And maybe the man doing the flogging feels that hitting is the only way he can reach an understanding with the woman. In every relationship there are simmering resentments. A less refined man might consider whipping an effective means of control, particularly a man who doesn't know how to communicate his frustrations any other way. But the idea of hewing to this kind of communication to elicit sexual desire made Stefan's blood run cold. The woman collapsed against a wall. To Stefan's surprise, Lady Cunegonde appeared to be basking in post-or pre-orgasmic bliss, a feeling he didn't share but longed for, with every cell in his body straining with a hard, cold hunger. Her well-padded back shone a bright red, but there was no purple bruising or breaks in the skin. He went up to the flogged woman and asked how she felt. She looked at him with the face of an angel, her cheeks flushed and rounded. How he envied her equanimity. She smiled but said not a word.

The man, who said his name was John, trained his manic eyes the color of icy marbles on Stefan as if they were weapons he'd unleash if Stefan wasn't careful.

"In the hands of a master flogger, pain quickly becomes pleasure." He said in a hushed voice.

"What'd you mean?"

"There are no words."

"Try me."

"There's a fine line between pain and pleasure," he said. "Keeping to that line is where pleasure is most intense. Over the years, I've developed this skill. Not many can do this. So you know I never go over that edge, I find where it is and I stick to the other side of it, always on that thinnest of lines." His eyes grew bigger still, until they were the size of cups. "I would do this for your woman."

"How long have you been doing this?" Stefan asked.

"I started as an apprentice in high school," John explained in a hoarse voice. "Over the years, it's become an obsession."

"You have a list of women who can recommend you?"

"I learned to give a woman exactly what she wants when she wants it," John said. "For a big woman, I know how to awaken the dormant nerve endings buried under the layers of fat. It takes a little more work on my part, but I'm happy to do this. For a slender woman, my touch is like a feather, to keep her hovering exquisitely at the edge before pleasure turns to pain. This takes practice. Not every flogger has my sensitivity and delicate touch. Ask Chloe. She'll vouch for me." His bushy eyebrows formed a dense, villous frown.

The vaguely sinister world around Stefan appeared to blur and swim before his eyes, adding to the compelling force of the master flogger's words as they spun around the room in an invisible vortex. Stefan turned to find Rick standing next to him.

"I'd love to learn how to properly whip," Rick said, brushed his hands through his hair, making it stand on end. "Mattie needs a good spanking."

"Geez...be my guest," Stefan said. "You won't see me playing that card. Pain doesn't turn me on." He tried to look disinterested, but he could see from Mattie's curious expression that he wasn't succeeding.

A few feet away, a woman with well-developed arm muscles dealt blows to a man's balls with a paddle. He lay on a stretcher, and didn't move.

Wincing, Rick wondered out loud how that could feel good to the man. Stefan pointed out that apparently the victim liked it, judging from the rapt expression on his face.

Rick's eyes locked on Stefan likely hoping for something deliciously shocking to hear. Stefan said he would have liked to have had the opportunity to apply a paddle to Rick's balls. Thankfully, Rick looked amused. They watched a dominatrix put a pale, dangling child-man on a leather horse, finding some solace in the gentleness of her gestures. Murmuring soothingly, like a nurse to a patient, she clamped plastic clothespins on the dazed man's nipples and rubbed the skin around them. Her victim looked to be in ecstasy. Stefan thought that the man probably couldn't get it up and this is how he coped.

"I hear you've become quite the Don Juan," Rick added breezily as if he were talking about the weather. His foot-tapping got obnoxious.

"I've played around during my marriage, nothing serious," Stefan said. "I just can't help myself."

"You think I didn't know? You announce it every chance you get."

"The urge is encoded in every red-blooded male."

"Lay off my wife."

"Your wife is a big fantasy of mine." Stefan attempted a chuckle. With an effort he managed to relax his facial muscles, and not give way to the cold fear numbing his belly, and blurt out the confession about the secret life he and Shelli led that lodged deep in his throat, like a burp that wouldn't resolve itself. That realization made his armpits heat up like little saunas, and his hair to stick to his brow like glue. Each time he swore up and down that Shelli and he were ensconced in blissful if boring monogamy, his skin got a little hotter until it started to feel like it was on fire. He was exceptionally good at lying; having perfected this skill in his sales job knowing to keep his voice warm and pleasant, and talk like he was joking in a bid to authenticate his claim that he had nothing to do with swingers clubs, but all anyone had to do was look at his eyes to know. "If you can stomach a visual of me masturbating to a picture of your wife," Stefan choked out these words, or maybe he swallowed them, as if, he too, questioned the direction they were going in.

"That's disgusting...I want to take that visual right out of my head."

"I'm playing with you. I think of your wife in the same hallowed terms as King David's first wife, Michal. I wouldn't desecrate her image that way."

"Admit you secretly want to shag my wife."

"All the guys do," Stefan said.

"Do you think I'd let any of you pervs have your way with Mattie? No fucking way." His tone was solemn, as if he wanted

Stefan to see that he was no mere dilettante, that he took this matter of guarding his wife's honor in as businesslike a fashion as he did analyzing securities.

Just then Mattie and Shelli appeared on the other side of the TENS machine exhibit. Shelli looked beautiful, a fragile doll. But the contrast: Mattie never looked better, her long legs accentuated by four-inch heels. Mattie said something that he couldn't catch; the chatter in his own head obscured everything else. But he could see that she whatever she said had the others laughing. Open-mouthed, they hung on her words as if she were doling out cake crumbs. Men were turning their heads, frankly admiring. Nothing like the slow smolder of fuck-me heels. They changed the sway of a woman's hips, the rotation of her pelvis and her stride, forcing her to adopt those mincing geisha girl steps. And the way Mattie's calves tensed on those heels, oh man, so hot. Stefan couldn't bear it. He reached into his pants to adjust himself.

The man operating the TENS machine called for volunteers.

"I'd love to give you a good shock," Stefan said looking at Mattie, his tone teasing.

"Get in line," Mattie said. "Rick could use help warming me up."

"My man," Stefan slapped Rick on the back. "What about it?"

"Hot candle wax, anyone?" Shelli said, looking at him as if she would like nothing better than to hear him say ouch.

Thankfully, at that moment, the dominatrix walked over, lightly smacking a whip against her own thigh. Shelli looked like she wanted to grab the whip out of the hand of the dominatrix and smash it down on his hands—clearly Shelli wasn't amused by his flirtatious ways, especially when it came to Mattie. Stefan wished that Shelli was less possessive, she cramped his style. He also understood that Rick considered Stefan's interest in his wife a compliment, as long as it remained all talk.

Right then, one of dominatrix's whips started crawling over Mattie's back.

"Doesn't have to be extreme," the dominatrix said. She was dressed all in black from the leather cat suit to the black nail polish accentuating her long, slender nails. "Subtle touches can be enough to arouse the most jaded lover. Black leather and garter belts may seem like routine fare, but they scream S&M. Even the simple act of giving each other a bath can be a light version of dominance and submission. Pinning another person's arms down is a mild form of bondage. You don't have to do much to turn something from the dull into the sublime."

"My husband's already amazing at foreplay," Mattie said. "Imagine what this'll do."

"I say this opens up a whole new world," Shelli said.

"It's all a tease, like being in a strip club," Stefan said, "and being told no touching, sit six feet from the dancers. What turns me on is flirting, followed by penetration, period."

"Yeah, well, so you say," Rick responded with a laugh, his face reddening. He always blushed easily, the color in his face changing with the ingestion of alcohol and with extremes of temperature. Right then his face looked like a ripe tomato.

"What I need is a cat-o'-nine-tails," Stefan said smoothly, having recovered his élan.

"Why don't you invest in a penis enlarger instead?" Shelli said.

"Take my wife, please," Stefan said. "Where have I failed?"

Stefan flashed on a picture in a magazine they had at home depicting one of Norman Mailer's wives grinding her lit cigarette into the author's bare ass at a sex orgy. Apparently a photographer was on hand to capture the moment. Stefan couldn't imagine why the fire from the burning cigarette didn't break the movement of Mailer's pelvis barreling into the woman he was fucking. Oy, maybe it turned Mailer on. He shuddered.

"I was thinking that, too," Rick said. "The one I want is sixteen and named Holly."

Sitting in the conference room of the middle school waiting for the principal to speak, Stefan looked across the polished pine conference table shiny with the defused light of the Jersey Shore and grimaced. Someone turned on the fluorescent lighting overhead and partially closed the blinds for what reason he couldn't understand, the sun wasn't bothering him in fact he liked it but that's how his parents did things, too, so it didn't question it as outlandish, a lot of people phobic to sunlight. Shelli opposed blinds unless there was a question of people looking in, they argued about it often. The fluorescent lighting made his tow-headed son with the impish face sitting directly across from him look unnaturally pale, almost ghostly.

Shelli sat on the other side of the table, next to their son. Her streaked caramel hair with the flecks of gold flowing down her back in an unruly mass. He looked upon her corded muscles, thinking she looked more like cyclist than he did, she was that lean. When he met Shelli he wasn't sophisticated about sexual things, back then he was merely happy if a girl was good looking, and laughed at his jokes. Extra points if she opened her legs for him. Today she looked good to him, but then she had to ruin it all, leaning forward, her face tense. Her panicked gaze flicked by Stefan with the insistence of a cornered animal, made him as fidgety as all hell, but he put his hands on his thighs, trying to still them. The woman needed to relax; she could use a sedative.

"But I didn't write anything bad," Seth wailed, scrunching up his eyes as if he wanted to cry. "No swear words."

The principal, a kindly looking woman with helmet hair, stopped writing on her legal pad and looked up with a ready smile, resting her plump hands over the pad. Amy Bloom arranged this meeting after Seth was pulled out of Miller's class for something he wrote on a flyer that had been passed around. One of the kids, a good friend of Seth's, had written: "everyone to run from school" under the typewritten words announcing an afterschool program and Seth had followed that up by scrawling underneath: "bring your guns." The first kid wasn't in any trouble, what he wrote was deemed unctuous at best.

Stefan straightened his shoulders, thinking it incumbent on him to ingratiate himself with the principal, and pasted on what he thought was the proper sort of smile to show that he was on her side, believing his son was at fault. His fingers itched to take the boy to task for it.

As the older woman spoke, he inclined his head, leaning in her direction, nodding every so often while listening to her talk in her emphatic way as if she was in front of a blackboard. Explaining why it's against the school policy to allow anything spoken or written that could be construed as inciting violence. He looked at his son. It seemed as if Seth didn't hear her words, he was so focused on his belief that he didn't mean any harm, under his breath complaining bitterly. Apparently he couldn't understand why his innocence wasn't obvious to everyone else. Stefan moved restlessly on the hard seat that ground into the tailbone, and thought back to his school days in Brooklyn, roiled by violence in the wake of people of color moving into the neighborhood. Both whites and blacks involved in the fighting. He had been frightened by the gun and knife toting gangs prowling the hallways and playground, the climate of fear that engulfed the school stifled communication. Back in the day, Stefan talked to four or five kids that he knew from elementary school and stayed away from the others. The school on continual lockdown.

Seth's school was ninety-nine percent white, a scattering of American Indians and blacks, you could count them on one hand. His school was never in lockdown, he had never been knifed; Stefan doubted Seth had ever heard the term used. The kid had no idea how bad things can get.

"You're so lucky to go to a school were you don't fear for your life," Stefan said with some rancor. He shot a look at Bloom to see how she reacted to his comment. She cocked her head in Stefan's direction, and then turned to Seth.

"Seth," Bloom said. "In the wake of Columbine we can't have any sort of talk about guns. It doesn't matter that you were kidding."

Bloom's hair looked sprayed on, and in her shapeless navy suit, she looked like she was bent on erasing herself, disappearing into the hodgepodge of faceless bureaucrats that peopled the administration building, but the shadowing effect was offset by her smile radiating genuine concern.

"What's Columbine?" Seth said.

"You haven't heard about the school shooting in Colorado?" Bloom said. "Really?"

"No, I haven't."

"Two students got ahold of some guns and murdered a dozen students and a teacher. A lot of other people got hurt." She looked down at her papers as if she saw something disagreeable there. "These kids didn't deserve to die."

"That happened around here?" Seth looked incredulous, like he couldn't believe that such things could happen. "I didn't hear about it."

Stefan straightened his watchband. "Well, you wouldn't have," Stefan interjected, still looking at his watch. "You don't read the papers." His eyebrows went circumflex.

"I watch Jon Stewart," Seth said, striking a plaintive note.

"Jon Stewart," Stefan repeated. "That's not news." He shifted his back and re-centered his weight.

"For the kids it is," Shelli said primly, wearing that holier-than-thou expression that he hated. She pulled her hair off her face but it bounced back.

At that moment Stefan wanted to slap her smarmy attitude right off her face, thinking she was so much smarter than he.

"It happened in Colorado," Bloom said. "You know where Colorado is, don't you?" She spoke as if she was willing to wait forever for the right answer. She idly scratched the back of her hand. Sharp, curved palm shadows moved slightly over the pine table's shine, and her head bobbed, a half moon.

"Yes, ma'am," Seth said. "Borders New Mexico."

Stefan's thoughts slipped to his lover. He texted Kay a few days ago and she hadn't texted back. He thought maybe she was mad at him. Just then he slipped into his daydream and his yearning. Stefan opened his mouth to reveal teeth shining radiant against ruddy sunburn, forgetting where he was for a moment.

Mrs. Bloom's voice broke in like a rusty saw.

"And on the west side?"

"Utah."

"When people do these crazy things, we have to put in safeguards," Mrs. Bloom said softly. "Keep everyone safe."

"I was only kidding with my friend," Seth said. "I wasn't trying to get people to actually bring guns." His face paled white as a sheet making his freckles stand out even more.

"We have to take all jokes seriously," Bloom said. "There's no way to know if you were kidding or serious, so we have to go on the presumption that you're serious."

"I didn't think others would see it," Seth said.

"What do mean you didn't think anyone would see it?" Stefan demanded, lifting his hands to his face in a gesture of mock despair. "Wasn't that poster being passed around the room?" He abandoned all hopes of resurrecting his daydream.

"Stefan, could you stop whatever it is you're doing?" Shelli said. "He's telling the truth. He's not trying to cover anything up."

Again, that holier than thou glance had Stefan bristling.

"I didn't know that people would think I was being serious," Seth said. His voice rose to a ratchety place. His body stiffened, his fingers holding tight to his chair. "It was a joke."

"You have to write things with the understanding that others may see your words," Bloom said, rearranging the papers in front of her and in the process sitting up taller. "And take what you write seriously. They're not just passing the poster to the next kid without reading the words you wrote."

After a pause the principal said that the only course of action she could take was to suspend him from school for the week, starting the next day. He could get his assignments online. Seth's jaw dropped. He looked like he wanted to cry, his mouth crumpling.

The rest of the week, Shelli worked at home and Stefan came home early so they spell each other. Both of them were in agreement on this. They told Seth he had to act as if he was in school, and read or do schoolwork until 3 p.m., the time school let out. Stefan told him to sit on the couch, or at his desk in their office, and do his work, the reading or whatever.

Seth said he missed his friends in school, and he couldn't wait to go back. At the end of his ordeal, he promised to go to class on time, do his homework, and not get trouble.

"It's crazy that my words would be taken out of context in this way," he said. "That now I have to be careful what I say or write in public."

"It's part of the price we have to pay for having our freedom," Shelli said.

"This is the lasting legacy of the Columbine massacre," Stefan said. "Our freedom to speak has been curtailed, maybe forever."

"You have a right to express your opinions as long as you do so in a way that doesn't "materially and substantially" disrupt classes or other school activities, according to the American Civil Liberties Union," Shelli said. "I think threatening to bring a gun qualifies as a disruption. And they can probably also stop you from using language that they think is 'vulgar or indecent.'"

"When people are upset about something there needs to be more opportunity for dialogue," Stefan said. "So you at least you know there's someone who would hear you out."

"Yeah, but I was just kidding," Seth moaned. "I meant nothing by it."

That Saturday, Stefan's thirtieth birthday, dozens of people came around dinnertime to help him celebrate. A winter chill was in the air and it started to snow, but no one seemed to mind. Big fat flakes fell softly in the still cold air making everything look romantic and beautiful. The news reports predicted a few inches, not enough to be a concern for folks having to drive home later that night. Shelli allowed the boys to stay up late so they could have birthday cake, putting them to bed at ten, and stayed with them in their room until they closed their eyes. Then she came downstairs, saying that they both caved once they got upstairs and with the door closed, everything was quiet.

And that's when the party really got going. A second cousin of his whom he'd met exactly two times in the past ten years, a

Miami lawyer in town on business, wowed the living room with a story about Cuban women and their legendary sex drive. The cousin spoke Spanish fluently, which got him a lot of action, apparently. Allegedly, they offered sex in return for his services. He laughed when Stefan asked if he took most of his business that way. Stefan enjoyed the banter, but could barely make out what the cousin was saying over the voices of the two yentas, Shelli and Leah, jabbering away nonstop, you should only know, talking and laughing as if they were vying for the grand prize as Most Obnoxious. With an abrupt about-face, Stefan talked the cousin into leaving where they had been standing around the fireplace and go with him to the kitchen for another drink. This entailed taking a meandering trail around couches and chairs brimming with people, not an easy thing to do. The hubbub grew more boisterous the closer they got to the kitchen. Shelli walked by carrying a load of empty wine glasses. How weird that she was always at his elbow, couldn't shake her if he tried. They have not scored in weeks and Stefan was not happy about it, the least she could do was let him talk with his friends and cousin without her interference. Get his rocks off verbally. He wanted to talk about sex without her judging. Beguiled by even the lure of the taboo, the suggestive conversation with the cousin had stimulated him more than he cared to admit even to himself, hungry as he was in a near-constant grip of carnal desire, possessed by an inflammatory force that he had to put the skids on if he was going to make it through the night. And he'd like to do it with a new woman, but it wasn't easy to get anything going, and he didn't understand why women were so protective of their so-called 'virtue.' Women were all whores, in one way or another, time they faced the facts, though it was also true that women's indiscretion is a joke invented by men, as Machado de Assis alleges. The truth is that in matters of love, at least, women never give themselves away with idle boasts; usually they are felled by an inability to control gestures and facial expressions. The man will smile or deny it in an offhand way while the woman will take great pains to claim she's been slandered. Having given herself out of love, either Stendhal's love passion or the purely physical kind, but in the case of infidelity, feels she's betraying her duty and in the words of de Assis: "… needs to disguise matters with even greater artifice and ever more refined treachery, whereas the man, sensing that he is the root cause of this transgression and the vanquisher of his rival, feels legitimately proud, and move on quickly to another sentiment that is less harsh and less secret; that fine fatuousness which is the shimmering sweat of merit."

The conversations around him multiplied, and the laughter grew louder. Mattie appeared in the middle of all this, beaming. He feasted his eyes on her curves, everything visible in her tight little dress, and with an appreciative nod, handed her champagne that he had opened specially for her, a Moet with shades of copper and an aroma dominated by wild strawberries, which she promptly downed, smacking her lips. He moved close to her, his hip touching hers, his nerve endings bouncing like yo-yos, making him shiver.

"Want to twerk?" he said.

"You want me to shake my booty?"

"Yeh." His voice sounded a husky note.

The scent of hibiscus floated in from somewhere. Daniel opened a bottle for people who wanted red. Daniel was quite the talker, and appeared to be sneering at people when he talked and pontificating like he was lecturing one of his classes at the university, but his wife Leah could match him both in volume and content, she was quite the yenta. The two of them surrounded Stefan and Mattie.

331

"I'll twerk it," Leah said.

"Not me," Daniel said. "I don't touch the stuff."

Get the two of them together and the stories would flow, drunken shenanigans at wild parties, mostly reminiscing about their college days, Daniel said nothing interesting seemed to happen to them anymore, they lived vicariously through their son; he helped them relive their youth.

"He's the twerker of the family now," Leah said.

In the flittering lights cast by the candles, Leah looked busty in her creamy silk tunic, downed her wine, talking nonstop, and not spilling a drop. As usual, Leah had a story ready about her life before she met Daniel in Britain on her semester abroad, the parties they used to throw there, her stories sounding wilder with each telling. This time, she did not disappoint.

"Just this morning, I heard from an old friend," she said. "He asked me if he could whisk me off to the Caribbean. I told him Daniel might have something to say about that."

Leah waited until all eyes were on her before proceeding. "He sounded so surprised to hear that I had married. What did he think I was doing all these years, waiting on him?" Her laughter tinkled like a dozen silver bells. "Back in the day, he wasn't much in the sack." With her overdone makeup accenting perfect features, she looked like a plus-sized Barbie doll, certainly not one he would throw out of bed. He enjoyed looking at the beautiful wives and imagining what he'd do with them, happy that Shelli wasn't there to put the lid on. It took a herculean force to rip his mind away.

"Come on. You were tempted by his offer," Mattie teased. "Admit it."

"He had a pecker the size of my little finger," Leah said. "I couldn't feel a thing."

"If he was more to your liking in bed, would you have stayed with him?" Mattie asked. She had gone to Britain for that infamous semester abroad, where she met Leah, so she could somewhat relate, having met the man in question.

"I don't know," Leah said, looking serious. "Daniel was poor when I met him, but in bed he outperformed on every score. Maybe the truth was that we clicked so well I thought everything he did magnificent, and I ascribed it to what happened between the sheets. But really it was in our heads…that undefinable sense that we fit each other's grooves.… more important than money."

Everyone laughed, sounding like a gaggle of geese squawking about societal mores as if Leah was vying for the prize of Best Conversationalist, Sharpest Wit, or Most Shocking.

Several drinks later, everyone had split up into twos or threes, the talk simmering. Julia showed up with her baby, a chubby girl with big cheeks and a double chin, and a thicket of wispy red hair. She said she left the triplets with her two aunts who lived close by and were only too happy to have them. Nice to see Julia plainly smitten with her child, kissing the baby's cheeks, and making cute noises, making the baby laugh. Shelli went up to Julia. Stefan inched away, thinking to make his escape.

"Dawn's gotten so big," Shelli said, her hands stilled, for once she wasn't carrying dirty glassware. "And that new baby smell is delicious."

Julia cooed at the baby. The baby's eyes lit up.

Mattie came over and exclaimed, "She looks like you, spitting image."

Stefan stopped his migration.

The baby exposed pink gums mouthing 'puh buh' and kicking her legs. And then just as abruptly, she began crying.

"Was it something I said?" Shelli said, stroking the baby's arm, "so soft."

"Feeding time." Julia took a fuzzy baby blanket and draped over herself, inserting the baby inside.

Stefan looked at Julia and imagined himself in the role of the child: his face shoved under the blanket, lips on that areola, swollen breast filled with warm milk practically spurting into his mouth. He thought he could detect a look of satisfaction on Julia's face that was almost sexual with the kid latched on. He imagined the silky texture of the skin and the warmth of the milk. Something to be said for motherhood, a state of mind he would never experience, nor could he imagine it, not really, he had no reference point for what it feels like to grow a child internally, birth it, and then suckle it. But truthfully he was not patient enough to be a mother. He was a man with a man's interests. There was always something he was striving for, something that had to be fixed, or made better. He watched Shelli say something in an animated fashion, her finger wagging over her drink. Julia, with the baby still latched on, looked contented with her role as listener, her mind not completely focused on Shelli; apparently that's what happens to women as their nipples are suckled. Shelli asked about the sucking reflex and Julia said it was amazing how strong the baby's suckling apparatus, like an industrial strength vacuum. At first it hurts then the nipples toughen and the sensations evolve into something better than sex, and can only be described as nirvana. Shelli had no experience with that, the boys had been born premature, never developed a suckling reflex, she had to feed them with preemie nipples; they couldn't suck worth a damn. Lucky medical technology had it down in the preemie department.

"I'd love to have another child," Shelli said, "This time it'd be a girl."

"Really?" Stefan said. "If you wanted that, we should have done something about it years ago."

Didn't she know by now that while she was the mother of his children, she by no means was the only woman in his life, and in truth he didn't think they were a perfect match, that illusion had died years ago, and while there were times he liked being with her, like when they went cycling, or involved with their children, apart from that her sense of humor didn't jive with his. He liked to throw out one-liners borrowed from others drawing from his days in acting school memorizing entire scripts from popular moves and plays, and he appreciated that his interloper recognize the show he took the line from, and understood why he mentioned it, and perhaps have one of their own in response. It was rare for Shelli to come up with any lines from popular plays or movies for that matter—nothing outside Shakespeare, and the classics like Ibsen and Chekhov, stuff he wouldn't touch.

Julia asked about Rick's new car, an elegant, sky-blue Jag, one in a series of such cars in his possession. Rick's love of cars was legendary in their circle, something that Rick turned into a preamble to a discussion of some new outlandish investment he had sunk his quite generous commissions into, mostly distressed properties. When it came to money, no one outperformed Rick. Talking about Rick's money didn't do anything for Stefan's libido; it merely rereinforced the lines of demarcation. Stefan suspected that Rick's money did a lot to spur Mattie's legendary sex drive, solidifying her unshakable loyalty. Women were cunts. All this talk about wanting a big dick, when we all know when there's a fat bank account all that all goes out the window.

"He loves taking that new car out for a spin," Mattie said. "Give him any excuse. He'll volunteer to fetch the dry cleaning, whatever; the destination doesn't matter. He guns the engine on the straightaways and zips around turns like a panicky racehorse. That's the only time I've seen him really happy."

"Mattie, you like the car?" Julia asked, pushing her curly red hair to one side with a plump hand.

"It's a sexy car. If I were the jealous type, we'd have a problem," Mattie said. "I swear Rick loves that hunk of metal more than me." Her smile turned to a grimace, her voice rose to a rackety place, and she began sounding like a petulant child who's jealous of the new baby in the family.

"I can't believe that," Stefan said, pouring her another drink, wishing his wife wasn't watching him with that critical eye. Later, he knew, she would quiz him on everything he said, what did he mean by this or that, and, as always, he would say he was just kidding and couldn't she accept a joke at face value?

"He buys cars the way I buy shoes."

"Why is it I can have as many cars as I want, but I can only have one woman?" Rick broke in with what was supposed to sound like amiable sarcasm, but a sliver of irritation seeped in around the corners.

"I concur," Stefan said.

"How'd you like it if I had more than one man?" Mattie asked pointedly.

"Go ahead," Rick said with a laugh. "We know how that would turn out."

"It's just like you to say that." If looks could kill, Mattie's would have reduced him to smithereens.

"Be careful what you wish for," Shelli said.

That drew a chuckle from Stefan, but was lost on everyone else.

Just then, Trudie, Mattie's good friend from Britain visiting for the weekend, came to life. In a series of jerky motions, like a windup doll, she grabbed Mattie by the hands with a great show of energy, turning the hedgerow of punk hair streaked pink and lavender that sprayed around her face into a hive. Trudie liked to play up her British mannerisms. She spent part of her childhood in Britain and fancied herself a representative of the best breeding of the Commonwealth. Together, they faced Rick.

"You're lucky to have her," Trudie said.

"She knows I'm pulling her chain," Rick said. "I love her deeply, madly. Every time is like the first time."

"That's the first time you've said you love me in how many years?" Mattie said with a smile.

"What, are we keeping score on that too?" he countered and kissed her puckered mouth.

Seth put his arms around Candy Gurl, and petted her soft pillowy coat as long as she allowed him. And then Micah took a turn at petting. She was comical, looking like an overripe ballerina prone to skittering across the tile on dainty feet that were oddly incongruous. They laughed at her antics. And Candy Gurl liked it too, running around the boys, picking up on their excitement.

Candy Gurl had this thing of pretending to sleep while they ate knowing that after they were done she would get the leftovers. Liking that she was well behaved, Stefan said nice things. But she had some bad habits, too, drooling when excited or exercising, which admittedly was quite often, and she was a shedder par excellence, strands of her visible everywhere she parked her tushe, so she was forbidden on the furniture people sat on. Whenever Shelli or the boys took her out to the forest her coat trapped all kinds of stickers and twigs, most of it ended up on the furniture. Most days for about an hour Shelli could be found on her knees, working the doggy brush, but it didn't matter to Candy Gurl, she still liked to rub against furniture. Shelli took it in stride, she loved Candy Gurl. The dog couldn't help that her coat was a magnet for all sorts of things. But Stefan made it into a joke, which was funny the first fifty times, than paled. Shelli said she was taking the dog for a walk and got the leash, and texted Wilhelm to say they got a dog and would be taking her for a walk later that afternoon. Seth and Micah said they wanted to come. Shelli asked Stefan if he wanted some ice cream. He said no, he was on a diet, and patted his stomach.

After they got ice cream they went to the neighborhood park. The frigid air seemed to impart some of its hoary winter frost to the narrow slices of the Atlantic that could be seen through the netting cast by densely furred black spruce. Bits of frost clung to the branches like the dollops of ice cream they had just consumed. Shelli was glad she had the boys wear jackets. They stopped to take Candy Gurl off her leash and watched her scamper after a black poodle. The two dogs barked excitedly, communicating in dog-speak, Candy Gurl looking like a big, furry, gray and white dandelion compared to the stylish poodle, and exhibiting her huge personality, lively, playful, and foolhardy, leading the other dog in circles, which made the black one go crazy. Shelli thought they were a lot like her and Stefan. And although Shelli felt a certain comfort in Stefan's company, it was also true that they rarely did anything alone anymore and only occasionally got together with their regular friends. That thought unsettled her.

Candy Gurl led the other dog to the edge of the ravine, and somersaulting, her nose pointed up to the sky, encouraged the other dog to bark forcefully at a tree that people in the neighborhood said provided a home for the nest of a nearly extinct breed of eagles. Nothing stirred out of that tree, no matter how loudly they barked. Candy Gurl braced her legs as if prepared to jump the ravine, the other dog bouncing like an automated windup toy, and getting more frantic by the minute. They barked loudly, insistently, shattering Shelli's delicate equilibrium. Out of the thin air it seemed Wilhelm appeared holding the hand of a blond boy looking like an exact replica of his dad, but softer, with the most angelic features. Behind them, a cute cinnamon labradoodle came up and jumped around the two, boy and man, as if he knew them, encircling them in a force field where the molecules vibrated with the displaced kinetic energy of Candy Gurl even though physically she had bounded out of sight.

Wilhelm hugged Shelli, leaving her gasping for air.

"Nils, meet Shelli," he said.

"Hello," Shelli said, sitting on her haunches and shaking the boy's hand. "Charmed, I'm sure," Then Shelli reached for the dog's paw, which was extended readily, and shook gently with a grave demeanor.

"Where are your boys?" Nils said.

"They're with Candy Gurl," Shelli said, "They'll be along."

As if on cue Candy Gurl appeared with a big stick in her mouth, shuffling like a bear, stray leaves dragging the verdant lawn, leading all the dogs to mill around and connect noses or asses, depending which parts were the most smelly, followed by lithe figures of Seth and Micah, both raring with energy, twirling sticks with the leaves still attached that they were handling like lacrosse sticks. Off in the distance, along the well-nourished albeit soggy lawn, a group of kids kicked around a soccer ball, their happy calls to each other bringing joy to Shelli's spirits.

The boys ran ahead with the dogs. Wilhelm and Shelli stayed behind. There were other dogs in the park, mostly tiny fluff balls on leashes, or peering out of baby carriages, stub noses sniffing the air. An occasional dog would happen by, but the dogs around Shelli ignored these others, the boys had their complete attention, petting and stoking their fur. Shelli talked about what they did that morning and Wilhelm spoke of the little things that occupied his days and avoided talking about the future. He took her hand in his and caressed her fingers, her nerve endings sparking as if his fingers had electrical current running through them. They went to the playground, a modern affair with a Wizard of Oz vibe to it. It was filled with fanciful giant metal trees and flowers in bright colors and cute little sculptures of frogs and birds, and mosaics to capture the imagination, and sweet little winding paths. The boys played on the jungle gym and took turns on the slide. Shelli rode the frog. Wilhelm put his arms around her shoulders, and bent down to breathe the scent of her hair, lucky she had just washed it that morning. Her muscles felt languid and wonderfully relaxed; her nervous system free-floating in a restful cocoon of zigging endorphins. She watched the children with a full heart, not speaking. She longed to kiss and touch Wilhelm but refrained, thinking to be careful not to put on a public display around her children.

After a time, a cold wind came up. Seth and Micah pulled at her arms.

"I'm hungry," Seth said.

"I'm hungry," Micah said.

They said goodbye to Nils. Wilhelm gave Shelli a big hug and looked at her with hooded eyes before breaking away. Shelli got down on her knees to hug Nils her eyes filling with so much nameless emotion that had been stirred up like a dust storm stirs up leaves and loose gravel, a result of a lifetime of never feeling fully understood. Shelli didn't mind leaving Wilhelm—though the fullness in her heart felt like it would burst like a balloon that had splintered. It was not so much a goodbye, as a regrouping, her sorrow enhanced by the thought that their parting was temporary, and in any case, tinged with the sweetness of memories. And when they got home the boys mentioned Nils and the labradoodle, but not Wilhelm, how did they know not to mention him? Shelli was relieved although she would have been fine talking about Wilhelm if he had come up in the conversation, she would have blown it off as coincidence. She started the boys on their homework and went to the den to ask Stefan to pick some a few bottles of wine along with some other things she needed, since he planned in any case to make a run to the hardware shop. He left the house and she began cutting the vegetables. The rain made a soft patter on the windowpanes, and then grew in force and velocity sounding like thousand nails hitting the windows simultaneously, as if all the moisture in the skies had been funneled to their corner of the world. Minutes later, a rustling at the door announced Stefan's return, his tall figure stepped into the room dripping water everywhere. He ran upstairs to get changed.

The homemade tomato sauce made a few days before was bubbling on the stove; the bread grilled to perfection, and the spaghetti would take mere minutes, the freshly cut salad greens simply waited to be drizzled with balsamic vinegar.

"You were gone a long time. Did you find everything?"

"I ran into Mattie," he said. "At the grocery store, of all places. Funny huh? All this time we've lived here, I've never seen her there." The tremor visible in his entire affect hit her like a ton of bricks.

The rain stopped abruptly as if a celestial faucet had been turned off. Through a crack in the window, the scent of rain-drenched flowers hung in the air.

"That's because you rarely do any food shopping. I see her there all the time." As she spoke, she felt her heart lurch at the unexpected direction the conversation was taking.

His eyebrows shot up like he couldn't believe what he was hearing, like he never suspected that Mattie did mundane things like shopping.

"So, what did you talk about?" In saying this, she decided she needed to bring the conversation back to the banal, where it belonged.

"Chase just joined the football team at his school."

"I didn't know he was into football." Her tone was soothing, inviting more discussion. "How old is he? Fifteen?"

"Yeah, that's what Mattie said." Stefan paused for a few moments, and Shelli returned to cutting tomatoes, thinking she had to focus on the task at hand to avoid cutting her fingers. Stefan looked at her expectantly as if he waited in desperation for her to say something first before the dam of his mouth broke, but couldn't help himself, he had to speak about it although it seemed to her that he didn't want to say it. "Did she ever tell you she's got a thing for LeBron James?" He looked excited, happy, as if he had made an extraordinary discovery, his eyes twinkling black opals. "She watches a lot of basketball, and she roots for the same teams as I do. She's a real Knicks and LA Lakers fan."

"Rick's just as much of a sports nut."

"I'd like to invite her to a game at Madison Square Garden," he added wistfully.

"Oh, really?"

"Well, you don't want to go and I already have tickets."

"Would you invite Rick too?"

"He'd only be in the way."

Shelli caught her breath sharply, unable to say anything, and stared out the window, her eyes filling. Even though she knew that Stefan made it more than obvious that he didn't love her in the way he used to, and knowing that she was in love with another man—obvious even though she said nothing about it —it still hurt to hear him talk like this. At the moment, it seemed that he viewed her with a critical eye, positioning her in the worst possible light from across a vast gulf where he picked apart

342

her every move. Knowing this made her sadness fall on her like a thick blanket, suffocating her. And although that knowledge made her feel unclean, this didn't change her desire to preserve her marriage for her children. She didn't think of it as a charade exactly, she thought of it as presenting a good front for her sons, and as a way of preserving everyone's sanity. How necessary was it for them to love each other in that way? Couldn't they simply respect each other and make it work?

But even while making that mute appeal to her more sensible self, Shelli couldn't help but wonder at Stefan's excitement over meeting Mattie at the grocery store. Mattie was a comely woman, imbued with a fiery spirit; Shelli was in love with her, too. At this very moment she wondered how much of his desire to swing was about his attraction to their best friend. And realized she was kidding herself, worrying about his interest in Mattie when no way could she stop her highly charged erotic correspondence with Wilhelm. Stopping would plunge her to the depths of depression. But the crazy thing, even as she lusted for one man, yet she couldn't stop caring about the other, she wished they could be friends. And that he would try to spare her feelings. Yet she knew there would be a day of reckoning, how long would they get away with it? Or was it possible for one woman to have two men? In either case, one thing was certain: Wilhelm, that soul-charmer, that witch doctor, had cast spells on her heart.

Shelli turned back to her dinner preparations, setting out the dishes and utensils, ignoring her trembling fingers, feeling like a hypocrite, knowing that the minute before Stefan entered the room—changing everything by saying he had bumped into Mattie buying groceries—she floated in a bath of erotic sensations, her mind on Wilhelm. That remark about Mattie, although she had suspected as much, was a shock, thrown like ice water to the face. What should she do about it, try to make nice? Ignore his lustful talk? Despite her dismay, she knew it was up to her to make everything right again. And that meant ignoring the little mean things he said. He didn't know how grab ahold of the errant stones that had been lifted up, and push them back into the cobbled pathway, the foundation of their lives. She would have to do it all by herself, easier perhaps because she had Wilhelm waiting in the wings, rooting for her. When she had everything in order, she adjusted her facial muscles before turning to face the father of her children and kissed him as if nothing was wrong—a quick, perfunctory brush on the lips— and in a twinkling it came to her. She suggested they buy extra tickets so the two couples could go together. And then she went to the den and put a smile on to call the boys to dinner.

At yoga class the next morning, she spotted Mattie in the fourth row; spandex clad, her flanks long and slender in the soft morning light, head in the downward-facing dog position, her pale hair hanging over her face in straight silky strands. Even when assaulted by humidity and all kinds of contorted positioning, Mattie's hair formed a satiny smooth marvel. Shelli couldn't quite manage her unruly locks, sometimes her hair curled like Wilhelm's labradoodle, and other times they pointed in crazy directions, like corkscrews. Outside, the cloudless sky stretched out ethereally, a translucent blue. The morning's fog, a milky veil, had just burned off, exposing the trembling luminescence where sky, water, and land meet. In the distance, a Wall Street ferry puttered along the choppy swell of charcoal-gray waters; a couple of fishing trawlers rocked in its wake. The silver-studded New York skyline sparkled like a necklace around the throat of the sky at the horizon line.

If Rick knew that Stefan was probably fantasizing that minute about his wife, would he have a problem with that? But

Shelli also knew that Rick loved having other men put Mattie on a pedestal, as long as they didn't act on it.

Shelli couldn't help herself; she told Mattie what Stefan had said about meeting in the grocery store and talking up sports.

"Yeah, he likes me," Mattie said.

"He wants to invite you to a Knicks game. He's got season tickets," Shelli thought that no one really knew anyone else, not really, even the best of friends.

"I told him to bring you over and we'll watch a game together in our new media room. Rick's a big fan too."

"I'd like that," Shelli said, feeling relieved that Mattie acted like it was no big deal.

But the truth was that Shelli had stopped watching basketball, too busy texting Wilhelm. Take away the beauty of the players' bodies, and the game itself seemed boring. Back and forth with the ball until she could scream. But she knew that sharing his favorite activity with him would create a bond more powerful than words could ever do. She decided she had to make an effort for her children's sake, show a modicum of interest. It was one thing they could do together, even if she didn't love their father with the same erotic fervor as when they first met. She resolved to learn the basics about his favorite players, and read enough gossip about their sexual lives to make it entertaining, and then settle back on the couch with the family to watch a game, book in hand to get her though the boring parts.

Ten

Shelli said not a word about Tequila contacting her, or their meeting over lunch, or her plan to join Tequila with whatever boyfriend of the day she had with her, and of course Wilhelm became part of it. Shelli loved nurturing her quasi-lesbian relationship, but they only acted sexual with each other when guys were present, spending considerable time kissing and fondling each other to the delight of male onlookers. Shelli found that whenever she applied her lips to Tequila's mouth and with Wilhelm moving inside her, she soared so high she became lightheaded and faint, setting the stage for the ensuing fireworks, each orgasm better than the last, in timbre and volume nearly matching what she experienced with Wilhelm alone. She lived for the precious few moments she could spend with Wilhelm— with or without Tequila. For a few weeks now she reserved at least one evening for Wilhelm, and anyone else they choose to invite, and hired a twenty year old who was well-versed in the things the boys were learning in school as their tutor/companion for the evenings she was away. It worked really well for them, they learned a lot from Emily, and enjoyed their time together. But the girl was beautiful, though Shelli noticed Stefan looking at her, and realized that she had to protect this girl, even though she knew that likely she could trust Stefan, but he was a man, after all, and it would be best not to test him. She offered to drive Emily several times but turned out her mother was always on hand to pick her up.

She knew that soon she couldn't hide all this from her boys, but the way she figured it, these were the last days of her hurly burly. And she couldn't imagine that she would want lovers in this way for much longer, after all, as a practical issue, there was a time limit on how long she would have her looks. They had advanced in one regard: Shelli had a wonderful boyfriend and lover, and a hubby who was a good provider. She didn't mind that her husband was constantly off doing things with other people, he had been that way even before they got into swinging and had often in the past criticized her for not having more of a social life. Mostly he seemed happy that she had things to do that didn't involve him and rarely asked her what she was up to. When he did inquire, she said she was going out with girlfriends. At times she worried that she had spread herself too thin, and other times, she thought things were as perfect as they could be. Shelli believed most of his evenings truly were taken up with board meetings and guy friends. He was never able to keep anything hidden, and if he had a secret lover she would know, although sometimes he flew into a funk that he couldn't explain and climbed out for mysterious reasons, and that made her pause at times, thinking how funny if it turned out they both had secret lovers. But if she opened up and asked Stefan to join their parties, she was afraid what he might do or say. The idea of going down that road again put a cold chill in her heart. She didn't want to go back to the days of him taunting her in front of others. Though having Wilhelm in her life made her hornier; not less; with the added complication that she was far picker now: none of the other guys would do. She was still happy to have sex with Stefan although there was a weird thing he started doing, demanding that she lay completely still while he performed sex on her prone body. That puzzled her. Maybe he thought the woman should merely do what she was told, and not think for herself?

Shakespeare has nothing but contempt for women who try to step out of their female role. Eleanor Duchess of Gloucester in *2 Henrik VI*, entreats her husband, the Duke of Gloucester, to seize on his power and influence to take the crown. When he rebuffs her with the Shakespearean equivalent of a pat on the head, the duchess laments her husband's lack of ambition and the limitations of her sex, which prevent her from acting in his stead:

Follow I must; I cannot go before,
While Gloucester bears this base and humble mind.
Were I a man, a duke, and next of blood,
I would remove these tedious stumbling-blocks
And smooth my way upon their headless necks.

There was historical truth to this scene: the real Duchess of Gloucester was famously arrested and imprisoned on charges of treasonable necromancy for consulting astrologers who predicted the King's death.

Going as far back in history as the written word there's these warnings to women who would make decisions that benefited their selfish needs over the good of their family. It was said of Helen of Troy, that her beauty was impossible to resist, and that she willingly went with Paris and abandoned her husband and daughter. Betrayal by taking up with another man even if the husband ignores you the ancients felt was the most heinous thing a woman could do, but okay for a guy to do, as it was in his nature to do so. She has the babies, and males prefer to invest in their own DNA.

She went to the kitchen where Emily, the babysitter, was making peanut butter sandwiches and got out the whey protein and made everyone strawberry smoothies. Stefan hung around sipping his smoothie and talking to Emily. In the time they had known her, she had grown taller, more mature, slim and fine-featured, and sporting an abundance of light brown hair that hung down the small of her back, blossoming into a vision of loveliness, possessing the aura of intense physicality peculiar to young people. It was apparent to Shelli that Stefan thought her beautiful, too. He had that appreciative look in his eye, and he started in with some light jokes, something a teenager might like.

"How do you drown a hipster?" he asked.

"I can't guess," she said

"In the mainstream," he said.

Shelli was reminded of "The Country Husband," a short story by John Cheever, about a happily married man with three lovely children and a pretty vivacious wife who doesn't feel he lacks for anything until he gives the winsome babysitter a ride home at the end of the night. She gets into the car crying about her father, a drunk who's called her up from a bar saying she's immoral. Leaning on the shoulder of Francis, the happily married man, and in the act of comforting her, Francis feels "… it was so much like a paroxysm of love that Francis lost his head and pulled her roughly against him." After that, his awareness changed and he started to act badly, as happens with all male animals in proximity of the nubile. People started getting on his nerves, and he said mean things to people when they did, things he never said before. He dreamt of Emily, but he knew that seducing her could ruin his life, so he visited a shrink, saying he needed a doctor to cure what ailed him. The "cure" was a mandate to work with wood. He made a coffee table, bringing him a measure of satisfaction.

Shelli couldn't imagine this happening with Stefan; he was the type who couldn't keep his mouth shut. Nor could Stefan work a hammer and nails. Nabokov's Hubert Humbert at least has the excuse of having spent time in a mental intuition when he seduces a prepubescent girl and runs away with her. These days, Humbert would never get away with it.

Stefan appeared the lovable teddy bear, lounging against the wall, tensing his arms to making his biceps pop. Wearing an indolent expression that Shelli recognized as his flirty look, he smiled at the both of them. His eyes spoke of lust, isn't that how it starts but then the urge would have to be fanned, by say, a late-night ride in his car. Shelli would do what she could to limit his time alone with that girl, without him catching on. Although she also knew he wouldn't force himself on anyone, however, like many men, he might fantasize about the girl and make a move if offered that chance. The thing about Stefan he could never hide his feelings. Shelli resolved she would be the unseen force steering him in the right direction, away from the girl. At the end of the night Shelli was relieved to see Emily leave with her mother and Stefan go to the den to watch a movie while Shelli went outside to walk the dog with the boys. Everything seemed so normal, no one displaying any untoward emotions. She took the leash but didn't plan to use it unless they went through a development, there were a few mostly toward the center of the island, though she hoped to confine their walk to the path along the perimeter of the greenbelt extending down the entire east side of the peninsula, some of it submerged forests of old-growth timber, a result of landslides from long ago. At the gate they were out of view of the house—and earshot—and the boys were running in the meadow behind the neighbor's house with the dog, burrs in their hair. Only then did she call Wilhelm to share a laugh. In her mind's eye, when he spoke to her on the phone, she imagined his big blue, Dutch-bred eyes boring through metal and wire like two frigid, ice-cold laser beams seeking to impale her.

She mentioned that Stefan wanted to find another couple for them and her dread of this happening, and her hope that she could delay that prospect indefinitely.

"Hit his prick with a hammer and come to me instead," Wilhelm lashed out in his throaty accent.

"Feeling violent today, are we?"

"It's my way of saying I want you, darling, I can't think of anyone else. When are you going to leave that bully to come and live with me?"

"Not yet, sweetheart, it's not time."

"We'll go all over the world, wherever you like—Spain and France, Bali. But really, it doesn't matter what happens between you and Stefan, I'll take you to these places even if you stay with him. I want to be with you regardless."

"Really? If I stay with Stefan you'd still make love to me?"

"I don't care about the sex. I have plenty of that with the women I've met through dating sites. What I want is intelligence and passion."

Breathing in the bittersweet smell of the woods, she urged him to date others during the times she couldn't be with him. "I understand you might fall in love with one of these women, I'll take that chance."

"Most of the women I've met on the dating sites don't thrill me, even the pretty ones, Most are chimeras, so caught up in defending their self-worth that they can't connect. But with you, I don't find that to be true, what I find, more layers that need peeling, more discoveries to be made. I want to be with you more than an evening or two a week; I want to be with you all the time."

"Building a relationship involves acceptance, understanding, and more acceptance."

"I'm eager to work on this with you."

"Give it a few more months; we'll see how you feel then. My love for Stefan used to be strong, or at least the memory of it was. So I owe him this."

"But what about me? Don't I matter to you?"

"You'll always be in my life in one way or another."

Candy Gurl burst out of the brush, accompanied by the sound of cracking branches, some of which were clinging to her coat. She'd have to comb out the girl's fur before they went inside. It was the price she paid for having a long-haired animal. She had trimmed the dog's fur before the summer heat, and the fur hadn't fully grown out yet. She imagined Old English Sheepdogs could die in one hundred degree if not sheared. In any case, she wouldn't break up the family—not yet anyway, and was totally happy with dog and children—now she was resigned to the notion that great sex with Stefan might be a thing of the past, and was willing to live with that but only because she had a lover who had proved to be more skilled sexually, and sent her into orbit every time he touched her, and turned out, lo and behold, to be fun to talk to. Even so, something about her secret life bothered her, as delighted as she professed to herself to be with it. Oftentimes she woke up in the middle of the night thinking that having a lover like this couldn't last.

Having enjoyed the athleticism of her walk in the cold wintery air, in the warmth of the house Shelli promptly peeled off her jacket and pulled the boys to her, and told them to hold still. Absorbed by the minutia of combing the burrs in the boys' hair, and checking for ticks as well, she had to ask them repeatedly to settle down, and let them go long before she was totally satisfied, but told herself that she got the worse of it.

Then she went through the dog's fur, getting the larger brambles out, and most of the burrs. The animal went to her water bowl, which Shelli discovered was empty and promptly filled it. The dog drank her fill, splashing everywhere. Shelli put the boys to bed and they quickly fell asleep.

Shelli found Stefan upstairs smoking his bong. He asked her if she wanted some. She smoked a few hits having decided to join him in the interests of solidarity, thinking it'd be more fun if they did it together, finding that pot made her more attenuated to the sensual. But Stefan had to get so stoned he could barely walk but this was not something they could talk about. Whenever she mentioned his addiction, he went on the attack, so she avoided talking about it. They scrubbed each other in the shower, with a fervor that reminded her of the old days. She did what she could to inspire the usual heat when they moved to the bed, and it seemed to catch after a worrisome beginning, though she felt the spark was slow to catch. Is it possible she simply hallucinated what happened in the shower? But then she pried the problem out of him. For the past weeks rumors that the bull market wasn't going to last had spread and Stefan couldn't shake it out of his clients, didn't matter what he said, and worried that he couldn't cover the withdrawals of people clamoring to withdraw their money all at once. He was working on delaying their requests as long as he could and pleading with them to leave their money in the fund at least for the short term. He said he felt like a fraud. How to tell people the company was overextended? She held him in her arms and rocked him for a time and felt empathy the same way she would if she had come across injured wildlife on the road, and his unhappiness slid off her like slick oil, there were parts of her that he couldn't penetrate, didn't matter how bad it got. She was just an actor on the stage, none of it felt real.

According to Seth, Miss Miller, the science teacher, singled out Alex, Seth's good friend, and picked on him a lot. Alex was painfully shy, at least a foot taller than the other boys and curled his shoulders to blend in, but he couldn't do anything about his debilitating stutter. The other kids picked on him, laughing at his extreme shyness and difficulty speaking. Alex was often called upon to repeat what the teacher had just said while the other kids giggled behind their hands. During class Alex drew on his notepad, clearly not listening, and having no idea what the teacher said. Seth sat next to Alex when they had class together so he could help him. Several times Seth tried to help Alex by passing him notes so Seth knew what teacher was talking about. He wrote *DNA* in big block letters, knowing that on his own, Alex would never guess what to say, not with the teacher standing a few feet away, arms crossed, tapping her foot.

Alex didn't look at Seth's paper and apparently his mumble was the wrong answer. The popular kids called Alex retarded and made fun of him right there in front of the teacher, who made no effort to stop them. When Shelli went to pick her boys up at the end of the school day, they told her everything.

"Seth is right to stand up for his friend," Shelli said. "It's about being a mensch." Shelli felt pride in Seth that he reached out to Alex and didn't join in the meanness of the others.

But that evening when Stefan heard about it he reacted the way he always did to any crisis involving his sons, big or small. The boys were his Achilles heel. "He's not your problem," Stefan said. "While it's regrettable that the teacher was acting like a cretin, don't pit yourself against the teacher. That's the way to get killed. Better to put your head down."

This was one of the things about Stefan that stuck in her maw. His advice was to act cowardly. And not to help others when they are put upon. Shelli didn't see this as constructive; she saw this as refusing to help their children learn the best way to approach to a problem. And to do it smart, with courage.

"Supporting his friend doesn't require confronting the teacher directly," Shelli said. "There's other ways of support."

Stefan was good at selling, but couldn't analyze problems worth a damn. Shelli lit into him, saying that name calling by other students was uncalled for. She thought that Seth's plan to offer Alex support was the right thing, as long as he did it in a way that didn't get him into trouble with the teacher. She said next time Seth might serendipitously record the event with an actual recording device, not his phone. If the teacher caught him using his phone, she would likely confiscate the phone, and delete his recording.

When she said that, Stefan looked at her with dismay, his eyebrows doing that pongee thing.

We all have flaws, she told herself.

"That was exactly what Aldous Huxley was talking about in *Brave New World*," Seth said, "people programmed to be so afraid of not fitting in that they don't question anything the establishment tells them, instead they blindly follow."

"That's a great book," Shelli said. "Huxley hit on a truth."

"In *Brave New World* people were given drugs to keep them complaisant," Seth said. "It's as if he was writing about life today."

"What are you saying?" Stefan said. "*Brave New World* was written over one hundred years ago."

"The message is timeless, sweetheart," Shelli said. "Do you remember Lenina's attempt to get Bernard to take soma to improve his mood, and his response: "I'd rather be myself, myself and nasty. Not someone else, however jolly."

Seth quoted the line that Lenina says, repeating the nostrums she learned in nursery: "'A gramme in time…' until Bernard tells her to shut up."

Stefan went off, mumbling under his breath about losers.

That afternoon Seth took action and excised from his phone the contact information of many of the children they used to play with, the ones whose parents were friends with their parents, the ones who didn't dare think subversive thoughts, even when away from parents and teachers, the ones who didn't say anything when the popular kids made fun of Alex. Micah liked those kids until Seth said he didn't, and he, too, started erasing these kids' names from his phone. Shelli complained, saying that they were shutting out some really nice kids, and asked why.

"I never seen so many haters," Seth said. "I can't even."

Shelli admired Seth for caring and being willing to do something about it. Micah said he wanted to support his brother on this.

"Warhol got it right when he said it doesn't matter what you do, everyone just goes on thinking the same thing," Seth said.

"You're growing by the day," Shelli said, putting her hands on his shoulders. "You're taller than me."

"Really, I don't feel any different," he said. "Shouldn't I have growing pains?"

"And your voice sounds a tad deeper."

"Really? But I don't have a beard. Not even a whisker."

"Not yet. Your chin is as smooth as mine."

"I want Dad to teach me how to shave."

"Wait until you have something to shave, okay?"

The mood on the trading floor was subdued; people looked like their best friend had died. Stefan's feelings a mishmash, not wanting to let go the sweet fantasy that had been sustaining him of late, i.e. the scene in the kitchen under the skylight where nothing happened and yet, at the same time, everything changed. Stirred by the grace and beauty of that teenage princess, a vision of loveliness that startled his jaded sensibility, in turning to her, he seemed to have come to a point of the deepest part of a submerged memory, something that surfaced from long ago. He had been on a date with a girl unattainable like this one, he didn't remember when it was exactly, but he was young, maybe on his first real job, and welling up inside, a sense of futility and desperation, concurrent with the feeling that if he could get this vixen to laugh all would be right in his world. Normally his heart would have plummeted looking at John's drab face, who just then was elbowing his way toward him, his tall figure framed by the fog pressing against the big bank of windows, a gray anamorphic mass. The sky and water looked like they were made out of the same whirling soft gray matter, moisture in its different forms befitting the funeral air inside the room. John passed him by with a nod, and Stefan saw that he was not the reason for John's look of concern. He saw a woman of exceptional beauty in that crowd of downcast faces which brought to mind the image of the girl; both seemed otherworldly, created without visible flaws. The woman was not a teenager but her beauty was vibrant and ageless, seemed to put him in a relationship with the world that felt mysterious and enthralling, and made the people around him sound terribly engaging, and made everyone look transformed, as if they had been shot through with a beam of light. Amazing what just looking at a beautiful woman can do for a man, never mind touching her.

Oh my god," someone on the floor cried. "Check these numbers."

"Shit hit the fan," said a guy whom Stefan liked for his acuity.

"We all knew this bubble was unsustainable," John said. "But the speed of the fall is breathtaking. Just this morning Cisco lost 86 percent of its market cap, Amazon stock fell from $107 to just $7. It's the 1920s all over again."

"I've never seen anything like it," a newcomer to the floor said forcefully as if he personally orchestrated the event.

"Remember back in March when the Dow sold at a phenomenal sixty-five times dividends," John said, "And we figured it had to be the right time to sell?"

"Most of my clients thought I was crazy to suggest such a thing," Stefan said, the rusty saw of his voice cracking, in a bid to be part of the conversation, feeling that he was late to the party. People were speaking at a speed that felt unsustainable.

Usually he was the most vocal but now in his altered state, he was reduced to a pale ghost of himself, at a loss for jokes, nothing in his head. It was as if he couldn't fully grasp what the newcomer was saying, he would rather hold on to the memories he hoarded, and dwell on the girl's perfume, and the music of her voice moving ethereally through the chambers of his mind. He shook his head as if to reorder his thoughts.

"I warned them," John said waving his hand in the air like instruments.

A few of the other traders had picked up their heads.

Stefan nodded his head dumbly, unable to break out of his haze to speak, his jaw muscles refusing to engage, and his eyes adopting an unfocused concentration for the few moments that he struggled to speak. And concurrently, he realized that if he could duck the worst that the dot.com bust meted out, he wasn't so bad off.

John's hands flew a mile a minute, swooping here, going high there, "I was at a lunch the other day and heard Druckenmiller say he bought into tech market in mid-1999 and sold everything out in January and was sitting pretty, smiling to himself, wondering when things would explode. Then some of his managers said they were making about five percent every frickin' day and he just couldn't stand hearing them talk like that, so Druckenmiller put a shitload of dollars in play…this was in early March…within hours of the top…. bought the top of the tech market in an emotional fit because he couldn't stand the fact that it kept going, violating every rule he learned in past 25 years. And, boy, did he get killed."

"He can afford to get killed. I can't." Stefan put his hands on John's shoulders, and gave his friend a gentle shake, and then let his hands drop. "A lot of my clients refused to get out of those risky stocks."

"I hope you recorded those conversations," John said.

"Of course, how stupid do you think I am?" Stefan said.

"Even the best minds weren't prepared," said the fresh-faced newcomer. "In just in five days, Soros's flagship Quantum Fund, in one fell swoop, saw what had been a two year-to-date gain turn into an eleven percent loss. By the end of April, the Quantum Fund plummeted twenty-two percent from the start of the year, and the smaller Quota Fund thirty-two percent."

"Ouch," Stefan said.

"A lot of companies got slammed, and not just in tech," the newcomer said.

"They're issuing pink slips and posting losses every day. Even weekends."

"Reminds me of something that happened to the US railroad in 1929," John said, "there were 163 'Class I' railroads in the U.S. Today there's seven."

"Thanks God for the circuit breaker regulations," Stefan said.

"Bubbles have to happen," John said. "It's a cleansing process. In the beginning of every bubble—precipitated by new technology—there's a free-for-all between the professionals and amateurs trying to pick the winners."

"When there's something to be gained, the companies selling the pickaxes and dynamite do well." Stefan had read in several of his history books that the merchants during the Gold Rush made out like bandits, as did the railroads.

"True," John stuck to his point, showing his characteristic stubbornness, the main reason he got so much business, he just wore people out. "But even then it's hard to predict ahead of time how it'll all shake out."

"Do you remember when HP acquired the Palm?" Stefan said.

"Yeah, the Palm," John said. "Cloud based, wasn't it?"

"HP thought the Palm could be a contender to iPad," Stefan said, "but they had such poor sales it was laughable, they weren't even listed on sales lists. Led to the sale of webOS to LG." The worst Stefan could imagine was being poor, and stranded without money, no money to buy food. In their line of business, only a fool wouldn't heed the warning. This was the stuff of nightmares.

"Now I recall," John said. "LG had wanted for a long time to move away from their existing app-based platform to cloud-based technologies, thinking it would save processing power, among other things, a smart move, on retrospect. But you know, practically everyone got hit," John said. "Luckily I put a sizable chunk into ten-year treasury bonds a long time ago."

"Of course you did." Stefan clapped his hands together. "Jesus H Christ." In his heart, raging despair: Why didn't he think to do precisely that?

Eleven

They sat near a bank of windows around a large rectangular table looking at the blackened, twisted trees and scarred earth fronting the gray foaming sea. Rick started a story about a summer trip he and Stefan took to Europe with just their backpacks and a few hundred dollars. They didn't money back then, life was simpler. Stefan took over the telling, as was typical of him, and everyone gathered around. His husky voice resonated, enthralling his audience, his face gleaming in the brooding light cast by the full moon as he recreated the summer that marked the end of their carefree life. Shelli found herself drawn in; he told that story better than Rick could ever do, the difference was striking. Rick hemmed and hawed, while Stefan colored the story with amusing details and asides. The upshot: They spent little, travelled on trains and hitchhiked, stayed in youth hostels, and ate cheaply. It was the kind of life that made Stefan happy. It worked out well, until the night both stepped out for a joint and everything they brought with them was stolen from the lobby of a youth hostel. How wonderful their parents had been, wiring them money to get home. He finished the story in deft strokes, his arms raised in his big, generous-hearted way.

Except for the rhythmic sound of waves there was silence all around. No one spoke at the conclusion of his story. It was as if he had sprinkled fairy dust over their heads. They stood around him, enthralled. Overhead, the moon waxed bright against a black sky, only a shimmer of stars visible. Shelli pulled her tangled hair back, exposing her face to cool night air coming in the open windows. Stefan's audience wanted more; they were visibly disappointed when he waved them off.

Rick changed the subject. "It's bad when McDonald's outperforms Microsoft," he said, his pale face reddening from drink. "I play tennis now. Golf's too expensive."

Shelli had to crank to see Rick, his face partially visible between the cut flowers that glowed like gems in the soft lamplight. He sat between Leah and Julia across the table. Strange to think about the stories of ruin: mansions abandoned in the middle of construction, former philanthropists reduced to taking charity from the institutions they had donated to, homeless shelters turning away the former rich. Shelli thought oh well, life's littered with minefields. But the crazy thing: at least among her friends, the calamity was mostly on paper, their homes still functional, electricity still on, the sun continuing to rise in the east and set in the west, the temperatures continued to warm as spring showed itself. To look around at the physical world, nothing had changed. Although their stock market accounts had been severely depleted and some cases completely wiped out, mostly it was paper money, and difficult to visualize.

"You didn't like golf anyway," Mattie cried from where she sat next to Stefan on the other side of the table. Her fork wrapped with noodles hung midair, dripping garlic.

"It's worse than you think," Joe said, his full lips mashed together, and eyes narrowed into pinpricks, as if he were the only one in possession of the secret formula and couldn't wait to let everyone in on it. He tended to be quiet, his manner innocuous and ingratiating in the way of someone whose main priority is to serve, but get him out of the pharmacy and he felt compelled to trot out his knowledge of *Barron's* and the *Wall Street Journal* at every opportunity. Typically he made everything out to be blacker than it really was.

Before the downturn Stefan and Rick tended to land on the sunny side of a trade, but after the crash Stefan didn't display the same enthusiasm anymore. He and Joe were agreeing on virtually everything, much to Shelli's dismay.

"One of my best candidates went belly-up," Stefan said. "And he knew his business better than anyone. Let his emotions take over."

"Spent money too freely?" Joe asked from the other side of the table.

"On top of everything else," Stefan finished with the coup de grâce with a slice of his hand to the table. He looked heated and pained, his eyebrows gyrating.

"How about Yahoo?" Rick said. "Jeff Mattel gave away their patent for Pay for Click advertising that they could have used to dominate the internet to Google for next to nothing."

"You heard about his next venture? A clothing business, I kid you not," Stefan said. "Never mind he totally fucked up Yahoo. Madrona Ventures handed over plenty of seed money, no questions asked. It's as if he had personally invented the internet. People like that always land on their feet."

"Crazy, huh?" Rick said.

"I knew there was going to be a market correction," Stefan said. "But I didn't pull everything out in time." Just that morning he had checked the market, and at breakfast, he had assured Shelli that he had hedged at least half of his bets correctly after all.

But what came out of his mouth next traveled the outer reaches of doom. "We could have made money on the downturn, but no, Shelli, the expert over here, convinced me to keep a presence in Microsoft, of all places. She was so convinced they weren't going to go down like the others because they ran a top-shelf business. I tried to warn her, but she made it her mission to talk me into holding some of the stock. And to keep the peace I did." He ran his hand through his thick hedgerow of hair, making it stand up on end, giving him a bedraggled look, like a witchy black cat.

"And you know the market will go up again," Shelli was an optimist in that regard.

"She's right," Rick said, looking at Stefan, his voice hardening, "although it might not be for another ten years."

"You just don't get it, do you?" Stefan said. "A million dollars vanishes, okay, but when the second million goes down the same way, I feel some pain. But you act as if it's nothing—a mere hiccup."

"You need to relax," Shelli said. "It's just money."

"Easy for you to say," Stefan said, "riding my coattails."

Shelli took deep breaths, thinking to herself that he posed this as a joke but underneath there was rancor. He liked to beat her over the head on this one: he made the money and she didn't. She tried to find her calm center, but her irritation backed up on her, and the treacherous muscles of the smile she was trying to force into submission kept betraying her. The pain of it all nearly caused her to cry out, nearly choking as she gulped it down, tasting its bitter dregs, the burn searing her throat. Her hair stuck limply to her neck.

"Are you okay, Shelli?" Julia asked. She leaned over, looking solicitous.

Behind Julia, the last rays of the sun sent streaks of orange marmalade across the room, wreathing a fiery halo about her head.

A tight smile played about the ends of Mattie's mouth. She turned to Stefan with her finger upraised, as if she were admonishing a child, her tone light. "I hope you're done now," she said. "Don't ruin our good time."

A man behind Shelli tipped his chair back. He appeared to be listening to their conversation.

"Talk to her," Stefan grumbled.

Everyone seemed to be staring at her, waiting for her response. She hoped they didn't expect her to keep repeating herself like a broken record, like her mother did to her father ad infinitum. She needed to wait for her emotions to subside before she could say anything as her jaw muscles refused to obey, and wished with the totality of her being that someone would introduce another topic, something uplifting.

"I've been playing damage control," Rick said, with a kindly look in Shelli's direction. "I talked the bank into a precious metals fund that's going gangbusters."

"Gas and oil, that's where it's at," Mattie cried.

"So, you're saying dump the precious metals?" Rick asked meekly, in a parody of total subservience to his wife.

"Yes, dear," Mattie said, glancing radiantly in his direction. "I've an advanced degree."

"And so you do, my dear," Rick responded, apparently pleased with himself at the positive message he was intent on delivering, his hand drumming the table.

"Alcohol," Daniel said. "People drink more in a downturn." He raised his wineglass as if he found all this subversive talk amusing.

"So you think attendance will fall at the sex clubs?" Rick asked. "Or is that category imperious to a down market?"

"I'd love to do the research," Stefan said with a wink and a hearty laugh.

Shelli looked at Stefan's radiating face, marveling that he could move so quickly to a happy place. She still smarted from the travesty of his charges. How could he blame her for thinking Microsoft impervious if the markets went belly up? Okay, admittedly an astute investor who wasn't consumed by greed would realize that no company was immune to disaster. She slowed her breathing, wanting to deflect the unhappy feelings she felt, and looked around at the others, thinking that she was her own worst enemy if she let it get to her. She hoped that when they were alone, she could talk with Stefan about what had just happened. She told herself to let it go—practice Tao. And so she worked at loosening the resisting bands of muscle, but they wouldn't cooperate, she just sat there with her wooden face of doom for all to see while they finished their meal. Stefan said he was tired, not interested in dessert, and wanted to go home. He hugged the guys and kissed the women with feeling, like a politician connecting with people in a way Shelli wished she could do. He exhibited a generosity of spirit that she admired and wished she could acquire; maybe it would rub off by osmosis? They went outside the restaurant into the chill air to fight the blowing wind with the waves crashing against the beach like timbales, part of nature's orchestra. The building stood all by itself on a stretch of undeveloped land that offered some relief from the overflow of look-alike housing sprouting all over New Jersey. In the darkness, all she could see was a crest of white foam. The wind whipped her eyes shut.

Shelli intended to wait until she got home to say anything, but she found she couldn't resist. Inside the dark and comfortable confines of the car, the question came as a feeling, not words. Her body, and the question inside it, was like a car filling up with the river it'd steered into. Her feelings rose, as waters do, through her body, leaving a pocket of oxygen compacting at the top. In these situations, she knew intuitively that she must break something to swim free, and said to herself: "Smash the window, idiot." Upon expelling her breath and breathing deeply, she asked Stefan if he was really mad at her about the stock market debacle, the dullness of her voice reflecting her low spirits. He told her she was being paranoid, he had been kidding. Couldn't she take a joke?

"I'd gladly give up everything if the welfare of our children demands it," Shelli countered.

"You're so full of shit. You'd be lost without your charge cards."

"I'm not saying it wouldn't be a big adjustment."

"Damn right."

Shelli didn't press the issue; they both made their points, better to back off and make a play at humor if she thought she had it in her. If nothing else, this is what she was learning about living with this man: much can be accomplished by listening to his gripes, as much as his pronouncements at times sounded overly harsh, and waiting until he was receptive to tell him her perspective without ramming it down his throat. She would attempt to moderate his stance by showing her willingness to work with him, and bottle her impatience.

The kids were not asleep when they got home. After paying the babysitter, Shelli heard that Emily's mom had a problem with her car, and the girl needed a ride home. Shelli briefly considered giving the girl a ride herself, and asked her boys who they would prefer putting them to bed, and they both cried "Momma," yet she vacillated, thinking she was going crazy with her fears about the girl, and not knowing what to do. Stefan had shown no signs of being anything more than his usual flirty self. And she thought the likelihood of Stefan acting on his impulses, unless he was egged on, was not going to happen, he was too much of a sissy. Berating herself for being too hard on him, she went to him and asked if he would drive the girl while she got the boys ready for bed. He readily agreed. She read in bed for a while and fell asleep before he got back. Stefan was up before her, so she didn't get a chance to ask about the girl, and then later it slipped her mind. The following morning Shelli bolted down her coffee and got the boys off to school before hurrying to her interview in West Orange. Her preoccupation with the fear that ran in underneath her consciousness like a subterranean river in the way that buried truths tend to rush along silently in some hidden place, informing decisions almost like they were preordained, she was beginning to realize that Stefan's verbal assaults had a lot to do with the problems she was having with self-esteem and connected with their secret life; but did that justify him making her the bad guy to their friends at the restaurant and elsewhere? She knew that no one would take her side, she was considered by people to be colorless, no personality. It dawned on her that sometimes she did start the fights, usually over some perceived slight or carelessness, leaving trash around for her to pick up for example.

After her meeting, driving past leafy trees through which could be seen filigreed images of houses behind the foliage, Shelli headed to the visitors parking lot at the school to pick up the boys, swerving past vans and gleaming luxury SUVs filled with screaming children, and parked under a big leafy maple. She stood near the car and waited outside. Seth asked if he could invite some of his friends' home for a few hours. She said yes as long as the parents approved. After making sure they all got permission, Shelli said she could take Amalie and Alex, but that was it. Alex carried himself as if he were a fragile and expensive piece of china, and took forever getting into the car, but Shelli understood that he was someone to handle gently. Amalie was one of those high-performing athletes, who, after exerting herself physically every day with swim practice following her two mile run, she would lose the energy to do anything when all words had failed her, she would flash her eyes, and lower her eyelashes, as if a heavy-lidded glance followed by fluttering lids conveyed everything she wanted to say.

Other kids got rides from other mothers. Everyone gathered in the kitchen to watch Amalie bake chocolate chip cookies, which largely consisted of standing around the bowl and swiping fingers in the dough, sampling. Good-naturedly she slapped their hands away and cut little squares to place on long cookie sheets. Candy Gurl's nose hovered nearby, sniffing the moist sweetness of freshly baked dough full of melting chocolate chunks issuing from the oven. The rich chocolate smell mixed easily with the sharp floral of plant life. Amalie was quieter than usual, her face marked by chocolate squiggles, but Shaun, standing next to her, made up for it with his loud talk and laughter. His soccer team had just won a tournament putting him in high spirits. He flexed his muscles, only too visible in his tight yellow tee, a thin tech fabric, the quick-wicking kind, which he made into a fashion statement by adding a pair of voluminous neon-blue track shorts and matching blue sneakers. At the other end of the counter, Alex huddled behind his camera, his hair hanging past his ears; chest and arms as slender as a young child's. He acted his usual shy self, snapping pictures, traces of cookie clinging to his white tee and denim pants. Candy Gurl appeared at Amalie's elbow, eyes as soft and moist as the melted chocolate she craved. Seth threw Candy Gurl a big hunk of cookie. The dog leapt in the air, her mouth opening like a steel trap, closing neatly over the delicacy with all the finesse of a gourmand.

After they had finished and the kids left for home, Shelli helped the boys with their homework and afterwards told them they were free to watch television or get on one of their videogames. They opted for both. Shelli was fine with it. A message from Stefan, saying he had gone somewhere with guy friends for a drink. What a pleasure to be alone with her thoughts. Something drew her to the cabinet in the den. On a whim, she pulled out one of Stefan's childhood albums. She stopped at the series of photos his father had taken of a seven-year-old Stefan and his friends splashing in their big above-ground pool. All the moms were seated in folding chairs on the lawn. Several of the photos showed tow-headed boys running around, throwing water-filled balloons at each other, mothers scattering. It looked like everyone was having a grand time. She noted how much like their dad they looked his build, eyes and thick hair, the rest of their features came from her, all of it created with much love. They were the warp and weft binding her to Stefan, creating a sense of community, giving her a sense of belonging to a family that she craved. She brought the album with her to the couch. What had she been like at that age: a tomboy who didn't like dresses and cut the hair off her dolls. And couldn't believe the quandary she was in, wishing she had faith in something, anything, but she questioned everything, that she couldn't change about herself. To think that she hadn't much advanced beyond the confusion of youth, still trapped in an endless series of choices, nothing clear-cut, decisions based on genetic coding and reactions to early childhood trauma. Every step of the way was endlessly fraught with difficult assessments, adjustments, nothing assured; things way easier for the religious. She might have liked Stefan back then—but then again, maybe not. Likely he had been a cowardly brat blaming others for things he started, not much different from now, having learned little in the interim. He had been a handsome boy. She found herself attracted to his amused grin, his mischievous eyes, and now, what she saw, Stefan's eyes and nose on her boys.

But if she could change her skeptical nature, she would happily get down on her knees, genuflecting and bowing her forehead to the earth, and ask God to tell her what to do. But even then the future would be murky, surprises at every corner. The only certainty was the love she had for her sons, and more tangentially, there was her love for Wilhelm. As for Stefan, her feelings were mixed, some of the time she felt a strong connection, and other times there was a feeling of rejection and shame. That sense of things seemed to have crystalized in recent weeks, as time went on she thought she detected a scornful twist to the lips, and words hanging like barbed wire, at first it happened when Wilhelm was around, and then it came up, it seemed, for no discernable reason. She quailed at the thought that eventually they would have return to the slog of monogamy, and the prospect of having to give up Wilhelm. And yet she couldn't imagine playing around indefinitely. But maybe she was wrong about her assumptions. Could such an eventuality be orchestrated?

On her phone, she found several messages from Wilhelm.

"When am I going to see you again?" he wrote.

"Things have been so hectic. Give me a few days, ok?"

Stefan came home went into the den to watch a television show on space travel.

"Funny, I dreamt of being an astronaut when I was a child," she said.

"Why?"

"I wanted to be a pioneer."

"It's the pioneers who get stabbed in the back," Stefan said.

"That's a cynical statement," she said. "You sound like your father when you say that." She knew that talking like that upset him; he didn't think of playing it safe as a bad thing, he thought of it as survival. She had been raised to understand that the only way to succeed was by taking calculated risks. They couldn't have been further apart in their outlook to life. But he was not one to dwell on things that had no clear-cut answers, to question the whys and wherefores.

"For you, a cynical statement is one you don't agree with," Stefan said.

"What's eating at you lately?" she asked. "You've got this low threshold when it comes to things I say."

"Sometimes you just don't know when to stop."

"If you could tell me in a nice way, I'd get the message."

"Excuse me, but I'm under a lot of stress."

"Come to mommy," She opened her arms. "I need a hug."

They connected briefly and split apart. In the warmth of the low light from the lamp it appeared that Shelli's tone and manner had a relaxing effect. Stefan facial features seemed to visibly relax.

"My boss said he's got to let go some of traders. I was latest hire, so I may get the axe."

"John likes you," Shelli said, hoping to sound conciliatory.

But then a shadow passed over Stefan's face and it seemed he had reconsidered his position, spitting his words like something disagreeable had lodged in his throat. "I wouldn't count on it." Apparently her ability to soothe was short lived. A few minutes later, he said: "I want to hear this, okay," and turned the volume up on the television. Shelli's stomach churned. The memory of Henrik, Stefan's father, walking away from an argument to rant at the television set came to mind. She wondered if the way they bickered was good for the boys to hear and couldn't hear him at this moment, but they heard him say similar things to her often enough, and she wondered how that might affect their sons—it was like they devolved to behaving like children themselves.

She daydreamed that Wilhelm came dashing into the room and with a flourish of sword and cape, swept her into his arms, promising he would rescue her. In her dream they walked out and Stefan didn't glance up from the television, not once. Without another word, Shelli left. Stefan followed her up to their room. She flopped on the bed.

"We can't talk without you biting my head off," she said, her head buried in a pillow, voice muffled.

"You shoot down everything I say."

"Hey, *kvetsher*, I could say that about you."

He wouldn't discuss their very real problems. Why that mattered now, she couldn't say, except that her conversation with Mattie had unsettled her, followed by that famous dinner with all their besties, making her feel about as together as a junkie headed for prison.

She sat up to, and thought to take a different tack. "What is it about me that bugs you the most?"

"You show no interest in my needs." He hadn't moved from his stance positioned in the middle of the room, his legs spread, arms folded across his chest.

"Okay, I have to watch that. I'll ask more questions. Is there something else?"

"You don't listen to me. I try to talk to you and you don't listen."

"I'm listening now."

"And now I forgot what I wanted to say."

"Let me know *shvitzer* and I'll be ready to lend an ear," Shelli said. "You used to be less prickly. I blame swinging. I don't like what it's doing to us."

"What? Like you're so easy to get along with?"

She went into the bathroom and brushed her teeth at the sink, her eyes flitting around the pink and white marble, the ornate trappings of her gilded cage, accompanied by her thoughts of Wilhelm, whom she didn't want to think about. Stefan she blamed for her current troubles, and at the back of her mind, the nagging thought surfaced that she should return that dress that she bought in a weak moment, immediately, on the morrow, before she changed her mind. The truth was she had plenty of clothes. As she wiped her wet hands flinging water on the bath towel, lost in daydreams, she realized that certain things might have escaped her attention. Did she merely think she'd become more loving, or had they become strangers to each other? Lately she'd been paying more attention to Wilhelm, Tequila and her lovers, and she had no idea how things really stood. And how much she'd come to depend on her virtual fantasy life she'd have denied vehemently. Was she fooling herself, thinking she could stop with the lovers and suddenly become the doting mother who gives and gives, asking for nothing in return? Shelli stepped out of the bathroom, took off her clothes and threw them on the bed. She sat on the bed on top of the clothes in her underwear.

Stefan sat down next to Shelli, scouted her clothes out of the way and put his arms around her. "Maybe if you could stop playing the victim card, we'd get along better."

She sighed heavily, feeling as if her heart were being sawed in two, knowing there was nothing she could say that he would care to hear, and instead asked a simple question, seeking answers.

"That's what I'm doing?" she said.

"Yes, and it's getting tired."

Briefly the film lifted and she realized it had been fun at first, but like any addiction, the sex soured and turned on them—having become potentially lethal, something like running a naked razor blade along her skin, knowing the danger, and continuing to do it anyway. She put up with Stefan's jealousy and his passive-aggressive bullying, knowing that everyone has faults. And in the meantime, she might have become less loving, perhaps even accusatory, wanting more than he could give. Her children were only a half of it. And there was this other nugget:

She didn't know Wilhelm well enough to know what kind of meshuga ways he hid from her. The stuff that people hide until they get to know each other well enough to relax their guard, the only way to know about those buried truths would involve spending a lot of time together. And truth be told, did she really have to choose between them, couldn't an accommodation be made? Although much of their love had been battered to a bloody pulp, she still loved Stefan.

In any case the boys needed their father. She didn't want to give up him up. She wanted it all. How to convince Stefan that she wasn't going anywhere but also that she wasn't willing to give up Wilhelm? Could they include other lovers? That would take some doing. Could she handle seeing Stefan with another woman, someone he cared about? She would have to be okay with that. With an incredible clarity of vision, Shelli knew that Stefan had blinders on when it came to knowing what to do; she had to be the one to show him the way. But also she needed to know when to back off. She recalled the ancient Greek myth of Nikaia, the magnificent girl who killed a harmless herdsman with her bow and arrow merely because he dared speak a few words of love to her. In defying the gods she ended up working the loom like any poor woman, sharing the same fate as Aura, another huntress that Dionysus had made pregnant. Dionysus had said that girls could take comfort in the thought that they formed part of a divine order. The truth of that wasn't lost on Shelli. Better to give a guy some slack, and realize guys are human, too.

With that in mind, she decided to do everything Stefan asked—which her therapist suggested, too—including responding with a simple yes or no to questions he posed. And to be more flexible when accepting what Stefan said were his limitations, even suggesting that she take what Stefan said at face value, and don't read weird or sinister motives into idle comments he made, the theory being that if she were to shed the mental baggage, he might follow suit. When he said something that caused her ire, the therapist suggested she wait and think about what she wanted to say, instead of reflectively saying something—and don't automatically think her assumptions were the correct ones, they could be wrong—circumventing the inevitable fight. Or if, upon reflection, she could think of a funny but banal comeback, she should go for it. The therapist also suggested she keep things light, and say the things that would solidify her willingness to cooperate—he had even used the words "willingness to cooperate." That meant, on her own, she'd take the extra step of picking up his trash and his half-empty coffee cups wherever he left them, and put things away without a word of reproach, and ignore the mean things he said. It got easier as time went on, but unquestionably it took considerable effort, the kind of effort a sedentary person would have to muster to get into the gym and maintain of habit of jogging every morning, not an easy thing to do, day in and day out. There were times she had to talk herself down from jumping the cliff. Sometimes her feelings clouded her good sense—the need to let go of her feeling that she had somehow been wronged. Make efforts to stop playing the victim, and think of the people around her, and make things better for them. But shutting her mouth was the hardest thing. The feminists had it all wrong.

When Shelli asked Mattie about it, Mattie said she was so certain this method would inspire him that she willingly staked her life on it. The therapist, however, wouldn't go that far.

After a few days of steadily increasing niceness, Stefan softened up considerably. One of those evenings after they had made the most passionate love in memory, Stefan turned to her, looking deep in thought, his mood pensive, not stirring. Shelli returned his gaze, not speaking. After a few minutes, with her lying quietly, looking at him, he fixed her with his impatient gaze.

"I know I have this nasty habit of taking out my shit on you," Stefan said. "I've been dispirited from the dotcom crash, made me feel roped to the mast." Seemly in a more reflective mood, he surprised her by suggesting they return to the safe harbors of monogamy, he said by way of explanation, "After going through this, do you feel any happier?" The look on his face was quixotical; his eyebrows and mouth forming a question mark.

She reached for a kiss, which he perfunctory returned as if he was on autopilot. He turned his back on her. "No more talk. I've got to sleep. Early call in the morning."

Tired from the day's work and tired with longing for something unattainable, something only a god from Mount Olympus could provide? Lying in bed only served to deepen her weariness, and with these questions swirling in her head, she fell into the deepest sleep.

Stefan was in his home office at his desk daydreaming in the fog-laced gloom, having forgotten to put the light on. He dreamt of something different for himself, but he no longer trusted that women would flock to him without him having to work for it, and the sense that he was somehow deficient filled him with sadness. He thought about Kay and Tequila and while he was able to get something going, in the end he felt they had rejected him. He thought his prick was big enough for most women, perhaps there was something else? He thought about the women he hungered for and never had a chance with, and the memories he called forth angered him. Couldn't understand why he wasn't more successful with women. They said he was handsome, albeit a little pudgy at times, and a good conversationalist. Why did he get so nervous that he couldn't keep it going in the sack? Before their marriage, he was shy around beautiful women, waiting until they made a move before making a move himself, and only started with Shelli when she wouldn't let him alone, and then the woman becoming as familiar as an old schmatte. He needed to be friends first, and trust was not easy to acquire.

This malaise about his own capabilities was starting to affect the muscles of his heart. Not so much a young adventurer robustly colliding with life as much as someone who just wants to get along. He felt none of his usual high spirits; instead he sank to new lows. Now he was just getting older and embittered; one of millions that likely felt this way. He blamed her. He was out of solutions. Shocking to see the men going berserk over his wife, his guiding hand never in evidence—this could not be tolerated, not even as a joke. And his struggles to find a new woman who would have him, he blanched at the memory of several women who refused to let him make love to them, even as their husbands were putting it to Shelli, and she, the selfish one, saw what was happening and continued with the man anyway, right in front of Stefan, the injustice of it made his stomach twist into a pretzel, and brought up an ugly acidic taste in his mouth. But there was no escape from his most urgent of urges: man programed to fuck as many good looking females as possible; what he was put on earth for. Investing in the highest most potent drive that nature endowed him with seemed the most reasonable of pursuits. Like a good Jew, he considered sex sacred between a man and wife; and as the biblical patriarchs had done, he'd extend that protection to concubines, but then he tended to the liberal side of these sorts of social arrangements. And finally he found Kay, who seemed to like him and just as he thought he had it made, Kay wouldn't answer his texts. An image of Tequila in the shower presented itself and he reflected on his enjoyment caressing her considerable charms, his excitement so profound he could barely contain himself. But that Alasdair was something else. At least he didn't dwell over much on the bad stuff, and tried to keep a positive attitude.

That thought led to others concerning Kay. He trembled as he dwelled on her infatuation with his dick, sucking and licking it like an ice cream Popsicle only matching his obsession with her weighty, sizable tits, crowned with pink aureoles the size of grapefruits, having the sole function of controls to her nervous system—flick there and this happens, or there, and something else transpires. He could control how much stimulus, and when and how she much she orgasms. He found that when he fantasized about Kay while fucking Shelli—never mind about the different body types—he'd grab Shelli's breasts and imagine he had Kay's in his hands, never mind that Kay's breasts were considerably floppier and soft as jellyrolls. He was able to transport himself and actually feel like it was Kay under him, precipitating the most delicious orgasm. And about that injunction in the Talmud not to fantasize about anyone but your wife when in bed with her…well, what if it? A natural human tendency, to think another person is in bed with you, and while Jewish sages were severe about sexual misconduct, and viewed conjugal intimacy as one of life's blessings and necessities, there is no universal prohibition on men having sexual relations out of wedlock although, as a nod to contemporary mores, modern rabbis frown on it. He never forced himself on anyone, and believed fervently in seduction as the only way, rape not his style.

Better that they remembered him fondly, even in their dreams. If that didn't work, he went without, and he didn't intend to break his record. When he was horny and she didn't feel it, he'd get irrational and act pissy like any red-blooded American male, but he liked the female to want it too. He aimed to please. Shelli usually saw through his moods and did something to put a smile on his face, why couldn't Kay be like that?

When pressed by the yogi master, Stefan acknowledged that Shelli had persevered, even though he put up roadblocks, and made things uncomfortable for her, yet she remained steady as a rock, willing to work with him on his issues, putting off her own gratification. Thinking like this brought tears come to his eyes, to think that Shelli was still able to give, even with all the shit he dished out.

He heard a sharp noise and realized that Shelli and the boys were home, making a hellish lot of noise. He left his office and went into the kitchen, discovered Micah buried in the icebox, and Seth pouring a glass of lemonade. His wife nowhere to be seen. Just then, the sun burst through the clouds, making everything seem brighter, chasing the gloom away.

Seth asked if they could go with Max's family to their cabin in the mountains for a weekend before school started. And Micah reminded him that Max had three siblings, and that they had been to Max's house multiple times. Seth said they liked Max's siblings. It was a three-hour drive but Shelli, who had just walked in the door carrying groceries and dumped them on the kitchen counter, said she didn't think that would be a problem, the chances of either boy being homesick with their good friends there was virtually nil. Plus Max's family had a speedboat. Stefan shrugged; he was fine with whatever the boys wanted to do. It gave him more time to do other things. Stefan wasn't keen on boats. He found them cold, windy, dirty, smelly, physically and mentally exhausting, not to mention dangerous, the list goes on. He preferred his feet planted on solid ground, but he wouldn't stand in the way of anyone who liked it.

"What's the big deal about boats?" Stefan said.

Shelli gave Stefan a nudge. To her credit, she didn't blow up as she usually did, which tended bring them to the boiling point and lash out with everything they had. He knew that he was partially responsible for Shelli's outbursts, some of his comments were off-putting, meant to make her or the boys feel his disapproval, like the time they went to the theater and Stefan insisted that he sit between the boys leaving her on the end where she couldn't speak to anyone other than Stefan. And as a twist to the knife, he reminded her he didn't like her talking to him even in whispers when the show was on, knowing that she would be bursting with comments. At the time his disgruntlement about the losses he sustained in the stock market and the swinging that didn't seem to go anywhere—vied for attention with the fantasy that struggled to stay alive, the hot babies he imagined would fall to him, and so rudely shut down by these loud-mouths.

"If Max's parents are okay with it, you can go," Shelli said.

The two were jumping up and down and creating a ruckus, their excitement bordered on frenzy. They might have gotten into a fight about it right then but underneath it all, heaving underneath his bowed shoulders, he admitted to himself that he was royally pissed that the whole swinging thing had not gone the way he wanted. Instead she wound up with a lot of guys wanting her and leaving him scrambling for attention. He was drained and such lucidity, coherence, and objectivity that he might have possessed was long gone. He had run out of everything that marked him as Stefan except desperation; of that he had superabundance.

By then, the boys had taken off to parts of the house, and with their exit, his spirit had sunk as low as he could go, signaling his great sadness and defeat. Rather, in a calm manner, she confirmed what they both suspected: they needed something to lift them out of the same old, seeing as swinging had become their new normal. Her sense of things seemed more in tune with his desires these days and not so plugged into fighting him on everything.

"Maybe we could do one last fling?" Shelli asked. "On the weekend the boys are with Max, before we make any moves to close the chapter on couple swapping?"

"Really? You'd want to do that?"

Shelli remembered what she had heard about ecstasy, but she wouldn't tell Stefan about it, not yet, not until she was certain she could score some, and maybe not even then. She liked what she heard about it causing people to drop their issues, become more loving, and provide incredibly prolonged orgasms. She hoped one of her old friends from college could find someone who would sell it to her, promising herself that she would make a few calls the next day. She knew how hard it can be for people who don't normally buy drugs to get any.

For a brief second, she entertained the idea of them trying meth, if she couldn't score ecstasy. She'd heard that gay men use it to prolong their ability to keep it going past all human endurance. But then she though that drug was likely too hardcore, from what she had heard, it was not a friendly drug, and had been linked to cardiovascular and Parkinson's, that's not to say other drugs are risk free. But from what she read about ecstasy, with proper dosing and judicious spacing between doses, there wasn't a downside.

"There's a new couple that looks amazing," Stefan said, heading to a corner table and turned on his laptop. He pulled up a profile and flicked on a picture of a beautiful couple. "What do you think?"

"Perfect." She said and whistled a cat call that she had learned from her brothers as a child. She was proud of that whistle, and for once Stefan didn't object.

He had to pinch himself; it was so strange to see her behave this way, so flexible, even suggesting they invite all their polyamorous buddies, including Ecuador and Kay, who admittedly as a couple they saw only once. She pointed out that it would be more interesting with a mix of people. He could tell she had no idea of his extracurricular activities with Kay; she said she was focused on making him happy, King of his Castle, the little chickadee trying to make things right.

The idea of seeing Kay again lifted him out of his funk. He had to remind himself to pretend he never saw her outside the meet-n-greets, and try not to look goony when she showed up, if she agreed to come, that is. To prevent himself from revealing too much, he flew to the fridge to do something with his hands. Head buried in the fridge, he covered up his nervousness by joking about them getting into a dogpile.

"A dogpile?" she said in a teeny voice behind him, "What's that?"

"You've never heard of a dogpile?"

"No."

"Did you really graduate college?" The sputtering of the open refrigerator drowned his voice to his ears.

"Okay, then; I lied, I didn't go to college," she said.

"Figures; your whole life has been a lie."

Shelli didn't react the way she usually did, no snide remarks and no calling him names, she simply bypassed what he said as if he hadn't spoken. "BTW, I thought to invite Ecuador to have a professor on hand to provide an academic take on the events to take place," she said.

Did she even hear what he said? Stefan could only laugh weakly, hand over mouth.

The next day Shelli got on the computer, feeling restless, and hopeful. She brightened when an instant message from Wilhelm appeared, asking to meet up for coffee. She responded by pouring her heart out, saying "the daily grind of living with Stefan's performance issues is fast wearing me down. The needy sense that he exudes; begging for attention, and then denying he has this obsession and telling everyone else it's them." After some thought, she added: "Your message is like balm to soothe my festering wounds. I love having you in my life and value you dearly, and can't wait to see you."

Twelve

A married woman rushes out to meet her lover, and finds herself standing alone on the end of the mostly deserted pier, her aching loneliness heightened by the mood of the place, weather-beaten and desolate, built of ancient wood planks that looked like it might fall apart in a strong wind. The only other visible life, the lonely cawing of seagulls joined with the whistling wind and crashing waves offering a sort of calming dissidence, offering a world apart, a poetic refuge for the stressed and lonely. Even as she gained comfort by the battering of wind and ocean spray, the early morning light shone on the trees like spun gold lighting up the gray terns singing nonstop among budding leaves, as if to say, *all nature is happy, why can't you be?* And yet, despite all this natural beauty, her spirits ebbed as if there was a hole in her heart that needed filling. She couldn't understand her disquiet, she had multiple lovers who cared for her, yet she didn't feel satisfied. None completely did it for her, she needed both, hence the rub. Now she had to manage it, to extract what she could out of both.

She entered the coffee shop, delighted by the exposed crumble of brick walls and reclaimed wood floor, and the big picture windows overlooking a watery purplish gray expanse that glittered from rays of sunlight striking the cresting waves just so, with clouds of blushing pinks and light grays lingering overhead.

She listened to the whooshing sound of coffee being made and breathed the earthy aromas and felt her spirits lift.

There were lots of couches and overstuffed chairs with plenty of space between tables. She thought when Wilhelm arrived, they would want privacy. She picked a table in a secluded corner.

There were a few other people sitting alone, most of them communing with their laptops or phones, busy absorbing the colorful multimedia images that appeared on their screens. She fought the urge to look at her phone, and gazed out the window instead. The deep azure brought her a measure of tranquility, and as she bent her head to sip the hot liquid, breathing in the steam of the coffee she felt more settled. For some reason she couldn't name she looked up from her cup, and there in front of her stood an apparition: Wilhelm, his blond hair slicked back, looking like he had just come straight from the shower, his collar still wet. Her eyes swept over his corded muscles with the sort of reverence she reserved for fine artwork. But what grabbed her attention: his expressive face; never could hide what he was feeling. Her heart leapt at the sudden shift of emotion around his hooded eyes and wide mouth as multiple smile lines appeared along the length and width of his face.

Shelli stood up and met him halfway, kissing him warmly on both cheeks, giving him a quick peck on his lips. She would have liked to linger on those lips but could feel the idle gaze of onlookers from nearby tables boring holes into her back. Still, she couldn't keep her eyes off him, lingering on his arms and shoulders, flashing eyes, and his laughing mouth. She felt as if she was seeing her friend for the first time. Her heart felt full to bursting. They smiled at each other as if they had signed a secret pact.

"I've missed you," he said.

"I live for the days we're together," she said, looking around the nearby tables. Satisfied that others were occupied with their conversations, she leaned closer and said softly, "I'm hoping we can do more of it."

"I would love that."

"The only thing standing in our way: Stefan has trouble connecting sexually with new people," she felt her face glow red in her embarrassment for Stefan. "You know this, right?"

"Camila told me."

"He's fine with me, but not with others. Camila, bless her heart, covered for him multiple times." Shelli's smile didn't falter and her voice dropped to a whisper. She looked around, but no one seemed be listening, other than Wilhelm.

"You care for him." He leaned across the table, the changeable color of his hazel eyes turning as varicolored as the swirling watery mass outside, with browns, golds and greens predominating, the whites of his eyes flashing like lightening in a storm, drawing Shelli in like a moth to fire. "To put yourself out like this."

"I care for both of you, I can't choose. I'm torn."

"I can't be around Camila for more a few days before I tear my hair out."

"There's the other issue of my children. I don't want my sons to suffer."

"Before I met you," he said, his cheek glinting in the sunlight as he spoke, "I was jaded and burnt out, and dragging myself through the days, but that's all changed," His voice enveloped Shelli with sweetness like soft honey as he recounted how much he appreciated her, "I could see myself married to you. But under these conditions: I'm your main man. I'm not saying you can't have others. God knows I've never been faithful to anyone, and I don't expect it of you. It's not in our DNA."

Shelli was gratified to hear that he wanted the same thing that she wanted, that here was a man who could have anyone but wanted something more, a stronger connection, that indefinable something. His declaration resonated with her.

"I know I can't be faithful to any one woman. I'll admit I have this problem. My ex- screamed at me when she found out about my affair and threw my clothes out the window. I wanted to try and work it out, but there was no reasoning with her."

A man behind Shelli appeared to be listening to their conversation, his head listing over as if testing the wind. A few other men looked her way, their smiles welcoming. Taking a deep breath, Shelli said: "I'm not hating on Stefan. He can be a lout but isn't everyone to some degree? I keep fantasizing that we could do it like the Europeans and I could have you both, less disruption for my sons."

"I hate to see you go home with him."

"At some point I may make an official break."

"Okay, I'm listening."

"I want Stefan to try a drug called ecstasy, or molly, or whatever it's called. I read about it in *Time* Magazine and looked it up: shrinks have been using it in marital therapy with good results. It's a feel-good drug that may help Stefan relax, and build trust in others, and maybe he can bottle his jealousy. I hope you know where I can find some. It might change his attitude for the better. And make it apparent what is true about us. It's not a moral issue; it's a something of the heart. I think then we will know what to do."

"I'm familiar with this drug," Wilhelm said. "The ego is totally immersed, and the concept of time vanishes. But don't rely on it too much."

"Oh. Why?"

"The brain needs time to repopulate serotonin levels. You do it once and then wait a month at least, the longer the better."

Shelli thought about what Roberto Calasso wrote in *The Marriage of Cadmus and Harmony*: "The Greek god imposes no commandments. How could he forbid anything, when he has already done it all himself, good deeds and bad? The Greeks did have maxims that aspire to the same universality as the commandments. But there were no rules descended from heaven. If we look closely at these maxims, at their insistence on *sōphroneîn*, on control, on the dangers of any kind of excess, we discover that they are of an entirely different nature: they are maxims elaborated by man to defend himself from the gods."

Which led to Shelli commenting a non sequitur: "Why the requirement that the most beautiful virgin is sacrificed whenever the ancients felt things were out of control?"

"What? You're feeling like a human sacrifice?"

"You know the story, right? In a nutshell, Helen went willingly with Paris to Troy though she left a young child and her husband behind. Soon after Achaeans led by Agamemnon gave chase, leading to the sack of Troy. Many are killed. Hector, the brother of Paris, boosted that they've killed over 30,000 Greeks. Helen in the center of the storm remained unscathed, though she played an active part, recognizing Odysseus in the streets of Troy though he dressed as a beggar. She convinced him that he could depend on her to act the traitor to the Trojans, saying she was homesick." Shelli picked up the book that she had brought with her, in case Wilhelm was delayed, and read from it: "Though almost giving away the position of the Achaeans hiding in the Trojan Horse "she insinuated her voice into the seething dark of the horse, shaking the souls of the Achaeans," writes Calasso. "…Then, just a few minutes later, while dancing on the Acropolis with the other Trojan women, she waved the torch that was to signal the other Achaeans on their ships that it was time to attack. Two incompatible actions, one right after another…performed with the same serenity." She paused and sipped her coffee. "This is what men think of women, that we're two-faced?"

"Ah, she loses Paris."

"Paris dies. Once the Achaeans scale the walled city of Tory, Menelaus searches the house of Helen's new husband, finds him asleep and kills him. Then he finds Helen in another room. He raises his sword, and Helen bares her breast. When Menelaus sees that, he lets his sword drop. And drags her in front of Agamemnon, who says "Helen isn't the cause of this." Menelaus heads to the Achaean camp holding Helen tightly by the wrist, his face grim. The warriors were prepared to stone her but at the sight of her, they dropped their rocks.

People began arriving in the half-light cast by the setting sun. The dusk had begun to settle, blurring the lines between flora and fauna, rock and outcropping. Distinctions between objects grew less defined, as jumbled as Stefan's emotions. Stefan spotted a red Mercedes coupe from the windows on the upstairs landing. He didn't know who it was, just that whoever was inside the car was coming to the party, and likely someone he hadn't seen in a long time. The female would be someone utterly delicious. They were all delicious. Stefan flew downstairs, nearly falling all over himself as he did so, and came hurtling out to see Tequila's glossy black hair bobbing as she popped open the car door wearing a dress showing off her curvy figure to perfection. She had lost weight in the belly and thighs, but her breasts were still nice and full, her nipples sticking out though the thin fabric like the knobs on his car radio. He drew her into a big bear hug, breathing in the smell of her, his moist breath on her neck, his chest pushing into her soft mounds. He thought he was dreaming, hard to believe he had the elusive Tequila wrapped in his arms, not that he had been chasing her, but even so, a new woman with whom he might have a chance made the blood shooting through his veins feel hot and blistery, loaded with a tango of dancing cells, causing his face to flush.

They stood outside near the rose garden where the last of the blooms on the rose bushes had been recently clipped. The naked rose hips clustered together, having just come back from a state of near death, some of them having died in droves over the winter. To combat the decay, Shelli put considerable effort in their revival, slowly improving nitrogen levels. Nowadays, they looked like they were on the rebound, a feast for the senses, adding to his lightheaded feeling.

Alasdair popped behind her, looking more ghostly than Stefan remembered, lean, his brow furrowed. Did she even like this guy? He couldn't figure her out; her face was that inscrutable; the dark pools of her eyes disappearing behind her curtain of hair. He couldn't decide whether her cheery façade was a mask or was it real? But it had always been that elusive quality that drew him in. She pulled back her hair, and that made all the difference. How capable she looked with her wide, toothy smile. Her smile filled her face, and her glittery eyes radiated warmth and confidence. She exuded something almost supernatural, glowing like a movie star or aura-shrouded celebrity. Stefan couldn't take his eyes off her.

"You've been avoiding me," he said.

"That's simply not true," Tequila said, her gaze piercing. "Alasdair called several times and each time you said you were busy."

"I'm thrilled that you're here in the flesh."

"Shelli wouldn't take 'no' for an answer."

Stefan led her into the living room. He wanted show her everything. Especially the pièce de résistance: wall of windows that ran across the entire length of the back of the house, looking out at the sheltering embrace of pointy volcanic hills rearing up on the other side of the ravine, thrusting at the sky, slanting, unlikely marvels. He wanted her to see what he woke to every morning. It wasn't just pride. He told himself how lucky he was to have such a beautiful home, and how lucky he was to live in paradise, and desperately wanted her to see how far he'd clawed his way up, moneywise, Shell riding on his coattails.

"How nice," Alasdair said, from where he had parked himself next to her like a sentry, an avenging angel wielding an imaginary sword, his hair as pale as new wheatgrass and fashionably askew.

Stefan noted with a shock that the man had a distinct lazy eye. How come he never noticed it before? Tequila turned to Alasdair, visibly softening as her hands went out to him. Stefan intuitively knew where her sympathies lay. His disappointment was palatable, not that he was entertaining absconding with her, but right that moment he had this fantasy that she might run off with him to a distant isle.

Shelli came down, wearing a pink silk slip dress and high heels, he imagined with something filmy underneath, her breasts bouncing, looking as sexy as hell, and calling out "hello," in her throaty voice as she came up and caressed Stefan's cheek, her fingers scalding, in passing. "Hey babe," she said. The old desire welled up, rendering him speechless. A thrill shot through his veins—almost felt as he had been electrocuted—and down to his toes. Stefan kissed Shelli with a loud smack.

"I'm going to the kitchen to make drinks," Shelli said.

The doorbell sounded. Stefan made haste to get the door for Kay and Ecuador.

"Now give Daddy a big hug." Stefan spread his arms wide.

Her smile was friendly but distant, nothing like what he remembered from their previous encounters, none of the lust that seemed to be oozing out of her pores in a nonstop outpouring at their last meeting. She seemed a contained young married matron who has accepted the heavy responsibility for the moral ambiguity of her role as polygamous wife and mother. It was obvious to him that there would be no wild grabbing of tit, at least not in view of her companion. Funny how much things seem to change, how they stay the same.

He hoped she would give him a sign that she was merely acting a part, but at that moment, there was none. He would have to wait to find a private moment with her later. He thought, no matter, and reached out to get his hug. Just then Ecuador waved to Shelli, and said, "Sorry old chap," and grabbed Kay by the arm. "Didn't you want to talk to Shelli?" Stefan registered his surprise at the term "old chap," noting to himself that there was no suggestion of a British accent and where was he from, anyway? Just as Ecuador turned toward Shelli, Kay winked at Stefan and his heart did a backflip, and gazed longingly at Kay's ass, thinking in every way that Kay was a fertility goddess with that ass, rounded as a full moon, and possessing thunder thighs to shake mountains. Stefan was moved to fall down on the floor and worship at her feet, but in the presence of Ecuador, he refrained, realizing he would have to defer his pleasure, and that spiked his interest, one image in particular sticking in his mind, that of her naked posterior dully gleaming as he prepared to enter her.

Stefan followed Kay and Ecuador into the kitchen in pursuit of Shelli. On the way, Tequila talked to him, and he tried to listen, but couldn't focus, he must have been leering because Kay and Ecuador left him abruptly, without explanation. He turned his attention back to Tequila. He tried to separate Tequila from Alasdair, but the man clung to her like Velcro. He hoped the Alasdair wouldn't raise any objections if Stefan attempted to get all sexy with Tequila. But his memory of Alasdair waxed positive on that score, likely he wouldn't mind. Thinking this way made Stefan feel more enthused about the whole business, thinking later in the evening he might get a chance to take Kay separately into another room, and would that be perceived in a bad light?

Kay's standoffish attitude disturbed him so much that he had trouble forming words, other times he couldn't speak at all, or he couldn't remember words and gestures he had exchanged with Tequila as recently as five minutes ago, leaving him at a loss for how to respond other than a 'yes' or 'no.' Tequila pointed out this sad fact several times, her frown deepening, and in a huff took off with Alasdair.

Stefan located Kay and pulled her aside, away from the line going for drinks, thinking he might connect with her now, after all he's been through, thinking that of all the things he could do, he would like to grab that massive ass and give it a few light slaps. He made off as if to squeeze them, but Ecuador's unblinking eye unnerved him, and his hands stopped moving of their own accord. He wondered what was going on with him, he felt so flustered. He tried to make small talk, something he was usually good at. But the things he wanted to talk about seemed inconsequential: what athlete was doing what, which movie star he was hot over, which new technological gadget he lusted after.

Someone tapped shoulder, and he turned around to see Camila's eyelashes fluttering like hummingbirds, her big blues looking like ice water he might dive into. She wore a slinky white dress with thigh high slits, her robust thighs on display. But she was still flat chested, which didn't inspire him. Didn't matter how beautiful her face. Stefan tried to think of something funny to say. Shelli gave Wilhelm a big bear hug which lingered longer than Stefan would have liked, and then she went to

Camila and hugged her as well. Everyone else gathered around making small talk about this and that. This was usually the time in a party, during the early hours when everyone was just getting comfortable, when Stefan would trot out stories to an appreciative audience.

If memory served him right, this was the very hour when once upon a time he talked a beautiful maiden into leaving a party at the company they worked at, took her out to a nightclub, and after a breathtaking, if brief, courtship six months later married her. Back then, they were so hot for each other whenever they were alone, he couldn't wait to do it; couldn't wait for the bedroom, had to pull her down to the floor in the vestibule. And he never thought his sexual need for her would subside, but it did. Those were the days he had thought everything was possible and believed that he would accomplish great things. A lot had happened to tarnish that dream—yet he still loved her, but he wanted new experiences, pack it in before he died. Right then he had his sights on getting his rocks off, something that these women never seem to understand, they think love always has something to do with it, when rarely does.

Later in the evening Stefan directed Alasdair to the upstairs bathroom instead of the downstairs to buy time, his eagerness spilling over. Tequila's tits were adequate for his purposes; he could fit comfortably between them, and right now he was despairing of his chances to sneak Kay out of the room for a private session. And he knew for sure that what he wanted to do had to be done in private. He didn't care who he did it with, he was flexible; he would see how things shaped up, maybe an opportunity with Kay would present itself, but he wasn't going to hold his breath. By the end of the night he expected to have both women, and hoped he was up to the task. In his excitement, Stefan spilled his drink. And left it for someone else to clean up along with his empty glass and led Tequila outside to a corner of the deck that wasn't visible from the house. He commenced with some naughty talk, thinking to raise the temperature, while his eyes of their own accord roved her body, massaging the glorious swell of her chest and sculpted shoulders, the cut of her toned thighs.

Swooning under a cloudless sky, but not completely relaxed; the pressure got to him; he felt the need to get something going before Alasdair showed up. Though this was a swingers' party, people still had feelings of ownership, even when they denied it to themselves, and only when presented with the actuality of the act powerful instincts hold sway, drumming out all good sense, and who knows what a cuckold husband might do, even though he agreed to it. There's that primitive injunction that a man answers to when another man is boning his wife. Thank God Shelli wasn't watching; they were all busy inside. He wasn't hiding from Shelli per se; he was merely saving her from the shock of seeing up close that her husband feels lust for other women and watching him in action. He knew that would bother her, no matter how enlightened she thought she was.

Right then if Shelli had demanded an honest answer, he couldn't deny his lust. Impatience flooded his consciousness; he wanted to dive in and feel the initial rush of neurons signaling intense sensual pleasure. Why was she pulling away? He saw that she wasn't in the mood to get intimate. He felt the impulse to overwhelm her physically and take her by brute force despite her protests. But he crushed the thought, realizing that she wanted to be seduced. It didn't matter how much strictures were removed women didn't change much from whatever kind of person that they were to begin with.

"You're beautiful," he said and brushed the hair out of her eyes, making sure that at the same time his fingers flicked her skin.

Training his malcontent orbs on a couple of ash-colored birds wheeling and diving over the thin thread of pail-gray water visible from where he stood, he imagined they were on the hunt, looking to feed. The pang of physic hunger was as real as if he was starving and denied food bubbling on the stove. He certainly wanted to feed on the morsel in front of him, and with a mighty effort he held back, hoping she was planning on giving in eventually. In his frustration, remembered a line from Jim Morrison of The Doors who said that pain is something to carry, like a radio. He knew he should take Morrison's advice, gain strength by shouldering his pain and wear it with pride. That would resonate with Tequila in a place where mere words couldn't reach. And he was trying to do that, but the pain was slowly killing him. Hoping against hope that he could rise to the occasion when called upon to do so later that evening with others in attendance—the plan was to avoid public humiliation. He dearly wanted to enlist Tequila's help. Maybe she would cover for him if needed.

"I've lost weight. Can't you tell?" his eyes filled. "People tell me I look sick." He blinked madly until his tears receded.

"What are you talking about? You look fabulous."

He jumped involuntarily, suppressing a cry, seeing Shelli appear on the deck, gesturing to them; saying they had to be part of this, whatever "it" was. He said he had been taking Tequila on a tour of the house and stopped for the view.

"Isn't it beautiful?" Shelli said.

"I love your view," Tequila said.

Wilhelm came on the deck behind Shelli looking like a prizefighter with his bulging biceps, his face friendly and open. "I have a happy pill for us. It lowers inhibitions and makes the world seem rosy." And so he spoke like a doctor with his patients, his expression serious, leaving Stefan bewildered, and wondering what kind of drug is this? How can I be assured the outcome will be pleasant?

"It takes roughly half an hour to come on," Wilhelm said. "I've dosed it perfectly for most people. If you think the dose is too small, wait an hour to make sure. You don't want to take too much."

Stefan hesitated, blinking rapidly as if a colony of mites had taken up residence there and holding a capsule up, and peering at the beige powder inside.

"Scientists looking for chemical compounds to control bleeding came up with it in 1914, but of course at the time they didn't know what they had," Wilhelm said. "Took a psychologist named Leo Zeff to spread the word. Therapists in the 70s and 80s used it in couples counselling."

"Alasdair and I did MDMA a few times," Tequila said. "Helped us connect with each other without all the bullshit."

"I thought MDMA is illegal?" Stefan said.

"When people started using it recreationally the Feds cracked down," Wilhelm said.

"Holy Guacamole! Isn't that always the case?" Ecuador said. "What about alcohol and tobacco? Why is that still allowed?"

"Shouldn't other vices — like being mean-spirited — also be illegal?" Tequila said.

Behind him, Stefan heard Shelli say, "Amen to that!"

Stefan followed Wilhelm's directions like a docile lamb, liking that he didn't have to make decisions, allowing him the space to work on his various half-baked seductions. He considered himself lucky, how many wives allow their husbands to participate in foursomes, or for that matter, to simply watch porn? Even so, boredom invariably sets in, as happens to everyone in long-term relationships.

Back in the kitchen, Shelli artfully arranged a cutting board with cheese and crackers. Camila dumped some grapes clusters, both green and purple, in a couple bowls. Kay put together a plate of cooked shrimp circling a bowl of cocktail sauce in the middle.

Wilhelm poured ice water into a pitcher, saying in a schoolmarm voice, "Your body temperature will rise, and you'll feel hot, be sure to drink plenty of water."

Tequila brought in a couple bottles of champagne from the pantry, scrawling on the face of each bottle: "Torpedo the water." Stefan was told to bring glasses for the champagne. Shelli led the way to the master bedroom, bearing the cutting board like it bore a load of precious jewels. The room was simply furnished, nothing extraneous, not much furniture beyond a couple of floor plants, the bed, and the dramatic floor-to-ceiling windows. The bed placed in the middle of the room as fitting a central devotional object and playpen.

In Hera's most majestic shrine, the Heraion in Argos, Stefan and Shelli ran across an image of Hera's mouth closing amorously around Zeus's erect phallus and agreed they wanted to get a copy of it made. No other goddess, not even Aphrodite has such an image in her shrine. Stefan was proud to show their guests this sculpture mounted in a place of honor on a beautifully carved round table in an alcove near the windows.

Shelli invited everyone to jump on the bed, or move to the mattress whenever they wanted, and pointed out the swing that she had just purchased for the occasion in a corner. She had also arranged a mattress on the floor in one corner of the room with soft pillows all around and said it was for "overflow."

Shelli took off her dress, and in her sizzling pink lace bra and panties she looked a mouthwatering pastry. Everything started to bounce a little, like his cells were dancing for joy. Stefan smiled at the sight of Wilhelm nuzzling her neck, his arms going around her waist, and yet he had to turn away, preferring instead to watch Alasdair making the moves on Kay, partially in amusement, thinking he could run circles around the smaller man, and bend him like matchstick. But then he realized this turn of events worked better for him than he had originally hoped for. He would bide his time, hoping Kay would be available to him sometime in the evening, and allow him to monopolize her for an hour or so after she had been warmed up by Alasdair.

Tequila whispered that she had ordered her husband to keep Kay occupied so Tequila could have her way with Stefan. He congratulated her on her foresight. Wordlessly, he extended his hands to her. She placed her palms in his much larger ones.

At Tequila's electric touch, Stefan wondered if their current intensity had anything to do with the fact that they had met in the world of swinging. Would he feel as charged if they met at a party geared to the vanilla crowd? Hard to say, he looked around the room and noted the anticipatory looks; smiles upended every lip. It was nice to see so much female beauty in the room, none off limits, and felt reasonably sure in the knowledge that he could have sex with any of them if he wanted. How many men can say they have their wife's blessing to screw other women in her presence?

Stefan watched Wilhelm take off Shelli's bra. Normally this would have unsettled him and made his stomach queasy, but he found that he was not offended by the sight of another man putting his ugly paws on his wife. It wasn't as gross that he imagined, especially if he occupied himself with Tequila's neck, kissing her warm skin, his blood rising with the heat of watching out of the corner of his eyes this obscenity of Wilhelm grabbing Shelli's tits, emblazed in electric lights on his retina.

He couldn't help the moan that spilled out, watching Wilhelm rubbing and kneading her nipples until they reddened into fine points making his blood rush, he found it strangely thrilling to play the voyeur with his wife, and watch her being fondled in this way. Stefan felt a corresponding jolt when Wilhelm's rock-hard cock popped out of his boxer shorts, as enormous as a horse's. Stefan could feel her excitement from across the room. Her smoky eyes glittered, and her breath came short and fast. Seeing that giant yam bumping her belly gave him a pang. When they had planned this evening, Shelli had assured him that she harbored no illusions; she had even called Stefan skittish. But Stefan thought Wilhelm looked way too eager.

Shelli crawled over to his side of the bed.

"Are you ok?" Shelli asked with a solicitous air.

"I demand he take his hands off you."

"Yes dear. Shall I tell everyone to go home?"

"You know I jest. Tell him not to look like he's enjoying it so much, okay?"

She went back to Wilhelm and Stefan directed his eyes on Tequila and concentrated on the soft flesh of her lips on his. The electricity of that kiss burned his mouth. His tongue flew away from her mouth to her chest where the top of her white lace bra peeked over the vee of her tiny black dress. She began fumbling for the buttons on his Hawaiian shirt.

"Do you need help?" Stefan squinted at her tousled head glowing blue-black in the soft light.

Eventually, Tequila got the hang of it, successfully undoing every button and pulling off his shirt. He leaned into her, kissing her lips, and attempting to unclasp her bra. Her full breasts fell into his hands like ripe peaches, and he stroked them as reverently as he's seen Wilhelm do with Shelli, hoping his wife was getting off on watching him do the exact thing, trying to will his fingers into softer, more pliant surfaces, and slowing his administrations, thinking that excruciatingly slow was more erotic to the woman.

With his help, she took off her dress and he removed her panties, running his fingers along the thin spray of black hair curling around her pudenda. She drew him to her, kissing him eagerly, causing pulsating waves of electrical energy to circulate his veins. His body continued to tingle even after they had stopped kissing. Soon they were on the bed, pawing each other, stopping every so often to smile at their own spouses, sending shivers down his spine.

Around Stefan, a veritable lovefest was happening in surround sound, the noises and smells of the air awash in endorphins; his cells dancing in time with the faint sounds of music drifting in the room from below. He breathed in a musky animal odor, the smell of sex. His lust for Tequila overwhelmed him, filling his eyes, overloading his brain, vying with his love for Shelli which had taken a backseat for the moment.

Wilhelm and Shelli were locked in a sixty-nine on the other side of the bed. Seeing Shelli in the embrace of another man made her seem more desirable, but the feeling was bittersweet. On the mattress on the floor Alasdair was grunting, sweat rolling off his forehead, thrusting into Kay doggy style. Stefan planned on taking seconds and felt good about it. On the swing, Camila straddled Ecuador, her ample thighs trembling. Seeing this in real life, not a porn movie, with the pheromones flying, ions coloring the airwaves in bright swaths of color was like seeing a volcano for the first time and experiencing lava's hot breath.

He missed being with Shelli, their jokes and rhythms, and pretended for the moment that he was with Shelli. He thought about the things they would say to each other. It would be intimate, whatever they thought to say, nothing held back. Everything slowed, he kissed Tequila's mouth and neck and breasts, buried fingers in her hair, and his tongue snaked down her belly. Stefan wondered if Kay knew he was thinking about her, missing her acutely, wanting both women to attend him, wanting them to take turns sucking his prick as Tequila arched her pelvis to meet him.

All around him, he witnessed a frenzy of touching and licking and kissing. He entered Tequila slowly, he didn't mind holding off, nor did he care about the passage of time, or what anyone thought of him. He knew just a few things to be true. That he was feeling in the moment, his heart dancing, full of ecstasy. The very cells in his eyeballs were doing cartwheels. And he realized that he loved to touch skin on skin, the heat of it, the slow march of it, and the light sliver of nervous energy that occurred in the passing—the briefest of moments to be treasured. But how to capture with all of his senses and preserve memory?

Tequila was his substitute lover, not his preferred lover, that would be Kay, but she wasn't half bad. He liked doing it with someone new, that was a given, and he reveled in an orgy of the senses with someone he didn't know as well as he knew Shelli. Tequila tasted good, and she was as passionate as he could wish for. He pulled out, he wanted it to last, and she kissed and fondled his balls and shaft, engulfing his swollen head until she practically choked.

He went back into her, taking it slow. Slower than he ever had gone, it seemed the right thing to do, to be somewhat aimless about his pleasure, enjoy every moment and not be working toward an orgasm. He wasn't nervous about his performance, just focused on having a good time. After a time he felt as if he had been doing this for an eternity, and realized that he didn't care about whether he had an orgasm at all, he was prepared to go on for hours with no end in sight, he could last as long as he wanted, like a marathon swimmer until he fell from exhaustion.

Overjoyed to hear Tequila say she had come several times, Stefan pulled out, needing a glass of water, and looked around at the happy, feverish faces. The air felt thick and moist, as if the air was a living, breathing entity. He felt an irrepressible, unaccountable joy infused his cells; each nucleus seemed to dance below his eyelids and cause him to want to hug everyone. But he didn't see Kay, though she was the only one he wanted to be with, and he went to the wall of windows feeling a strange sadness, lasting only brief moment, his joy was too much for sadness to stay long. The room was lit by several candles perched high and out of the way, and made it so all he saw was his reflection. Kay came up to him.

Stefan turned to her and felt no need to hurry, without saying anything started to kiss her slowly, her skin tasting like spun sugar. He said he wanted her to go with him away from the others to the guest room, down the hallway. She agreed readily, but neither of them moved, he kept kissing down to her breasts and fondling them, kissing and sucking.

He stopped to say he was thirsty, and went to Shelli and offered her glass of water. She asked if he would be okay being one half of a sandwich. The idea was that she wanted be fucked by two men at the same time—with one qualifier—she preferred not to have a cock in her asshole, doing her bunghole would be a last resort, and only when well-lubed, and only if she had trouble getting two cocks inside her vagina, provided the two men could manage thrusting with all that was going on. She thought the experience on ecstasy would be more interesting with two cocks going at warp speed, and asked him to choose who would be underneath her, and who would go on top. Stefan told her he didn't care and asked her to choose.

When Shelli was ready, she took both penises in hand, and took turns sucking each until they were rock-hard. She lay on her back on top of Wilhelm and placed his cock in her vagina, rubbing its base, and then squiggling and up and down his shaft. He was lying down, her legs opening like a frog's. Stefan got excited seeing Shelli's labia draping itself around Wilhelm's large cock, enfolding him like the petals of a purple iris. Her engorged clit stood up like a stubby penis. Stefan placed his mouth on Shelli's clit and sucked it. Spasms shook her body. She ejaculated something sticky and squishy. Stefan learned later that this fluid comes from the Skene's glands near the urethra, it isn't pee, and doesn't originate in the bladder, and is surrounded by tissue that includes a part of the clitoris extending up into the vagina. It balls up with blood when aroused, enabling the vagina to get wet and to squirt. The fluid produced by the Skene's glands is very similar in composition to prostatic fluid, and both the male prostate and Skene's appear to operate in a similar way.

Stefan stood over Shelli and shoved his aching cock into her wet, tight hole, which still housed Wilhelm. It gave him no end of pleasure to enter that tight space. He thought he'd have trouble getting inside, but her vagina stretched to accommodate him. He didn't feel Wilhelm's cock at all. It felt like any other skin, nothing that marked it as a cock. Her tunnel felt warm and soft all over, and dense with vibrating nerve endings.

Stefan and Wilhelm moved at different tempos. Shelli began laughing and babbling incoherently, yelping, and carrying on.

And then suddenly they began speeding faster, climbing together in a shuddering journey into outer space that melted the stars. Stefan was ecstatic that he had been able to hold off coming, and he had felt so incredibly relaxed until the friction took hold and created the impetus for a slow build. Stefan came with a great jerking and heaving like a runaway freight train. Stefan had never come so hard. The three of them screamed their joy at the same time.

They lay in a tangled heap for what seemed hours, until Shelli pushed Stefan off her. He couldn't summon the strength to lift his head, he felt as if he was still in a trance. Wilhelm and Shelli also were looking quite spent, limbs falling every which way.

Shelli kissed his shoulder, slowly tracing her lips down his arm, and wondered out loud if perhaps he had passed out. Wilhelm and Shelli agreed it was the best orgasm of their lives. His mind blank, Stefan could say nothing, eyes at half mast, and he melted into Shelli's arms, falling into a light sleep, and waking to candles that had gone out, leaving them in partial darkness. Shelli's face was so shadowy he couldn't make out her features. He gathered what little strength he had and asked about their guests. She said that everyone but Wilhelm left, and she gave him a quick kiss before demanding another kiss that left him feeling heady and amazed, and sad; wondering at his shortness of breath, each emotion overwhelming what came before. Primarily he was amazed at the love he felt for this woman, and his shock, too, at the events that had transpired, and the way he had handled everything. And that he accepted that Wilhelm was in bed with Shelli, his arms around her. Immersed a state of utter joy as he had been the past few hours, gone were the rancor, jealousy, and feelings of inadequacy, or the feeling that he had missed out not having fucked Kay.

Stefan's love for Shelli could easily have died from malnutrition or drought, but right then it began to blossom into the kind of hothouse flower that never dies—sometimes it falters, true, and has to be coaxed again—and each time, his love grows stronger, nourished by all this new understanding.

About the Author

Joanna Kadish's short fiction has been published by Potato Soup Journal, Literary Orphans, Cultured Vultures, Quail Bell Magazine, Citron Review, Urban Arts Magazine, and Crack the Spine. She was a finalist in the Black Coffee & Vinyl Presents: Ice Cultures project, summer of 2018, Cutthroat 2016 Rick DeMarinis Short Fiction Contest, and received honorable mention in GlimmerTrain's Emerging Writers Contest for 2015 and 2016.

One of her essays won first place in Adelaide Literary Award 2019 Contest, and she was a contest finalist in the creative nonfiction category in the Spring 2019 Pinch Literary Awards.

Her work appeared in an anthology by Riverfeet Press, titled *Awake in the World, V.2.* Another essay was published in the Catamaran Literary Review for their summer issue 2019, as well as in the Adelaide literary magazine June 2019.

Years ago, Joanna was a regular freelance contributor for the New Jersey Regional Section of The New York Times, and several regional newspapers and magazines, including The Cleveland Plain Dealer and Asbury Park Press. She received a few awards for her essay and feature writing from the Society of Professional Journalists. After self-publishing two novels, she went for her MFA at Bennington College in Vermont. Her BA is from UC Berkeley.

Made in the USA
Middletown, DE
02 March 2022

61998023R00243